spaz

Also by Bonnie Bowman
*Skin*

# spaz

A Novel

Bonnie Bowman

Anvil Press | Vancouver | 2010

Anvil Press Inc.
P.O. Box 3008, Main Post Office
Vancouver, B.C. V6B 3X5  CANADA
www.anvilpress.com

First Printing.

LIBRARY AND ARCHIVES CANADA CATALOGUING IN PUBLICATION

Bowman, Bonnie
    Spaz / Bonnie Bowman.

ISBN 978-1-897535-27-1

    I. Title.

PS8553.O907S63 2010        C813'.6        C2010-906956-0

Printed and bound in Canada
Cover design: Mutasis Creative
Interior design: HeimatHouse
Author photo: Lisan Jutras
Author caricature: Malcolm Jamison

Represented in Canada by the Literary Press Group
Distributed by the University of Toronto Press

To my parents,
who raised me in that most carefree yet insidious
of settings: suburbia

# 1 }

If it weren't for his most unfortunate gait, Walter Finch would pass through life virtually unnoticed in any North American setting. He was of average height for such a citizen and weighed comfortably within the dictates of the standardized height-weight chart. He kept his flat brown hair trimmed and tidy and his slightly myopic view of the world was witnessed through benign hazel eyes. Sometimes Walter wore prescription glasses for driving, particularly at night, and especially if it was raining. His singing voice was passable but lacked passion, a serviceable combination that lent itself to other activities in Walter's life such as cooking and sex. He was not fastidious, nor was he slovenly. Walter Finch did what was necessary to keep up his appearance. He used nail clippers. He had never used a loofah.

Aside from a noticeable gap between his front teeth, Walter's walk was the only remarkable thing. It wasn't a limp, at least not in the manner of most limps that display themselves as a forward-and-backward lurching motion. Nor was it a step-drag-step pattern. It was more a tilting, really. A wobble. This came about because Walter Finch tended to walk on the outer sides of his feet, an action that caused him to affect a curious side-to-side, choppy, swaying motion and promoted a rather coy twitching of his bottom. He had done this forever.

On occasion, bystanders had thought him drunk as he bob-waddled along the sidewalk. But Walter Finch did not typically consume alcohol above that demanded of him by a social occasion, a wedding or a funeral. His liver was intact and average in size. It would be useful to someone else should he die in a car accident. Other onlookers had, at times, believed him "mentally challenged"—an overeager assessment on their part, but one absolutely without merit or other evidence to support such theorizing. Walter Finch was certainly no genius, at least not in the matter of academics, but he was possessed of an uncanny eye for detail and trivia if he put his shoulder into it. And his memory was quite excellent, if an event or task warranted subsequent examination. He, however, did not drool or roll his eyes about wildly or wear tinfoil hats or mumble incoherently when he stumbled along, and as such, an assessment of mental deficiency was way too hasty. Perhaps most amazing to Walter Finch were the times he was pegged as a homosexual, merely because of the hitch in his hindquarters. He, of course, was not. But he had nothing against them.

For as long as Walter could remember, he had walked like this. As a child, he had been banned from most sports activities—if not by doctors then by cruel team captains. Later on, he had suffered it in the silent tragic way mastered by teenagers and it had only gone unnoticed when his friends were drunk and walked the same way. When Walter grew to be an adult, he mostly ignored it. His mother said he was special. His mother's mother suggested Walter's "deformity" was the reason his father had run away. Walter wanted to believe the former and had doubts about the latter, but having no memory of Bradley Finch, he couldn't be sure.

Shortly after Bradley's vanishing act, Joy Finch, Walter's mother, found herself in the unfortunate but necessary position of having to secure a job. This she found easily enough at the Eaton's Catalogue store, a sprawling warehouse where she spent her days drinking industrial coffee laced with artificial creamer, taking phone orders and cataloguing gossip with a roomful of similarly disadvantaged women from other neighbourhoods. In Joy's own neighbourhood of Agincourt, "housewife" was the moniker worn by the bulk of the adult female population, a role never questioned until years later, when the women tried on different titles—homemaker, domestic engineer—and when magazines told them they should be paid for their housework. Walter's mom was one of the few women with a job, but because it was thrust upon her, she didn't feel enlightened in the least. She, in fact, felt put upon and cursed Bradley Finch's name, wishing she could do to his face what she did to her time card every morning.

This was also the time when Joy's mother, Clara Potts, moved in. In the 1950s, this was all quite risqué. As a neighbourhood unit—a suburb of Scarborough, which was a suburb of Toronto—Agincourt could have been held up as a poster child for the times. A newly built, orderly, tree-lined subdivision of young families in stucco bungalows, that pinned its hopes on its children, a solid pension, and future migration to Florida. If there were dreams, and naturally there were, they were buried as deep as the septic beds in everyone's backyards, covered up with a well mani-cured lawn. The mom who could have been a dancer would instead waltz with her vacuum cleaner on a stage of broadloom. The dad who might have been a great landscape painter would instead spend his weekends pruning back his subjects and painting their trunks with rings of toxic chemicals. If there were no dreams, neighbourhoods like Agincourt would remain forever idyllic.

This seemed particularly true of the Agincourt denizens, who, perhaps because Agincourt was in its infancy, tried to set an example. Indeed, in Agincourt's early days, the sub-suburban bungalows were filled to the uncluttered eaves with young white families—moms and dads and kids. Single-parent families were virtually nonexistent, and in that respect the Finches were setting a trend. And in the mid-fifties, before the inevitable implosion of the shiny nuclear families, it was considered unusual to have only one child. As such, Walter was a bit of an oddity. And he did, after all, have that most unfortunate gait.

In the early days, when he kept falling over every time he tried to walk, Walter would have been the oddest kid on the block if it weren't for Adelaide, the retarded girl down the street. Adelaide was a huge, white lumbering thing who, at nine years of age, had the breasts of a Sumo wrestler and a vocabulary to match. She couldn't seem to wrap her tongue around multi-syllabic words and she referred to Mrs. Finch, for example, as MITT INT. Adelaide didn't speak so much as *boom*. She might have been partially deaf, no one was sure. Walter was WAH INT. Her washed-out blue eyes would have been considered attractive on someone else, but because of her unfocused gaze, Adelaide had the appearance of being blind. She wasn't, at least not in the ocular sense. And despite all her obvious setbacks, Adelaide was an extremely pleasant girl, or so her perpetual goofy smile would seem to suggest. Everything about Adelaide was a would-have, might-have, or a could-have been. Her shoes were invariably on the wrong feet, her nose always seemed to be running and her blouses or dresses were consistently buttoned up wrong. But the neighbours learned her language and were patient with her while she stood on their back porches, braying on and on in a loud barrage of single syllables, happy to have an audience. To an untrained ear, it would sound like: AH-GOB-NOO-BAY-YET-DAY-MITT-INT. To Mrs. Finch, the translation was: I got a new baby yesterday, Mrs. Finch. At which point, Adelaide would hoot and fling her new doll around by its hair and Joy would exclaim and clap. But by far the worst exhibition performed by Adelaide was the act of eating food, as it soon became apparent to everyone that the admonition to "chew with your mouth closed" was completely lost on the girl. The neighbourhood learned what not to give her. At the top of the list were egg salad sandwiches.

Adelaide had free rein in the neighbourhood and scant supervision from her mother, Lillian Vanstone. At first, the Agincourt moms thought it a disgrace and would cluck and klatch about Mrs. Vanstone's lack of interest in her poor daughter. But Lillian Vanstone was so much older than the other moms, having given birth to Adelaide in her forties, they didn't have much in common with her anyway and were relieved she kept to herself. Although everyone saw way too much of Adelaide, they saw virtually nothing of Lillian, who kept her drapes drawn even in the daytime and had a strange boy cut her lawn once a week in the summer and shovel her driveway in the winter. There was no Mr. Vanstone—word had it he had perished in a mining accident up north, maybe Sudbury—and Adelaide's rumoured older brother was grown up and living in another country, maybe Greece. Compared to the critical attention levied at Adelaide and her weird mother, Walter got off relatively easy.

When he was born, Walter appeared completely normal. His baby feet and toes curled up like most baby feet do. Joy would tickle the soles of his feet and he would gurgle and giggle like any baby would. He was in the average percentile for his age group and Joy would wheel him out every day in an oversized grey carriage with shiny chrome fenders, happy to show him off. Robin Mooney, who lived across the street, had given birth to twin girls around the same time as Joy Finch had pushed Walter out of her womb. The two young women had shared a couple of days in Toronto General Hospital's maternity ward. The Mooney girls were per-fection, both blessed with a halo of white fluff on their tiny round heads. Nina and Tina, they were called. One would grow up to be head cashier at the local A&P and the other, a cocktail waitress at a biker bar northeast of Scarborough. They would both wrestle with substance abuse problems, but remain annoyingly beautiful throughout their lives. Had they moved out of the subdivision, great things might have happened for Nina and Tina, according to local wags. Speculation ran to supermodels at best and highly paid twin porno queens at worst. Staying in Agincourt appeared to be the kiss of death for the second generation, but no one would rec-ognize that until it was too late.

It was no surprise therefore that Robin Mooney and Joy Finch became fast friends, due in part to their coincidental proximity and their shared new-motherhood. Before Mrs. Finch was forced by circumstance to enter the workforce, the two women spent the better part of their days drink-ing coffee from stainless steel percolators, eating cinnamon buns, and talking about their children. They were adding vodka to their coffee years before the kids started adding acid to their Kool-Aid.

"Wouldn't it be neat if Walter married Tina or Nina?" Robin Mooney mused one day, back when suburbia still harboured the illusion of hope.

"Yeah, then we would be in-laws," Joy replied, pouring a coffee and un-rolling a cinnamon bun.

"We would have the same grandkids."

"And maybe they would live on the same street too. Like us."

Sip. Chew. Sip. Chew.

"I wonder which one of my girls he would marry?"

Shrugs.

"I don't know. They're identical though, aren't they?"

"Uh huh. But they'll probably have completely different personalities when they grow up. I think they already do."

Sip. Chew.

"Mmmm. Guess it's too early to tell."

"Yup. It would be fun, though."

"I know. Let's *make* them do it."

Muffled giggles, crumbs spitting out.

"You mean, like an arranged marriage?"

"Yeah. Like India."

"That would be *so* weird."

"I know, they're weird over there."

And then the women would talk about more ordinary things like the colour and consistency of Canadian poo, while they sipped and chewed and licked sticky brown cinnamon off their fingers.

Nina and Tina learned to walk on their first birthday. They were adorable in their identical pink puffy-sleeved dresses, white lace ankle socks, and shiny shoes. Everyone said so. Like matching, miniature ponies they would toss their blond manes and prance prettily for anyone who cared to take their picture or bestow a compliment. Which was unfortunate in a way, because the girls never did learn to see beyond flattery. A compliment, for instance, got Tina knocked up when she was sixteen and compelled her to tell people she had to drop out of school because she had a stomach tumour. Things like that.

When Walter was still ambulating on all fours at eighteen months, Joy got anxious about his apparent lack of motivation for getting vertical. She would stand him upright, hands in his sweet armpits, and cautiously remove her grip, making encouraging cooing sounds. Walter would invariably teeter a bit, then either fall forward on his hands or end up sitting abruptly on his bum. He would look bewildered, but never cried, and would gather himself into crawling position and motor off somewhere else. When he was still doing face plants at age two, all talk of arranged marriages ceased.

Walter eventually got the hang of moving about upright, but he couldn't seem to perform the standard heel-to-toe manoeuvre or find a use for the balls of his feet. He scuttled about on the sides of his feet, an act that created a bowlegged effect but was an altogether efficient means of getting from point A to point B. Joy took him to the doctor who did not seem concerned.

"There's nothing wrong with his feet," said Dr. Cleghorne, pulling Walter's socks back on and giving his chubby calves a reassuring pat.

"What do you mean there's nothing wrong with his feet? *Look* at them. They're crooked or something," said Joy, her voice rising.

Dr. Cleghorne shook his great buffalo head and raised his wide shoulders helplessly.

"His feet are fine Mrs. Finch. Structurally sound, average size for his age, perfectly formed—"

"But—"

"But nothing. Like I said, there's nothing wrong with Walter's feet. There's something wrong with his walking."

Joy glared at him. "No kidding. Do I have to take him to a walking doctor, then? What the hell does that *mean?*"

"Why don't you ask Walter? Ask him why he walks like that. Maybe there's a psychological reason or something."

"Are you telling me my son needs a shrink? Is that what you're saying?"

Dr. Cleghorne gave a loud snort and Joy half expected him to paw the ground.

"I'm not telling you anything. I think Walter has chosen to walk this way. There is no medical reason for it. If he doesn't snap out of it, you could try some support shoes or braces."

"That's it?"

"I can't do anything else for you."

Joy picked Walter up in her arms and set him on the floor. "Let's go, Walter," she snapped.

Walter hobbled out of the examining room, his mother at his heels. "Bye doctor," he called out over his shoulder.

"Never mind that," said Joy, giving him a push.

The trauma of the doctor's visit called for a trip to Robin's place for coffee. Joy, having taken the afternoon off work, relished the idea of relaxing and rehashing the day for her friend. The two women reclined on chaise longues and kept an eye on Walter, Tina and Nina who were playing in the Mooneys' backyard. It was early summer and, thankfully, not too humid yet. A brisk breeze was doing its business with the sheets on the clothesline and the hummingbird feeders were swinging. The coffee was freshly perked and everything was in order. Robin, as usual, looked far too elegant for an Agincourt housewife. Her sleek, platinum blond hair was swept up in a pastel chiffon kerchief and she wore slim white Bermuda shorts with a matching strapless top. Robin was described by other women as petite. Or pretty. Or precious. All the P words. Men used other words to describe her, but never within earshot of her husband, Allan. Beside Robin, Joy always felt a bit monstrous, mainly because of her extreme height. At six feet tall, she towered over all the other women on the street and a lot of the men, and she still carried with her the slouch she had cultivated as a teenager, despite her mother's unrelenting rants on good posture. Unlike Robin, Joy had noticeable hips and boobs, which was all fine and good until Twiggy came on the scene and voluptuousness was shot right into the toilet as a feminine ideal. When emaciation became stylish, Joy's slouch became more marked. She never wore high heels. But she did have a beautiful head of curly chestnut brown hair, reminiscent of the Breck shampoo models in the magazines, and a fresh pretty face, resembling all the Ivory soap girls on television commercials. To an appreciative male eye, both women had their individual charms that did not go unnoticed in Agincourt.

About Robin:

"I'd like to bounce her up and down in *my* lap."

About Joy:

"I'd like to bounce up and down in *her* lap."

Between the two of them, they were a fantasy for every man.

Today, Joy hadn't changed from the doctor's visit and still wore her sleeveless A-line shift—a yellow print affair—and matching strappy sandals which she kicked off before unfolding her length into the chaise longue. She poured a coffee, lit a cigarette, and told Robin about the doctor's visit.

"So, there's nothing wrong with his feet?" asked Robin, pushing her sunglasses down her nose to peer at Joy.

"That's what that asshole Cleghorne told me. If you can believe anything he says," said Joy, taking a fortifying drag of her Benson & Hedges.

Robin settled back in her chair and watched the kids, secretly relieved Nina and Tina were leaping about like gazelles. Walter, bless his heart, tried his best but couldn't help looking like a jerky wind-up toy. She could afford to be magnanimous.

"You know," Robin began. "There's a new Foster's Shoes in that mall the other side of Kennedy Road. You know, across from the A&P?"

"So?"

"So, Foster's apparently specializes in orthopedic type shoes," said Robin, choosing her words carefully, not wanting to offend.

"Orthopedic shoes?" Joy said. "Aren't orthopedic shoes for old ladies?"

Robin sat up straighter and flipped a stray corner of scarf off her face. "No, Foster's has kids' shoes too. I mean, maybe they might help his walking. I don't know. Maybe it's worth a try?"

Joy mulled this over and watched the kids tumbling about. They were playing a game they called Magic Carpet where Nina and Tina were princesses and Walter was Ali Baba. Their magic carpets were the ever-rippling shadows on the grass caused by the sheets flapping in the wind on the clothesline. Walter had explained it to Joy one day, proud to be Ali Baba. It seemed no matter what game the kids made up, Tina and Nina were always princesses. If they played Cowboys and Indians, the twins were Indian princesses. If they played Detective, they were kidnapped princesses. Joy considered orthopedic shoes while she watched the kids flying around the yard and screaming when the shadows took an unexpected and violent turn, throwing them off their carpets and plunging them to their certain death. As she and Robin were drifting into a companionable silent reverie, they were jolted into awareness by a familiar bellowing.

"HI-MITT-INT! HI-MITT-MOO!"

Joy and Robin looked at each other and shrunk down in their chairs, mouthing: *Oh no.* Adelaide flopped into the yard, sucking on a grape freezie, her lower face a bright purple colour and her corn-yellow hair in scraggly, uneven pigtails. She was wearing sneakers with no laces on the wrong feet, and her white dimpled knees were scabbed and bleeding. A dirty Band-Aid hung half off one knee. Her striped cotton blouse looked two sizes too small and rode up her plump tummy. She looked like she always did. The women squinted up at her as she towered over them, picking her bum and grinning (or grimacing—it was hard to tell).

"Hi Adelaide," they said politely. "How are you today?"

"AH-FINE-HAH-YOU-MITT-INT-A-MITT-MOO. AH-GOB-MITT-FEEZ," thundered Adelaide, shoving the dripping Mr. Freeze in their faces.

"Mmmm," said Joy.

"That looks good," said Robin.

Adelaide's mouth hung open, and after a couple seconds, her laugh erupted like the delayed sonic boom from a jet plane. She took her fingers out of her bum and smelled them, then offered them to Joy and Robin.

"No thank you," said Joy.

"Don't pick your bum, Adelaide," said Robin. "It's not polite."

Adelaide held the offending fingers in mid-air, examining them. She looked at Joy and Robin quizzically and then hooted with laughter again.

"BAH-BUM-BAH-BUM!" she screamed with delight.

"That's right," said Robin.

"That's a good girl," said Joy.

With that, Adelaide plopped her bulk down on the grass and watched the other kids, contented. At that precise moment, Joy decided to make a trip to Foster's Shoes, although Walter was looking comparatively normal right about now. She even found his unsteadiness a bit endearing and vowed to take him to Dairy Queen later as a treat.

# 2 }

**Thus began Walter's relationship with Foster's**, the results of which would impact his life into adulthood. Until he became acquainted with Foster's, Walter's footwear had not been of any concern. He had the requisite sneakers, a pair of black dress shoes and a pair of sandals, all of average quality and comparable to those worn by the other boys in the neighbourhood. Brand names and style were not huge selling points for boys of his young age, and shoes didn't merit much notice one way or the other. What they put *on* their feet was not nearly as important as what their feet did *in* them. Running shoes were for running—the faster, the better. Skates were for breakaways and scoring goals. Footwear served a purpose. No more, no less.

**FACT**: The more times you could get away without wearing any shoes at all, the more esteem you were held in. If you could walk barefoot on broken glass, you were King.

Naturally, the girls had a different take on these matters. Nina and Tina would spend hours diligently polishing their white patent-leather dress shoes, adjusting the bows, looking at their faces reflected in the shiny leather. They would push thumbtacks into the heels and toes to make tap shoes, or wrap ribbons around their ankles and pretend they were ballerinas. They made puppets out of their furry slippers, and put tinkly bells in the laces of their figure skates. The colour of their running shoes was of far more importance than how fast they could run in them and knowing how to fashion a perfect loopy bow was way more inspiring than being able to tie a neat double knot.

**FACT**: The prettier your shoes, the more esteem you were held in. If you could walk in your mom's high heels without falling over, you were Queen.

Within the Agincourt community, a kid had to be pretty outrageous to attract any lasting ostracism. It went without saying that Adelaide was an easy target, but Walter was soon privy to another sobering—

**FACT**: Shoes from Foster's suck. There was no esteem whatsoever.

Straight last shoes. That's what Mr. Foster called them. Straight last shoes only came in one style—ugly—and one colour—ugly brown. Straight last shoes had round, heavy looking toes, thick laces, solid chunky heels and durable soles. They were worse than dress shoes, and on the list of things detested by boys, dress shoes ranked pretty much near the top. Bad enough his wacky walking had excluded him from sports or anything else remotely cool—and, not to mention, earned him the nickname Spaz—he sure as hell didn't need to call more attention to his feet. Had he known about straight last shoes, Walter might have tried to walk sensibly in the days leading up to the big shoe-buying spree. But when Joy and Clara hustled him into their secondhand Ford Mercury, Walter had no idea it was a conspiracy.

"Well. Here we are!" exclaimed Joy, as they pulled into the strip mall.

"This is just a waste of time," Clara grumbled, squeezing her square body out of the car. "And money. Ain't no shoe made that'll fix that boy's walk, mark my words."

Joy collected her purse and looked heavenward for strength.

"Come on, mom. It can't hurt to look," she said, slamming the car door.

Clara let out a muffled belch and gripped her purse tight to her side.

"Foster's," she harrumphed. "Well, don't sound like no Jew name, anyhow."

"Jesus, mom."

And with that invocation of the Lord's name, the unholy trinity stepped into the light. A bell tinkled, heralding their arrival. The store smelled suspiciously of leather and the overriding shoe colours appeared to be browns and black. One circumnavigation of the joint and Walter had seen enough. He sat on a chair and tried to look small. Soon Mr. Foster himself swept out of the backroom, wiping his hands on a towel. The shoe salesman looked to be about the same age as Walter's mom, and he was as thin as the pencil moustache swiped across his upper lip. His ultra-shiny black shoes made no sound on the carpet and he slithered up alongside Joy like an unexpected shadow.

"May I help you?"

Joy, startled, dropped the shoe she was holding. Mr. Foster snatched it in mid-air and replaced it on the rack, quick and quiet as you please.

"Uh, yes. I hope so. I need to buy some shoes for my son."

"Mmhmm," said Mr. Foster, glancing over at Walter and giving him a creepy wink. "Did you have anything particular in mind today?"

Walter shrunk further down in his seat and tried to avoid eye contact, but Clara had no such hesitancy. She strode up to Mr. Foster and planted herself square in front of him. Everything about Clara was square.

"Look, the kid can't walk proper," she said. "Some quack of a doctor says there's nothin' wrong with his feet. My daughter here thinks maybe you got shoes that'll help. I don't think you do."

Mr. Foster recoiled slightly from Clara, but kept his cool. His mouth moved in what was supposed to be a smile, the effect like oil spreading across his face. Flexing his long, bony fingers with great deliberation, he swiveled in Walter's direction and raised one tweezed eyebrow.

"Stand up, boy," barked Clara. "Show the man how you walk."

Walter looked at Joy, who gave him a tiny nod of encouragement. He stood up and wobbled to the end of the store and back. Joy watched anxiously, switching her gaze from Walter to Mr. Foster and back again. Clara stood firm, legs planted apart, arms folded across her square bosom, checking her watch. Only Mr. Foster seemed completely at ease. He nodded when Walter sat down.

"Good, good," he said in a voice as cool and smooth as melting ice cream.

And like that, in a flash, he went from standing to sitting on a midget stool in front of Walter, his nimble cartoon fingers flying on the laces of Walter's shoes. Before Walter could say a word, his bare feet were planted in Mr. Foster's professional lap. Despite his bewilderment, Walter felt like his feet were finally in good hands.

Mr. Foster's slender fingers caressed Walter's instep, his outstep—if there is such a thing—his heel, the balls of his feet, and finally his toes, which Mr. Foster tweaked playfully before standing up. He winked at Walter again, but this time it didn't seem creepy at all.

"Why don't you take another wee walk down to that mirror, son. Then we'll measure your feet."

Walter hopped off the chair and tottered down the store. He tried walking straighter, standing taller, wanting to make Mr. Foster proud. He had called him *son*.

Although Walter had always been conscious of his walk, this was the first time he felt he was being tested on it. He wanted desperately to pass. Joy watched him with motherly benevolence, Clara with impatience, and Mr. Foster with narrowed assessing eyes. Walter made his way back to his chair where Mr. Foster waited, hunched over on his stool, a black and silver measuring plate on his lap, and a nylon sockette dangling off one spatulate finger. Walter winced at the girlie nylon, but Mr. Foster slipped it on his foot in a businesslike manner and at least there were no other kids in the store, *thank God*. Walter had experienced the foot measuring device before, but never so thoroughly or with such reverence. Mr. Foster moved the sliders, gripping his foot in a snug lock. He pressed Walter's toes, flattening them out, adjusted his heel, ran a finger down his arch, and not once did it tickle or hurt. Mr. Foster's breath was the only sound, and he effortlessly switched feet, performing the same manoeuvres on both. It was calming, and despite Clara's frantic pacing, Walter felt dreamy.

"What do you think?" asked Joy, almost slipping and calling him doctor.

Mr. Foster slid the measuring device under Walter's chair and removed the nylon from his foot. He looked up at Joy, who was twisting her purse strap around one finger, and he stood up.

"I think we can help the boy out," said Mr. Foster, patting nonexistent creases out of his slacks. "It's not some kind of cure, you know. It's going to, hopefully, train his feet to be more upright, so he won't tend to fall over on the sides of his feet. Really, it's just more support, more preventative than anything."

Clara walked over to interrogate Mr. Foster. "So, what are you saying? He's still going to walk like a monkey?"

Walter was mortified, but stared hopefully at Mr. Foster for his answer.

"Maybe. Maybe not," said Mr. Foster. "Time will tell. But if nothing else, the shoes I'm recommending will stop any further collapse while his feet are still growing and vulnerable."

Mr. Foster gave Walter a reassuring look, but spoke to the adults. "He's toe-ing in, did you notice?"

Clara rolled her eyes around like wet bowling balls and Joy squeezed hers almost shut.

"He's what?" Joy asked.

"Toe-ing in," pronounced Mr. Foster with authority, turning to look at Joy. "Mostly the left foot, nothing to worry about. It's to be expected, considering his gait."

"Jesus Christ," intoned Clara. "What next?"

Mr. Foster leaned into Clara, closer than anyone had ever dared before. Walter got new respect for the shoe aficionado.

"Why don't we try a pair on and see what happens?" Mr. Foster breathed into Clara's puffy face. "Then, maybe, we could find something for your bunions."

With that, Mr. Foster spun on his polished heel and glided into the backroom, leaving Clara to sputter and turn red.

"The nerve!" Clara huffed, but she did sit down and tuck her feet under her chair, out of view, before Mr. Foster blew back in with a tower of shoeboxes.

Walter had been so captivated by Mr. Foster he had almost forgotten how ugly the shoes were going to be. He bit his lip when he saw them but Mr. Foster was ahead of the game. He wasn't stupid enough to extol their virtues, he got downright professional and deft, almost daring Walter to question him. Once again, Walter's feet were manhandled, shoe-horned into tough brown casings, massaged, squeezed, caressed. *Stand up. Sit down. Walk over there. Stop. Turn. Run down the store. Jump up and down. Come back. Let's see. How does that feel? Is this your big toe here? Does your heel lift out when you walk? Where does it rub? Is this too tight? Too loose?*

It was an unspoken truth between Walter and Mr. Foster that these shoes sucked. The odd thing was, the shoes felt good and supportive. Walter felt safe in these shoes. Here, in this store, with Mr. Foster coaching him and Joy beaming at him, Walter felt powerful. These shoes wouldn't let him down. They would carry him anywhere, get him through anything. Somewhere in the back of his mind, a voice was piping up, a voice he ignored. The voice was saying: "Everyone's going to laugh at you. You look like a retard." Walter could hear that voice, but he pushed it from his mind here in Mr. Foster's shoe store where the sight of Walter in these shoes seemed to make everybody so happy.

By the time they left Foster's, Walter had brown, ugly, straight last shoes in a box under one arm and he wasn't the only one clutching a new purchase. Mr. Foster had hypnotized Clara into low-heeled shoes that would help her bunions. They were all climbing into the car when Mr. Foster stuck his head out the store's front door and called to Joy.

"Mrs. Finch!"

Joy paused, her body halfway into the front seat of the Ford.

"Mrs. Finch, could you come here for a second? There's something I forgot to tell you."

Joy stepped out of the car and shaded her eyes, peering at him. Clara was looking at her new low-heeled shoes in disbelief, and impatiently waved a chubby hand at her daughter.

"Well, go on," she said. "Go see what the man wants."

Walter watched his mother and Mr. Foster conferring and saw his mother slide an uneasy glance at the car. He didn't make much of it at the time, and soon enough Joy was back and Mr. Foster had disappeared into the store with a tinkling of the bell.

"Well, what did he want?" asked Clara, as Joy turned the key in the ignition.

"Nothing, really. He reminded me about what kind of polish I should buy," said Joy, looking in the rearview mirror at Walter.

Clara cackled. "That's a likely story. He probably wanted a date."

The car rolled backward out of the parking spot and Joy glared at her mother. "He did not."

As soon as the car pointed in the direction of home, Walter's misgivings were beginning to kick in and Clara was referring to "that nice Mr. Foster" in a voice she seldom used about anyone. Walter peeked in the shoebox and shuddered. The little voice in his head had multiplied into a chorus, full-blown and raging.

A few days after Walter got his straight last shoes, he was sitting on his front lawn, wearing them. He was digging clods of dirt from around the birch tree and rubbing them into his shoes, trying to make them look less new, less noticeable. Joy and Clara were in the backyard, relaxing on the ever-present chaise longues, drinking iced tea. Clara was dressed in shades of green and pink. Her sunbathing attire consisted of a floppy straw sun hat, extra-large green-framed sunglasses, a full skirt, and a long-sleeved cotton blouse, mint green with a baby pink rosebud pattern. God forbid she would be exposed to the sun. She didn't want to look like no goddamned Indian. Joy, on the other hand, was bareheaded and wore bright red shorts hiked up to her underwear line, and a red and white sleeveless polka dot blouse unbuttoned to her bra. She was developing a nice patch of freckles on her chest and a bit of a burn on her nose. Clara regarded her daughter with disapproval as she leaned over to refill her iced tea from a pitcher.

"You can see your brassiere, you know," Clara said with a sniff.

"So. Who's looking?"

Clara stared intently at Joy as she put the pitcher back down. She settled her bulk back into the straining chaise longue and took a noisy sip, dentures clacking against the glass. Sometimes she couldn't figure where her daughter got this attitude. Clara patted her necklace, a single strand of bloated green beads, and her matching bracelets rattled with the motion. After her formidable layers of underwear, jewellery was the first thing she put on every morning. Face powder was the next thing and, lastly, perfume. If she was going out somewhere, the list of personal ablutions grew considerably more involved. Nobody knew when Clara had spotted her first grey hair. But after stifling a horrified gasp, she plucked the wiry interloper from her scalp and ate the evidence. That very day, Clara made the acquaintance of Miss Clairol, and religiously renewed their relationship on a regular basis. She would keep her unnaturally black hair into the grave, and Joy had no doubt Clara's corpse, should it be exhumed, would forever boast a full head of coal-coloured hair, curled and meticulously set. Clara believed there was no excuse for not looking your best at all times, a credo she could never get her daughter to embrace. To do otherwise, she would say, was pure unadulterated laziness.

"You're going to burn," she said now, staring up at the cloudless sky.

"I don't burn. I tan," said Joy.

"It's not very attractive. You're not getting any younger, you know. Your skin is going to look like old leather in a couple of years and men don't like that look."

Joy smiled to herself. Obviously her mother was unaware of the popularity of the California Girl look. Not that Joy gave a shit what men thought. Not that men were on her mind. No, Joy and her girlfriends had always been very into tanning. When she was a teenager, all the girls would mix baby oil and iodine together and smear it over their bodies. Instant tan. They would squeeze fresh lemons into their hair to get the sun-bleached look and lie outside all day while their mothers rocked on covered porch swings, swathed in material from head to toe. Nothing had changed. She ran one hand through her chestnut curls, and sat up running her other hand down one long leg.

"I need to shave my legs again," she said, peering at the hairs dotting her legs. It looked like her legs were covered in blackfly poop.

Clara grunted, her own legs covered by a rose-coloured voluminous skirt. Only her ankles and feet showed, and despite her squarely solid torso, Clara had slim legs with shapely calves and ankles. Her legs were by far her best feature, which she attributed to wearing high heels for as long as she could remember. Clara's shoe collection was extensive, the smallest heel being about two inches. Even her slippers had high heels. But because of this predilection, years of pedal abuse with pointy-toed pumps had taken a toll. Her feet, once narrow and long like her daughter's, were now squat and wide, with horny bunions that resembled polished pebbles. Today she was wearing nothing on her feet but bright red toenail polish. She was pleased to see Joy's toenails were painted too. It was something at least.

"If you keep shaving your legs, the hair only grows back in thicker and darker," Clara said. "You never should have started. I never shaved my legs and you can't even see the hair, it's so fine."

Clara pulled her skirt up, flashing a shiny, white shin. Joy gave the obligatory look and nod, not mentioning that she could definitely see hairs on her mother's legs. Every summer, she got the speech about sun damage and leg shaving and slutty bathing suits. She waited for the next comment, knowing already what it would be.

"It's different raising a boy," said Clara, smoothing her skirt back down over her legs, unsuccessfully suppressing a belchy hiccup. "You have to be more careful about these things. You can't be showing your bosoms all over the place. You want young Walter growing up with the right attitude about women, you want to show some respect for yourself."

"Jesus, mom."

"Jesus don't have nothing to do with it."

"Well, neither do you. Walter's *my* son."

Clara shut up for a minute and played her final and predictable card. "He's Bradley's son too, Lord help us all. Look how he turned out. Couldn't keep his whaddya-call-it in his pants for love nor money. He didn't have no respect for women, now did he?"

Joy closed her eyes and listened to the sparrows and the clinking of the ice in her glass. She willed herself to *burn*.

Walter was now scuffing the burnished leather of his straight last shoes with gravel from the driveway. It was painstaking work as he worried the leather with infinite care, trying to dull the sheen without damaging the leather. He was so involved in his task, he didn't notice Johnny Carmichael until he felt a friendly kick.

"Hey Spaz, what are you doing?"

Johnny Carmichael lived three doors down and was one of a family of four black-haired boys. Of the four, Johnny was the closest in age to Walter. He was also the only boy on the street who wore glasses, which didn't endear him to his brothers but did create some sort of bond with Walter. Johnny's eldest brother, Ray, would grow up to be a petty hood and never do jail time. Which is exactly where the second eldest brother, Billy, would wind up after being interviewed on television with a black bar over his eyes. It was the best thing for him, some would say, as Billy found God in jail and upon his release became a counsellor for drug addicts. The youngest of the Carmichael clan was Clive. As a child, Clive was sickly and forever getting ill or hurting himself in weird ways. Clive would grow up to be a marine biologist who was sickly and forever getting ill or hurting himself in weird ways. Clive would be one of the few who made it out of Agincourt.

Too late to hide the shoes, Walter took one off and handed it to Johnny, who kneeled down beside him.

"I have to wear these stupid shoes and I'm trying to make them look worn in," said Walter.

Johnny dropped the shoe on the lawn, repelled.

"God. Did your grandmother pick those out?"

Walter shook his head, realizing now that no matter how much gravel he rubbed into the leather, they would always look worse than dad shoes. It was hopeless.

"I have to wear them 'cause of my walking," he said.

Johnny threw himself backwards onto the lawn and lay there. He squinted through his thick lenses and felt one of those secret thrills you get when someone else is hurt, or fails a subject, or gets thrown off a team.

"Why don't you throw them away?" Johnny suggested. "Say you lost them."

Walter considered this. His grandmother would no doubt smack him on the head for being careless. His mom would get that sad look. That was the worst. She would look at him the same way she looked at the one remaining picture of his dad—the one she kept hidden in her underwear drawer. Walter had caught her, on occasion, staring into that drawer for minutes at a time. She would stand there, not moving, gripping the drawer with both hands and leaning her weight against the bureau. He had watched her, unseen, wondering what was in there until one day he climbed up on a chair and peeked inside. He pawed through panties and slips and brassieres, mostly white, until he found the photograph. It was black and white and creased. Walter stared at it and knew it was his dad even though his father was never mentioned, only insofar as his mother conceding that he had one somewhere. His supposed father was standing outside in what looked like a forest. He had a rifle in one hand and was holding a bunch of birds in his other hand. The birds, which Walter would later learn were partridges, were obviously dead and Bradley Finch was holding them upside down by their feet. His face was partly shaded by a cap and he was wearing a plaid shirt, baggy pants and big rubber boots. Walter wanted to feel something about the photograph, about his dad. Part of him wanted to steal it and run outside to show all his friends who had dads. Until now, he hadn't known what his father looked like, let alone where he was. Now he knew what he looked like and that he lived in a forest. But if he stole the photograph, he knew his mother would have to tell him stuff. He would have opened far more than a drawer full of underwear. And he knew she would get that sad look, which is finally what made him replace the photograph and close the drawer and keep the information to himself.

Now, sitting on the lawn with Johnny Carmichael, he knew he wouldn't throw his shoes away. Even if he could bear the sad look, he knew his mother would take him back to Foster's and buy another pair. He also knew money was in short supply and that the shoes were expensive, compared to normal shoes.

"I can't throw them away," he said to Johnny.

"Why not? I won't tell."

"She'll buy another pair."

Johnny digested this information along with the grass he was chewing. It had never occurred to him. Almost everything he owned was handed down from his older brothers. Getting something—anything—new was a treat. Getting it twice was unheard of. When he was feeling a twinge of jealousy about the benefits of being an only child, he glanced over at Walter's shoes again. It made him think that he'd rather have ten brothers and wear snowmobile boots in the summer than be caught dead in Walter's shoes.

"Do you have to wear those to school?" he asked, hoping for an affirmative response.

"Yeah, I guess. She'll make me."

"God."

"I know."

# 3 }

**The train was going around and around the track,** through the tunnel, past the grove of plastic trees, over the trestle, around and around. Walter watched it stupidly. He had thrown his straight last shoes out his bedroom window into the backyard and was sitting on his bedroom floor in his usual awkward position. Thighs pressed together, knees touching and lower legs skewed outward at right angles. Walter had been in his room all day and refused to come out. There was plenty here to keep him amused for days, weeks even. He had books, a large boxy cream-coloured radio, toy soldiers, and a live turtle in a bowl, Timmy. Hanging from the ceiling was a marionette dressed like a pirate with a parrot glued to its shoulder. And he had crayons and paper and glue. He didn't know how long he could survive without food, but there was a jug of water on his desk that he could drink. Walter was hiding out and no amount of coaxing from Joy or bullying from Clara could get him to leave his sanctuary. He needed time to think, that's all. Walter had received some new information and it wasn't sitting too well. It was information about his shoes, and it was bad, bad, bad. Joy had sprung it on him a week after the visit to Foster's, having first given him some time to adjust to the new purchase. After breakfast, which, in retrospect, was suspiciously over-the-top with blueberry waffles and whipped cream and thick pink slabs of back bacon edged with yellow cornmeal, Joy had asked him to stay seated for a minute. Walter looked at her solemnly, a blot of whipped cream at the corner of his mouth.

"It's about your shoes," she began.

Walter braced himself, thinking he was going to catch holy hell for messing them up with dirt and gravel.

"Mr. Foster said you have to—ummm," Joy said, her voice trailing off.

So it wasn't about scuffing them up. What then?

Joy fiddled with her paper serviette, twisting it into a rope. "He thinks, Mr. Foster thinks, that it would be best if you…"

Walter was curious now, but anxious to get outside. When Joy opened her mouth to continue, Clara bustled into the kitchen. She stood there, hands on her hips.

"Come on, child," she barked. "Get on with it. I've got to clear the table."

Joy looked at her son, trying to will him into understanding and acceptance. Clara couldn't take it anymore.

"Oh, fer Christ's sake," she said, throwing her arms in the air, and looking pointedly at Walter.

"You gotta wear them damn shoes on the wrong feet, is what."

Joy appeared to shrink and Walter was confused. He looked from Clara to Joy and back again, not comprehending.

"What?"

Clara started picking plates off the table and clattering about. Joy grabbed her mother's arm and stilled her with a firm grip.

"Mother, please get the hell out of my kitchen."

"I just—"

"NOW!"

Clara untied her apron and threw it on the counter, hustling herself out of the kitchen and muttering things about mollycoddling.

"What did she mean?" Walter asked, getting worried.

Joy composed herself and put on her no-nonsense mother voice.

"Walter, you're going to have to wear your new shoes on the wrong feet. Mr. Foster said it will help straighten your feet out better."

Walter felt dizzy, like when he rode the spinning teacups at the CNE. He wasn't hearing this. Or he was hearing it wrong. Wear them on the wrong feet? No *way*. She didn't say that.

"It won't be forever," Joy was saying, speaking rapidly now that the worst was over with.

"Just for a while. Then you can wear them on the right feet. I don't think anyone will even notice. They both sort of look the same anyway, right? Why don't you go get your shoes and we'll see how that works. I bet you won't even know the difference."

It was sinking in. She was serious. Walter couldn't believe it. Those shoes were bad enough on the right feet, and now he had to wear them on the wrong feet? The *wrong* feet? Like *Adelaide*? Holding in tears, he tumbled off his chair, running for his bedroom, tripping over his stupid feet, skidding on the polished hardwood hallway in his socks, nearly crashing into Clara on the way.

"Never, never, never! You can't make me! I'll run away!"

He slammed his bedroom door, and began barricading it with chairs and books and his desk. He stuffed T-shirts into the crack under the door, in case Joy called the police and they used tear gas. Then he picked up the hated shoes and climbed onto his bookshelf to reach the window. Tears were blurring his vision as he cranked open the window and threw the shoes outside as far as he could. He closed the window and pulled his drapes shut. He lined the windowsill with marbles that would roll off and wake him up if the police tried that route. Finally, he placed thumbtacks in strategic locations throughout the room. These preparations had all been completed about six hours ago—an eternity. Walter watched the train go around and around and felt hungry. The turtle pulled its head into its shell.

Walter's seclusion lasted nearly twenty-four hours. Joy worried in silence, leaving trays of food outside his bedroom, and stroking the door before padding back down the hall. Clara had never been good friends with silence and considered it her duty to let the ungrateful grandson know how his actions were affecting the population in the outside world.

"You're giving your mother a nervous breakdown!" she screeched at the closed door. "Your mother's in her bed with a migraine! Do you have any idea what you're doing to your poor sainted mother? Well, *do* you?"

Walter crawled into his bed and put a pillow over his head whenever he heard Clara's familiar stomping down the hall. Clara had wisely chosen guilt as the first weapon of choice from her arsenal. The initial assault was an important one. But when that strategy didn't move Walter to surrender, her subsequent attacks became increasingly less effective, deteriorating into empty demands and culminating in weak clichés.

"You get your ass out of that bedroom NOW!"

An hour later:

"You don't know how lucky you are! When I was a kid, we didn't even have shoes! We had to wear moss!"

A further hour:

"Those shoes cost good money! Do you think money grows on trees? Well, *do* you?"

Three hours:

"Stay in there then! Starve to death! All the more dinner for us!"

Four hours:

"We'll give those shoes to the orphans—who would be quite happy to have them, mister—and you can wear socks to school! How would you like THAT?"

And finally, perhaps predictably:

"If your father were here, he'd haul you out of that room so quick, your head would spin!"

Walter thought about that one. He pictured the man in the photo, crashing through the bedroom door, splintering his barricade into sticks, and kicking aside the debris with his big rubber boots. Walter would scramble up his bookshelf to the window, desperately trying to crank it open and flee, but he would hear the hammer cock on his father's rifle and freeze in mid-flight. There would be a scuffle. When his grandmother and his mother finally came rushing in, they would see his father standing in the middle of Walter's bedroom, rifle in one hand, and the other hand holding Walter upside down by his feet. Clara would run to get the camera.

"Say cheeeeeeese!"

Walter wondered if his mother would keep the photo in her underwear drawer and if she would be sad when she looked at it.

Walter had never before realized how long nights were. They must be a hundred times longer than days, he thought. When it got dark out, and he heard the sounds of the women going to bed, he turned his light off and tried to sleep, but it was impossible. He got out of bed and turned on his desk lamp. He found his flashlight and brought it back to bed with him. When he turned it on, it made crazy slanty shadows on the wall from the dangling pirate, which was kind of fun but also kind of spooky. The radio was his salvation. Sound was crucial in this dead zone of night-time, and as each radio station left the air, he frantically spun the dial through a static mesh until he heard a clear tone. One by one the stations went dead. The ones from the States were the last to go. By the time that happened, Walter had memorized quite a few *Hit Parade* songs that he had never bothered listening to before. But it was scary when the dial went all the way around and there was nothing left but static. It was like everyone had abandoned him, as if they had all died or something. He felt eerily alone. *What if everyone on earth was dead?* For a heart pounding minute, he considered removing the barricade and rushing into his mom's room to see if she was still alive. He got as far as standing in front of his bedroom door, touching one of the chairs jammed under the door-knob, but he couldn't do it. Walter didn't know what would be worse—finding everyone gone or discovering everything was okay and he was mental. He walked back to his bed and crawled under the covers. It was so quiet with his window shut, he couldn't hear the crickets. But the red light on the radio dial had a comforting glow and the soft hiss of the static was reassuring. Timmy *plooped* into the water, and Walter felt more at ease knowing Timmy was still alive. But the surreal stillness in his immediate surroundings bred extreme activity in his brain. He was restless in an anxious kind of way and forgot about being hungry.

To pass the time during the night that wouldn't end, Walter started looking through some of his storybooks with the flashlight. He came across *Cinderella* and pushed it aside. But then he picked it back up, turning the pages, the familiar story running through his head. Considering his current situation, *Cinderella* was far more interesting. He wondered if the prince would have been so in love with her if she had to wear her

glass slippers on the wrong feet. Doubt it. Straight last glass slippers probably weren't even invented in those days. But shoes must have been pretty
important back then. Cinderella could have left anything behind at the
ball. A glove, a hankie, a purse. But she left a shoe. That prince walked all
over the place holding her shoe, looking for her. Everybody tried that shoe
on, everybody wanted it to fit. The world hung on a shoe. Walter knew all
about trying to make a shoe fit. His straight last shoes were, in a way, like
those glass slippers. They would fit only his feet. God, now that he
thought about it, his grandmother had called Mr. Foster a prince of a
man. Was he? He wondered how come the glass slippers didn't break
when Cinderella danced in them. He wondered if you could make shoes
out of glass in real life and thought his mom would look pretty in them,
if you could.

Walter lay back against his pillow and stared up at the pirate puppet
shadow snaking up the wall and folding itself onto the ceiling. He crumpled up a piece of paper and threw it at the puppet, watched it dance, its
black wooden pointy boots swinging back and forth and clicking together.
It reminded him of something. He shot up in bed, whispering: *There's no
place like home, there's no place like home.* Dorothy, he thought with satisfaction. From *The Wizard of Oz.* She had those sparkly ruby slippers that
she clicked together. He couldn't stop thinking about shoes now, and
struggled to remember anything he could about the movie that had
scared the shit out of him. And yes, once again, shoes had been totally important in that story too. Shoes had saved the day for Dorothy. The ruby
slippers were magical, they had powers. The Wicked Witch didn't want
Dorothy *or* the Scarecrow *or* the Lion *or* the Tin Man. She wanted the ruby
slippers! Walter was astounded with this revelation, the importance of
shoes. He recalled the feeling he had, for a minute, when he first put on
his straight last shoes in Foster's. He had felt...invincible, almost like
he had super powers. Was it possible they were magic shoes? He wondered what they were doing out on the lawn in the backyard. Were they
walking back to him? Walter couldn't think about anything else. Why,
think of all the stories with shoes in them. He thought about the old
woman who lived in a shoe and had all those kids stuffed in there. That

had to be a magic shoe, for that to happen. And didn't Hans Brinker have some kind of magic skates or something? And Puss 'n Boots, what had happened there? He tried to remember every story he had ever heard that had shoes in it. And there were *tons* of shoes he had never given thought to. He closed his eyes and pictured them all, they danced or walked or skipped through his brain, on a treadmill that sounded like static. Wooden shoes, moccasins, flippers, workboots, roller skates, golf shoes, ballet slippers, cowboy boots, Roman sandals. He looked at his bare feet with new interest. All those shoes for all those feet in the world. Shoes made out of glass, wood, rubies. The only thing he still couldn't figure out was why, with all those different kinds of shoes in the world, were his the ugliest? His gathering excitement degenerated into dismay again and he fell into a troubled sleep. While he slept, the radio static crept into his brain and wove itself around his dreams, strangling them. He dreamed that he married Adelaide and everybody at the wedding wore their shoes on the wrong feet. He danced and danced until he threw up. It would be the last time Walter would dream at night.

When Walter woke up in the morning, things were different. His room was stuffy. At first, he didn't know where he was and he sat up in bed staring blankly. There was music coming from the radio, no more static, and somehow he knew all the words to the song that was playing. The walls were free of shadows and the pirate was motionless. It hung, head looking down at the bed, arms and legs at odd angles, frozen in mid-dance. Walter blinked. The flashlight had fallen off the bed, its beam so weak you could hardly tell it was still on. Walter's books were strewn about, on the bed and on the floor. He had marks on his skin where he had lain on them. It was darker than usual because the drapes were still drawn. On normal days, his mother was in here before he woke up, throwing his drapes wide open and chirping: "Rise and shine! Out of bed, you sleepyhead!" But not today. Today was different and Walter knew everything would be different from now on.

He could hear his mother and grandmother moving about in the rest of the house and he smelled breakfast cooking. His stomach growled. Walter rubbed his eyes and yawned. Yesterday's events were recalled, but something had changed overnight. His world had shifted. He climbed out of bed and wobbled over to the window to open his drapes. The bookshelf against the window was empty, all the books being piled up against his door. Walter climbed up the bookshelf and pushed the drapes aside. Marbles went flying, hitting the floor like bullets, startling him. He looked down at them in a fog and cranked the window open. His shoes were no longer in the backyard, a fact he registered without emotion. Maybe they ran away. Walter clambered down the bookshelf and landed right on a thumbtack. Wincing, he pulled it out of his foot, seeing a tiny prick of blood appear. It hurt, but not as much as he thought it would. He calmly fed Timmy, like it was a normal day, and made his bed. He noticed a pile of pennies on the desk and then remembered the penny jar was now under his bed, half full of pee. Then he walked over to his door and began dismantling the barricade, piece by piece, in a completely orderly fashion. There were thoughts in his head that had never been there before. New thoughts tumbling about in a haze, leaping about like clothes in a dryer. More static. But Walter wasn't trying to dial them in. He left them alone and went about the business of putting his room in order. He needed everything back to normal right now, because somewhere in the static, he knew nothing would ever be normal again. The night had done that. Walter now knew that his room was a lie—it wasn't really blue and red, like it looked during the day. It wasn't a colourful painting of a boy's bedroom. He had seen his real room last night and it was black and white and grey. His room was one gigantic photograph that you really lived in. And the only other thing Walter knew for sure, as he dragged his chair back to the desk, was that he couldn't tell anyone about the shadows, or the static. It was his secret that everyone died at night and that other things woke up. Things like that were far more important than wearing your shoes on the wrong feet.

He opened his door and went into the bathroom. His pee went on forever.

Joy and Clara heard Walter in the bathroom and looked at each other.

"Thank God," said Joy, pushing eggs around a frying pan. "Do you think he's come out for good?"

Clara was at the counter briskly spreading margarine on toast like she was stropping a razor, her bracelets jangling. "I knew he wouldn't last," Clara said, squaring her shoulders. "He's like his father that way. No commitment."

Joy turned the heat off on the element, ignoring her mother's last comment, and walked to the fridge. But Clara wasn't finished.

"You still gotta deal with those shoes. You're not going to back down are you? Mr. Foster said he's gotta wear them on the wrong feet."

Joy poured orange Tang into three plastic tumblers, listening to the sounds Walter was making in the bathroom. She had found the shoes last night out on the lawn and sneaked them into her bedroom without Clara seeing.

"We'll see," she said. "I think Walter and I will have to have a talk."

"What's to talk about?"

"For starters, we'll talk about why he locked himself in his room. Then we'll talk about his shoes."

Clara shook her head. "Talk, talk, talk. What you need is more action."

"What I need is for you to shut up."

And surprisingly, Clara did. She brought the stack of tortured toast to the table and set it down. She looked at her daughter who was hovering by the kitchen door, peeking around the corner and down the hall.

"Did I ever tell you how my mother, your granny, used to make me walk around with cookbooks on my head?"

Joy looked over at her mother. "What?"

Clara sighed: "She used to make me walk around with heavy books on my head. For good posture, she said. Once, she tied me to a kitchen chair for hours because I was slouching at the table."

Joy stared at her. "You never told me that before. That's horrible."

"I know. But I've got good posture. It accentuates my bosoms."

Joy, of the perpetually rounded shoulders, initially thought Clara was taking a shot at her. But Clara was looking out the window and speaking quietly.

"You know, she never told me why it was so important to have good posture."

"Didn't you ever ask her?"

"I don't know. We never talked about those things."

# 4 }

**Predictably, the shoe thing didn't go too well.** The kids at school were ruthless. But Walter appeared to have resigned himself to wearing his shoes on the wrong feet and Joy was relieved he hadn't put up more of a fuss. As to the actual wearing of them, they felt okay on the wrong feet. Walter clumped along and endured the abuse he had expected to get. The taunts were buried in static, and if somebody pushed him, his miraculous shoes actually kept him from falling over half the time. When he was at home, he found himself spending more time with Nina and Tina and the other girls on the block. For some reason, they didn't tease him as much as the boys did. Which was odd, he thought, because when it came to tormenting Adelaide, the girls were way worse than the boys. Walter was developing a new appreciation for Nina's and Tina's penchant for dressing up like princesses and when he discovered they had brand new glass slippers, he was sold. They weren't real glass, they were clear plastic with silver sparkles, but they looked believable enough. It didn't take much convincing on Walter's part for the twins to act out the Cinderella story, taking turns being the title character. It became their favourite game and, happily for Walter, he got to be the prince. He would run all over the yard, holding the plastic shoe, and getting the neighbourhood girls to try it on. The girls loved this game and called on Walter every time they wanted to play Cinderella.

Johnny Carmichael remained his friend but even Johnny got a bit weird on him, not because of the shoes, but because Spaz was over at the girls' houses a lot. Johnny was not thrilled with his friend's defection. But he wasn't sure how to approach it with Walter, who didn't seem at all bothered by the growing ostracism from the other boys. This put Johnny in a delicate position. Walter was his best friend, but hanging out with him now was tainting his own precarious standing. Ray, Johnny's brother, had even called Walter a queer once. Thankfully, no one else had picked up on that nickname yet, but Johnny knew it was only a matter of time. Yes, Johnny thought, Walter needed a serious talking to.

Ever since Walter had barricaded himself in his room, and before Johnny lured him into the woods for a serious talking-to, Walter had begun living in two different worlds. Colour during the day and black and white at night. It wasn't something he was conscious of, it was something he accepted. In a way, it was like death. You knew it was looming, it was real, but you didn't dwell on it because you couldn't. It was *such* another dimension. Always an average student, Walter surprised himself thinking about smart things, things like death and dimension. But not IQ smart, like being on a quiz show. And not cunning smart, like knowing how to make a bomb out of household ingredients or crack the combination on a safe.

After having discovered the nighttime transformation of his bedroom, Walter would stay up later and later, eagerly awaiting the fading of the primary colours into a grey wash. There was nothing to do that late at night except listen to the radio and think his new smart thoughts when all the stations went off the air. His initial panic at the suspension of all activity lessened and evolved into the thrill of a secret, the only witnesses being the people on the radio and Timmy. He knew Johnny and Nina and Tina would be sleeping, unaware of this world he now inhabited every night. They would know nothing of the photograph that developed within the shadows, the radio voices, or exactly how a second was pulled, like bubblegum, and gradually blown into a minute. They would never understand how you could feel time. How you could let it get inside you, know it better than you know your best friend. He could tell Johnny about the *Hit Parade* songs. But he could never tell him what they meant, how they were like a gateway into another world. How the radio people spoke directly to him. How the songs about war made Walter understand what it was like to die. You can't tell people stuff like that. Besides, Walter didn't want to. If he talked about it, it wouldn't be special and it wouldn't be his anymore. And he was afraid if he talked about it, he would lose the feelings. So Walter kept his secret, and maybe it was his new smartness or maybe it was something as simple as a consistent lack of sleep, but things were different. And unbeknownst to him, soon the static would drift into his coloured world and attach itself.

When Walter emerged from the woods with Johnny, he carried with him yet another thing he couldn't talk about. But at dinner that night, which was meatloaf smothered in ketchup, mashed potatoes and canned green beans, his injury did not go unnoticed.

"What happened to your finger?" asked Joy, as she passed the margarine.

"Nothing," said Walter, tucking into his cone of potatoes.

"It doesn't look like nothing," said Joy, taking his hand and examining it.

"You should put some Mercurochrome on that. And a Band-Aid."

Walter gulped down his potatoes and nodded his head.

"Okay."

"How did you do it? Did you cut it on something rusty?"

"Nope. It was a knife. It was really clean."

"A knife? How did you cut it on a knife?"

Walter eyed his mother, wondering if it was okay to tell her about the pact. Johnny, as he was slicing Walter's finger and his own, had said it was top secret.

"I made a pact with Johnny. We're blood brothers now."

*Press your finger against mine. We have to mingle our blood.*

Clara choked and her own knife clattered noisily onto her plate. She hacked something up into her napkin.

"You mean you sliced your finger open on purpose?" Clara asked. "To make a pact? Why'd you do some stupid-ass thing like that for?"

Walter sighed. "That part's a secret. I can't tell you."

*You have to stop hanging out with the girls so much, Spaz. You and me, we watch each other's backs.*

Clara swivelled her head around so fast her necklace bounced. She directed her accusing gaze at Joy. But Joy didn't have a problem with the pact thing and returned the stare levelly.

"Mom, I did that when I was a kid too. With Mary-Jane."

Joy gave Walter a fond look.

"We're blood sisters for life," she said to him.

*Okay, now we're blood brothers for life.*

"Really, mom? You made a pact too?"

Joy cut a perfect tiny triangle off her slab of grey meatloaf.

"We called it an oath. And you're right, Walter. You can't tell anyone the details. But I still think you should put a Band-Aid on when you're finished dinner."

Joy was actually relieved. Like Johnny, she had been harbouring concerns about Walter's recent interest in playing with the girls. It pleased her that the boys had become blood brothers. Clara felt left out and had to have the last word. She shovelled potatoes into her mouth and looked at Joy with narrowed eyes.

"You hate Mary-Jane," she protested, bits of potato flying from her lips.

"Well," said Joy. "That's not the point."

*Swear, Spaz.*

Walter knew the pact meant more to Johnny than it did to him. It occurred to him that he now had a brother and a dad he couldn't talk about, which didn't seem fair.

*Okay, okay, I swear.*

Saturday afternoon in mid-July. Clara and Joy had taken up their usual positions, side by side on chaise longues on the back patio. They were drinking ginger ale from the Pop Shoppe, and about to do their nails with a new shade of frosted pink polish. Pink was a radical departure for Clara, but her daughter had convinced her to walk on the wild side. Walter was beside them, playing with his marble collection, separating the different sizes of marbles into royal purple drawstring bags made of felt. He was still wearing his shoes on the wrong feet. Clara and Joy were barefooted and studiously removing their old nail polish with cotton balls. The smell of rubbing alcohol made Walter look over. Joy was humming, all efficiency and grace with her long fingers dabbing at her long toes, her knees brought up to her chin. She was wearing a black plastic hairband that caught her curls up and made her look young, Walter thought. While Joy hummed, Clara grunted and puffed, her face red. It looked like she was going to have a heart attack, her hulking body straining the seams on her shiny blue-flowered house dress, with the effort of bending over to reach her swollen feet. Walter watched in amazement and a kind of horror, expecting Clara's dress to rip open at any minute and expose her girdle and god knows what else. While Clara was still trying to remove the last of her toenail polish, her fingers weighted down with big garish rings, Joy had finished placing clean cotton balls between her long, tanned toes. She started to open the pink polish and noticed Walter observing her. She held the bottle out.

"Cotton Candy," she said, tilting the pyramid-shaped glass bottle at him.

"What?"

"That's what colour this is," said Joy, palming it. "Cotton Candy. Sounds delicious, doesn't it?"

"Yeah," agreed Walter. "Does it taste good too?"

Joy laughed up at the sky, one hand shaking the bottle in quick, sharp motions. Walter could hear the tiny crack of a bone in her wrist every time she shook it. It was the same cracking sound as when she shook a thermometer.

"No, no, no," Joy said. "You can't eat this, it's poison."

While Joy unscrewed the white cap that looked like the Eiffel Tower, Walter considered this new information. His mom was putting poison on her toes. Pretty poison called Cotton Candy. He wondered if Nina and Tina knew they were putting poison on their toes and fingers when they painted them. And because Nina bit her nails, he figured he should warn her. So Walter watched the procedure with interest and got caught up in it—the precision, the smell, the fluidity with which his mother wielded that tiny brush, never painting outside the lines. And the intentness of her expression as she did it, her bottom lip caught up in her top teeth. The pink polish had sparkly things in it, like the glass slippers, and it made his mother's toes look beautiful, like a princess or a queen. After she finished the first coat, Joy lay back and passed the bottle to Clara who had finally managed to scrape the harsh red paint off her own toes. She was panting and perspiring with the exertion. Walter's stomach took a turn when he looked at Clara's creature feet. Her toenails were yellow and big and thick looking. They looked like nasty hooves. He realized he had never seen her toenails naked like that.

"What are *you* looking at?" Clara said, spreading her cramped toes apart.

Walter gulped, but couldn't tear his eyes from her feet.

"Nothing," he said.

"Didn't anyone tell you it's not polite to stare?"

While his mom's feet reminded him of graceful, high-stepping flamingo toes, Walter could only think of roadkill when he looked at Clara's mangled puppies. His own toes curled uncomfortably in his straight last shoes as sudden static kicked in, raking his gut, and he blurted out something he never expected to say.

"Can I paint your toes, grandma?"

Joy covered her mouth with her hand to hide a grin, and Clara looked as shocked as Walter was. But it was out there—the invitation—large and ugly. Clara sucked air in through her dentures, sounding like a tea kettle, and for once, was at a loss for words. Walter was horrified he had volunteered for such a task. Time took on the stretched-out quality of Walter's nights. It was so quiet, you could almost hear the robins pulling worms out of the lawn, and Walter thought he would rather drink the entire bottle of pink poison than touch his grandmother's feet with it.

But much like his mouth had moved without his permission, Walter's limbs began a life of their own. His legs retracted from their splayed out position and vaulted him upright. Then they started walking him over to Clara's chaise longue. Joy's eyes were bugging out of her head and Clara was holding her breath, one big wheeze working itself up in her mammoth bosom. Walter was helpless to stop anything about himself.

He sat down at the foot of Clara's chair and held out a grubby hand for the nail polish. Clara handed it over without so much as a jingle or a jangle. Everyone was still and subdued, like Walter was about to perform a miracle, heal the feet or something. He shook the nail polish, quickly and smartly, like his mother had done. A ball bearing rattled around inside the bottle, the only sound. But inside Walter's head was another sound. Full-on static. He couldn't claw through it. Grey noise, scratchy and tumbling about like it had just woken up in his head. The ball bearing clicked, *clickety-click*, and the static mesh hung behind Walter's eyes like a curtain, but he could see into it, he could see backwards into his head. And while his inside self was trying to harness the ecstatic static, his outside self was unscrewing the crusty cap of the nail polish bottle. His outside eyes were staring at his grandmother's grotesque feet with their dull yellow claws. He leaned in, his nose mere inches from his canvas, brush poised in the air. Both women leaned in too. Walter narrowed his eyes and lodged his tongue in the gap between his front teeth. The static was swirling and whooshing, and somewhere down the street a lawn mower started up. Walter touched the tip of the brush to the base of Clara's big toenail, hesitated, and then swooped a big fat Cotton Candy pink stroke up the nail and off its edge. It was brilliant. Perfection. No globs, no streaks, no cuticle stains.

Ahhh, breathed the women, nodding appreciatively.

And Walter dipped for the second stroke. Again, the women leaned in. Could he match his initial genius? Was it a fluke? Sometimes the second stroke is the most difficult, and the ladies knew this. If they were holding fans, they would have fluttered them nervously. Walter didn't hesitate on the second pass. The brush dove unerringly to its proper starting point beside the first pink stripe and flew up the toenail, and off its edge, this time with a decided flourish.

Oooh, breathed the women, nonplussed at the boy's obvious flair.

Two bold pink lines, half the toenail, now gleamed in the sunlight. There was no telling where one stroke touched the other, it was that smooth and even. Walter was onto his third dipping—the static had mellowed out and now rocked gently inside his head, swinging like a hammock. He was soothed. He was all-powerful. He was a friggin' *artist*. One by gnarled one, Clara's vicious talons were painted with equal skill. Even the wretched baby toenails, all curved and ingrown from the pressure of skinny-toed stilettos, were expertly shellacked with Walter's confident touch. By the time he got to the second foot, the women had relaxed, their initial disbelief settling into bewildered pleasure. Walter was on a roll. He almost wiggled one of Clara's toes and almost said, *this little piggy*. When he was done, he sat back on his heels and looked up at his grandmother. She looked stunned, like she had discovered she had a bullet hole in her forehead. Walter felt pride in a job well done. His grandmother's toes looked grand. The transformation was amazing and he had done that. It made him feel accomplished. Joy laughed, which made Clara laugh. And the static blew away, out Walter's ears like thin, grey smoke. Colours and sound filtered back in—the lawn mower, kids playing, the distant whine of a saw, birds chirping and tittering. His name.

"Walter?"

It was Clara. He focused. The animal feet were bearable to look at now because he had *touched* them.

"Thank you, Walter," Clara was saying. "You did a perfect job. I should get you to do my nails all the time."

"You're welcome, grandma," said Walter, fully immersed in colour again and wondering what the hell he had done.

There was a bit of an awkward silence. Joy cleared her throat. Clara stared at her toes. Walter swallowed. Everyone seemed uncharacteristically shy. But it was a good kind of shy, tentative, respectful. Walter manoeuvred himself to his feet and looked at his mother.

"Can I go to the Mooneys', mom?"

"Sure, honey. Be back for dinner, all right?"

Walter clomped off. He had to go see Nina and Tina's feet. And he had to warn them about eating the polish. After he left, Joy and Clara looked at each other.

"My stars," said Clara, patting her hair.

# 5 }

**After the incident with the toenail polish,** his grandmother started treating him differently. She still swore at him sometimes and ignored him other times. But she was giving him glimpses into her life, starting with her bedroom. Clara had a padlock on her bedroom door and Walter had never been allowed inside before. Of course he had always been curious, but it wasn't high on his list of discoveries to make. His mother's bedroom was pretty nondescript and he figured his grandmother's would be even more drab and boring. But it wasn't. It was like a museum or a mausoleum— a *musoleum*. The first time he saw it, she had been closing her door, on her way to breakfast. Her bulk took up the entire narrow hallway, and Walter stopped, waiting for her to snap the padlock shut. While fiddling with the lock, she dropped the key onto the hardwood hall floor and Walter picked it up for her.

"Thanks," said Clara, taking the key from Walter.

But instead of pocketing the key in her housedress, Clara held it in her palm and looked at her grandson.

"Do you want to see inside?"

Walter was surprised. With all the new thoughts roiling around in his head, he had stopped thinking about Clara's bedroom and what lurked within. First he had imagined a house of horrors in there—a torture chamber, a dungeon, Hell. Then as he got older, he figured it was very plain and probably smelled like his grandmother. Now here she was, a bejewelled giantess with garish pink toenails, dangling the key to her lair in front of him. Walter shrugged and looked up at her.

"I don't know," he said. "Sure. I guess."

Clara snorted. "Well, don't get *too* excited about it," she said, snapping the lock open and pushing the door ajar.

"Go on," she invited, one beefy arm holding the door open. "Take a gander, boy."

Walter blinked as he stepped inside, his eyes adjusting. It was nothing like his mother's room, which was all light and airy with off-white furniture and sheer curtains. If his mother's room was day, his grandmother's was night. Heavy brocade drapes in a dark blue and gold peacock pattern were closed over the window and the room did smell like his grandmother, a musty mix of talcum powder, lavender, and age. He got that part right. But nothing could have prepared him for all the stuff in there. He stepped inside, half expecting things to jump out at him. It might be a trick. This was like a whole other house. For starters, there was a ton of furniture crammed in. Dressers and a high-boy and a vanity with a velvet stool, and a bookshelf and a writing desk and a loveseat and the bed with a gigantic wooden headboard and footboard. Everything was heavy dark wood, polished and shiny, and somewhere in all the smells was lemon. There was a Persian rug on the floor and Walter had never seen one before. The floors in the rest of the house were either bare hardwood, waxed tile, or covered with wall-to-wall dull green broadloom. This rug had designs on it. It was dark red, like blood, with blue and black and white swirls and leaves and flowers. It was a magic carpet.

"Wow," he breathed.

"Look around," said Clara, pleased with his reaction.

There was enough china in the room to stock a store, painted plates, fat-cheeked porcelain dolls and a barnyard's worth of animal figurines.

"Them are my knick-knacks," said his grandmother, watching Walter take it all in.

There was a souvenir spoon collection in a locked glass case, embroidered satin pillows, an old-fashioned wash basin with a pitcher, stacks of scented floral stationery—lily of the valley—and about a million pictures of the Royal Family. There were doilies everywhere. It was nuts. Clara sat on the high bed and Walter heard the springs groan. He stood at the vanity, a fancy affair with a huge speckled mirror shaped like a fan. The vanity was littered with perfumes and make-up and jewellery, which glittered and shone in the muted light. It was splendid and rich looking. A jewellery box made of worn black leather was open, lined with red satin and overflowing with baubles and trinkets and rhinestones. Walter was overwhelmed and he sat on the velvet stool, staring around. He had no idea this place existed inside the house.

Clara burped noisily. "So? Whaddya think?"

"This is great!" said Walter. "Where did you get all this stuff?"

Clara crossed her legs, pulling her dress primly over her knees. "Oh, here and there. Some of it I've had since I was a girl."

Walter looked at her questioningly. She glared at him. "I *was* a girl once, y'know."

Walter couldn't picture it. He turned around and looked in the vanity mirror. He saw Clara lean over and open a drawer on her night table. She fumbled around for a minute, her bracelets clanking. Walter picked up a hairbrush with a thick engraved silver plate on the back and a heavy silver handle. It weighed a ton. The bristles were dense and soft, like fur. He brushed his face. There was a matching comb in an identical silver casing with gems embedded into it and a hand mirror of the same design. Walter ran his hands over everything, it all felt so rich and important. He heard his grandmother get off the bed and watched her approach him.

"There," she said, tossing a photograph onto the vanity.

Walter picked it up. It was older than the black and white photo of his dad. This one was brown and white and not very clear. A young woman and a tall older man stood side by side, staring straight into the camera. Neither one was smiling. The woman was wearing a sack of a dress and her hair was parted in the middle and pulled back off her face in a severe bun. The man wore a suit and a hat.

"Is this you?" Walter asked, pointing to the woman.

"Yup. Pretty skinny, huh?"

"Yeah. Who's the man?"

Clara leaned over the vanity and picked up a tube of red lipstick. It too was in a jewelled silver case. Walter watched her unroll the lipstick, and run it over her lips which already had lipstick on them anyway. Clara pulled her mouth into an "O" shape and slicked the colour on, speaking in a mumble.

."That's your grandpa. His name was Rusty."

More news. Walter absorbed it, like Clara's lips drank in the colour: Rich Red. Yet another man in the family that he knew nothing about.

"Where is he now?"

Clara smacked her lips together, an unpleasant, wet sound.

"He's dead," she said, reaching past Walter for a Kleenex.

Walter watched his grandmother blot her lips with the Kleenex and smack them together again.

"How did he die?"

Clara stopped her mouth ministrations and looked down at Walter.

"I killed him," she said matter of factly, picking up a jar of Vaseline and opening it.

What? Walter didn't think he heard correctly. Clara dipped a lacquered fingernail into the Vaseline and began applying it over her lipstick.

"You what?"

Clara reached across Walter for another Kleenex, her brassiere digging into his shoulder like an armoured breastplate.

"Killed him, I said. What, are you deaf?"

"How...uh," he stuttered.

Clara wiped the Vaseline off her finger and picked the photo up, examining it. She laughed, a brittle sound.

"Poisoned him, I did. Killed him with my cooking, I guess you could say."

Walter stared up at his grandmother, mouth agape. She kissed the photo now, leaving a greasy red smear that she wiped off with her thumb.

"Ah, Rusty, you old fool," she said.

Humming a cheerful tune, like she hadn't just confessed to *murder*, Walter's grandmother walked back to the night table and returned the photo. He was speechless. Clara sat back on the bed and looked at him.

"Cat got yer tongue?" she asked, seeming pleased with herself. "Guess you want to know what happened, don't you?"

Walter nodded, not entirely sure he did want to know.

Clara cleared her throat, a phlegmy, bubbling sound, and clasped her hands in her lap like she was about to recite a poem or The Lord's Prayer.

"Well. We was sitting down to dinner one night, me and Rusty, and I had made this rabbit stew, y'see. Rusty had come in the night before from his traplines. That's where we got the rabbit from. We didn't have no grocery stores back then, way up north. We had to kill our meat. Anyways, there was turnips and onions and carrots in the stew, and I think, if memory serves, I might have made dumplings too."

Clara stopped speaking and closed her eyes, thinking back. Walter was getting completely grossed out. First of all . . . *rabbit* stew?

"Yes," she said now. "Yes, there was dumplings, I remember now. Anyhoo," she took a breath. "Yer grandpa had no more 'n three bites of that stew and keeled over. Right there at the table. Dead. His face in the dumplings. That's how I remember them 'cause I had to wipe them off his face."

Clara snapped her fingers in the air. "Dead. Like that."

Walter jumped. Clara eyed him closely.

"Hah!" she chortled. "Don't believe me, do ya?"

Walter lifted a boxy green ring off the vanity and slipped it over his thumb, twisting it. He shrugged his shoulders and Clara got up off the bed.

"Well, sonny boy," she said. "It's true. Ask your mother, if you don't believe me. She was there, too. Mind you, she was just a wee thing then. But, she was there. Good thing she didn't eat none of that stew or you wouldn't be here either. And shut your mouth, you look like a bass."

Walter swallowed with effort. God, his grandmother was a murderer. When he was about to ask her what she put in the stew, besides dumplings—toenail polish?—they both heard Joy calling them to breakfast and that was the end of that. On their way out of the bedroom, Clara nudged him with her elbow and winked.

"You won't be telling the cops about our little talk now, will ya?"

"No way, grandma."

"Good. I wouldn't want to have to cook you up a little bunny."

And with that parting comment, Clara strode down the hall like a general, her brooches glinting like medals.

From the day of the confession onwards, Clara never locked her door again. As time passed, Walter became comfortable going into her bedroom. It got to the point where he would perch on the bed and watch Clara putting on her war paint, as she called it. And Clara got so used to his presence she didn't mind bustling around the bedroom in nothing but her underwear. But it was hardly revealing. Clara wore more things under her dresses than Walter wore over his clothes in the wintertime. Her brassieres went all the way down to her waist and somewhere in that vicinity the massive expanse of girdle started. Over top of it all was the obligatory white full slip. And then there were the underarm pads, oval pieces of flesh-coloured material that nestled in her armpits, looped over her shoulders with thin elastic. Dress shields, she called them. Clara had so many different straps digging into her shoulders, Walter wondered how she could lift her arms. It looked really painful and left grooves in her skin. Seeing her in her underclothing didn't bother Walter, there was so much of it. But her skin did, at first. Like that initial sight of her feet, it took a bit for him to get used to looking at the previously unexposed parts of her body. For instance, he never knew she had big black moles on her back or freckles on her shoulders. He never knew she dyed her hair black until she showed him her roots one day. And he was fascinated to learn she plucked a *hair* out of her chin on a regular basis. There was so much for her to do, it was no wonder she was always tired.

"Being a woman is hard work," she would say to Walter, and he believed her.

Once he got accustomed to his grandmother's appearance, Walter loved watching her daily preparations. She would sit at the vanity in her brassiere and girdle and slip, and paw through her jewellery box, selecting different rings and brooches and a necklace and clip-on earrings. Sometimes she would let him choose something. After she was gussied up with beads and stones, she would "put on her face." First the moisturizing cream, Nivea, which she would also rub into her wrinkly elbows. Then the foundation, the pancake, she called it. CoverGirl. Then, the powder, the rouge, the lipstick, the eye shadow. Again, CoverGirl. Finally, the perfume. White Shoulders or Chanel No. 5. Walter found out that she brushed her hair with the fur brush every night before she went to bed and that she wore a sleep mask and a hairnet. It was too much. When he asked his mom if she did all that, she had laughed.

"No, honey. I basically wash my face and comb my hair, and go," she said.

He wondered how they could be so different. And why it was his mom who was beautiful and his grandmother who looked alarming. He thought his grandmother might look prettier if she didn't do all that stuff. When he suggested it one day, Clara said she wouldn't be caught dead without her war paint.

"Why do you think I'm letting you watch me?" she asked Walter.

"I don't know."

"So's you can do me up proper when I *am* dead," Clara said, and leaned over to whisper in his ear.

"I want to be wearing my dusty rose dress, remember that. I guess you can pick the jewellery."

Walter looked forward to it. Sometimes he forgot she had killed Rusty.

In Clara's bedroom, Walter was an explorer. It was like being out in the woods with its different air and smells and shadows cut with shafts of light. He would lie on his stomach on the Persian rug and trace the patterns with a finger, then turn over onto his back and stare at the ceiling, that had way more interesting shapes than his own bedroom at night. The wallpaper was green and gold leaves and branches, and if you crossed your eyes it was like being outside. If you touched the wallpaper, the branches and leaves felt like velvet moss. But this was better than being in the forest. Instead of grey and brown rocks, there was a glittering treasure of stones to discover and turn over in the jewellery box. There were animals, real ones that had been stuffed, presumably by the long-dead Rusty. A great owl hung from the ceiling, wings and talons spread, mid-swoop, and a black squirrel sat on the writing table clasping a fountain pen in its tiny paws. Walter wondered if Timmy could be stuffed when he died. He thought Timmy would make a fine brooch, if you painted his shell bright colours and glued silver stars on it.

Although there always seemed to be something new to explore in his grandmother's room, by far the best day was when Walter discovered her closet. In the beginning, Clara had shooed him out after her accessorizing and before her final dressing. But one day, she either didn't mind, or forgot, and opened her closet for the first time to choose a dress. Walter didn't notice at first, he was busy looking at photos of his mother and grandmother having a picnic at Lake Simcoe, which could have been the ocean, it was so big. They were wearing one-piece bathing suits and bathing caps, his mother tall and slim, his grandmother well on her way to being a large square. There were no men in any of the pictures, except those from other families in the background. By slyly asking his grandmother how old she was in the photos, Walter figured her current age to be around sixty-something, an estimate never to be confirmed because Clara deemed it unladylike to discuss one's age.

"Here," she said, handing over a large pink conch shell with Niagara Falls written on it and a sticker of a hula girl.

"Put this to your ear. You can hear the sea while you look."

Walter didn't hear his grandmother open the closet door. He was wrapped up in sounds of the sea, which sounded vaguely familiar to him. The hollow echoey sound penetrated his brain, and it didn't take much effort for Walter to imagine he was at the seashore. He wondered if he would have to wear his straight last shoes in the water should he decide to go swimming in the ocean. And thought they would probably drown him with their weight, and fill up with sand and leave mysterious footprints leading to the water's edge. Lifeguards would track them, and wonder why the left shoeprint was where the right one should be. It could throw off the entire rescue effort while Walter was being dragged under, kicking futilely, trying to undo his laces. All this would happen while his mother and grandmother ran back and forth on the shore in their one-piece bathing suits and bathing caps, leaving two sets of normal footprints—long and narrow, short and fat. And when the lifeguards finally dragged his limp body back to shore, they would shake their heads with regret and say:

"If he wasn't wearing those shoes..."

Or maybe the shoes would save his life. Maybe he could kick a shark in the face. Then everyone would want a pair. He would be a hero and on-lookers would shake their heads with disbelief and say:

"If he wasn't wearing those shoes..."

And the sea whispered all these things in a hollow, steady voice, as he turned the thick black pages of the photo album.

It wasn't until he got to the last page and closed the book, removing the shell from his ear, that he heard the clattering of hangers. Walter looked up to see the broad backside of his grandmother sticking out from the closet, her flabby arms flailing through a jungle of dresses. He stared dumbly. The closet was new territory. While his grandmother kept up a steady stream of cussing and bracelet jangling, Walter wobbled over to watch. There must have been a billion dresses in the closet. No slacks.

"Trousers are for men," Clara would say to Joy whenever Walter's mother wore slacks. "You want to look like a man?"

But dresses, well, Clara had a department store's worth of dresses in that closet. Flouncy frocks, A-line shifts, sunny sundresses, sleek gowns, everyday housedresses—you name it. A few skirts with matching jackets or soft sweaters, but mostly dresses. Walter sat down on the floor beside his grandmother while she rustled through her collection. He noticed her armpit dress shields were already getting a good workout. Finally, she seemed to settle on something and pulled out a sleeveless white dress with big black daisies on it. She held it out to Walter.

"So? This one?"

She shook it in front of his face.

"Okay," he said.

"Okay? Okay? That's it?"

She stared at him, waiting.

"It's pretty, grandma. I like the flowers."

Clara looked at the dress, debating.

"Hmmph," she grunted. "I'd have to change my necklace."

Walter nodded knowingly when she looked at him. Clara laid the daisy dress on her bed and smoothed her slip down over her bulging girdled stomach.

"You poke around in there and find me some nice white shoes to go with it," she said. "I'm going to get another necklace."

With that, Clara thudded over to the vanity, leaving Walter in charge of her footwear. He crawled closer to the closet on his hands and knees and peered inside, under the dresses. There they were. Shoes, millions of them. His mouth hung open. Rows and rows of high-heeled shoes, lined up like polished soldiers ready for their marching orders. He reached out a hand and ran his fingers over the pointed toes. He crawled deeper into the closet, the hems of the dresses grazing his head. He was in shoe heaven and temporarily forgot his assignment. Nina and Tina would go crazy in here, he thought, picking up dazzling shoes and stroking them. And the smell. His grandmother used baby powder in her shoes and Walter breathed it in—powder, polish, leather, and a hint of mothballs. The smells and the closeness of the closet aroused in him a feeling of expectation, looming adventure. And the shoes were deformed, which endeared them all the more to Walter. His grandmother's bunions had warped the entire collection of footwear in the same manner, bulged them out at the seams. Now that he had been intimate with his grandmother's feet, Walter pictured them in detail inside these shoes and saw where every malformed toe had moulded the leather to its shape. He desperately wanted to try one on.

Later, his grandmother would tell him the names of all these shoes: slingbacks, mules, pumps, stilettos. All high heels, except for the pair Mr. Foster had sold her. Those were simply called walking shoes and they were still in the box that Walter recognized. Each pair of shoes roused an emotion in Walter. The high-heeled silver backless slippers with pink fuzz on the toes made him want to laugh. The black leather plain pumps had a sober, quiet air about them, like church or like a pact in the woods. There was an entire row of identical satin pumps in unbelievable colours. Those were wedding shoes, his grandmother told him later, dyed to match the material of her dress at the time. They were part of what was known as an ensemble. It was becoming clear to Walter why his grandmother placed so much importance on her "ensembles." They made her feel different ways. As Walter picked up each pair of shoes and caressed and inhaled them, he felt like a psychic who could conjure up images of a person merely by holding one of their belongings. When he held the gold high heels with fine elastic straps, he could see his grandmother curtsying and waltzing in a ballroom with a prince. In the green wooden-soled sandals, she was strolling a seaside boardwalk, twirling a matching green parasol and eating an ice cream sundae. With each pair of shoes examined, his grandmother became a character in a story, and it didn't matter a bit that she was so fat and had to yank a hair from her chinny-chin-chin. In these shoes, she was a fair maiden, a witch, a farm girl, or a gypsy.

Of course Walter had seen his grandmother in some of these shoes every day and never given a thought as to her dancing or strolling. It was only when the shoes were off her feet, only when they were all laid out, that a connection was made. It wasn't so different than the connection of electricity that arced and zapped and brought Frankenstein to life. Much like that experiment, this connection jolted Walter into awareness of possibilities, new visions, deep within the closet laboratory. But still, like a dumb, stupid monster, he had no idea what it all meant. These new feelings were primal, urgent, but beyond his grasp. For now the shoes merely delighted him, filled him with glee. Some were like candy, the colours delicious. There were lemon meringue pie shoes, blueberry shoes, bubblegum, and canteloupe. They stirred an intense craving in Walter and his toes curled up in his own clunky clodhoppers. Walter felt like eating his grandmother's shoes, devouring them. Or something else. Licking them at least. Or wearing them—on his feet, ears, hands— or sleeping with them. Crawling inside them, if he could, and being the little boy who lived in a shoe. He felt a need to get intimate with them, in much the same way he had been moved to paint his grandmother's toes. Walter wasn't exactly conscious of these feelings, they floated around like dandelion fluff, aimless and bouncing off the undulating static. And he pressed one hand firmly into his crotch, unaware what he was doing but feeling a need to hold something back. He had confidence that he would figure it out in time, and until then, he would clump along in his Frankenstein shoes, bumping into new things and experiencing unfamiliar feelings.

He knew something would come of this, because here in his grandmother's closet the static was rocking and rolling, folding in on itself, seesawing, collapsing and expanding. It was like an accordion in his head and hundreds of tiny perfect shoes danced on the sharp edges, to a tune from the *Hit Parade*. The connection put Walter into a kind of paralysis and Clara's shoes breathed and glowed, pulsing in time to his inner rhythms.

He stopped touching the shoes and simply sat still, waiting for something to happen, something to give. Then, Clara happened.

"Hey! What are you doing in there? *Making* the damn shoes?"

The accordion ground to a halt and Walter's outer eyes adjusted to the closet. Shoes. White shoes. He grabbed some slingbacks and crawled out of the closet. His grandmother was sitting on the bed, squeezed into her daisy dress and sporting a strand of white pearls as big as ping pong balls.

"Here, grandma," Walter said, holding out the shoes. "Are these okay?"

Clara nodded in the affirmative and turned her back to Walter.

"Fine, fine. Now, be a dear and zip your old granny up, would ya?"

"Okay."

And newly zapped, the monster zipped. Another new thing to do.

# 6 }

**When Walter was an adult,** he would pinpoint the revelation of his calling to the day he discovered his grandmother's shoes. In retrospect, the moment was simply a coalescing of other telling factors that had been present since the day he first fell on his bum when he tried to walk. More probably—if you believed in nature over nurture—since birth. Others would call his epiphany less flattering names, like obsession or fetish. But to Walter, it was neither. It was the springboard for a purpose, and according to everything Walter had been taught, a purpose is a good and positive thing. It moves you forward, makes you count. He, after all, did not ask to be born with such feet. Nor did he beg for straight last shoes, and it certainly wasn't he who suggested wearing them on the wrong feet for those formative years of childhood.

People were always saying things like: If life hands you a lemon, make lemonade.

Well. So there. So *fucking* there. Now, shut up all of you. I have to bury my grandmother in her dusty rose dress and pick out her jewellery. And she will wear the grandest shoes in the world, shoes of my design. Did you know she was a murderer? Does that scare you? It should. I will wear her highest heels and dance on her grave. And, yes, maybe I can't walk but guess what? I can sure as *fuck* dance. My feet are to dancing what Mel Tillis's voice is to singing. And what of substance do you people with no connection have? I help people. I help people walk their roads. That is my purpose, not my obsession. It is my *calling*.

Walter began his calling in his grandmother's closet. Unbeknownst to either Clara or Joy, he would crawl into the closet and spend hours with the shoes. Sometimes he would fall into a trance with a shoe over his face, breathing in the scent to help his visions. He did lick the shoes on occasion, but stopped short of chewing them because the polish came off and stained his tongue with even the gentlest of slurps. His grandmother had given him permission to polish and buff them, which he did on a regular basis, with fastidious precision. Her shoes had never been so pampered and Clara could find no fault with the job Walter did. Inside the closet, he was free to let the static run wild. Sometimes it was sketchy and elusive, other times, plump and pulsating like an organ. Walter scrutinized Clara's shoes, every stitch, buckle, and strap. He stuck his hand inside and explored where the leather had strained its seams, felt his grandmother's ghost foot in every one. Sometimes when the static obliterated everything, when his stomach felt the most anxious, his hands would curl up inside the shoes and he would scratch with his fingernails so hard he would lift the insoles right out. It was only when his vision cleared and the straining in his stomach eased, that he realized what he had done. He would return later with glue to fix the damage, a task he enjoyed performing. While other boys were taking apart clocks and engines, Walter was engrossed in the workings of shoes and feet. It seemed an entirely rational exercise, given the attention, mostly unwanted, paid to his own. His grandmother was appreciative of the high gloss he managed to coax out of her older shoes, or the extra holes he punched in the straps for greater comfort. He loosened up her newer shoes without her knowledge, kneading the stiff leather, flexing and bending their joints. There was never a shortage of things to do, whether it was a major repair job like fixing a broken heel or the fine detail work involved in retouching a nick in the leather or reattaching a feather with a pinprick of glue. After he got his mother to teach him how to sew—a request that surprised the hell out of her—there wasn't much Walter couldn't do to keep his family's shoes in good repair. He was a natural.

The calling urged Walter on to greater deeds. It stirred humanitarian impulses deep within his soul. To hell with the name-calling, the taunting, the sidelong glances. They were easy to ignore after awhile, particularly after a session in the closet. Eventually, people would come around. They all had shoes that needed fixing. They all had feet. Walter came to believe he had been given the ugly straight last shoes for a reason. They humbled him, ensured he wouldn't get too cocky. And, in a way, they were like a calling card. Heck, if he could manage to get around in retard shoes, *especially* on the wrong feet, it would stand to reason he could overcome any obstacle, be sympathetic to anyone's dilemma. That should inspire confidence. If he could withstand the jeers, ignore his awkward clumping, he *must* know something other people don't know. He *must* have powers. The shoes would keep him honest. Otherwise, his obvious superiority might be visible and you can't work miracles if people resent you. Subdued confidence is better. It makes people wonder what your secret is, and why you don't cry when someone pushes you hard enough so that you fall over because you're wearing your shoes on the wrong feet and you're always off-balance anyway because your walking is crooked. Why you pick yourself up, dust yourself off, and duck your head in acknowledgement before shambling off down the street. Why you have the nerve to look back over your shoulder with a straight gaze into your tormentor's eyes, once. Those things command respect, but not the kind of slavish devotion that gets heaped on the football captain or the tough guy. It's the kind of respect born of fear of the unknown. That's what Walter was going for. But that was only a side bonus. His main thing was the calling. And what better place to start than with Adelaide.

He called on her. It was the first time anyone had called on Adelaide. And barring Jehovah's Witnesses or Fuller brush salesmen, it was one of the few times someone had ever knocked on the Vanstones' front door. Walter took a deep breath, looked around to see if anyone was watching, and walked up the driveway. The lawn boy was falling down on the job, Walter noted, observing the weeds and patchy grass. It struck him that there were no flowers. He took stock of the house as he approached, noticing the drawn drapes in every window. It looked deserted and for a minute, he got nervous. There were stories about Mrs. Vanstone, told by the neighbourhood kids and overheard in adult conversations. But more and more, Walter was identifying with Adelaide. After all, she had no dad, no visible sibling, and her mother looked almost as old as his grand-mother. Not to mention the obvious. The damn shoes. He flexed his shoulders and plodded up to the front door, consciously pushing back the creeping static. He knocked and waited, staring down at his feet. He didn't see the living room curtains move and didn't see Mrs. Vanstone's beady eyes peering out at him. Walter knocked again, starting to get second thoughts about his grand idea. But then he heard footsteps and the front door opened a crack.

"Yes?" croaked Mrs. Vanstone.

Walter tried a big smile that didn't quite make it, and he stepped back a pace.

"Hi, Mrs. Vanstone. Is Adelaide home?"

Lillian Vanstone stared at the boy. It was the Finch kid. If it were anyone else, particularly one of those Carmichael boys, she would have slammed the door in his face. Nobody ever called on Adelaide, it would have to be a mean trick. But because it was the kid with the limp, she hesitated.

"What do you want with Adelaide?" she asked, suspicious.

Walter thought about the question. He couldn't very well say he wanted to experiment on her. It wouldn't do to divulge his purpose to Mrs. Vanstone. She could hardly be expected to understand the purity of his intentions. Trust no one.

"I wondered," he said, "if Adelaide wanted to come out and play?"

Lillian ran her tongue over her chipped teeth and considered this. The kid looked harmless. And although she felt she had to protect her overgrown daughter, she didn't want to stunt her social development in any way. Maybe Adelaide had made some real friends while she was out gallivanting around the neighbourhood. If so, she had done better than her mother. Things hadn't been going well for Lillian, what with her boy, Rory, gone overseas, and her husband lying somewheres at the bottom of a mine shaft. Adelaide used up all the strength she had. Caring for that child, she had nothing leftover to extend in being neighbourly. But if they came to her...well, that was a different thing. Lillian pushed the screen door open.

"Come on in," she said. "Adelaide's in her room, I guess."

Walter stepped into the small foyer. The Vanstones lived in the most expensive of the three models, the one with four stairs leading up to the living room. Almost a split-level, but not really. Mrs. Vanstone plodded up the carpeted stairs and Walter followed, looking at her feet. She was wearing burnt-orange knitted slippers that were unravelling. At the top landing, Mrs. Vanstone waved a hand at the living room.

"Have a seat. I'll go see what Adelaide's doing."

Walter watched her trudge down the hall and he sat in the nearest armchair that was covered in plastic, hands folded in his lap. It was dark in here, like his grandmother's bedroom, but the smell was different. It smelled like food, but not like the cooking smells in any other houses he had visited. More of a rotting smell, like sour stew. And there were plants absolutely everywhere, which was weird considering the lack of outdoor foliage. This was long before indoor plants became a must for every home. Long before Boston ferns, spider plants and wandering Jews became household pets. Modern housewives of the day cultivated clean, bright living spaces rather than terrariums. They kept their plants outside. But Lillian Vanstone was ahead of the times. Her place was so twisted up in ivy and vines, you couldn't tell where one plant began and another ended. It was, well, crazy. Walter liked it. He pictured Adelaide's brain to be like that, all overlapping with so much information it got lost in the maze. Maybe if she lived at his house, she would be normal. If she stayed away from the closet, that is.

Then he heard Mrs. Vanstone's tired shuffle and he looked over his shoulder with what he hoped was a winning smile.

"I like all your plants," he said.

She stood there, stooped over with the beginnings of a severe dowager's hump, her hands shoved into the pockets of a stained apron.

"Yes, the plants," she said.

Walter struggled out of the deep chair to his feet. He was beginning to think this was a bad idea. It was easy to be around the other moms on the street, to know what to say, to predict what they would say. They were all like catalogue cutouts, interchangeable. But Mrs. Vanstone was cut from a far different catalogue.

"Um, is Adelaide in her room?" he asked.

Lillian stared at him blankly. "I'm making pie," she said.

"What?"

"Pork pie. It takes all day."

She pulled a pack of Export Plains out of her apron and offered him one.

"No, thanks. I don't smoke," he said, trying not to think about pig pie.

Lillian tapped the smoke on a tarnished Zippo lighter before firing it up and convulsing in a coughing fit with her first inhalation. Walter watched the ritual with morbid interest. Having recovered from her lung spasms, Lillian disappeared into the kitchen without another word. Walter followed her, but not without some degree of fear. The kitchen, the source of the sour smell, was as dark as the living room except for a weak light over the stove. A huge pot bubbled with brown foam that spit and hissed as it hit the hot element. Walter saw things bobbing around in the sludge, grey gristly knobs of unknown origin, and turned his head away. Lillian Vanstone was sitting at the red Arborite table, pouring a cup of tea. She motioned Walter over.

"Sit down, young man."

Walter sat and watched her pour him a cup of tea from what resembled a rusted watering can for the plants. He never drank tea, but had no desire to argue.

"One lump or two?" asked Lillian, pulling off a passable coquettish voice.

"One, please," he guessed.

"One, two," said Lillian, dropping three cubes into his cup.

She leaned right into his face then, and cackled: "Buckle my shoe."

Walter shrank back into his chair. Why did she say buckle my shoe? How much did she know? Maybe this crazy lady shit was all an act. And where the hell was Adelaide? He looked closer at Mrs. Vanstone, looking for a wart on her chin or some other sign she might be a witch. But she had shifted her focus to her cup of tea and was madly stirring it with a tiny spoon, the kind his grandmother had in the locked glass case. Tea was slopping over the sides of the cup onto the saucer and drowning the lit cigarette she had rested on its edge.

"Biscuit?"

Walter blinked. "Pardon me?"

Lillian was holding a bag of Dad's cookies out to him and furiously shaking it back and forth, the cookies audibly breaking up into chunks with the force.

Walter shook his head. "No, thank you."

Lillian looked like she was going to cry. "You don't want a Dad?" she asked, tearfully. "Every kid should have a Dad."

*Jesus.* Walter sipped his tea for something to do. It was like drinking hot rusty sugar water. Mrs. Vanstone was slurping down her tea with great zeal, when she wasn't dissolving cookies into it. It was like she forgot he was there. He sat very still, wondering if he should get up and leave.

"Adelaide's outside," she said.

"What?"

"Adelaide. She's in the backyard. Isn't that why you came over?"

Lillian looked him up and down. It was the Finch kid. The one with a limp. He was probably okay. Now, if it was one of those Carmichael boys, that would be another story. But she didn't want to stunt Adelaide's social development, now did she? It wouldn't do not to be neighbourly. Maybe she should offer him some tea. But Walter had risen from the table and was already opening the back door.

"Thanks for the tea, Mrs. Vanstone," he said, and clumped down the back stairs.

Lillian sucked as hard as she could on her cigarette, but nothing happened. And then she remembered it took all day to make pork pie. She better get busy.

Adelaide was wearing a thin one-piece white bathing suit that showed way more of her body than was comfortable for any observer other than a pervert. She had been running through the sprinkler and now sat in her sandbox, covered in wet sand and all manner of the other goo that she seemed to always attract. When she saw Walter coming down the stairs, her face lit up and her slobbery mouth hung wide open.

"WAH! AH-GOB-SAM-BOX!" she shrieked, grabbing fistfuls of sand and throwing them up in the air.

Walter hesitated on the last step, and stood still for a second, gripping the shaky wooden banister. He couldn't remember why he was here. This kind of memory skip was happening more often and it was distressing, frustrating. But Walter was learning to obey his compulsions, not to argue. Usually the lapse was short-lived, an unsettling moment while the static knifed into his brain and divided it into easily digestible portions. Adelaide was oblivious. While Walter swayed on the bottom step, Adelaide was lying on her back in the sandbox making sand angels and bleating nonsense words. Walter shook his head and walked over to the sandbox where Adelaide was having the time of her life, although a stranger might have thought she was engaged in a seizure. Walter perched on a corner of the sandbox and looked around the yard. He saw her running shoes lying a few feet away and the connection, the zap, was made. He relaxed.

"Hey, Adelaide," he called.

She stopped flopping around and sat up, gritty snot covering her upper lip, pale eyes zeroing in on Walter. There was a quiet spell, where both kids assessed each other. Adelaide's customary exuberance was suspended momentarily while she struggled with the realization that Walter had come to her, that she hadn't had to force her company on him. It clicked into place in her mind. Walter, for his part, took clinical stock of Adelaide. He noticed things like one strap of her bathing suit had fallen off her shoulder and her titty was showing. Not that it mattered. You could see everything through the transparent white bathing suit anyway. This state of affairs did not excite him in any way, nor did it disgust him. It made him wonder about stuff. Like how come Adelaide's brain was so much younger than other girls her age, but her body was older? It was exactly the opposite of him, with his overly mature brain and his immature walking. He felt kindly towards Adelaide at this moment.

"Adelaide," he said. "Go get your shoes."

Adelaide bobbed her head up and down, yellow pigtails flying.

Walter pointed to her running shoes lying on the grass.

"Can I see your shoes, Adelaide? They look like really nice shoes, I'd like to see them."

Adelaide turned and looked at her shoes. She pointed at them.

"SOOZ?"

"Yes! Can I see them?"

"HAAA! MAH-SOOZ-MAH-SOOZ-YOU-PAY-MAH-SOOZ?"

Walter inclined his head towards the dirty sneakers. Adelaide got it and scrambled to her knees. She was panting like a dog, her tongue hanging loosely out of her mouth. This was, for Adelaide, a very happy moment. She rolled herself out of the sandbox and ran awkwardly over to the shoes, her chubby pale thighs squeaking together, bathing suit rammed into her crack, her jiggly white ass cheeks entirely exposed. Walter nodded encouragingly when she reached her shoes and looked back at him for approval. She trotted back holding the running shoes and gurgling with pleasure.

"Put them on," urged Walter.

Adelaide stared at him.

"Put your shoes on," said Walter. "I want to see how pretty you look in them."

"PITY?"

"Yes, pretty," said Walter, smiling.

Adelaide nearly turned herself inside out with glee and actually blushed. She dropped to the grass with a thump and began struggling to pull her shoes on.

"PITY-PITY-PITY," she grunted loudly, getting her fingers tangled up in the frayed laces.

Walter observed. Adelaide automatically put her shoes on the wrong feet, which made him feel a bit sick to his stomach. The laces were a disaster. No way she could manage the intricacies of doing them up. She gave up and finally yanked the laces out of her running shoes altogether. She sat there, legs stretched out in front of her, admiring her shoes, slapping them together. Walter cleared his throat.

"What colour is your bathing suit, Adelaide?"

She whipped a triumphant glance at him.

"WHY!" she yelled.

Walter grinned.

"Right! Good girl! Now, what colour is…my shirt?"

Adelaide clapped frantically and howled: "BOO! BOO!"

"Verrry good," Walter said. "What colour are your shoes?"

Adelaide thought about that for a minute.

"PAD! PAD-SOOZ!" she yelped, thrilled with herself.

"Good! You're right Adelaide! Plaid! They're plaid shoes!"

While Adelaide went into writhing contortions on the grass, hugging herself, and kicking her feet in the air, Walter was pleased with himself. Good, he thought. She knows her colours. He pulled the nail polish bottles out of his pocket, the ones he had swiped from his mother's bedroom.

"Come here," he said. "Let me see your feet."

Adelaide stopped humping the lawn and pulled herself into a sitting position. This was too much fun. She liked Wah. What did he want her to do now?

"Your feet," said Walter again. "Can I see your pretty feet?"

Adelaide calmed down and obligingly pointed her feet in Walter's direction. She was out of breath and started sucking her thumb, looking at her new best friend, wondering what was coming next. Walter sat on the grass and pulled Adelaide's feet into his lap. As soon as her running shoes nestled onto his thighs, Walter felt a rush of giddiness. He pulled her right shoe off and for once Adelaide was silent. She sucked her thumb and watched, trusting. Walter understood this. It was the same way he had felt with Mr. Foster and it caused him no end of pleasure, sensing he was having the same effect on Adelaide. This was power, the good kind of power. God, he loved this, all these thoughts. He was expanding his horizons. What started in his room alone at night had replicated itself in the closet, and now he was able to bring it out again in the daytime, out in the open. He could see the progression, how it worked.

He looked at Adelaide's bare foot. It was a lot bigger than Nina or

Tina's feet but smaller than his mom's. Adelaide's was the whitest foot he had ever seen. White and soft and plump with blue veins. So blue, for a second he felt like slicing open her foot with a knife and doing a pact— a thought that died as soon as it flickered. He did recognize, however, that Adelaide would probably have let him do anything he wanted. But Walter had other things on his mind. He held both feet in his hands for a second, feeling their weight. All Walter could hear was the sucking sound of Adelaide's mouth on her thumb and the distant sound of the ocean. Walter picked up the bottle of red nail polish and held it out to Adelaide.

"What colour is this, Adelaide?"

"WED," she said, from around her thumb.

"That's right," said Walter, shaking the bottle.

"I'm going to paint your big toenail, okay?"

Adelaide nodded furiously, eyes wide. She *loved* Wah.

"Now, don't move, okay?" he said, brush at the ready. "Be very still."

"KAY."

Walter painted her toenail perfectly. It was an odd toenail, very little nail on quite a bulbous toe. Walter blew on it when he was done and cautioned Adelaide not to move. Then he picked up her right shoe and on the inside of the tongue, he painted a round red dot with the polish. Adelaide watched it all with interest and kept quiet. She knew something important was going on.

Walter picked up the second bottle of polish and held it out to her. She was ready for him this time.

"PEEK!" she shouted, pulling her thumb out of her mouth for a second.

"Right," said Walter.

And, with the pink polish, he performed the same procedures on her left big toe and her left sneaker. Now, the defining moment. Would she understand? This was more exciting for Walter than it was for Adelaide. His voice got serious, but he kept a gentle tone.

"Look Adelaide," he said. "Now you can know which shoe goes on which foot."

He wiggled her right toe, and looked at her hopefully.

"WED," she announced proudly. "WEH-HED. WED-DOH."

Walter put both shoes in her lap with the tongues rolled back so she could see the dots.

"See the red shoe?" he asked. "Where's the red shoe?"

Adelaide scrunched up her eyes and her nose and leaned forward, visibly concentrating. Then, unexpectedly, she farted. Not a polite fart either. A whooping, screeching fart that exploded with such velocity and violence, it caused Adelaide to topple over onto her side. Which is where she lay, shrieking with laughter, punctuated with the aftershocks of her volcanic fart. It went on forever, eruptions that sounded like someone driving on a flat tire. Flub, flub, flub, every time she laughed. Normally, Walter would have been in hysterics. But this pissed him off. He had wisdom to impart, and Adelaide wasn't cooperating. He felt like grabbing her and shaking her. He felt nauseated.

"PEE-YEW!" screeched Adelaide, trying to shove all her fingers up her nose at once.

"PEE-YEW-BUM!"

Walter buried his head in his hands and tugged at his hair. She was right about that. But despite the unpleasantness of the situation, he still had a job to do and setbacks were to be expected. For the first time, he tried consciously increasing the static to take his mind off strangling Adelaide. Turning up the volume, finding the perfect midway point between stations and then cranking it up to ten. Unbelievably, it worked. Adelaide faded into tiny black and white checkerboards. Her kicking legs strobed out and her obnoxious volume got buried in the pounding surf that smashed up against the back of Walter's eyes. It was so sudden, he didn't have time to appreciate what he had done. He sat there, outwardly immobile but inwardly scrambling for control. He felt like he was madly running around inside his head, adjusting knobs, spinning dials, flipping levers. Scanning fast-moving data. Making phone calls, yelling at secretaries to file, file, FILE! This was some serious static he had conjured up and he wasn't at all sure he knew how to make it stop.

Adelaide sensed something was amiss with her friend. She sat up and looked at him. She reached out a chubby hand and touched his knee.

"WAH?"

But Walter was too busy cartwheeling through the tickertape parade. He didn't see Mrs. Vanstone's witchy face pressing up against the kitchen window. He did see Adelaide, though. She was there on the sidelines, faint and blurry around the edges. But first he had to contend with the marching band that had struck up a discordant, crashing version of "When the Saints Go Marching In." This was all wrong. There shouldn't be music. He was supposed to be between stations and he frowned with the effort of dialing back.

Adelaide saw him close his eyes and thought he was going to sleep. She took a deep breath and sat back, not wanting to wake him. She crawled a few feet away, looked at Walter, and picked up her shoes.

"Wed," she whispered, and put the right shoe on the right foot.

When both shoes were on, Adelaide crawled back to Walter's side. She put her feet in his lap and waited for him to wake up. Her beaming face with its perma-grin was the first thing Walter saw when he gained control of his head. The shoes were the second. Adelaide bounced them up and down on his thighs.

"Wed-peek-wed-peek-pity-sooz."

He smiled at her and fell backwards onto the lawn, arms stretched above his head.

"Ahh," he said with satisfaction, and felt a thrilling warmth creep into his loins.

Adelaide threw herself down beside him with a shuddering thud. She stretched her arms over her head, mimicking Walter.

"AHH," she bellowed. "AHHRRGHHAARRHGARH!"

Walter looked sideways at her and grinned.

"You're having fun, aren't you?" he said fondly.

Adelaide wrapped her arms tight around her chest and stuck her legs straight up in the air, wiggling her feet, her shoes, proudly.

"WHEE!" she whooped.

Nobody mentioned the fact that she had crapped in her bathing suit at some point. One thing at a time.

# 7 }

**Walter kept his triumph with Adelaide a secret.** But everyone knew something had happened. When Adelaide would pound into their yards, she would zone in on Walter and act far too familiar with him. Nobody took any notice that her shoes were now on the right feet, a fact that annoyed Walter. Wasn't it obvious? He didn't care about taking credit, he only wanted people to see. He pointed it out to Nina and Tina one day, when he had been roped, literally, into being the necessary third for double dutch. Adelaide was off to one side yelling the entry mantra for skipping.

"ONE-DOO-FEE-GO-INNNN-SO, ONE-DOO-FEE-GO-INNNN-SO."

Nobody ever let her skip, but she would lunge at the ropes anyway, close enough to get her nose clipped by the pink plastic and her chin elbowed on the upstroke. Tina was skipping, facing Walter.

"Hey, Tina," he yelled, over Adelaide's bellowing.

"Did you see Adelaide's shoes?"

Tina was counting in her head as she hopped from one foot to another, canary yellow sneakers flashing. She was getting close to breaking her sister's record of unbroken skipping and clearly did not need any distractions right now.

"What?" she asked distractedly, out of breath.

"Adelaide's wearing her shoes on the right feet! Did you see?"

Tina ignored him. She couldn't risk a look and really, who cared? But Adelaide heard. They were talking about her, about her shoes. It was *so* obvious it was her turn. She could hardly believe her good fortune and rocked back and forth on the balls of her feet, readying herself for entry, vibrating with excitement.

"One-doo-fee-go-innnn-so," she repeated under her breath, eyes all over the place, looking for her opening. She had seen the twins skip together in double dutch before, so she knew that's what was expected of her now. For a second, she got anxious and looked behind her. But there was nobody else to go-innnn-so. And Walter had said her name. Reassured, she focused on the pink ropes arching against the blue sky and slapping down like whips on the asphalt. It was mesmerizing, rhythmic. She started to drool. Nobody paid any attention to Adelaide jockeying in her plaid sneaks like she was about to crash their party because she was always lurking somewhere on the fringes. Walter should have been aware though, of the electric intensity gathering itself like a storm around Adelaide. He should have smelled the ozone in the air. But he was too pissed off at Tina for not looking at Adelaide's feet. Instead, he sped up the ropes, hoping she would falter. But Tina merely gave him a nasty glance and stepped lively. No way she was going to lose this record. Nina felt Walter pick up speed but didn't correct it. It really wasn't in her best interests for her sister to win and she matched his rhythm, staring at Tina's feet, hoping her shoelaces would come undone. So nobody noticed Adelaide working herself up into a lather, her pale eyes blinking furiously, fists clenched. It was her moment and she owed it all to Wah. Adelaide knew they were going to let her skip because she had learned how to put her shoes on the right feet. That must be the secret. You can't skip unless your shoes are on the right feet. She decided she was going to marry Wah. But first, she was going to skip with Deen.

Tina was getting tired, but the record was within her reach. Walter and Nina speeding up would only make it happen sooner. She was golden, and to prove it, she spun around in mid-hop to face Nina without missing a beat. That's when the truck hit her from behind. Adelaide had found her moment and with a roar, she charged the ropes and slammed into Tina. It all happened rather quickly, as these things do. Tina went flying and ended up face down on the street, looking like a broken blond Barbie doll. Walter and Nina stopped, letting the ropes go as slack as their jaws. And Adelaide was oblivious, hopping up and down, flapping her arms and getting tangled up in the pink ropes, bawling out some nursery rhyme that had nothing whatsoever to do with skipping. Walter couldn't believe it and felt like it was his fault. Tina was alternately whimpering and screeching at Adelaide as she picked herself up off the pavement. Nina felt guilty for wishing ill on her sister and began hurling abuse at Adelaide and pushing her. And Adelaide got scared. She was all wrapped up in the rope and began shrieking and clawing at it, while Nina pummelled her. Adelaide howled, looking around desperately for her friend.

"WAHHHH!"

But Walter was all tangled up too. Tangled up in guilt, in divided loyalties, static. He put his hands over his ears and closed his eyes. He was counting, and would keep counting until he hit the number of skips that broke the record. Mrs. Vanstone's voice crackled beneath the static as he counted: *One, two, buckle my shoe.* He walked in tight circles, his shoes hurt, his head hurt.

"WAHHHH!"

He cringed and counted louder: *Three, four, shut the door.*

Yes, could you please shut the door on your way out? I said, shut the goddamn door, I can still hear you.

The twins were both on Adelaide now, trying to get their skipping rope off her. Adelaide had stopped yelling for Walter and was reduced to loud blubbering as she tried to help the girls untangle her. It was a mess and the one common thought all three girls shared was: What the crap is Walter doing?

It was a fair question, and one that Walter was also asking. Nothing was working out the way he would have liked. You try to help someone and look where it gets you. It was his fault Adelaide jumped into the ropes. She had felt powerful in her shoes, thanks to him. But it wasn't her fault Tina and Nina couldn't appreciate it. And it wasn't Tina and Nina's fault that they were perfect. Walter found himself feeling sorry for all three of them. He kicked a stick.

*Five, six, pick up sticks.*

He may have felt sorry for all of them, but he didn't like any of them, now that he thought about it. He didn't like the way the twins excluded everybody from their inner circle—they wouldn't let him skip, either—

and he didn't like the way Adelaide couldn't make lemonade out of a lemon, even when he handed her the sugar and the water and the ice all wrapped up and tied with a bow. No, Adelaide would take a lemon and make something worse, like what? Like lemonade that tasted like liver. That's what she would make. Liverade.

*Seven, eight, don't be late.*

Adelaide was lying on her back on the street, arms stretched out at shoulder height, legs tight together, motionless, staring at the sky, breathing noisily through her mouth. Walter thought she looked crucified. The twins were having an argument about the skipping record and what number Tina had reached, while they worked at freeing their rope from Adelaide's heavy limbs. Walter started walking backwards in circles. He didn't like this at all. Something had gone terribly wrong and he caused it. He had managed to transfer some of his own power to Adelaide. It had hopped right off him and onto her. And look what happened. She couldn't handle it. He would have to be more careful from now on, he supposed, as to whom he helped. Or at least warn them of their potential. Rather than scaring him off, the skipping rope incident began to excite him. The more he thought about it, the more overwhelmed with possibilities he became. He could affect outcomes. He would not back down.

*Nine, ten, do it again. Do it again. Do it again.*

He moved on in a most natural fashion, yesiree. Step right up, folks, see the boy with the backwards feet. It will shock and amaze you. See what he can do. This is no gimmick, folks, there are no mirrors. See the boy with the backwards feet.

Walter stepped right up, ticket in hand. The calling was seductive, it moved through his head like a fur brush. He was being groomed. There would be no going backwards, no second-guessing his path. It was time to make some killer lemonade and he knew exactly what to do. Because as his grandmother said, those who can, do. Those who can't, teach. He already saw where the teaching had gotten him. It was time to do.

He made his first pair of shoes from wood. Walter hammered short pieces of rope into chunks of two-by-fours and fashioned a sort of sandal.

He slipped them on his feet and fell flat on his face when he tried to walk in them. Undaunted, he practiced every day in the garage until he could walk the length of it without tripping. The wood shoes made his feet drag more than usual and gave him severe toe cramps and splinters, but he persevered. He had to affect a kind of high-stepping gait, bringing his knees up more than he was accustomed to, but he made it work, somehow coordinating it with his side-to-side wobble. Walter found some leftover paint from his bedroom in the garage and painted the shoes blue and the rope red. He glued bird feathers on the sides near the back, resembling the wings Mercury had on his heels. His straight last shoes sat on a box, a watchful witness, as Walter clumped back and forth in the garage working up a sweat. Once he got the hang of them, he wanted to try them out on the street, on grass, on carpet. He wanted to see if he could run in them, go up and down stairs. Reason told him he would get laughed off the block. This much he knew from his experience with the straight last shoes. But things like reason and good judgment got lost in the swells of static whenever he wore the wood shoes. Plus, they made him taller.

It's a funny thing when you're proud of something you've accomplished but you risk complete humiliation by showing it off to the world. This is what Walter was thinking as he stood in the garage one afternoon in his wood shoes, gearing himself up to walk outside. He felt like how he imagined the Wright brothers must have felt the first time they showed the world their flying machine. Poor old Orville and Wilbur probably got laughed off their own block when their rudimentary airplane crashed and burned on its maiden takeoff. But look at all the planes now. Those Wright boys had vision and Walter was sure as shit that they knew they were onto something big, despite their initial clumsy efforts. He braced himself and looked down at his red and blue shoes. They had wings too. Walter understood that these shoes were like the Wright brothers' first airplane. He knew that as soon as he revealed them to the world, they too would crash and burn. But, like all great inventors, Walter had vision. If they could tolerate the snickering and name-calling, so could he. He had built up immunity to that sort of thing anyway. His straight last shoes had toughened him up, served a purpose. With one last look down at his new shoes, Walter inhaled deeply and walked outside. He could feel the static simmering, lying in wait, on the verge of exploding into a full boil. Walter ignored it and concentrated on his calling. He goose-stepped down the driveway, a proud inventor wearing bunched-up shorts with an elastic waistband and magnificent winged shoes. He felt like he was walking down a runway. Only this was an airport runway and he was ready for takeoff. Let's see if this bird will get off the ground, he thought grimly. He walked purposefully through the gently billowing static. It was like flying through clouds.

Naturally, Walter's maiden flight was a disaster. Nobody gets it right the first time. He sat in his bedroom, holding a washcloth full of ice to one eye, and looked at his winged shoes with the good eye. Some feathers had come off the right shoe, he noted. Needs fixing. The girls had laughed, as expected, but a couple of them had petted the feathers and Walter knew they were envious. The boys, well, they were boys. It's for your own good, they had said as they punched him behind the Becker's store. Things have gone too far, they said. Johnny had tried to intervene, but all that got him was a pair of broken eyeglasses. Walter winced as he reapplied the washcloth. They were right, after all. It's only when things go too far that anything gets accomplished. Only when you take a risk. Walter figured his black eye was like getting a gold star. It was recognition that he had done something so extraordinary, it made people nervous. The beating only served to strengthen his resolve. But he would never wear the winged shoes out in public again. Not until everyone understood. One day he would get an award for being an inventor and then he would pull out the winged shoes and show them to his audience.

"These are my first invention," he would say. "People laughed at me when I wore these, but I persevered. And I don't think anyone's laughing at me now."

Deafening applause would fill the theatre as people rose to their feet, standing in their own wing shoes, overcome with emotion. Great fashion designers would put his shoes on models who would never trip in them. People with deformed feet would wear his shoes and walk straighter. He would give them away to kids in Africa. Design special shoes for the circus fat ladies to help their bunions and withstand their weight. Make astronaut shoes to walk on the moon. Shoes for kings and queens made out of diamonds. And maybe one day he could make real flying shoes, *rocket* shoes.

A black eye was a small price to pay, when you thought about it, and Walter wasn't about to give up. He never wore his wing shoes out again, but he did show them to different people. He had never heard of marketing surveys before, but instinctively knew he had to get reactions.

His grandmother:

"Jesus H. Christ on a cross, what the hell are those things? You've been hanging out in my shoe closet too long, boy."

But Walter knew his grandmother secretly liked them. She was heavily into shoes.

His mother:

"They're very nice, Walter, but you can't wear them. You have to wear your straight last shoes all the time. These, whatever you call them, will destroy your walking."

Secretly, she thought he was a genius. No bout adoubt it.

Adelaide almost barfed with excitement and pawed them with her fat, greasy fingers.

The only neighbours who seemed genuinely impressed were the Quayles, the lone couple who defied suburban convention. This had not so much to do with Mr. Quayle being a drummer in a swing band, nor with Ivy Quayle being the neighbourhood Avon lady (a preoccupation much loved by the other housewives), rather what set the Quayles apart was their lack of children. For that reason alone, they would have been considered complete outcasts if it weren't for the sympathy Mrs. Q engendered by the speculation she might be barren. That distressing and tragic possibility made Avon sales skyrocket and secured Ivy's standing.

When Walter showed them his wing shoes, Mrs. Q tried putting one on. She stuck her toes through the rope loops and wiggled her foot.

"My, my, Walter!" she beamed. "These are about the prettiest shoes I ever did see in my life!"

Mr. Q set the other shoe down on his workbench under a bright light. He examined it with much thoroughness, murmuring as he turned it over.

"This is fine work, Walter," he said. "You've got a real knack."

The Quayles obviously recognized his talent. They must be visionaries too, Walter thought, as he said his goodbyes and wobbled out their back door.

"Poor kid," said Mrs. Q to her husband, waving to Walter.

Mr. Q hugged his wife close.

"That's what happens when you don't have a father figure," he said.

They watched until Walter disappeared and then they walked back inside. Their house seemed the tiniest bit more empty now.

"Shall I fix you a drink?" Mr. Q asked, already pouring rum into a couple of glasses.

Mrs. Q nodded absently. "Sure, honey. You know, we should spend more time with Walter. Have him over sometime, don't you think?"

"I think that's a fine idea, Ivy. Maybe I could teach the boy some woodworking. Start him off with a birdhouse or something."

Ivy took her glass of rum and smiled up at her husband.

"I'll speak to Joy about it."

The Quayles settled in beside each other on the couch, pleased with their decision. It would be nice to have a child around the house. Ivy decided she would let Walter loose in her bag of Avon leftovers. He was obviously a creative kid.

Walter had one more person to try. He stuffed his wing shoes in a bag, strapped it onto his handlebars and peddled off. Down Kennedy Road past the Tam O'Shanter golf course, skirting through the parking lot of Agincourt Mall. He walked his bike through the busy intersection of Kennedy Road and Sheppard Avenue, and wound his way through the Lynnwood Heights neighbourhood, keeping clear of the traffic on the main streets. He was exhausted by the time he swung past the A&P and into the strip mall where Foster's Shoes was located. He dumped his bike on the sidewalk and burst through the front door, sending the bell into a tinkling frenzy. The store was empty. Walter slowed his breathing and walked around.

"Mr. Foster?" he called out.

The curtains to the backroom swept open and Mr. Foster breezed out. He stopped short when he saw Walter.

"Walter Finch," he stated. "How are you, my boy?"

Walter sat on a chair and put the bag with his wing shoes underneath. Mr. Foster picked up a feather duster and walked over to Walter.

"I see you're still wearing your shoes. Is there something wrong with them?"

Walter shook his head. "No, nothing. They're great."

Mr. Foster knelt down in front of Walter and brushed the tips of his straight last shoes with the duster.

"Well, then. What can I do for you today?"

Walter reached down and pulled out the bag.

"I made some shoes," he said. "I wanted you to look at them."

Mr. Foster sniffed and his eyes widened.

"You made some shoes? Well, let's have a look, son."

Walter gratefully handed the bag to Mr. Foster, the expert. The shoe magnate held Walter's wing shoes with respect. His long fingers ran nimbly over the ropes, and caressed the feathers like they were real baby birds. Walter's stomach did a flip. It seemed like an hour before Mr. Foster looked up.

"You have made straight last shoes," he said, holding them up in the air.

"See? You can wear these on either foot. They are completely straight."

Walter swallowed. "Is that good?"

Mr. Foster stood up, still holding the wing shoes.

"It's not good or bad," he said. "It's just...let's say, it's a wonderful beginning. What made you decide to make shoes, Walter?"

Walter looked shyly at Mr. Foster.

"You did," he said.

Mr. Foster got a funny look on his face and handed the wing shoes back to Walter. He seemed to be thinking deep thoughts and snapped his fingers.

"Walter. Would you like to see the backroom where all the shoes are stored? Maybe it will inspire you when you make your next pair of shoes."

Would he? Would he? That would only be the best thing that could ever happen. Walter couldn't speak, and tried nodding his head. Once he started nodding, he couldn't seem to stop. He felt like his head was going to snap right off and go sailing across the room. Mr. Foster allowed a smile to leach into his face.

"I'll take that as a yes," he said, executing an abrupt about-face. "Follow me."

Walter scuttled as fast as he could after the great man who had disappeared behind the curtain. Walter's heart was thumping. He was about to glimpse the inner sanctum of the shoe store. The place where all the shoes were kept, where decisions were made as to size and colour. Where all the brand-new shoes, straight from the factory, sat in their boxes wrapped in tissue paper, untouched by anyone. Unworn by any foot. Walter paused for a moment to deal with the onslaught of static that washed over him like a waterfall. A scene from *The Wizard of Oz* popped into his head. Mr. Foster was the Wizard and Walter was about to invade the control room where all would be revealed. He pulled back the curtain and stepped inside.

In here, if Mr. Foster was the Wizard, Walter was a Munchkin. The ceilings were a billion times higher than in the front room and shelves of shoeboxes climbed all the way to the top. Walter felt dwarfed and insignificant but his heart swelled with rapture.

Mr. Foster watched him shrewdly. It wasn't often someone showed any interest or respect for his chosen profession. In the parlance of the times, Mr. Foster was considered an odd duck, a confirmed bachelor. No wife, no kids. His dream was to have his own shoe store one day. He didn't own Foster's, it was a coincidence that the store bore his name, and he didn't bother correcting anyone who assumed otherwise. He saw in Walter something of himself, even on that first day he had fitted the child with straight last shoes. As Walter clumped unevenly down the towering shoe corridors of the backroom, fingers drumming on the boxes, Mr. Foster picked up one of the wing shoes and studied it. A weird smile slanted across his face, shifting the sharp contours like geological plates shuffling and settling under the earth's crust. A wing shoe, he thought, and looked down at his own polished shoes. Wingtips. Mr. Foster watched Walter lifting shoebox lids and peering inside the boxes, smelling the leather. He, of course, knew nothing of the radio station that blasted through Walter's head, but he wouldn't have been surprised. He had his own version of static when he was around shoes, but it was more localized. It swooped and tumbled about in a much lower location, rippling through his Fruit of the Looms like hiccups. His hand curled around Walter's wing shoe. While Walter gazed with wonder at the emporium of footwear, Mr. Foster made a decision. He would take Walter under his wingtip and become his mentor. Teach him everything he knew about the shoe business, help the kid out, let him into his world. Finally, he knew he had found someone to share his passion. He could see it all now. Foster and Finch. F & F. It was a good solid name for a shoe store, he mused, as he ground the wing shoe into his crotch.

"Mr. Foster?"

The shoe king wrenched himself out of his reverie to see Walter standing before him.

"What's this, Mr. Foster?"

"Oh. Yes. That's a shoe stretcher," said Mr. Foster, sliding the wing shoe off his crotch and setting it on a table.

Walter was clearly excited about the shoe stretcher and Mr. Foster figured he might as well start Walter's apprenticeship now. No time like the present. He knelt down to Walter's height and took the shoe stretcher from his hands. It looked like a wooden replica of a foot with a pointy toe. Walter thought it looked like a life-sized version of one of his pirate puppet's feet. There was an iron loop sticking out of the heel end of the foot. Mr. Foster turned it slowly and as he did, the polished wood began to split open down its length.

"Wow," Walter said, his mind racing with the logistics of it.

Mr. Foster's mouth twitched.

"Go find me a size eight man's shoe," he said to Walter. "There are some men's shoes in the second aisle, third shelf from the floor."

Walter sped off. A shoe stretcher! What an idea! He was already thinking about asking Mr. Quayle to help him make one. He found the correct shelf and pulled out a size eight box. Before returning, he knocked the lid off to make sure there were shoes inside. The smell of new leather assaulted him and he reeled. Nobody had touched these shoes before, it was so obvious. The white tissue paper was smooth and clean and Walter carefully folded it back. Black, glistening men's dress shoes lay spooned together like lovers in a cardboard coffin. Who would buy them? Walter wasn't nearly as familiar with men's shoes as he was with women's. Maybe a businessman would buy them and wear them to his office in a skyscraper downtown. Or maybe someone like Mr. Q would wear them to take Ivy dancing in a ballroom. He turned one over. He could see himself reflected in the soles. They were like amber glass. How do you walk in shoes like these without sliding all over the place? Walter folded the tissue paper back over them, like he was tucking them in for the night. Regret flickered. He would never be able to wear shoes like these.

"Did you find them?" Mr. Foster called.

Walter put the lid back on.

"Yes, sir, I'll be right there."

And Walter had his first lesson. Mr. Foster slid the wooden puppet foot into the size-eight men's fancy shoe and turned the iron loop. The only sound was breathing and a barely audible creaking of new leather. How simple, thought Walter. How amazingly simple. He watched, suspended in a web of static, clinging onto the filaments with fingers and toes, balanced precariously. With every long breath Mr. Foster took, the web swayed imperceptibly. With every creak, Walter tightened his grip. He was afraid if he let go, the web would wrap itself around him like a cocoon and suffocate him.

As Mr. Foster carefully turned the iron loop, he watched Walter with interest. The kid looked dazed. He wondered what Walter's reaction would be if he kept turning, kept the tension building, kept going until the stitches popped and the shoe split open. It was tempting. He hadn't had this much fun stretching shoes in a long time, although he had always found the exercise disturbingly sexual. Slipping the smooth wood inside the virgin leather. Cranking it, feeling the resistance, but persisting. The groaning leather always sounded to Mr. Foster like small cries or whimpers. Protestations. It's for your own good, he thought. I'm breaking you in for someone else. Sometimes it worried Mr. Foster that he had these thoughts, but he couldn't seem to help it. He humanized shoes. He was a matchmaker, setting up the perfect fit. It's what made him the world's greatest shoe salesman. And he believed he saw the same qualities in Walter. Perhaps the feelings Walter was experiencing weren't as overtly sexual as his own, but that could be due in part to Walter's young age. No matter. It was obvious that something got stirred up in the kid, a passion of some sort, a longing. Mr. Foster grimaced and executed another excruciating quarter turn of the loop, bending it to his will. But anyone could go too far. What made this exercise special, what made it satisfying, was exerting self-control. Knowing how much the shoe could withstand. Holding back. Knowing when to withdraw, no matter how much you wanted to explode inside the shoe. Because if Mr. Foster knew anything, he knew his job. And his job was to prepare shoes for others' enjoyment. Usually, he was an expert at self-control during working hours. But having Walter here, seeing the childish awe on his face, made Mr. Foster feel reckless, made him feel like showing Walter all that he was capable of. But that wouldn't be wise. Mentors didn't do that sort of thing. Mr. Foster fought his urges and stopped tightening the shoe stretcher. He handed the bloated shoe to Walter with the stretcher sticking out of it.

"See how that works?" he said.

Walter reached through the web and took the shoe with both hands. He understood. It was all about tension.

The bell tinkled in the front room, breaking the mood. Mr. Foster stood up.

"I've got a customer. Why don't you come back next week and I'll show you how to do the same thing, only with a broom handle."

Walter got to his feet and stuck out a hand to shake Mr. Foster's. He turned to go.

"Walter," said Mr. Foster.

Walter paused.

"Don't forget your wing shoes, son."

# 8 }

**When Agincourt Mall first opened its doors,** it was a godsend to the good people of Agincourt. Anchored by a Woolco department store at one end, the enclosed mall offered year-round shopping comfort for the local population. And when they tired of browsing for sewing patterns or camping flashlights or board games, they could take a load off in one of two restaurants, the pool hall or the public washrooms. It was all very civilized and everyone welcomed its presence in their midst. In time, mega malls like the Scarborough Town Centre would infiltrate the neighbourhood and overshadow their smaller counterparts. The Town Centre itself arrived in due course with much fanfare, ballyhooed as a multi-level retail mecca with escalators, live plants, piped in music, and chrome and enough glass to blind shoppers to any other destination. It made Agincourt Mall's lustre degenerate to that of a shabby relative who had hit the skids. After the advent of super malls, the consumer population at Agincourt Mall took a sharp nosedive, although it got enough overflow business from the Brewers Retail outlet that opened up later in the parking lot.

But in its heyday, Agincourt Mall was considered the place to shop, as it was indeed the only place. As years went by, and the Agincourt kids grew into teenagers, it also became the place to hang out. And the best thing of all about Agincourt Mall was The Red Grill, Woolco's cafeteria-style restaurant. What better place to while away the hours, drinking Coke and eating cheeseburgers and fries, smoking cigarettes and skipping school. What better place to escape the parents for an afternoon, although one always had to keep an eye open for their presence in Woolco. If there was a parent-spotting, cigarettes were hastily butted and ashtrays moved to an empty table. The only thing separating The Red Grill from the rest of the store was a metal bar that acted as a waist-high fence, running around the perimeter of the cafeteria. And the only thing more frightening than a parent-spotting was a parent spotting you. It was never a good moment if a parent executed a squeaky U-turn with their shopping cart and zeroed-in on The Red Grill. Ten times worse if they lined it up against the metal fence and struck up a conversation.

Fortunately for the teens, their parents never suggested having dinner at the mall, these outings being reserved for restaurants beyond the immediate neighbourhood. A perennial favourite for this activity was Swiss Chalet, home of that great Swiss delicacy, barbecued chicken. In fact, the only thing remotely Swiss or chalet about the chain was the milkmaid-style uniforms worn by the pimply teen waitresses who never quite managed to fill out their white, gathered bodices to any great effect. It was a great day for Swiss Chalet, therefore, when Nina and Tina were old enough to secure part-time employment as waitresses. The twins took no time developing into both their peasant blouses and their stations in life. With their blond, fresh-scrubbed presence, it came to pass that more and more fathers were suggesting family dinners at the Chalet and the Mooney girls took full advantage by pulling their blouses off their shoulders much lower than regulations allowed. Tips increased exponentially with each inch of milky flesh exposed. And even more predictable, the other waitresses hated the sisters and eventually ratted them out for stealing gallons of the special Chalet barbecue sauce and taking it home. Normally, this would be an indictable offence worthy of instant termination. But the twins were only put on probation. Mr. Carr, the manager, knew what side his lightly toasted bun was buttered on. As he told his supervisor, it was strictly good business to keep the twins on in their positions.

"I give you my word I will keep a close eye on them," he promised.

Mr. Carr was, if nothing else, a man of his word. He neglected to tell his supervisor that he had some special sauce of his own he dreamed of slathering between their buns. So tormented was Mr. Carr by the twins' burgeoning voluptuousness, it got to the point where he sat in the back storeroom holding a warm, headless chicken, seriously considering the logistics of jerking off inside the bony cavity. While he watched the twins hustle their round asses in and out of the kitchen, he imagined them rotating on his own greased spit. When finally he couldn't restrain himself any longer and laid more than a close eye on them, it was Mr. Carr who ended up being terminated. As he was led out of the restaurant by one of Scarborough's finest, Tina flashed her tits and stuck her tongue out. Mr. Carr promptly fainted.

These were but some of the stories Walter was privy to during that time in Agincourt's adolescence. And a worthy confessor he was, as Walter not only knew how to keep his mouth shut, he seemed genuinely interested in such tales. As the twins grew more and more radiantly beautiful, Walter steadily evolved into his averageness. As a teen, he no longer wore straight last shoes but retained his jerky walk and his nickname. Nobody seemed to know if the shoes had helped at all, not even the worldly Mr. Foster who only said: "Couldn't have hurt."

When the crop of Agincourt teens reached the age of employment, many found their first job at Agincourt Mall. As did Walter, who, at age fifteen, secured his first part-time job at Kinney Shoes. Although Walter's first choice was to work at Foster's, he was told by Mr. Foster that, regretfully, there was no budget. That's when Walter discovered Mr. Foster did not, in fact, own the store.

"But you should get a job in another shoe store," Mr. Foster said. "You should learn as much as you can, because I have great future plans for you."

The manager of Kinney's, Mr. Bardolini, ignored the fact that Walter was underage by a year and had that clumsy walk, because Walter not only came to the job with years of unpaid experience, he also was possessed of a real respect for the shoe business, something none of the other kids had. Mr. Bardolini believed Walter would be an asset. And armed as he was with all of Mr. Foster's insight, it didn't take long before Walter was the top-selling salesman at Kinney Shoes. With Mr. Bardolini's guidance, Walter learned how to stock shelves, operate a cash register, and create displays. He did everything from vacuuming the store and cleaning mirrors to counting receipts and closing off the till. It was rare that a customer left the store without polish, insoles, laces, and a matching handbag to supplement their shoe purchase. He never had any returns and Mr. Bardolini thought he was a genius.

"You have a real good head on your shoulders," he said to Walter. "One day, you'll probably replace me as manager."

Walter bobbed his head at this comment and loped off down the store, lining the chairs up and dusting their seats. He didn't have the heart to tell Mr. Bardolini that he had far greater plans than managing Kinney Shoes at Agincourt Mall. Kinney's was boot camp. He knew he would rise steadily through the ranks and command his own platoon one day. That was a given. If he wanted to, he could probably own a fleet of stores. He had choices. Even Mr. Foster had talked about opening up a store with him some day. Walter was beginning to see his world open up and he was in no rush. He had confidence that things were unfolding as they should and all he had to do was be patient and keep learning. Some day he would realize his purpose. He could feel it beneath his skin. One day, he would outdo Mr. Bardolini and Mr. Foster put together. They had a career. But Walter was born to this.

# 9 }

**Nancy Jean Nova moved into Agincourt** when she was twenty-five years old. By that time, most of the woods had been levelled to make way for a new subdivision and the outlying farmers' fields had been completely built up. The new subdivision of Agincourt was sparsely treed with massive houses that boasted features nowhere to be found in the old Agincourt bungalows. When the new subdivision was being built, Joy and Clara and Robin would tour the model homes and wander about, wide-eyed at the luxury. Sunken living rooms, by god. Family rooms with sliding glass doors and separate dining rooms with archways and peekaboo windows. Fireplaces, breakfast nooks, decks, multiple bathrooms, not to mention the *ensuite*, for chrissakes. And the model homes were furnished in the utmost extravagance. Who had ever seen lavender wall-to-wall carpeting before? And crystal chandeliers twinkling over rosewood or mahogany dining tables. Cathedral ceilings in the entranceways, circular staircases. Skylights! Built-in ironing boards! Dishwashers! Doorbells that played music!

The women went crazy with delight and no small amount of envy. The best they could do was tart up their dark, dank basements and fashion them into rec rooms with fake fireplaces made out of Styrofoam. Or wait until one of their kids moved out, knock out a wall, and make a family room. Ambitious handymen could install a second bathroom in the basement, but despite their best efforts, the original Agincourt moms knew they couldn't come close to the splendour of the new subdivision. The women would chatter about the model homes as they walked back to old Agincourt, indulging themselves in fancies as to which model they would buy if they had the money. They would talk about how they could duplicate the colour schemes and rip off decorating ideas for use in their own homes. They would walk up their driveways, assessing their houses anew, noting with selfish pleasure their larger yards and abundant foliage. Then they would turn the key and step into their house. Ding. Dong. Bit by bit, their enthusiasm would wane, as the tight confines of their homes closed in around them. Things would stand out, like the worn patches on the arms of the couch, the thinness of their broadloom. Things they had loved only yesterday would look drab in comparison. The pole lamp in the corner looked foolish and cheap, with its three tri-coloured plastic cones pointing off in bizarre directions. The MODEL homes had TRACK lighting. The MODEL homes had DOUBLE sinks and DOUBLE garages. The MODEL homes had EVERYTHING.

The model homes were the bane of every father's existence.

Nancy Jean Nova's family moved into the new subdivision and straight into the original model home with the sunken living room and lavender carpet. This did not impress Nancy, who had always lived in large houses. In fact, Nancy was of the age and temperament where she would rebel against anything with a whiff of the bourgeois. Her first order of business upon moving to Agincourt was to find a job and make enough money to get her own pad. A dump, preferably. In downtown Toronto, assuredly.

Nancy was a bright girl, much too bright for college or university.

"I'd rather learn in the school of life," she would say to anyone who asked.

This impressed her parents about as much as their upwardly mobile lifestyle impressed Nancy.

That is how it came to be that one day Nancy Nova strode confidently into the Scarborough Town Centre, clutching a résumé. She wasn't going to leave the mall until she found a job. She steered clear of anything to do with waitressing, bypassed anything academic, like bookstores, crossed off clothing stores because she abhorred fashion, and didn't go near the department stores that seemed custom-made to swallow up a person's individuality. Nancy believed if you worked in a large department store you would have to be a joiner, a team player. Pet stores made her sad, gift stores were too precious with all their glass and crystal, and the scent from bath boutiques made her ill. As Nancy Nova walked through Scarborough Town Centre, she saw her options dwindling. She sat down on a bench and scrounged in her purse for a cigarette. As she flicked her lighter and leaned into the flame, she heard Bob Dylan singing "The Times They Are A-Changin'." It was one of her favourite songs and she hummed along, looking around for the source of the music, which as it happened was right in front of her. Bob Dylan was drifting into the mall from a shoe store. Nancy looked up. Maher was the name of the store and she had no choice but to take it as a sign. She pulled her résumé out of her purse and stood up, tucking her straight black hair behind her ears and butting her cigarette out in a planter. She could sell shoes. It's not friggin' rocket science. And from the looks of the place, it wasn't some high fashion, trendy joint either. It looked reasonable. She took a deep breath and walked inside, determined not to leave until she landed a job selling shoes.

"Can I see the manager?" she asked the harmless looking guy at the front counter.

"I'm the manager," he said.

Nancy slapped her résumé on the counter and made hypnotizing eye contact.

"I was wondering if you needed any help. I'm looking for a job in the shoe business."

The manager stared back at her. He didn't look at her résumé.

"Do you have any experience?"

"Yes. But not selling shoes. How hard can it be? I know I'd be damn good at it."

"Really? And how do you know that?"

Nancy leaned back. This wouldn't be easy. He wasn't melting like most guys she pinned with her gaze.

"Because I'm not stupid. Because I really, really need this job. Because I like the music you're playing. And because all the other stores in this mall creep me out."

She tried out her famous smile. "And because I have lots of experience *wearing* shoes."

With her last comment, Nancy Nova lifted one leg up in the air and laid her foot on the counter to demonstrate. She was wearing black leather Mary Janes, which she wiggled back and forth.

The manager held his hand up as if to ward her off, while he bent down beneath the counter.

"One sec."

When he surfaced, he had a piece of paper and a pen in his hand, both of which he slid across the counter.

"Why don't you put your foot down, have a seat and fill out this application form."

Nancy shrugged and removed her foot.

"Okay, sure. But do you need someone or are you going to file this in the garbage when I leave?"

"I would never do that. If your references check out, I'll personally call you and let you know where things stand with the schedule. We might be losing someone tomorrow, as it happens."

"Okay, whatever you say. You won't regret it."

She grabbed the application form and pen and sauntered over to a corner of the store where she sat and wrote, sneaking curious looks around at the other staff, the shoes, and the customers. An Elvis Costello tune was playing now. Must be a mix tape. She wondered whose it was. Her foot tapped while her pen scratched out embellishments to her sketchy career, which consisted of working in a dry cleaners, a pizza take-out and a rental car company. In minutes, she was finished and back at the counter. She waited until harmless guy finished ringing in a sale.

"All done," she said, pushing the application form towards him.

He glanced at the form.

"Nancy Nova?"

She looked down at her feet and lifted her shoulders.

"Yeah, that's me. But I hate my name. My friends call me Nova. You can call me that."

The manager held out his hand.

"Pleased to meet you, Nova. My name is Walter Finch. My friends call me Spaz."

She raised her eyes, startled at the manager's admission, and found herself looking into inscrutable hazelness. They shook hands and Nancy Nova went home to the new subdivision. She couldn't help but wonder why that nice guy was called Spaz.

Walter watched her leave and wondered why he had impulsively divulged his childhood nickname to her. He tidied the counter and looked at her application. He noticed that she lived in the new subdivision and realized she probably lived with her parents. Considering her age, which was pretty close to his own, Walter found that odd. She didn't seem like the type of girl who would still be living at home. The store tape switched to Leonard Cohen and Walter decided to hire Nova, if Teddy left. He liked her spirit. And he couldn't get past the fact that he had told her his nickname.

# 10 }

**To an objective observer,** things looked fine and dandy for Walter as he grew into young adulthood. Although no one would ever call him handsome exactly, he had a pleasant enough countenance that never offended. His presence was often requested at social functions in much the same way one would ensure the presence of a cheese platter. A good hostess always knew the importance of a solid standby—a filler-upper, if you will. Walter was such a standby, and perfectly suited to the role of balancing a lopsided girl-boy ratio if warranted. One could always count on Walter to make small talk, circulate, and perform his guestly duties in an unobtrusive and polite manner. Parties always seemed to boast at least one wildly exaggerated, engaging guest whose mere presence promised a successful affair. Walter was not this type, although he did appreciate the magnetic energy of such characters. There was also usually at least one loner. The brooding poet or guitar plucker who sat in a corner all night observing, simultaneously drawing people in and repelling them, with his or her air of intrigue and contempt. Walter was not that either. He didn't dance jigs on tabletops, never got drunk and loud, was never discovered in the spare bedroom making out under a pile of coats, and was usually never alone for long. Walter was cheddar. He would never be as flamboyant and raunchy as Stilton, or aloof like brie.

His funky way of walking, of course, was noticed by newcomers. But after a couple of drinks, even that feature would dissolve into a party blur. As long as he didn't knock anything over or step on anyone's feet, Walter's walk was only cause for eyebrow lifting in the beginning. After awhile, it became like a stutter, or an eye tic, or a missing finger. Not to be talked about: initially out of politeness, later because there were always more interesting people to circle and devour.

Because of his easygoing nature, acquaintances were plentiful for Walter Finch. The bulk of his friendships were with women who found him to be a good listener, completely non-threatening, and, for a guy, oddly understanding of their own natures. This, they surmised, came from Walter having been raised by women. It would happen that a few of these female acquaintances also felt some degree of pity for Walter. Sometimes they would say things to each other like:

"Y'know, if Walter walked normal, I'd even consider going out with him."

"I know. He's such a nice guy, really."

"But that's part of his problem too."

"Yeah, I never really look at him that way. I wonder if he's ever been laid?"

"God, I hope so. He'd make a great boyfriend for somebody."

"He'd probably be so grateful."

"He'd never fuck around."

"Isn't there anybody we can set him up with?"

"Nobody I can think of. Everyone we know is too shallow."

"Like us, you mean."

"Yeah, poor Walter. Hey, why don't we have him over for drinks Sunday night."

"Okay. Do you want me to bring anything?"

"I dunno. Maybe some cheese."

Truth was, Walter had been laid. He was a bit late out of the gate, but having sex was a rite expected of him as a healthy, red-blooded Canadian male. Walter always did what was expected of him, but not always in the way one would expect. His high school years were lean in this regard, consisting only of sporadic gropings at the drive-in or bowling alley, exhausting bouts of French necking in the CNE horse show stands or in subway stations, and mutual fingering and hand jobs a couple of times at the Mooneys' cottage. Not, it should be mentioned, with Tina or Nina. The reasons this activity never went all the way were several. Not many girls ever pursued Walter with any vigour and the frenzied fumblings that did occur were usually due to alcohol consumption. For his part, Walter wasn't attracted to any of the available girls, at least not the ones who were sensible enough to see past his walking problem. It didn't help that he had grown up across the street from two of the most sought-after knockouts for miles around. They were like his sisters and beauty such as theirs never did turn his head. He wasn't on any sports teams during high school, which ranked him as a loser right off the top for half the female students. And most of Walter's time was taken up with extra shifts at Kinney's, when he wasn't doing homework. Any free time he did have, he either spent in Mr. Quayle's workshop or with Mr. Foster. He also made a conscious effort to try and maintain some semblance of a relationship with guys, especially Johnny. Chicks weren't a priority, but he casually dated enough to save him from the label of homo, which had threatened deflating him as a kid.

When Walter did get around to *it*, he had moved on from Kinney's and into the Town Centre where he was soon promoted to manager of Maher. This was safer territory, further away from the prying eyes of Agincourt Mall. Once he was officially declared Maher's youngest manager at age nineteen, Walter decided it was time to experiment with the grownup activity of sexual intercourse. He began his further sexual education with Daphne Fox, the plump woman who worked at A&W in the Town Centre's food court. Walter was a regular customer and a big fan of the A&W Teen Burgers and throughout his tenure at the mall, he and Daphne had developed a rapport. Daphne was in her mid-thirties when the union occurred. She had not had much luck in the romance department for years, not since she started working at A&W and packed an extra fifty pounds onto her five-foot-two frame. Walter saw Daphne as a very shiny, round, jovial woman, emphasis on woman. She had a babyish voice that belied her age and a tendency to giggle overmuch, but Walter didn't mind this trait. Daphne also had a habit of petting Walter whenever he sat in the food court and she joined him on her break. She would pat his head before she went back to the grill, stroke his forearm when she sat down and massage his shoulders if she stood behind him. None of this Walter minded, not even when her hefty breasts pushed up against the back of his head when she performed a spontaneous neck rub. He couldn't tell if Daphne was flirting with him or not, and until the day he decided he needed to expand his sex life repertoire, he had never considered the burger fox as any kind of potential fuckmate. At *all*. But once he mentally set himself up for initiation into the manly rite of passage, he chose Daphne as a suitable instructor. He saw his opportunity looming when she told him she was quitting her job and moving to Uxbridge, a small town outside of Toronto. There would, of course, be a party in her honour. There would, of course, be booze. Walter doused himself with Brut and, with all confidence, attended the party packing a condom in his wallet. He knew his target audience. And his audience responded with exuberance.

Walter never told anyone about it. But despite his lack of devotion to Daphne, he had quite honestly enjoyed having intercourse with her. It was like fucking a greasy, fat Mama Burger. Afterwards, they lay in Daphne's waterbed and drank mugs of rye and root beer while she petted him. It was fine. Both of them were grateful.

His second stab at the old in-and-out was with someone much closer to his own age: Melanie Johnson. Melanie was a sweet, freckled nympho. Your basic slut with heart. She was pretty in a cross-eyed, kooky kind of way. She chain-smoked Craven M menthol cigarettes and Walter liked the smoky mint taste of her tongue. He received his first blow job from Melanie, an act he watched with interest and some concern for her well-being. He wasn't sure if the retching sounds were normal and had the feeling that foxy Mama Burger would have gobbled him up, no problem. *Yeah, I'll have a side of thighs with that. And could ya Super Size it?* His blow job anxiety weakened more than his resolve for this activity and, much to his relief, Melanie eventually gave it up and did what she did best. She nimbly hopped on and rode him like a Barcalounger. Again Walter would have to admit that, all things considered, he enjoyed this whole sex thing. And again, Melanie left town the following day to return to her home in Bracebridge, Ontario. Walter couldn't help but wonder if all his sexual activities would be with women who left town the next day for places that ended in "bridge."

Only one person knew about his encounter with Melanie, and that was Johnny who had set it up for his buddy.

"So? What'd I tell you?" Johnny said the next day, adding: "You know, Spaz, I'd do her myself if she wasn't my cousin."

Walter believed him. But unlike Johnny, who got his pecker wet every chance he could, Walter was willing to lay low. He didn't know what he was waiting for exactly, but figured he'd know when it happened. Besides, he had a shoe store to run. Everything else—a relationship, a cool apartment, a car—was there for the taking whenever he was ready for it. All those other things were scurrying about under the surface, like scabies, itching at him. Walter acknowledged this, but until he suffered a festering outbreak, there was no point wasting energy on it. And there was something else he mostly ignored. Ever since becoming gainfully employed at Maher, the static that used to torment him as a child had lessened to occasional crackles. This state of affairs brought with it both a sense of relief and, contrarily, a vague longing. Walter believed the static might have been a childhood aberration, like having allergies that mysteriously vanished in adulthood. If he thought deeper about it, he wondered if the static had helped enlighten him to his calling, and disappeared because it wasn't needed anymore. Mostly, he tried not to think about it because he was afraid it would come back. With its absence, he had accomplished many productive things.

# 11 }

**Sometimes all it takes is one simple thing,** like a phone call, to set up a domino effect of life-altering moments. For Walter, this happened in 1985. This was the year the static came back, stronger and more insistent than ever. It was the year Walter's life took a sharp turn, veering forever out of the safety zone of Agincourt. He didn't go far geographically, only a few miles south to Toronto's lakeside. But it shifted something. At first Walter embraced the changes as they occurred, certain he was being steered into his true calling. After all, on the surface, they seemed a normal progression—moving out, changing jobs, becoming more responsible. Things everyone did. He hadn't accounted for the reoccurrence of static, but if he had, he would have accepted its place in his life. There was nothing he could do about it anyway. Had he known what awaited him, Walter would have appreciated more the brief respite he had been given during those carefree early years at Maher.

The phone call was from his mother, inviting him and Nova over for dinner. Walter had been living with Nova for a year in a walk-up apartment in the Beaches area, on Toronto's eastern waterfront. This strictly platonic living arrangement worked on several levels, not the least of which was Nova being able to drive him to or from work. In fact, Nova took the call at Maher.

"It's your mom," she said, handing the phone over.

Walter talked to his mother, hung up the phone and looked at Nova.

"We're both invited for dinner tonight."

"Am I still supposed to be your girlfriend?"

"Whatever. You know my mom. She'll think what she wants to think."

"Do you want me to come?"

"If you don't have anything else to do. She sounded kind of weird, actually. Like something was going on."

The minute they pulled into his childhood home, Walter sensed something different. He felt anxious. While Nova busied herself with the rearview mirror, reapplying her lipstick and combing her hair, Walter looked at the house. It had a foreboding appearance, despite the warm yellow light filtering through the sheer curtains in the living room and the orange glow from the fake carriage lanterns on either side of the front door. The birch tree in the front yard was taller than he remembered, its silver bark glinting in the moonlight. Everything appeared normal, but something was off. Walter took stock. He wished he could see something new to explain this feeling of dislocation. A grotesque garden gnome, an evil topiary, anything. But there was nothing different, and this unsettled him more than anything.

"Hey, are you okay?" Nova asked, finished with her touch-up.

Walter wasn't okay at all, but he didn't know how to explain it.

"Yeah, I got this weird feeling all of a sudden."

"Like what?"

"I dunno. Like déjà vu, or something."

"Do you want to go in?"

"Yep, let's go. It's nothing."

Nova hopped out of the car and watched Walter clumsily exit the passenger side. She frowned. In all her years of knowing Walter, she had come to respect his intuition. It was like he could predict things, like who would buy what shoe. The only thing she knew for sure about Walter was that there were things about him she would never know for sure. She also knew that she trusted him like no one else, and if somebody fucked with Walter, they would have to fuck with her too. His uneasiness disturbed her. She followed him up the driveway and noticed his walking was more uncoordinated than usual. Nova didn't like it. The closer he got to the front door, the stronger Walter's apprehension got. He felt a bit sick, but plodded on, almost tripping up the three cement steps to the front walkway. Nova hit the doorbell when they reached the front door because Walter seemed incapable.

"I don't know what's wrong with me," he whispered.

Nova took his hand and squeezed it.

"Don't worry about it. We can do this," she said.

"Do what?"

"I don't know."

She gripped his hand harder as they heard footsteps approaching and felt protective of him. The door opened, allowing warmth and cooking smells to envelop the two guests standing on the stoop, and Joy Finch opened her arms, beaming a motherly welcome. Nova sighed with relief, not knowing what she had expected. She let go of Walter's hand to shake Mrs. Finch's as she stepped into the hallway. Walter followed, unable to shake the bad feeling. He hugged his mother and smelled a new brand of perfume on her neck. That was different. And she felt thinner. He observed his mother as she chattered away to Nova, hanging up her jacket and tucking her shoes into the hall closet. She was wearing makeup. Her hair seemed longer, curling down past her shoulders. When had all this happened? Walter hung his jacket up, feeling unsteady again.

"Walter, you look great," Joy said now, hands on his shoulders. "I'm so glad you could both make it. Although I have to warn you, you'll both be my guinea pigs tonight."

Nova glanced at Walter, who looked faint.

"What?" Walter asked. "What do you mean?"

"Don't look so alarmed, honey! I meant I'm trying out a new recipe, that's all. Jesus Walter, what did you think I meant?"

"Nothing, mom. Sorry, I've had a long day."

That was when Walter noticed another new thing. The smell coming from the kitchen. It was curry. His mother had never made curry in her life. He couldn't imagine his grandmother touching it.

"Where's grandma?" he asked.

"Oh, she's in the rec room watching television."

At least that was normal. The three of them walked into the living room and that's when Walter saw the reason for his anxiety. There was a man sitting on the couch. A man he had never seen before who was rising and walking toward them, hand outstretched. Time receded. He saw his mother batting her eyelashes—were they false?—and looking nervously back and forth between him and this man—was she blushing?—and he saw Nova shrink into a tiny version of Cleopatra—why had he never noticed that resemblance before?—and he felt the man's smooth paw scoop up his own useless hand that felt boneless. His mother was speaking.

"Walter. I'd like you to meet…"

The rest was lost. Like that, the static was back with a vengeance. There was nothing Walter could do to stop it. The domino had toppled.

Walter and Nova fled the dinner party the first chance they got and were sitting in a tavern on the Danforth.

"Oh my god," Nova was saying. "When I saw that guy, the first thing I thought was that it was your father. I nearly shit myself."

Walter drained his glass of beer and poured another from the pitcher. He would drink more than usual tonight.

"I know," he said. "That's what I thought too at first. It totally freaked me out."

Nova peered at her boss and friend with admiration.

"You had it pegged, though. You knew as soon as we got out of the car that something was up. Didn't you?"

Walter sipped thoughtfully. It was true. He had known.

What he didn't know was how he felt about his mother having a boyfriend. On the surface, it didn't seem so bad. David—for that was his name, David Nussbaum—seemed a decent sort. And David Nussbaum had money. That much was obvious, if not by his meticulous manners, then by his wardrobe and accessories, items whose value Walter was kept apprised of throughout the evening by Nova.

"Did you see his watch?" she had whispered when they had a minute alone. "Did you check out his cufflinks?"

Walter hadn't noticed. Too bad the shoes were in the closet, they would have been the only thing Walter could have judged David Nussbaum's paycheque on. But since Nova seemed impressed by his attire, Walter could only imagine the shoes to be of European design. Mr. Nussbaum's apparent worldliness must have been the reason Joy had prepared curry. No doubt she was trying to be continental. But neither the watch nor the impeccable manners had any effect on Clara.

"I'm not eating no Paki food," Clara sniffed when she ventured out of the basement and into the kitchen to get another Tom Collins.

Joy couldn't risk a look at David, who was leaning against the sink with a martini glass slung between two manicured fingers.

"Mom," she said in a warning growl.

Clara ignored it and squared off against David. "You like Paki food, I suppose, Mister, uh, whatsyername," she said.

David nodded and sipped his dry gin martini.

"Nussbaum, but please call me David. And yes, I do enjoy Indian cuisine."

Clara furrowed her brow. "Nussbaum. That's Jewish, ain't it?"

"Yes it is, ma'am."

Joy was in a controlled state of panic, looking back and forth between Clara and David, twisting a tea towel around her wrist, wishing she could cinch it around her mother's neck. God, she should've sent Clara out to bingo.

Clara put her hands on her hips and rocked back on her heels.

"I hate dill pickles," she said pointedly.

"Mother," said Joy, grabbing her elbow and steering her out of the kitchen.

"I always said dill pickles tasted like Jew's piss, didn't I?" Clara said to Joy, as she was being dragged into the living room.

"Jesus Christ," Joy muttered, pushing her mother into an armchair. "Stay there."

Clara patted her hair innocently.

"Do Jews believe in Jesus Christ? I think Pakis believe in cows. You better watch your mouth, young lady. You might scare that nice looking man away."

"Me? I might scare him away? Jesusss…shit, mother. Can you please keep your mouth shut for the rest of the evening? Can you do that for me?"

Clara clapped a hand over her mouth and lifted her pencilled eyebrows in mock disbelief.

"I'm not doing anything wrong, what's the matter with you? I'm trying to help you not screw up the first date you've had in years. And where's my damn Tom Collins. I think I left it in the kitchen."

As Clara moved to get out of the chair, Joy pushed her back into it.

"Never mind. I'll get it for you. You stay put."

Clara obliged, but began howling for her drink by name.

"Tommmmmy! Mister Coll-llins! Where are yo-ooou, you bad, bad boy! Get out here, now! Mama's waiting..."

Joy raced back into the kitchen to make her mother a double, hoping it would knock her out. David had seated himself at a kitchen chair and looked amused.

"I'm so sorry, David," Joy said, squeezing a lime into Clara's drink. "It's not you. She's always like this, although I think she's getting worse as she gets older."

David Nussbaum opened his mouth to speak, but saw Clara filling the doorway, and thought better of it. He cleared his throat in an attempt to alert Joy, who was babbling on in a string of apologies. Clara got there first.

"So David. What are your intentions towards my daughter?" she asked, then burst into spasms of heaving laughter, setting off a clattering frenzy of necklaces.

Joy froze, shoulders hunched. David merely smiled.

"Well, let's see. I intend to take your daughter to the opera, maybe the theatre, and treat her to some fabulous restaurants, if that's okay with you."

Clara pondered this and lumbered over to Joy's side, directing her gaze at David.

"You're rich, ain't ya?"

"I'm well off," David agreed.

"I bet you're a doctor."

"Then you would be right."

Joy handed the drink to Clara who took a dainty sip and then belched like a longshoreman.

"What kind of doctor are ya?"

Joy cringed, and tried running interference. "Come on mom, don't bother David. Why don't you go back downstairs and watch T.V.?"

But Clara wasn't having any of it. "What? What's the matter with you? I only asked a simple question."

"I think your show is starting now. Hurry up, you don't want to miss the beginning."

Clara stood rooted to the spot like an old-growth oak. "Get your hands off me! Is he a goddamn *women's* doctor? Is that what he is? That's it, isn't it?"

Joy was near tears and David stepped up to the plate.

"No, I'm not a gynecologist, Mrs. Potts."

"Thank Christ for that!" Clara gurgled into her glass as she took another swallow.

"I'm a psychiatrist."

Clara choked and sent a wide spray of Tom Collins across the room. Joy wished she were dead.

"A shrink? You're a shrink?" gasped Clara. "That's not a real doctor! That's a bunch of malarkey, mister. But, I gotta admit, it's a good scam you boys got running with that. People pay a lot of money to blab about their problems, don't they?"

"Actually, I *am* a real doctor. And yes, people do pay a lot of money. But I try and take away their pain, like other real doctors."

"But you don't save lives."

"Sometimes I do, yes."

"But you don't see a lot of blood."

"Sometimes."

"But you don't slice 'em open."

"No, some of them do that for themselves."

"Hmmph. Well, don't be getting any ideas about shrinking my head. It's screwed on right, buddy boy."

Joy viciously stirred the curry and the doorbell rang.

"That's got to be Walter," Joy said, breaking the standoff between her mother and her date.

Clara grunted. "I'll be downstairs. And don't expect me to eat none of that food, neither. I'll make myself a sandwich later. If we've still got bread in this house."

Clara began her descent, Joy wiped the hair off her face and headed for the front door, and David slid into the living room. He wondered if the son would be like his grandmother. He hoped not, but was sure Walter would be affected on some level by living with that woman all those years. It might be interesting, in a purely professional sense, to meet the lad. But mostly, he wanted to get the family duty meetings over with, so he could whisk Joy off to an expensive hotel and finally feel those beautiful, long legs snake around his own. Tall women had always been a turn on for Dr. David Nussbaum, who stood shy of five foot seven. Tall *shiksa* women, especially. It made him feel dirty and wrong. Why should his patients have all the fun, with their anxieties and guilt complexes, phobias and addictions? In point of fact, tall *shiksa* women made Dr. David Nussbaum *cra-aaazy*. And when it came to crazy, he was the expert.

Nova and Walter were onto their second pitcher of beer.

"He seemed all right, didn't he?" Walter asked.

"Yeah, for a shrunken shrink," said Nova. "Your mom seemed to like him, anyway. I thought it was nice to see your mom with a guy."

Nice. Walter supposed it was. So why did he still feel vestiges of static clinging to the periphery of his consciousness like a stubborn crust? He drank another glass of beer, hoping it would soften those lingering bits like moisture would a scab. Loosen them up, dissolve them, and slough them right off.

When Walter got home that night, he lay in his bed and stared at the ceiling. It reminded him of when he was a kid and he used to spend hours thinking his thoughts, and how he knew they were smart thoughts, and now he couldn't remember the last time he had enjoyed a smart thought. His mother had a boyfriend. On the surface, it didn't seem like much, like how his ceiling seemed like a ceiling on the surface. But he remembered that his smart thoughts had shown him there was much more to a ceiling, or a wall, or an entire room, than what appeared on the surface. He stared at the ceiling with its white squares and tried to open it up. But the only thoughts that came to Walter were ordinary. How much business Maher had done last week. How it was his turn to buy groceries. The last movie he had seen. Nova getting six holes punched in her ear. The ceiling was still a ceiling, not so much as a ripple.

He could hear Nova moving about in the kitchen, doing ordinary things like opening the fridge door and closing it. These reassuring sounds were not. The solid looking ceiling was not. Walter's room, in all its simplicity and straight lines, was not. Not reassuring in the slightest. Walter hung onto the thought about his mother and her fancy boyfriend, like he was hanging onto a child that someone was trying to take away from him. He needed to explore this thought because it had caused the re-emergence of the static. So he held on tight, while ordinary thoughts threated to snatch it away, whisk it into a waiting car and give it a new identity in another country. He blinked. Now, that was a smart thought. And if he tried really hard, he believed he could hear the distant crackling of static. But it was all so much effort. He used to *swim* in this shit.

He tried again, wondering what was so important about his mother and her boyfriend. But this time he tried stretching the thought, in an attempt to make it more transparent, to see into it. His mother had a boyfriend and Walter was no longer the only man in her life. Walter considered the significance of this, but still the ceiling didn't waver. He sighed. It was an ordinary thought. The kind of thought any young man would have when his mother started dating. It was predictable, linear, most likely. He concentrated. His mother had a boyfriend, he wasn't the only man in her life anymore, and his mother didn't need him? Nope. Linear. Ordinary. And probably not altogether true. His mother would always need him. The thought would only stretch so far and then snap back to its original shape. Walter was frustrated with the non-elasticity of his thinking. He used to be able to stretch his thoughts so wide that they would expand beyond his reach and he would be forced to let go. Back to the beginning. His mother had a boyfriend, he wasn't the only man in her life anymore, but she would always need him...and...and...the only question remaining was obvious. Did Walter need his mother? Now that she had a boyfriend to take care of her, did this free Walter?

He shook his head and felt his eyeballs roll from side to side. It still didn't make the ceiling move, but it felt good. It took a few hours of lying still and trying to force a conclusion, but eventually he did come up with one thought and it was this. He should move out of this apartment. Get his own place. Get a driver's licence. Be his own man. Grow fucking up. His mother had moved on, it was time he did the same. As soon as he thought this, Walter knew it was the right thing to do. It wasn't a *smart* thought necessarily, but it was a *right* thought.

# 12 }

**Nova remained in their old place,** which was kitty-corner to Walter's new apartment. But he had the deal. His new digs were above the small Fox movie theatre, in a building so old that the original stable doors on the main floor were still intact, but now opened onto a caretaker's office. His kitchen opened up onto a porch which led directly onto the roof of the Fox, allowing for a huge gravel and tar backyard. Walter didn't know why he had chosen such a large three-bedroom apartment that would suck an even larger portion of his paycheque. For its size though, the place was a steal, probably because of its state of disrepair, and he figured if he couldn't swing it, there was plenty of room for someone else to move in. Not that he had any intention of that happening. The whole idea was to try being a man first. See if he could cut it. And somewhere, way back in his mind, those smart thoughts he thought were lost forever had started churning and rumbling the instant he had opened the door to look at the place—it happened like a train approaching from a distance. If he put his hands to his temples, it felt like he was laying his hands on the cool metal rail of a train track, feeling the faint tremor heralding an increase in volume and shaking until the roar and the full weight of the train burst into being and if you didn't snatch your hand back and leap out of the way, you would be crushed. Better to stand as close as you dared, arms spread wide, eyes closed, and feel the controlled power of the hulking black metal and embrace the vortex of wind that it stirred up, and let the maddening, relentless, and deafening noise engulf you.

This is one image that came to Walter while he was being led around the apartment by the landlord. To his amazement, it came like that. Like a snap or a zap, the smart thought zeroed into his brain with no effort at all. He had to sign the lease. There was no question. It became a matter of his survival, and he couldn't explain this to Nova or Johnny. He could only say lame things like:

"It's a good deal, I can't turn it down."

"I'm thinking of turning one bedroom into an office."

"I ..."

Walter got off the packing box in the living room and walked down the long hallway, past the bedrooms, to the back end of the apartment. His footsteps echoed and the bathroom door creaked when he opened it. These noises were fine and sounded as if they'd been there his entire life. He washed the moving grime off his hands, gripped the cracked sink and stared into the mirror. He didn't see his face. He saw his past. Years were in there, memories. It was like he was mentally thumbing a deck of cards. Images flipped by, one by one, partially glimpsed, but enough to recognize the card. *Flip*, a face card. Adelaide. And with it, an image of her wide trembling mouth and pale eyes. Then, *flip*, a numbered card. A ten. Ten years old, playing street hockey with Johnny, *flip*, a joker, Tina telling everyone she had a stomach tumour, *flip*, Mr. Foster, *flip*, Kinney Shoes, *flip*, *flip*, *flip*. The cards flipped faster and faster until the images blurred and his face disappeared in the mirror. The quicker the cards snapped, the less he could see, until they were flying by so rapidly, the last ten cards, the last ten years, were blank. Blank. What had he done those years? Walter's eyes hurt from staring and he rubbed them with his damp hands. His face swam back into view. It was still an entirely average face, without so much as a noticeable flaw to give it distinction or character. Not a hook or bump in the nose, no mole or pockmarks on the cheeks, not an overhanging brow, an overbite, or a receding chin. Feature by feature, Walter's face was completely and utterly proportioned, the sum of which served to render the whole almost invisible. Had Walter's face possessed a singular skewed detail, even so small a thing as a scar or a flush or dark circles under his eyes, it might have brought to life all the other proportions. It might have made him handsome, or at the very least, remarkable. He smiled. The gap between his front teeth flashed and for a moment, he looked different. It helped.

Walter tilted his head, half expecting his reflection to remain fixed—half expecting his mirrored self to remain stalled somewhere in the last ten years that, sadly it now seemed, were a blur of work and friends and life and life and uninspiring life. And now, finally, here he was by himself in his own apartment. This *huge* apartment that echoed and creaked and make him feel awake again. Made him feel like he was about to live in colour. Like maybe the cards would slow down to a reasonable click, so he could actually see the hand he was being dealt.

His face may have been unremarkable, but in the final analysis, there was no question it was the face of a man that stared back at him. Finally, at thirty years of age, Walter Finch knew this to be true.

# 13 }

**Visitors to Walter's apartment** could stretch out in the spacious living room or cozy up in the tiny cluttered kitchen. In between was where people felt the emptiness. In that long uncarpeted wooden hallway, sporadically lit behind old cloudy wall sconces, where their footsteps were loud if wearing shoes, and where they felt like they could slip and fall at any given moment if they were wearing socks. The entire place was crazily sloped and the hallway proved difficult to navigate for some, particularly after a few drinks—a combination of the slanted floor and the shadows, all of which could shift perspective and cause a sort of tunnel vision. It was also colder in the hall for some reason, and at night you could hear the movies through the floorboards. Everyone suggested Walter brighten up the hallway with better lighting or at least buy a hall runner to warm it up and muffle the sound from the Fox, but he never did. He liked the hall the way it was and when no one was around, he would take a running start from the living room and slide all the way to the bathroom in his socks, as if he were on skates. For Walter, it was a glorious feeling. He wasn't a spaz when he flew down the hallway. He was smooth. He was whipped butter.

He had been living in the hotel for a few months when the first thing happened. Walter had settled in to dinner, which he almost always ate in the kitchen at the card table. Although his mother had donated some wobbly T.V. trays with white elk painted on them, Walter preferred dining in his kitchen where he could look out at his roof and the neighbouring rooftops and chimneys. It was like a scene from *Mary Poppins* and some nights he imagined the shadowy figures of chimney sweeps cavorting and leaping from building to building.

On this particular night, he was having pork chops cooked in Campbell's mushroom soup, Green Giant corn niblets, and a baked potato. He had returned from the beach and was ravenous, forgoing his bathing and jerking-off activities in favour of dinner. Walter didn't eat fast food much, barring takeout from the Goof restaurant across the street, but his cooking was pretty standard. Tonight, he was reading the paper while chewing and swallowing his pork chops in his typical fashion—unhurried, but not what one would call leisurely. You cut, you chew, you swallow, you drink, you get full, you're done. This was the same approach, if one were to think about it, that he took with his increasingly frequent masturbation bouts. You grip, you pull, you grow, you speed up, you spill, you're empty, you're done. Move on.

So it was while Walter was chewing and swallowing, not pulling and spilling, that the phone rang.

"Hello?" he mumbled, in mid-swallow.

An hour later, he hung up the phone, the remainder of his dinner cold and untouched. Walter scraped the food into the garbage and rinsed off his plate. He was humming, but not aware of this, as he shrugged into a jacket and pulled a toque over his head. Winter was on its way out, but there was still enough of a bite in the air down by the water to necessitate a bit of bundling. Walter pulled on his gloves. Fifteen minutes later, he was sitting on his preferred bench staring at the lake. A wind was up, and the water looked restless, which was exactly how Walter was feeling. People were out at this hour, moving past him in various modes of transport. If they weren't jogging or power walking, they were rollerskating or pushing strollers or being led by dogs. Like lightning, they sliced against the grey windy waterfront, and Walter found them irritating for the most part. But whereas he would usually concentrate on dissolving them into harmless molecules, tonight they weren't worth the effort. He had other things on his mind, more important things. The water hit the shoreline in regular intervals and slunk away. His underlying thoughts were like that. Rolling, relentless, reassuringly predictable and bumping up against the shoreline of his consciousness, only to recede, reconfigure, and return. The man part of Walter was feeling pretty confident right about now. Thanks to the phone call, he was about to move up in the world, forge further ahead with his career. This meant he would be engaging in more manly things like carrying personalized business cards, and perhaps it was time to finally buy a car. Walter hadn't expected the phone call, yet it wasn't a complete surprise. He rubbed his gloved hands together and squinted at the grey lake. It's funny how things you don't expect are only surprising when they don't fit into your plans. Like if someone knocks at your door and offers you free chocolates or free money. Now, *that's* a surprise. But if the surprises feel right, if they seem to be fitting, you think of them more as destinies, inevitable occurrences. This is why he hadn't been completely surprised by the phone call from Mr. Foster. It fit. It made sense to Walter. If you believe your life is following a certain path, these types of things are like highway billboards:

DESTINY! FIVE MILES AHEAD!
DESTINY! TWO MILES!
NEXT STOP! DESTINY!
LAST EXIT BEFORE DESTINY!
DESTINY! YOU ARE HERE!

That phone call was Walter's exit from Maher Shoes. Signal your intention, slow down, and make a hard right. Lean into it, baby. He hunched forward on the bench, gripping his knees. I'm taking that exit, he thought. I've done my time on this highway, and lately I've been falling asleep at the wheel. I've been driving by rote. Gearing down on the curves and the hills, going into overdrive on the straight stretches, comfortable enough to drive with one hand, sometimes one finger. I don't need a map. I need new terrain.

Walter stood up. He would cut short his lakeside vigil tonight. There were things to do. First, call Nova and tell her he was taking tomorrow off. Get her to open the store. He had an appointment with destiny after all, and you don't fuck around with that shit.

He walked back up to Queen Street, into the hotel, and began running a bath while he called Nova. No, I don't have time to explain, he said to her. I'll know more tomorrow and I'll fill you in. I've gotta go, I'm running a bath.

Walter sat naked on the edge of the tub while steam filled the room and purpose filled his being. The apartment seemed to murmur to him. He slipped into the hot water and lay back, eyes closed, pores open. Getting his own place had been the right thing to do. Tonight he didn't jerk off, although Mr. Foster's news certainly would have been cause for celebration. But Mr. Foster's news filled a greater need which served to diminish the libidinal one. Instead, Walter simply held onto his dick, the same way you'd keep hold of a tiller on a motorboat even if you weren't changing direction, or rest your hand on a stick-shift in a car even though you weren't changing gears. It just felt good to keep it there. Nobody said you had to use it.

While Walter relaxed in his bathtub, Mr. Foster was unwinding in an entirely different manner. He was drinking a glass of wine and smoking the last of the five cigarettes he allowed himself per day. The years had been kind to Mr. Foster. He hadn't changed much and didn't look his age, which now hovered somewhere in between fifty and sixty. No extra weight had found its way onto his scarecrow-like frame, and he still retained a full head of hair, which remained slicked back off his forehead with a distinctive widow's peak, but was now dyed a rusty brown colour. His pencil moustache remained a fixture on his upper lip, meticulously dyed to match his unnatural hair. Tonight, glass of wine in one hand, cigarette in the other, he was striding through his new shoe store, admiring the design, the colour scheme, the glorious hand-picked stock. His own shoe store, the grand opening of which would take place in about a month—the dream turned reality. It had been a lot of hard work, but even now it seemed impossible. Mr. Foster executed a flawless pirouette without spilling a drop and bowed to his reflection in a full-length mirror.

"Monsieur," he said, lifting his glass to his reflection. "To our success."

·And he took a dainty sip, watching himself over the rim of the wineglass. He looked splendid, if he did say so himself. Trim. He noted with satisfaction the snug fit of his black evening gown that shimmered and twinkled with hundreds of midnight-blue sequins, and the velvety richness of his white elbow-length kid gloves. He thrust a bony hip out to the side and one skinny leg showed itself through a side slit. The shoes he had chosen were marvels, like glistening spiderwebs, barely there, but supportive enough to withstand hours of dancing. Women would go crazy for his selection of shoes, he thought, turning his foot this way and that, admiring the style. And although he had spent years researching the stock he wanted for his new store, he had far greater plans. His own line. That's where Walter would come in. Mr. Foster had vision when it came to business, but he knew Walter was possessed of something extra. The kid had creative vision. Mr. Foster had thought about this for years and had it all worked out. He would give Walter a piece of the business and the freedom to create a line of shoes. And though Mr. Foster had never walked down the aisle, he knew a perfect marriage when he saw it.

He leaned over to butt his cigarette out before it burned his gloves, loving the feel of silk stretching tight over his ass. Naturally, no one would know about his alternate wardrobe. And, Mr. Foster thought, compared to all the other deviant behaviour out there in the world, his predilection was quite harmless. But still, not acceptable for an up-and-coming new businessman. It wouldn't do to let the secret out of the closet. Besides, Mr. Foster knew Walter harboured something deep in his soul. He didn't know what it was, but he could sense it was there, in much the same way an abuser can sniff out a victim a mile away. He smoothed the dress down over his slim hips, regretfully. Time to change and go home. Mr. Foster began turning off the lights and preparing to leave.

He was stepping out of his spiderweb shoes while Walter was stepping out of the tub. It may have taken years for Walter to feel comfortable wearing the skin of a man, but Mr. Foster had always revelled in the skin of Audrey Hepburn. Dressed now in slacks and a sweater, Mr. Foster wrapped a scarf around his throat and took one last look at his new store before stepping out onto Queen Street East. He turned the key in the lock and walked to his car, shoulders back, but stopped in his tracks half a block away. He couldn't resist one more look. Hands clasped in front of him, Mr. Foster gazed at his store as if he were an art lover studying a favourite painting. He wanted to relish the moment before it became public domain. For years, it had been his little secret. Now, it was his and Walter's. Next month, it wouldn't be a secret anymore. Next month, the female shoe-buying public would become aware of the existence of Go-Lightly Shoes, the store. Hopefully, in a year or so, they would become aware of GoLightly shoes, the shoes. Mr. Foster clicked his heels together and spun around. He was whistling "Moon River" as he walked to his car.

# 14 }

**Events were piling up in Walter's world.** Not only had he secured a new job at GoLightly Shoes, he was in charge of designing a line of ladies' footwear. What may have seemed an overwhelming and daunting task to anyone else was welcomed by Walter with gratitude. He was never more certain of anything in his life. One of his extra bedrooms now had a purpose, as did he. A designing room, a studio. Walter decided to call it the Drawing Room. Every hotel should have one. He purchased a large drafting table and all manner of supplies, including a collection of books on shoe design. Mr. Foster had secured the services of an elderly Italian cobbler on Spadina Road in the old jobber district and Walter had been introduced to Remo within the first week of his employment at GoLightly. Remo was of the old school and Walter's designs didn't have to be complicated architectural blueprints. They only had to be clear enough for Remo to understand. As long as Remo understood Walter's drawings and as long as Walter understood Remo's heavily accented English, all would work out. Walter set to work with his pens and pencils and imagination in hand and found himself to be quite an adequate artist. Perhaps he couldn't draw a bowl of fruit or landscape to save his life, but he could replicate the form of a shoe without any problem whatsoever. Remo showed him what perspectives and angles he would need and Walter practised diligently, starting with skeleton forms and working towards more detail and structure as his skills progressed. This is what he was absorbed in one fine day when someone knocked at his door. He looked up from his drafting table, annoyed at the interruption. He was in the middle of designing a sandal with knee-high laces and intricate overlapping leather straps. Concentration was key.

"Fuck," he swore, gripping his pencil tightly as the knocking continued.

Had he known who was on the other side of his door, he might have thought twice about answering it. But as it was, the knocking was driving him mad and there was only one way to stop it. Walter waddled to the door and opened it. His mouth fell open.

"Well, don't just stand there. Take my bags," said his grandmother, as she pushed her way past him in a cloud of White Shoulders to stand in the hallway, hands on hips.

"Come on, what are you waiting for? And where's my kiss?"

She stood, bright red lips puckered—in more ways than one—and Walter leaned over to kiss her powdered cheek.

"Grandma, what are you doing here?" he asked to her back, as she marched down the hallway towards the living room, yelling orders as she went.

"Get those bags, will ya? You can put them in my bedroom and I'd like a nice hot cup of tea. I had to take the bus and the subway and the streetcar to get here. I'm parched."

Walter watched his grandmother's receding back. He bent and slid her luggage into the hall and closed the door. The pencil he was still holding in one hand clattered onto the wooden floor. He began inching down the hallway towards the living room, nervously, as if some creature had flown in the doorway, a bat, and was now circling the living room. Walter had no idea what she was doing here. In fact, since moving to his new apartment he hadn't seen much of either his mother or his grandmother. It seemed they lived in another world, another dimension. But here she was, large as life, and Walter didn't know what to do with her. There was only one thing for it. Ask her. But he didn't get to the question quick enough.

Clara looked up from her spot on the couch at Walter who stood in the doorway. "Where's my tea?" she demanded, pulling off her gloves.

"Uh, sorry. I'll go make you some. Be right back."

"RED ROSE!" she bellowed. "None of that HERBAL CRAP!"

He practically bounced off the walls as he skidded down the hall into the kitchen where he plugged in the kettle and began dialing his mother who, as it turned out, would give him more bizarre news. Turns out, his mother had accepted a marriage proposal from David Nussbaum—"I was about to tell you"—and upon hearing that news, Clara had run away.

"I'm not living in this house if he's moving in," she had said to Joy, while packing a suitcase.

"Mother," Joy pleaded.

"I'm not living in a house with a man, let alone no Jew-boy shrink. He'll probably gaslight me and send me to the nuthouse," Clara muttered, causing Joy to tear up.

"Mom, please. Where will you go?"

Clara snapped the suitcase shut and started on another one.

"Like you care where I go. I raise you, I move in to help you when your no-good husband leaves you high and dry, I help you with your boy, and this is the thanks I get. Thrown out on the street like a dog."

"I'm not throwing you out! You're leaving! I want you to stay!"

Joy sat down on the bed and put her hand on Clara's arm. "Look mom, David said he would build an in-law suite in his basement. You'd have your own private apartment down there, but still be close to us. What are you doing? This is crazy!"

"See? Already I'm crazy. Well honey, you're the crazy one. Now I know why you're marrying a shrink."

Joy looked at the ceiling, exasperated. "Look, we'd be moving into a much bigger and nicer house. With a pool! And not right away or anything. It's not going to happen overnight. He's going to renovate a whole suite for you!"

Clara stuffed a picture of the queen in her suitcase. "Well, I guess he don't have to bother now, do he? You can both move to a castle on an island. I'm leaving."

After half an hour, five suitcases were bulging and Clara realized she couldn't carry them all. She began unpacking them and repacking everything into two. She may have been within spitting distance of eighty years old, but she was strong as an ox.

Walter poured boiling water into the teapot with one hand while he opened the fridge with the other to grab a beer. He leaned against the counter while the tea steeped, holding the cold beer bottle and staring at it blankly. Beer wasn't the answer. He put it back in the fridge. So many complex questions called for a more definitive answer. Scotch, maybe. Straight up. He grabbed a bottle and began pouring the whisky into a coffee mug—no need for his grandmother to know he was drinking— one finger, two fingers, hell, let's put a whole goddamn fist in there.

Walter placed everything on a platter: the teapot, a cup, milk, sugar, his drink, and some stale peanut butter cookies. He took a deep breath and walked down the hallway like he was walking to the gas chamber. It was surreal. The seven o'clock movie had started up at the Fox theatre and dirge-like music was playing over the opening credits, reverberating under the bare wooden floorboards of the hallway, a fitting accompaniment to his walk of doom. Walter reached the living room and stopped. His grandmother had arranged her massive bulk so as to appear to take up the entire couch. While he was in the kitchen, she had taken off her fur-lined, suede high-heeled ankle boots and set them neatly on the radiator, draped her full-length muskrat coat over one arm of the couch, moved the trunk, which served as a coffee table, over by the window, and set up one of his mother's elk tray tables in front of her knees. She sat, arms crossed over her jutting, missile-silo breasts, looking for all the world like a big perspiring buddha in drag. Walter walked over to the window and laid the platter on the trunk. He then dragged it back over to the couch so Clara could pour her tea and he pulled up a straight-backed chair to a safe distance away from the painted behemoth. He gulped his Scotch and waited.

Clara poured herself a cuppa, as dainty as you please, and took a cookie which she first sniffed suspiciously before laying it on the tray table beside her cup. She gazed around the room, taking scrupulous note of its failings. Walter couldn't help but do the same. It was sparse, compared to his grandmother's bedroom. It was neat enough, but not immaculately scrubbed. And compared to her dark and crowded musoleum bedroom, he thought she might be feeling at odds with the spacious and minimalistic setting. Her constant rattling would echo in here. Some plants would soften up the edges, he mused. He pictured a few shelving units filled with books and knick-knacks. And then he couldn't stop rearranging the place. He imagined things hanging from the ceiling, dead animals. He thought about framed photographs placed on the window seat, brightly embroidered cushions, magazines scattered about—*Redbook, Chatelaine*—rolling ottomans on casters, a ceiling fan, boxy end tables with tall lamps, a console television, brass horse ornaments, a bamboo room divider, gilt-framed oil paintings from mall displays, crystal vases, potpourri sachets, candy dishes filled with sticky humbugs and licorice allsorts, dried floral arrangements, mirrored wall tiles, ceramic bowls of waxed fruit, lace tablecloths, and doilies, doilies, *doilies*.

He rubbed his eyes and took another drink. Walter felt the Scotch settle in his stomach as if it were the hot flame of a pilot light. Each gulp of whisky was like turning up a temperature knob. If he drank fast enough, the pilot light would eventually whoosh into a shooting flame and heat up his entire body and head. If he went too far, he might explode.

His grandmother blew on her tea and took a sip, leaving a bright red lipstick stain on the rim.

"That's good," she said.

"It's Red Rose."

"I know. I thought you might have that fake tea, that herbal crap."

"No. I don't really drink tea much. Red Rose is the only kind I know because that's what you and mom drank all the time."

Clara smiled then, an astonishingly contented smile.

"You're a good boy, Walter," she said, dunking a cookie into her tea, looking like she had lived there for years.

She chewed the cookie, crumbs falling unnoticed onto the protruding ledge of her bosom. She didn't mention that it was stale or store-bought. Walter was relieved but her lack of concern made him uneasy. He expected her to give him shit about something. He shifted in his chair and took another belt of booze.

"I talked to mom," he said, bracing himself.

Clara waved one porcine hoof in the air, bracelets clanking. She allowed a belch. "I don't want to talk about that woman."

Walter forged doggedly ahead, the pilot light spearing his chest cavity.

"Do you know when she's getting married?"

Clara shoved an entire cookie in her mouth and talked around it, brown sludge pooling in the corners of her mouth. "How long can I stay?"

Walter stared at her. In her own way, his grandmother was asking a favour of him. There's a first time for everything. Maybe the long trip down here had tired her out, made her vulnerable. Walter believed he should take advantage of this because sure as shit she'd be her old ornery self come morning. But as he looked at her over the rim of his Scotch mug, he noticed things. She looked older. Her roots were grey, something he never thought he'd see in her lifetime. He thought he detected a wheeze coming from her chest and her hand shook when she raised the cup of tea. It was like the fight had gone out of her, despite her barging into his space like a bull a few moments earlier. Walter decided to set aside any questions about his mother, for the time. He also decided to be charitable, although somewhere deep beneath the pilot light, it occurred to him he might regret it later.

"As long as you want, grandma," he said. "There's plenty of room."

Clara perked up a bit and poured another cup of tea.

"Hell sonny Jim, if we're gonna be roommates, you shouldn't call me grandma anymore."

"What should I call you?"

"My name, what else?"

"Clara? I should call you Clara?"

She leaned back into the couch and stretched her legs out in front of her.

"I need a footstool. You're living like a monk here," she said.

Here it comes, he thought grimly, getting up to slide a box under her feet with a cushion on top of it. He set her pudgy feet down gently. They were damp and he squeezed them briefly before sitting back down.

"Are you tired, grandma? Do you want to go to bed?" he asked.

"I think a nice loveseat would go perfect over there," said Clara, pointing her cookie towards the fireplace.

"I guess."

"Do you remember my loveseat? I could bring it here, maybe. Fill up the room."

Walter remembered it all right, all spindly and curlicued in white antiqued paint with gold trim and a royal purple velvet seat. It looked like a throne for two monarchs, or an extremely fat one. As he recalled, it was positively the most uncomfortable and garish thing he had ever sat on in his life, the seat hard and the back sharp. And it wobbled to the point where you expected it to collapse if you crossed your legs or sneezed. He could only nod again, mutely, and turn up the flame.

Clara would never admit it to anyone, but she was bushed. Forget the bus, the subway and the streetcar. Those damn stairs up to the kid's apartment were enough to wind an Olympic athlete—one of them skinny gals that looked like a man. When did women stop wanting to look like women? Clara thought about that as Walter excused himself to go to the bathroom and duck the loveseat question. She knew that's what he was doing. She wasn't born yesterday. Nope, Clara Potts was born when women were women and men were men. Clara used to be a knockout. A dame. She had always wanted to be a dancer, but in her day, dancers were all whores. She still had the gams though. And the boobs. The rest, well nothing a good pantygirdle and a long-line brassiere wouldn't set right.

She held the plate up to her bosom and brushed the crumbs onto it. Clara hoped Walter had feather pillows. She couldn't sleep on them foam ones. They were all hard and springy. Nothing like a good feather pillow that you could mould to your head, sink into. Like a good woman, she thought, patting her belly.

Clara closed her eyes and rested her head on the back of the couch. This was quite comfortable with her feet up, now that she thought about it. The radiator clanged and she could hear traffic down below and the faint sounds from the movie theatre, all noises she wasn't used to, but everything considered, the kid had a comfortable place that you could hear yourself think in. It would do nicely.

Walter was making up his grandmother's bed in the middle room. *God, I'm already calling it my grandmother's room.* Luckily there was a pull-out couch already in there, a score from Nova's parents. He put his own quilt and chenille bedspread on her bed, busying himself with house-keeping thoughts to keep the others at bay.

I'll use a sleeping bag myself. Tomorrow I'll buy some extra blankets and pillows. I know she likes feather pillows, I've heard her rant enough times about the evils of foam. I hope this small dresser is big enough for all her stuff. God, there's no closet in here. Where is she going to keep all her shoes? Her shoes, her shoes, her shoes...

He sat on the edge of the bed as a wave of dizziness crested and broke, the undertow dragging him under and back into his grandmother's closet. Baby powder, he smelled. He swallowed with some difficulty, his tongue thick with polish. The high ceiling appeared to have dropped significantly as he gazed up at it, not entirely surprised to find himself now lying on the bed. Hems of colourful dresses danced and swayed, hangers rattled, and his fingers clenched and clawed at nothing. As he was pulled deeper into the closet, Walter struggled to maintain some sense of reality. I'm remembering, he thought. People do that all the time. There's nothing wrong with it. My grandmother showed up and it's only natural I would be remembering things about her.

As the hotel bedroom blurred and rippled, Walter hung on. He focused on the room's window with its peeling paint and one cracked pane. The moon was shining through it and the window became a lighthouse, a beacon. As long as he could still see it, he hadn't gone under. But he was getting tired now, and oh, it was soothing in the closet. In the closet, there is no time, no worries. In here, I invent things, fix things, get ideas. The closet *nurtures* me.

He could hear the ocean now, as if he had a big pink conch shell to his ear. As long as he could still see the window—and yes, he could—what would be the harm in letting the occasional wave wash over his head? Other sounds now, a motorboat. The coast guard, perhaps, come to save him. They would never find him, he was too deep. Dragged under by his heavy straight last shoes. But the coast guard got closer, the motor louder. He put his hands over his ears and hoped he was deep enough that he wouldn't get chopped up in the propeller. It was right over top of him. So close he could hear the radio. They were probably calling for help, he thought. The sound of the radio crackled and spit, the dial spinning him back into his black and white boyhood bedroom. The radio was between stations, blaring out static and bits of the *Hit Parade* as the dial spun around and around, all the way to DEE-TROIT, ladies and gentlemen. Comin' to you all the way from the MOTORRRR CITY!

Walter let it all roll on by, this black and white spool of film, this movie of the week. He tried opening one eye and realized his eyes were open. He looked for the lighthouse. There it was, cracked pane, peeling paint. The film receded into a wash of grey, backed with a minor clicking sound that gradually slowed. He sat up on his elbows and aside from feeling he had just woken up, everything was normal. And then he saw his grandmother in the bedroom doorway, holding the tea platter and looking at him.

"Where were you?" she asked.

Walter sat up, disoriented. "In your closet," he said.

Clara stared at him and flung one arm at the bedroom. "Really. Well then, maybe you could tell me where it is, because from where I'm standing, I ain't got one. Where the hell am I supposed to hang my dresses?"

Walter started to laugh, but composed himself. He was afraid if he started laughing he wouldn't be able to stop.

"I know, I know. That's what I was thinking about. Only one of these bedrooms has a closet. Maybe I can rig up a pole across one corner that you can use to hang your clothes on."

Clara balanced the tray on one hard-packed hip, as she scanned the room.

"What kind of place has no closets?"

"A hotel."

Clara blew a noisy blast of air from her nose. "I never heard of no such thing."

"I think these rooms were rented by the hour," said Walter, wondering if she'd catch on to the implication.

"Hmmph. Guess you got some pretty interesting ghosts in here then," she said as she heaved herself out the door, heading into the kitchen.

"You said it," said Walter under his breath, as his grandmother yelled a parting comment from down the hall.

"You better not be chargin' ME by the hour!" she bellowed. "Or you ain't gettin' no ROOM SERVICE!"

Walter smiled weakly. Maybe this could work out. If she would keep out of his way and leave him alone when he was working, maybe it would be all right having her around for a while. And then he remembered what brought her to his door in the first place. God, later for that, he thought, and pushed himself off his grandmother's bed. He walked towards the kitchen and could hear Clara starting to wash the dishes. She was singing "Bicycle Built For Two" in a high, warbly voice as she snapped on the rubber gloves with a surgeon's authority. Walter watched her from the doorway, her broad-beamed behind and strong-looking, shapely calves a reassuring sight.

He still couldn't believe she had chosen him as her safe harbour. She had plenty of friends her own age, most of who lived in the seniors' apartment building at Birchmount and Sheppard. Her bingo pals. Walter had met a few of them when he had driven her over there on occasion. Most of them widowed or divorced, living in identical, tiny one-bedroom apartments, filled to overflowing with mementos and crafts, much like his grandmother's bedroom. All the apartments smelled the same too. There was nary a speck of dust to be found in any of them, but a film of age had settled over all the furniture and clung to the walls. That's what you could smell, over and above the air freshener, the Pine-Sol, the perfumes and lilac soaps, the cooking smells. It was the smell of decay, Walter thought. A sobering smell, peculiar only to senior citizens. He wondered if his apartment would begin to smell like that with his grandmother living here.

"What are you standing there for?" his grandmother barked over her shoulder. "Grab a dishtowel boy. Get those bandy legs over here and help your old granny out."

And so he did. Side by side they stood, his grandmother grumbling about everything from Walter's lack of SOS pads to her lack of an apron, and Walter agreeing pleasantly with everything she said. The basic hotel kitchen felt like a real home kitchen and Walter was content. He looked out the window onto the rooftop, saw the chimneys and lit windows in other buildings, and wondered if anyone with binoculars was peering into his own kitchen and thinking how homey the scene was. And then, for the first time ever in this apartment, he thought: What if it wasn't my grandmother standing beside me? What if it was my wife?

The unexpected pang of this thought sucked all the contentment out of Walter for a moment, replacing it with panic. He could picture his grandmother living with him for twenty or thirty more years, because god knows, she would live to be at least a hundred. And he would be one of those men who remained tied to the apron strings—if she had thought to bring an apron—a career bachelor, the male equivalent of a spinster, whatever the hell that was, a Peter Pan, someone to be pitied, never to have children, and in his case, never to be a favourite uncle, and what woman in her right mind would want to date someone who lived with his grandmother? A grandmomma's boy, oh my god. What peeping Tom worth his telescope would linger over *this* domestic scene for more than a second?

Walter looked down at the top of his grandmother's head, noting the grey roots clearly, and wondered if she had always been that short. She must have sensed him staring at her and she looked up at him. Her eyes were cloudy with the beginnings of cataracts, and Walter thought he could see a tear track on her powdered cheek.

"Thank you for putting up with me Walter," she said, brushing her cheek with the back of her rubber-gloved hand.

And just like that, all the panic and anxiety he had been feeling went down the drain with the last of the soapy dishwater.

# 15 }

**For Walter's purposes,** GoLightly Shoes couldn't have been better situated, being just a couple of blocks from the hotel. He was utterly free from the clutches of Agincourt and it felt damn good. There were no malls, mega or otherwise, here in the Beaches and that felt good too. He relished strolling along Queen, peering into individual storefront windows, each business an enterprise unto itself. The Queen Street shopkeepers supported each other, with the pubs being the most favoured recipients of the bulk of their spending dollars. But GoLightly was in the unique position of being the only shoe store in the immediate vicinity. It wouldn't take long before almost every female working the local stores would be strutting her stuff in GoLightly's footwear. It was amazing to Walter that he now worked with Mr. Foster and had been entrusted by the great shoe man with GoLightly designs and the co-management of his pride and joy. They were on a first-name basis and every time Walter called his boss Reginald, he got a kick out of it.

Nova had also joined the GoLightly crew, a good move for all concerned. Being so much more outgoing than Walter, Nova brought with her a ready-made clientele of local residents she had met since living in the Beaches. Her vitality and Walter's expertise made them an invaluable team for Mr. Foster.

Not surprisingly, Clara was one of GoLightly's best customers, taking full advantage of Walter's employee discount. Her presence in the hotel had never been questioned and she and Walter had fallen into an easy alliance. Walter had fashioned some brick-and-board shelves in Clara's bedroom and her new shoe collection was growing at a fantastic rate.

Once Walter's designs got serious, he decided to keep his drawing room locked and Clara had found this most amusing.

"Well, ain't this a reversal," she had said, watching him drill holes in the doorframe.

"I guess it's true what they say," Clara yelled over the drill. "Life goes full circle, don't it? Guess you're gettin' back at me."

Walter fit the plate against the door, mumbling around the screws in his mouth.

"I only want to lock it when I'm out, Clara. Once I get some finished designs, they're going to be top secret. Can't have anyone stealing them, can we?"

Clara digested this information, along with the fact that he had used her first name.

"So, I can go in there sometimes? See what you're up to?"

"Sure, maybe you can help me someday. Once I know what I'm doing."

Walter screwed the plate on the frame and Clara watched with interest.

"I've got lots of ideas, you know," she said. "I remember all the shoes from when I was a teenager. They're coming back into style now, I'm seeing."

Walter finished installing the lock and turned to his grandmother. She was right. Retro was huge. And if anyone would remember specific touches, she would.

"You're right about that," he said. "Why don't you start making a list of your favourite shoes and we can talk about it later?"

She fingered the newly installed lock, and looked at Walter.

"Y'know, I remember a pair of sandals that had hinges on them, like this here lock. Bet you never woulda thought of that. They were wood soles, cut into sections and hinged together. I've never seen nuthin' like them since. Red leather straps on top."

"They were hinged? Could you draw me a picture?" Walter asked.

"Maybe. Those were some shoes, boy. I LOVED those shoes. And comfortable? Cripes, they moved with your feet. Opened and closed, opened and closed. Why, I bet you could put teeny locks on them so no one else could walk in them! You could lock people out of your shoes!"

Walter watched her face light up as she described the shoes.

"You got any paper?" she asked.

"What?"

"Paper. Foolscap paper or something. I only got my good stationery and I'm not gonna waste that."

"On what?"

"On my designs! Hurry up, time's a wastin'. I got ideas, boy, ideas. Chop, chop. I'll need a table now too. And some of your fancy drawing pencils."

She reminded Walter of Adelaide at this moment, childlike. Maybe he had created another monster.

"I'll set you up," he said.

"Good. The sooner the better. I'm all excited now, and you don't want to know what happens when you get an old lady all excited."

"What happens?"

"We pee our pants," she said, and walked towards the kitchen to start dinner.

Her cackle floated down the hallway. Walter had a nagging thought underlying all this camaraderie, but it was hard to pin down. It was wrapped up in thoughts of commitment. He seemed to be digging himself in deeper with his grandmother, fixing up her room, letting her manage the meals, and encouraging her to draw shoes. On the one hand, it all felt right and good. But this feeling of contentment with his grandmother was moving him to question his lack of another kind of commitment. Walter had never given much thought to a love relationship when he had plenty of time and freedom to dwell on such things. But now that his head was full of business and grandmothers and, god, his mother getting married, there it was.

Walter slumped to the hall floor. *Commitments.* His life was full of them and soon, his mother would be making one to David Nussbaum. He still hadn't wrapped his brain around that nugget of information, but as he had no say in it and no loyalty to his biological father, there wasn't a lot to think about. Besides he had shoes to design, a grandmother to deal with, a best friend to spend time with, rent to pay, and a day job to continue. He tugged at his hair. What about commitment to his personal life? What about that, anyway?

"HEY! Get in here and peel some spuds, why don'tcha?" Clara yelled from the kitchen.

Walter struggled to his feet, and pushed relationship thoughts aside. Clara never asked for help making dinner. She probably wanted to talk more about the hinged sandals or other shoes she remembered wearing. He tottered down the hall, thinking about shoes. Wing shoes, actually. He wanted to ask Clara if she remembered them. If the love of his life were out there somewhere, she would have to wait. Shoes came first.

**Sleep, for Walter, was still a luxury.** For most of his life, Walter had gone to bed at a reasonable hour, but lain in a semi-conscious purgatory until dawn. Now, intent on his designs, Walter didn't darken his bedroom doorway until the sky lightened it. This cut down on the hours spent in bed rolling around in a grey wash that obliterated dreams. Instead, he used those magical hours to draw. It was acceptable to dream then, part of the creative process, and when the nighttime static trickled into his consciousness, he used it. Sometimes it pricked at him like barbed wire, and opened up a tiny slit through which he could glimpse a solution to a nagging design flaw. Other times it seemed to fall over his vision like a burlap hood, but he used that too. When that happened, when the room and the drafting table melted away, Walter's hand moved without his permission and mysterious lines and swirls would appear on the paper. It was akin to the automatic writing performed by psychics when they tapped into the other side and spirits spoke through them. Those wee hours, when the sky lightened, those were Walter's most productive times. He would come out of his reveries and instead of seeing written messages in the swirls and flourishes and dots he had drawn, he would see shoes. Never an entire shoe, but bits of them. A curiously shaped heel, a cunning series of eyelets, or sometimes a distinct pattern that could be duplicated with either fabric or embossed leather. It never let him down, never. And Walter began to push for these out-of-body experiences. The inspirations that came from them were far superior to anything he could dream up in a conscious state.

Things were easy when objectivity took a vacation, when perspective bounced around like a pinball until lights flashed and sirens blared and everything screamed TILT! TILT! TILT! That's when his hand moved, swooping and diving in what felt like random movements but weren't. It would start slow, always. He would be hunched over the paper, fine-tuning some previous idea, when the room would begin to soften up around the edges. It was like a fine mist would creep in and hover midway in the room, encircle him and his table, pool around the lamp, his pencil, and his fingers. The mist was cool and it swept up in tiny eddies and currents. Baby cyclones formed and they would dance on the tabletop and disappear inside him somewhere. He never saw them streak into his eyes or ears or nose, but he could feel them in his head—they were singing without sound. The light would change in the room. It would become intensely bright on the paper, so bright it would have blinded any other mortal. So bright, it didn't hurt his eyes anymore because *he* was the light. And throughout, that old familiar friend the static was there. Sometimes the static felt like a metal cage that clanged open and shut, allowing only enough light in so as was bearable. Other times the static lay still but watchful, a guardian at the ready in case Walter needed to call upon it. And as his cognitive brain began to shut down, compartment by compartment, other untapped zones opened up, bloomed. It was like he had a big can of paint in his head and it tipped over, the inspirations pooling out and onto the paper, spreading like a slow stain. And then, as the static roared to a loud scratchy thrum and the room dissolved into flickers, things picked up momentum. Walter's hand flew, and his eyes held on, following every arc and dip like obedient students. The shoe spirits were speaking through him.

When the static lessened and the desk light diffused, when his hand slowed to vague drifting and his vision focused, streaks of pale were licking the sky. Walter wouldn't look at what his hand had drawn. He would turn off the lamp and go to bed. By that time he could sleep, and all those aimless hours of static and unproductive thoughts that used to keep him half awake and tossing were channelled into art in the drawing room.

When he came home from work, that's when he could find things in the illustrations left by the shoe spirits. Design clues would emerge like tiny angel footprints, and Walter would copy them into a separate folder. On his days off, when Clara was out grocery shopping or indulging in her new hobby of placing bets at the local horseracing track, he would flip through the folder and mix and match the pieces to see what felt right.

But drawing fantasy shoes was only the first step. He had endured countless arguments with Remo about structure and materials and feet. What looked good on paper wasn't always possible to manufacture. It was frustrating, but Walter kept at it.

"The foot, she no bend so high!" Remo would wail, shaking Walter's designs in his face.

The phrase "back to the drawing board" was becoming all too real. But Walter persevered. Despite Remo's histrionics, the hunchbacked gnome was grudgingly impressed with the drawings and would often perform the same mix-and-match procedure Walter went through at home.

"Ah, you see? This shoe? She full of life now. Remo fix."

Remo would kiss the drawing and then grab Walter's face and kiss each cheek.

"Bella," he would say, beaming at the sketch as if he drew it himself.

The only problem Walter had with Remo was dodging the cobbler's insistence on altering Walter's own shoes.

"I make you walk good," he would say, clucking and shaking his head every time Walter clumped into Remo's office.

"I need to focus on women's feet, Remo. Not my feet."

"So then. You need woman foots to practice on."

"That would be great, but where am I going to get woman foots?"

"You make them," Remo stated, as if it were the most obvious thing in the world.

"Out of what?"

"Out of the plaster, what else?"

"Like, plaster casts?"

"Yes, yes, like casts."

Yes, yes, Walter thought. "Remo, you're a genius."

# 16 }

In all his years of selling shoes, and despite his fixation on women's feet, Walter had never found his job to be an erotic experience, at least not in the way most people would imagine. Back when he had worked at Kinney's in Agincourt Mall, Johnny had been the first one to suggest the carnal possibilities in such an occupation.

"You mean you never look up their skirts?" he had asked, incredulous. "What's the matter with you? You've got the perfect angle."

At the time, such comments only amused Walter. Business was business. Snatching random snatch peeks would never occur to him. But explaining that to Johnny was impossible. Selling shoes was hard work. Most women were determined to cram their bloated size nine feet into AA-width, size seven shoes. With only a cursory glance, Walter could judge the size of a woman's foot. He didn't need a measuring plate. And for those deluded women convinced their fat flippers were actually dainty sparrow feet, Walter wouldn't use the measuring device to convince them. He knew the worst thing you could do was confront them with their lie. After all, the customer is always right. Walter couldn't count the number of times he'd watched a woman approach him, her size tens slapping and flapping, holding a fragile evening sandal in one hand.

"You got this in a size seven?" she would ask, lowering herself with a thud into a chair.

Depending on the shoe style, Walter had ways of making the shoe fit. Some he could stretch into an entire size larger and wider. It was laborious and delicate work. He would warm up the leather, work it with his hands to make it malleable, and ever so gently bulge it out. First with the shoe stretcher and then by pushing the end of a broom handle into the toe and moving it back and forth, opening up the leather wherever he needed the room. Slingbacks and open-toed shoes were the easiest to fit, because these women didn't give a shit if their heels hung an inch off the back or their toes dangled off the ends. They would stand defiantly, their feet overflowing the shoes, and look haughtily at Walter.

"See? I told you I was a size seven!" they would pronounce with a sniff.

He would agree and watch them teeter out of the store, a sprained ankle waiting to happen.

Sometimes even Walter couldn't stretch a shoe enough. In those instances and if the customer was adamant, he would get a larger shoe and remove the size entirely. Scratch it off the sole, black it out on the inside. If the woman took a ten, get rid of all signs it was a nine and deliver it as a seven or eight, or whatever they claimed to be. This made the women happy and that was his job. They would slide their feet into the shoes, which were always a bit tight, otherwise they wouldn't want them, and prance around the store. Again they would say: "See? I told you I was a size seven!"

Again, he would agree.

Other times, it worked the opposite. Popular stylish shoes would be the first to sell out, leaving only larger sizes in stock. It seemed the size ten women would buy out the sevens and eights and leave the tens behind for women with size six feet. These small-footed women had no illusions about their shoe size.

"Can I get this in a six, or a five?" they would ask.

Walter couldn't lie in these circumstances.

"I'm sorry, we're sold out. That's the last pair, size nine."

While some women would demand he phone other shoe stores to try tracking them down, other women were in a hurry and wanted instant gratification.

"Let me try it on and see how big it is on me. I know sometimes, depending on the country it was made in, I can wear a seven or eight."

Hopeful women. Ever hopeful.

Walter would hunker down with these women and sometimes he

could make the shoe fit. But in these circumstances, open-toed slingbacks were the most difficult, impossible if the heels were high. Tiny feet would slide down the slope of the arch and pop right out the end. Half their foot would be sticking out and there was nothing anyone could do about that. Pumps were easier to deal with. Walter would lift the manufacturer's skimpy insoles right out of the shoes and lay thicker foam insoles underneath. By using half insoles on the ball and toe area of the shoes, the foot would automatically be pushed back into the heel. Fucking around with insoles could keep a size six foot nice and snug inside a size eight or even nine shoe. Walter had dealt with a lot of Asian women, many of whom had the narrowest baby feet he had ever seen, who were quite happy with a larger shoe. Maybe they thought it Westernized them, he didn't know. But with a full insole, a couple half insoles, and some heel pads at the back, you could bulk up a size five foot and balance it into a size nine shoe, if you really wanted to. It would look retarded, but the women didn't care. It was only the size ten women who suffered from low foot esteem.

It wasn't easy to explain any of this to Johnny, whose sole obsession was Walter's position on the floor.

"Don't you ever slide your hand up their legs? To see what they'll do?" he had asked.

"I can't do that," Walter said.

"Sure you can. How about when they're trying on boots in the winter? You gotta do the zippers up, man. It's the perfect time to cop a feel or sneak a peek."

Walter could only sigh. How do you explain the boots? The worst part of the job, by far. The knee-high boots made for stick legs, and the meaty calves that had to literally be pushed and prodded, pummelled and stuffed bit by bit into those sleek sausage casings as you ground the zipper up inch by inch, ripping the flesh off your index finger that would eventually harden into a callous, and praying the zipper wouldn't break. Oh yes, the boots. Shoe salesmen hated the boots more than anything. And there was nothing anyone, not even Walter, could do about it if a gigantic calf wouldn't condense its mass enough to strap in.

Walter could struggle with a boot zipper for fifteen minutes and finally get it done up only to have the mid-part of the zipper burst open and a ball of flesh spring out the side. But the women demanded he try. If they were wearing pantyhose, he would have to slide a finger behind the zipper to protect the nylon from snagging as he sweated and worked the zipper up with his other hand. It was hard to believe, with all that trouble, that women would insist on buying these instruments of torture. On particularly insane fittings, he knew for a fact that once these women got home, they would never be able to put their boots on by themselves. This is one reason women had tons of shoes.

And as far as the boots went, not only were they the hardest to fit, winter was the worst time of year for odorous, clammy feet. There was nothing remotely romantic about it, but all Johnny could think about was being eye level with a living, breathing female crotch. Walter knew he would never convince Johnny that being a shoe salesman was work. Like he could never convince a woman she was a size ten.

As much as Johnny might have enjoyed sticking his nose up dresses and sniffing around, Walter liked the smell of feet, even the winter ones. It didn't bother him—in fact, it relaxed him. And how to explain that? No way. He couldn't tell Johnny of the hours he had spent in Clara's closet snuffling and licking her shoes. Or that he used to nap in the closet with shoes over his face and how it had transported him. In fact, if anything was going to get Walter horny while he was at work, it wouldn't be the panties, it would be the feet. Johnny would never get it.

Nova had an entirely different attitude about selling shoes. There was no way in hell she would spend time padding a large shoe to fit a tiny foot or stretching the hell out of a too-small shoe. She would fix the women with her dead-eye gaze and say things like:

"Are you nuts? If you're a size seven, I'm Elizabeth Taylor."

Walter had cringed when he first heard Nova's selling style, but she got the job done. After attacking the women's vanity, Nova would do what good salesmen or women were supposed to do. She would talk them into buying something else, if not a pair of shoes, then a handbag. To Walter's ear, her style sounded dangerously close to bullying, but Nova managed to tread a fine line that usually ended with the women thanking her profusely at the cash register and talking like they were old friends. For her part, Nova would roll her eyes whenever she witnessed Walter in the backroom, struggling and sweating to manhandle a shoe into a completely different shape.

"You're wasting your time," she would say to him, as she dashed by with six shoeboxes in her arms. "I'll sell four pairs of shoes in the time it takes you to sell one."

This was true. Nova consistently took home the top commissions. But Walter wasn't in it for the money. He was trying to make a square peg fit a round hole, and the greater the challenge, the more he wanted to rise to it. Mostly, to his mind anyway, he cared. If customer A wanted shoe B, there was no way she'd be walking out of the door with shoe C, not if he could help it. And on those rare occasions he simply couldn't manage a fit, Walter was better than anyone when it came to suggesting and then selling something else. Because he *knew*. He understood the connection between women and their shoes, and he could tell by a woman's posture, her clothing, her attitude, what she was all about. He knew how to treat her, and most assuredly what to sell her. If nothing else, he could tell by the shoes she was already wearing—the manufacturer, the heel height, the state they were kept in. He would examine the bottoms of their shoes and note the places with wear. Details would coalesce into one big picture, nothing was too small to escape detection. All those years of observing his grandmother's scrupulous attention to ensemble, his mother's *laissez-faire* attitude about fashion, Adelaide's complete ignorance, Nina and Tina's competitiveness, not to mention his own struggle with the straight last shoes, all of it was put to use.

Whereas Nova would say to a customer, "Those make you look like a cow, try these," Walter would say, "Those don't do you justice, these are much more flattering."

But both Nova and Walter were impressed with the other's methods.

"I don't know how you get away with it," Walter once said to Nova.

"'Cause I'm a chick," she said. "I don't know how you can grovel like that."

"'Cause I'm a guy," Walter said, and they both laughed.

Once Walter figured out what made Nova's style work, his insight was put to further use. After only a few minutes with a customer, he could sense if she would be better served in Nova's camp and hand her over. When GoLightly's developed a steady clientele, it seemed to divide naturally between the two of them. Walter would typically end up with the older ladies who had a lot of time on their hands and craved attention, or he would get the ego-driven, vain women who were always right. And his wacky walking seemed to go over best with those groups. The old ladies tsk'ed and felt like taking him home and feeding him chicken soup and the vain women found in him an excuse to act superior. Nova did best with the vulnerable ones, the indecisive women.

Overseeing all this was the great and powerful Reginald Foster, who despite his exalted position and exhausting load of paperwork, would also on occasion be getting his knees dusty in the storefront. Walter still felt a thrill when he would find himself kneeling side by side with Mr. Foster. Sometimes they would conclude a sale at the same time and stand beside each other at the cash, simultaneously bagging the shoeboxes, tossing in cans of polish or sets of laces, and spiking the receipts to the ding! of the register. Occasionally Mr. Foster would wink at Walter and he would feel like a kid again. Other times, they would sit shoulder to shoulder in the backroom after hours and discuss Walter's design ideas. Those times, Walter felt like a man who had earned respect. He had no idea Mr. Foster was dreaming about dancing in Walter's shoes.

It was a busy Saturday afternoon at GoLightly's when another domino fell. Walter had three customers on the go. One elderly woman was surrounded by a flotilla of slippers and was taking forever shuffling around the store, humming to herself. He only had to check in with her every now and then to slip a different pair on her ancient feet and flash her a smile. She was no trouble. The second woman, who was about forty or so, was trying on designer sneakers and sprinting up and down the store. Walter had often seen her jogging on the boardwalk and knew her name to be Judith. She was the type of woman who refused to let him help, other than to bring out an endless parade of runners for her perusal. She would tie her own laces, thank you very much, and no need for him to hover. I'll let you know when I decide, go on about your business with the others, I'll be fine, you don't have to worry about me, I can see how busy you are. The third and youngest woman looked to be about twenty-five and Walter knew she was Nova's type. Quiet, indecisive, easy to manipulate. But Nova was busy juggling five other customers and the girl fell to Walter. Everything about her was soft, her voice, her gaze, her walk. She looked, to Walter, like a soft brown mouse. He had watched her tiptoeing around the store, brushing the toes of shiny shoes with her fingertips, eyes half closed, like she was in a dream. She never picked any shoes up and her body language gave no hint she wanted attention. She drifted through the store, shroud-like, her expression bemused. While Walter's slipper lady shuffled and his sneaker lady sprinted, he approached the mouse girl to ask if he could help.

"Yes, I believe you can," she said, looking up at him with half-lidded green eyes.

"What are you looking for?"

"May I sit?"

"Of course," Walter said, directing her to a seat at the back of the store.

Mouse girl floated down into the chair, skirt billowing, and Walter crouched in front of her, balancing his butt on his heels, rocking a bit. He waited, noting her shoe size with a sliding glance at her feet.

"I need some shoes to wear at my birthday party next week," she said.

"Did you see anything you like?"

She leaned forward.

"Not yet."

"Nothing?"

"No. That's why you're going to help me."

A small smile, ankles crossed, mouse girl arched her eyebrows. Walter enjoyed her presence and sat there a moment considering things, while behind them, Judith was basically doing handsprings and cartwheels around the store and slipper lady was trying furry mules on her hands like mittens and clapping them together. Nova had been in and out of the backroom at least three times while Walter and the mouse communicated telepathically about her needs.

"Any specific colour you're looking for?" he asked.

"No. I trust you."

Her comment made Walter's heart open up and he felt like lying on the carpet with mouse girl beside him, both holding hands and staring at the ceiling. The madness of GoLightly's on a Saturday afternoon was but a distant soundtrack to a simple script in a two-person drama. Walter rose to his feet.

"I'll be right back."

"Thank you."

"Let me deal with..."

"I know."

Within minutes, Walter had dispatched of slipper lady and Judith with more efficiency and speed than ever before. Before either lady knew it, they were being hustled out the door with their new purchases. Walter then tore into the backroom and climbed the rolling ladder, zipping back and forth along the rows of shoes, grabbing boxes by instinct and tossing them onto the floor, where they would fall open and their contents spill out. When he clambered down, shoes were scattered everywhere, cherry red shoes, shiny black patent shoes, sparkling white and silver shoes, all of them he gathered up into his arms and ran back into the storefront, panting. Mouse girl was still there, sitting peacefully in her cloud, hands clasped on her lap. Beatific. He had not imagined her.

Walter knelt at her feet to remove her simple canvas deck shoes, plain brown and white. She was wearing brown knee socks. Walter noted all of these things. Women didn't wear knee socks much any more, and for some reason Walter was pleased she was wearing them. He undid the white laces and slipped the deck shoes off her feet, looking up at her face.

"Would you like to take your socks off? I have some fresh nylons here."

Mouse girl didn't say a word, but placed her feet on Walter's thighs and leaned back in the chair. She stared at the ceiling. Okey dokey, he thought, and grasped the tops of her knee socks to roll them down. It wasn't entirely unusual to remove a woman's socks. Sometimes he would grab an ankle sock while removing a shoe and slip them both off together.

And he had experienced his share of women who had flirted with him and asked him to remove their socks, giggling and squirming in their seats. But mouse girl wasn't flirting. There was nothing suggestive in her demeanour or her body language as Walter rolled her knee socks down and slipped them off her feet. And that's when it happened. A lurch in his stomach, a flutter, he wasn't sure. Her feet were exquisite. They were breathtaking. And they were lying on his thighs, naked and soft and excruciatingly white, like ghost feet. Her toenails twinkled, painted with silvery glitter. He had never seen such feet and could only stare. How could this elegance come out of such plain shoes? Walter felt like he had cracked the nondescript brown shell of a coconut and discovered the rich creamy milk inside. He wanted to drink her feet, suck her toes, scrape the glitter off with his teeth. Everything he had ever felt like doing with his grandmother's shoes so long ago, he now wanted to do with these feet. The feelings were the same and the static was back. It gut-punched him. Her feet were cool to the touch, but their presence on his lap burned like frostbite. All he wanted to do was cradle these feet, bring them up to his face, touch each toe with the tip of his tongue. For starters.

He couldn't bring himself to think further than that, because there were things that needed doing. He had to hack through the static somehow and put the nylons on her feet. The thought of slipping sockettes on these feet paralyzed him with fear. And then he would have to slide her stockinged feet into GoLightly shoes, a fearful thought. Walter flexed his fingers to make sure they still worked. And her toes curled, grasping the fabric of his pants and hanging on. This served to do two things to Walter. It blasted a clear path through the static while simultaneously giving him an instant erection. The static was still present, but it was having a party around him, not inside him. He could feel it close by, like a rolling thundercloud, but it had opened up enough to see green sky that was her eyes. And to feel the pressure in his pants. And to be able to unwrap a nylon and slip it on her right foot without keeling over. No words were exchanged, but Walter felt like a steady conversation had been going on between them. He picked up a red shoe with a vicious high heel and a toe like an ice pick. It had satin ribbons that wound around the ankle and as he placed her perfect stockinged foot into the shoe, he heard the whispering of the shoe spirits. Walter reverently looped the ribbons around mouse girl's ankle and did something he never thought he would do. He looked up. Up her slender shin to her bare knee. She had a small scab on her knee, and the sight of it made Walter's heart split open. He slipped her left foot into the red shoe without taking his eyes off her knee and began wrapping her left ankle. With a mighty mental effort, Walter wrenched his gaze off her knee and found himself between her thighs. He thought of Johnny and was helpless to stop his visual journey. Mouse girl moved in her chair, a mere fraction, but enough that Walter glimpsed a flash of white cotton. His throat seized up and he felt like he was losing it, the only thing keeping him grounded being the ecstatic pain of the high heel digging into his thigh.

"Shall I stand up now?"

Walter swallowed. Mouse girl had spoken and he realized her shoes were all done up and he was kneeling like a penitent, his hands gripping the backs of her calves, holding onto her legs as if they were the bars on a jail cell window and he was staring beyond them to freedom, to the promised land. The land of cotton. Look away, look away, look away...

So he did. Mouse girl stood up and stepped over his sinner's lap in one fluid motion, red spikes flashing. When Walter mustered enough courage to lift his head, he didn't see her anywhere. She was gone. And like that, everything changed. The static dissolved and the sounds of GoLightly's picked up volume. The cash register dinged, he could hear Nova's voice complimenting a customer on her haircut, the babble and gabble of shoe-shopping women, and Reginald's laugh cutting through the ambient jazz music playing through the store speakers. Walter felt like he had run a marathon and everything was now slowing down—his heart rate, his breathing, the blood pulsing through his dick. He had no idea how much time had passed and felt guilty that he had not taken up his share of customers. But everything appeared normal and no one seemed to be paying any attention to Walter as he sat on the floor surrounded by shoeboxes. He took advantage of the space that had been cleared in his mind and got to his feet. Mouse girl was nowhere to be seen. Her brown canvas deck shoes lay underneath her chair, and Walter scooped them up and tucked them under one arm. Figuring she must be in the bathroom, he cast his professional eye about the store to see if anyone else needed help in the meantime. But everything was under control. He picked up a feather duster and strolled about the store, nodding at familiar faces, dusting spotless displays, and waiting for the mouse. The bathroom door thudded and he spun around, but the woman coming out of the bathroom wasn't her. It was a young woman leading a child by the hand. Walter stared at the woman, trying to make her into the mouse girl. Was she wearing a wig? Had she changed her clothes? It was stupid.

"Can you help me?"

Walter turned, excited and relieved, only to face a buck-toothed teenage girl who was holding a handbag out.

"What?"

"Do you have something like this, only smaller?" asked the rabbit-faced girl.

Walter stared dumbly at her for a second. Everyone was turning into a forest creature today. He took the handbag.

"Yes we do," he said. "Wait here, I'll be right with you. Same colour?"

"Yeth," she lisped, and corrected herself with precision. "Yesss."

Normally Walter would have felt empathy with this girl. Anyone with an impediment usually earned extra care and attention from the Spazman. But not now. He wobbled to the far wall, looking for a glimpse of the red shoes, and nearly tripped over Nova sitting on the floor.

"Hey!" she said, punching his leg. "Watch where you're going!"

Walter mumbled an apology, then knelt down beside her.

"Have you seen my customer?"

"What customer?"

"That chick I was serving. She was trying on the red ribbon shoes."

Nova shook her head. "Nope. Didn't see her. What's she look like?"

Walter couldn't very well say she looked like a soft brown mouse.

"I don't know, normal. She was wearing these when she came in," he said, holding out the deck shoes.

"I don't know. I don't remember her."

Walter could feel sweat seeping into his collar. "She was sitting right over there!" he hissed. "How could you not see her?"

Nova looked at the empty chair and shrugged. "Sheesh, take a pill, Spaz. I don't keep track of your customers. Maybe she left."

"But...but she's still wearing the red shoes. She couldn't have left," he said, his voice taking on a begging tone.

Nova laughed at him. "God, maybe she stole them. Right out from under your nose."

Walter got to his feet, considering this. "Thanks," he said, and walked to the purse wall.

Rabbit girl ended up being a good sale. She bought two expensive handbags, a box of all-weather protector, and a couple of belts. Walter rang up the purchases with a sinking heart. It had been half an hour at least and mouse girl was most definitely gone. What the hell had happened there? He cleared up the shoeboxes by her chair and spotted her knee socks underneath. These he picked up and rolled into balls that he shoved into her deck shoes. When no one was looking, he snuck the shoes into his knapsack in the backroom. For the rest of the business day, all he could think about were those brown shoes and socks hiding in his bag. He didn't dare think about the triangle of white cotton though it seared his retina like a V-shaped brand, flashing every time he blinked. But when he found himself whistling "I Wish I Was in Dixie" all afternoon, he realized he had given the mouse girl a name.

# 17 }

**It was Sunday, the day after Dixie had vanished** with the red shoes, and Walter was standing in his living room looking down at Beech Avenue. The hotel seemed to inhale and exhale at irregular intervals like an asthmatic, creaking and sighing, occasionally coughing up a clang. Walter felt nurtured and warm, despite the weakness of the sunlight. Clara was out with her new pals at Greenwood racetrack, and Walter took advantage of her absence to get reacquainted with the embrace of the hotel. He also took this opportunity to reacquaint himself with his dick, which had managed to sneak out of his pants at some point. Walter looked wonderingly at it, all stiff and sun dappled, stirring up the dust motes every time it twitched. He wet his index finger with spit and rubbed it lightly around the head of his penis, enjoying the multiple rushes this caused. But he felt no sense of urgency. And something about the emptiness of the hotel, the tree branches scraping the window, the sounds of brittle laughter rising up from Beech Avenue—there was something about all these things that Walter treasured.

Once his grandmother returned, the hotel would absorb her personality, and he valued this time alone. He was afraid if he jerked off, he would lose the intensity of this atmosphere. And the longer he immersed himself in anticipation, the more vivid everything became. The stiffer his dick, the warmer the sun, the more resonant the noises. By holding off on physical gratification, he could appreciate everything with greater clarity. He put his hands in his pants pockets and straightened his back, staring out the window like a sentinel, everything at attention. Nobody could see him, the restaurant across the street wasn't tall enough, and it fronted onto Queen, not Beech. The tree in front of his window was camouflage, and Walter gave no thought to the fact that his cock jutted out from his pants like a diving board, bouncing slightly as the spit cooled, as if miniature swimmers were jumping off its end. But he wasn't ready to release his own swimmers yet. He wanted to cherish the moment—the exhilaration of standing alone in his living room with a naked defiant erection, to be his own man in his own place again. Cocksure.

As Walter stood at the window, indulging himself in what was beginning to resemble rapture, he was not unaware that all along he had been thinking about Dixie. Somewhere behind the hissing and clunking of the radiator, the groaning of old wood, the life sounds of the hotel waking up and stretching in the early afternoon sun, were other sounds. Her voice, soft and breathy, teasing his ear. The faint sucking sound of her bare inner thighs as they unstuck when she uncrossed her legs. And the sound of his own breath yesterday afternoon, harsh and shallow, as her feet were unveiled in all their glittering glory. How could she not have heard him—gasping like a floundering fish, a desperate salmon gaping glassy-eyed up her skirt, driven by a need to hurl himself at her crotch. To spawn and die.

The clarity of that moment hit home as Walter realized he was panting, hyperventilating, and he let out a cry as he collapsed against the window seat, his cock in his hand, hot semen pumping out and splattering the window like seagull shit. His breathing slowed as the hotel wheezed and whispered in understanding.

But that wasn't the end of it. Clara called to say she was staying overnight at her friend's place—*You sure you can get along without me?*—and Walter spent the entire rest of the afternoon, and well into the evening, in a masturbating frenzy. Nothing came close to the intensity of his first bout at the window, but it was still astounding. Walter figured he masturbated more times on Sunday than he had the entire time since his grandmother moved in. And he knew why. Dixie had interrupted his hibernation.

By eleven o'clock at night, Walter was exhausted and hadn't done anything productive all day. He hadn't tried to draw, he hadn't gone outside, and he had unplugged his phone. He lay on his bed, wondering if he would be able to sleep tonight. His dick felt like it had been through a meat grinder, but otherwise he felt rejuvenated. He wondered if he could get it up one more time. And then he remembered the brown socks and shoes. He sat up and looked around for his knapsack. Walter tumbled out of bed and crawled on his hands and knees to the knapsack. He opened the zipper and her foot smell wafted out. He nearly swooned and could feel his poor dick trying to rise to the occasion. Walter couldn't believe he hadn't thought of the shoes and socks earlier. The motherlode, he thought, as he dug them out of his bag and held them aloft like trophies. To make this wank special, he decided to prolong the joy and take a walk to the beach, get his blood moving. He tied the laces of her deck shoes together and slung them around his neck and pulled her brown socks onto his own feet before lacing his boots up. As he walked down to the beach, a lilt in his crooked step, shoes bouncing on his chest, it occurred to Walter that this was probably what one would call an *erotic* experience. He felt attractive, not average. And Beech Avenue looked different too, sexier, like it was a street in another country. Somewhere romantic, say, Paris. And he, Walter, was a suave Parisian lover, strolling down to the edge of the Seine to meet his mistress. He peered in the windows of the homes he passed, and pictured the inhabitants to all be French and sitting around eating croissants, chainsmoking Gitanes, and drinking red wine. How very cool, he thought to himself, as he plodded along, shoes bouncing off his chest. *Trés* cool.

When Walter reached his favourite bench and sat, he was delighted to discover a full moon and a clear black sky shot through with brilliant stars. Everything was black and silver tonight, the sky, the water, all glittering and winking like sequins. And nobody was around. Aside from a gentle rustling of tree branches and the wet sound of water lapping the shore, all was still. When the wind shifted, Dixie's shoe smell slid up his nose. God, here he had thought he would be twisting himself inside out, battling against delayed gratification impulses. Building the pressures again so he could stumble back up the hill to the hotel and ram his dick inside one of her shoes for the crowning achievement of the day. But he was as calm as the waters of Lake Ontario and for once his mind wasn't consumed with snarled thoughts that he felt compelled to pick at, to unravel. Tonight, with his toes curled up in Dixie's socks, and the comforting weight of her shoes draped around his neck, Walter's thoughts were like smooth ribbon, *red ribbon*. Impossible to tangle. Cool, liquid, sliding thoughts, like mercury, *the wings of Mercury*.

He sat like that for an hour before finally trudging back up the hill and the steep stairs to his apartment. Then he sat in his drawing room, naked except for the brown knee socks on his feet, for half an hour. He did not, as he had suspected he would, have a pressing need to immediately ram his dick inside her shoe. For some reason, it felt disrespectful to be so bold. Instead, he held her shoes in his hands, lifting them occasionally to his nose or holding them just above his penis and letting the laces trail up and down its length. He was introducing them in a civilized manner. Friends first. But soon enough, the sniffing turned to chewing and the laces lay inert on his thighs while his cock inched its way inside. Eventually his entire length was gripped in canvas, his hand squeezing. The other shoe was halfway down his throat and saliva poured out of the corners of his mouth, his eyes rolling back in his head. Could this be *any* better? As he squeezed and pulled the dick shoe, and tasted Dixie's foot essence run down the back of his throat from the mouth shoe, Walter was finally realizing the full potential of those feelings he had experienced, but not understood, in Clara's closet. Only this time he wasn't holding back. This time, he was going in. And Dixie's shoes were the perfect fit.

He didn't wake up until noon and when he saw the time, he wondered why no one had called him from GoLightly's or why his grandmother hadn't woken him. In the kind of daze that comes from having overslept, Walter walked into the bathroom to shave, still wearing the brown socks. Several facial nicks later, it all started coming back to him. The masturbation olympics. The unplugged phone. Clara's sleepover. Wearing the shoes and the socks. The walk to the beach. The final introduction (dwelling on that for a bit). The only thing he couldn't remember was sleeping. But apparently that's exactly what he had done. Walter wasn't so sure he liked sleeping that much, considering how drained he felt. While he was getting dressed and wondering if he had mopped up after himself last night, he heard Clara's heavy tread coming up the stairs. By the time her key turned in the lock, he had scooted into the kitchen and put the kettle on. Knowing she wouldn't expect him to be home, he called out.

"Clara!" he yelled. "I'm still here, I'm in the kitchen!"

"Walter? What are you doing home?"

"I slept in," he called, hearing her approach.

The kettle began whistling as she reached the kitchen. Walter grabbed it off the stove and gave her a big smile.

"Tea?"

She plopped into a card chair, causing it to wobble, and leaned back against the wall. "You never sleep in. What in hell did you get up to while I was gone?"

"Nothing," said Walter, pouring water into the teapot. "How was your sleepover? Was it a pajama party? Did you girls have a séance or anything?"

Clara ran a pudgy hand through her newly dyed hair. "Can't leave you alone for a minute, can I? Didja have a girl over? Get laid?"

Walter sat on the counter while the tea steeped and regarded her with amusement.

"No, nothing like that."

"Hmph. Too bad."

"What about you? Any hot guys at Millie's last night?"

"Oh yeah, sure. Dean Martin, Kirk Douglas, James Bond. They were all there. King Kong."

She eyed him closely as he brought the teapot to the table. "You sure you didn't get lucky? You look all happy or something."

Walter sat across from her. "I'm sure. Do you want some toast?"

Clara poured some milk into her cup and tapped her fingernails on the teapot. "Lord boy, it's after noon. I had breakfast hours ago. It's lunchtime for us decent folks. Do you want me to make you a sandwich? I think there's some chicken salad in the fridge."

"Thanks, but I've gotta get into work. I'll grab something on my way," he said, getting up. "See you later?"

"Sure thing, buddy boy. I'm making stew for dinner."

Walter looked sideways at her, and she chortled.

"*Beef* stew, don't worry."

He squeezed her shoulder as he walked out of the kitchen. It was good to have her back, it was good to have banal conversation. After last night, he didn't think he would need the same sort of privacy for quite a while. If he didn't already walk funny, he'd probably be walking funny today. But his head felt clear and uncluttered. He knew he'd face a lot of questions when he walked into GoLightly's, but this didn't bother him. It was like he was above it all, flying over a battlefield, the sounds and bloody action distant and dim to his senses. He wasn't part of it. He wasn't part of anything. He was a shoe salesman on his way to work. Hi ho, hi ho.

As expected, Spaz got the razz once he arrived. He took it good naturedly, as he took most things. Nova grilled him more than anyone else did.

"Did you hook up with the red shoe girl?" she asked, when his vague answers weren't satisfying.

That startled him. "No," he said. "Why would you think that?"

They were in the backroom and Nova was taking a cigarette break. She blew a perfect smoke ring and peered at him through its centre. "I don't know. You seemed pretty obsessed with her yesterday."

"I was not," Walter denied, realizing he was still wearing the brown socks.

Nova smirked. "You're blushing."

"I am not."

"Are too."

"Aren't not."

"You are *such* a loser," Nova said. "You've got a thing for her don't you?"

Walter lifted the cigarette from her fingers and took a drag. "You are *such* a pain in the ass," he said, exhaling and giving the cigarette back to her.

"I wish I had seen her," Nova said. "I'd like to know what kind of girl turns you on. What did she look like anyway?"

Walter made a face, but Nova persisted.

"No, really. I mean it. Tell me what she looked like."

"I don't remember," he said. "She had brown hair."

"Long? Short? Curly? Straight? What kind of hair?"

"Um, straight, I think. To her shoulders, maybe longer. I really don't remember."

"Okay then, what was she wearing?"

"She was wearing a dress and knee socks. And deck shoes. I showed them to you, remember?"

"Brown. Like her hair, right?"

"Right," Walter confirmed.

Nova hopped off the table and butted her smoke.

"You're not telling me everything, Spaz-man. I know you. Are you sure you didn't get together with her last night?"

"I don't even know her name," he said.

How could he tell Nova that he truly didn't remember anything about Dixie except her feet? Those he could describe in detail if asked. Those feet had pushed him into his orgy of self-love the night before. Oh yes, the feet had been there. They had danced in his head like sugar plums, they had pitter-pattered up and down his spine, they had kicked his *ass* last night.

"Okay, I'll let you off the hook for now," Nova said. "But if she ever comes in here again, I want you to point her out to me."

"Sure," Walter said, peering out the doorway. "I should get out there. We've got a couple customers."

"You go. I'll be out in a minute," said Nova, pushing him out the door.

She watched him wobble into the store, her eyes narrowed. Something was up with him. When a man changes his pattern, even the slightest, you know something's going on. And Walter had never been late for work before, ever. Too bad it wasn't the red shoe girl. Nova would like to see Walter interested in someone.

Walter's customers were easy. One was only browsing, thanks. A looky Lou. The other seemed content to only try on the display shoes. I'll let you know when I need help, thanks. Walter didn't push it. That was Nova's style. GoLightly's had received a new shipment and he decided to design a display of the new arrivals. An image of the lakefront came to him, the way it had appeared all black and silver last night. He began selecting right shoes that were either black or silver, size sevens, and walked armloads over to the front display shelf, a shiny chrome, multi-level box.

"Black and silver," a voice stated.

Walter was removing the old display shoes and turned to see Reginald.

"That'll look good," the boss said, chin in hand.

"I think so," said Walter, his head full of stars.

"Maybe I can help."

Walter began spritzing the chrome with Windex and wiping it down. "You think?"

Reginald twirled and glided into the backroom. When he returned he had one shoe and a square of black velvet in his hands.

"Here," he said, dropping them on the carpet.

"I forgot about these," said Walter, picking up a spiderweb shoe. "This will be perfect."

"We only have a couple sizes left, but I thought they'd fit in," said Reginald, pleased.

Walter picked up the black velvet and ran his fingers over it.

"Where do you get all these pieces of fabric, anyway? You always seem to come up with them."

"That's my secret," said Reginald. "Will it work?"

"It definitely will," said Walter, already visualizing his midnight tableau.

The black velvet was perfect. He would ripple it like waves, and sprinkle silver glitter over it. Stand the shoes on end, balanced on the backs of their heels, toes skyward. Fan them out, black, silver, black, silver. Hang a silver shoe from the top bar by its stiletto heel, a spangly crescent moon. This would work.

Reginald stepped back and watched him. Walter's displays were always the most creative in the store. He wondered what had inspired this one. It was certainly inspiring him. Tonight he would bring out the black velvet gown and rhinestone tiara and wear them while he listened to the soundtrack from *Anything Goes*. He would make a Waldorf salad, yes, with a nice glass of chilled Chardonnay. It would be delightful, delicious, delovely. Mr. Foster would create his own display.

While Reginald minced through the store picturing himself in his black gown, Walter put the finishing touches on his display. An adjustment here, a tweak there, and it was done. He stepped back and closed his eyes for a second, so he could get the full effect when he opened them again. But when he opened his eyes, expecting to see a glorious, glittery black and silver scene, he saw something else. Smack dab in the middle of his display was one of the red ribbon shoes. He blinked, but it was still there. He reached out his hand to touch it, see if it was real. It was, and he picked it up, turning it over in his hands, feeling stunned.

"Gotcha," whispered a voice in his ear.

He spun around, heart thumping, and saw only Nova. She was standing with her arms crossed, eyeing him.

"Just checking," she said.

He handed the shoe back to her and shook his head.

"Don't do that, you freaked me out."

"Really," said Nova, taking the shoe. "Would you like me to put a pair of these on and walk around so you can re-live your fantasy?"

"You're sick," he countered.

"You're deluded."

"Diluted?"

"That's what I said."

Walter started to grin. And then he had a thought. Something Remo had suggested, that Walter had pushed to the back of his mind for future reference. As Nova started to walk away, he called her back.

"Hey. How would you feel about me making a plaster mould of your foot?"

She turned.

"A what?"

"A plaster mould. Like a cast. Remo suggested I make some plaster feet to help me with my designs. You know, so I could either paint the designs right on the feet, or actually wrap pieces of leather or whatever around them."

"Are you serious?"

"Yes I'm serious. Either that, or you could come over and I could use your real foot. But then you'd have to move back in."

Nova tossed the red shoe in the air and caught it behind her back.

"Sure, Spaz. If it'll help. Just tell me where and when. Although, as you know, I don't have the prettiest feet in the world. Are you sure you want to use mine as models?"

"Your feet are fine," he said. "I like your feet."

Nova stuck her tongue out. "Flattery will get you everywhere."

Walter smiled, but Nova could tell his mind was elsewhere. He was probably deep in thought about the foot plastering now. It might be fun, she thought. Maybe she could learn how to do it and make a mould of her tits to hang on her wall. That would be funky. She'd make sure to have it front and centre when her parents visited. She would paint her boob statue in zebra stripes, she decided. Or leopard print. Something in animal.

# 18 }

**The stuff was called alginate.** A white powder, that when mixed with equal parts water, became a smooth paste that quickly firmed up into a rubbery jelly-like substance. Dentists used alginate to make impressions of teeth, and it was perfect for Walter's purposes. Remo had somehow got his hands on a mess of it through an orthodontist friend of his. There was no shortage of alginate, it was made readily available to Walter, and with this, some plaster, and a bucket, he had all the necessary supplies to make foot moulds. It turned out to be a very simple and extremely effective process. The end result would produce exact foot replicas, right down to ragged cuticles, uneven toenails, or plantar's warts. The first time Walter tried it, he used his own foot. Not only did it prove benign in nature, it was amazingly quick to do. He got Clara to witness his initial attempt, in case anything went wrong. In case he couldn't get his foot out of the bucket and needed someone to saw the thing off. Clara found the procedure so interesting, she wanted one done of her hand, which he obliged her with. She painted the hand bright pink and set it on top of her bureau, using it as a necklace tree.

Nova came over the following Sunday to have her own foot immortalized and Clara greeted her at the door.

"Come on in, missy," Clara said, holding the door open.

Clara was wearing a white wool cardigan and had the pink hand sticking out the end of the sleeve.

"A pleasure to see you," she said formally, holding it out to shake Nova's hand.

Nova shook the plaster hand solemnly.

"You too," she said. "Walter here?"

"Yup. He's in his studio. Go on in."

Nova walked down the hall and Clara followed close on her heels, running her plaster hand up and down Nova's back, like a claw.

"I'll get you my pretty," she cackled. "And your little dog, too."

They both entered Walter's drawing room together.

"I see you've met the hand," said Walter.

"Yeah, we've been introduced."

"Now, meet the foot," said Walter, handing over the mould of his own foot.

Nova held the replica of Walter's foot and found herself surprised that it looked so normal. She thought it might have been lopsided or curved in some fashion, accounting for Walter's walk. But it looked like any guy's foot. Size eleven. No noticeable aberrations.

"Wow, this is pretty cool," she said. "It looks exact."

"I know!" said Walter. "It works great, I can't believe it, really. And it doesn't hurt at all and it only takes about a minute to make the mould. That's all. It's wild."

Nova set the foot down.

"Well, let's get started then," she said, pulling up a chair and unlacing her boot.

Clara spoke: "Do you kids want something to drink? A Coke or something? A beer?"

"Sure," said Walter. "I'll have a beer, thanks."

"Me too. Thanks Clara," said Nova.

Clara lay her pink hand down on the table and moved towards the door.

"You better not get drunk. Who knows what you'll end up making moulds out of," she said, watching Nova peel her sock off.

"Hope you washed your feet first, young lady," was her parting shot.

Nova threw her sock at Clara. "Get me the beer, old lady."

"Hah!" Clara snorted, but clearly was amused.

Walter didn't understand the relationship that had developed between Nova and Clara since his grandmother had moved in. It was one of respectful antagonism. They were constantly baiting each other, when they weren't hugging each other like girlfriends.

"I'm starting to like your grandmother a lot," Nova admitted to Walter about a month after Clara had deposited herself in the hotel.

"You are?"

"Yeah. She's a riot. I never really knew that about her before. I used to think she was crotchety."

"She is crotchety."

"Well sure, she is a bit of a curmudgeon," agreed Nova. "But aside from that, I'm starting to think of her like a buddy. You probably don't see it because she's your grandmother. It's like my parents. I can't stand them and you like them."

Walter thought about this. "I guess. I mean, she does make me laugh. But I can't think of her as my buddy. I guess it's because I never think of my buddies dying."

"She'll probably outlive all of us," said Nova.

"She wants me to dress her when she's dead. You know, for when she's in the coffin."

"Really? That's grotesque."

"Well, I don't have to actually *dress* her. I have to make sure they dress her *right*. I told her I'd do it."

"Maybe I could do her makeup."


Walter mixed up the alginate and water in the bucket and once it was smooth, motioned Nova over.

"Now, stick your foot in here up to the ankle and don't let it touch the bottom or sides of the bucket."

"It's cool," said Nova, sliding her foot in the goop. "It feels kinda neat."

"It'll only take about a minute," he said. "You can almost see the stuff getting firm. Feel it."

Nova reached down and felt the mixture. It was starting to feel bouncy to the touch.

"This stuff's amazing," she said.

In about a minute or so, it had set.

"Now, wiggle your foot a bit. Enough to break the seal," said Walter. "Then you can slip it out."

As Nova was removing her foot, Clara tromped in with a tray. There were three Carlsbergs on it and a bowl of Hostess potato chips.

"All done?" she asked. "Thought I'd join you in a beer if you don't mind."

Walter was mixing up the plaster, which he poured into the hole left by Nova's foot.

"Now what?" asked Nova, taking a slug of beer.

"After it hardens, I jiggle it out of the bucket and peel the alginate off. It's super easy. Then, voila! Your foot will be famous."

Clara gulped her beer and let out a belch.

"You gotta wash that crap off your foot, though," she pointed out.

Nova looked at her foot. Bits of the rubbery white alginate were stuck all over it. They rolled into snot-like balls when she rubbed them. She flicked one at Clara and it bounced off her face.

"Hey! Keep your toe jam to yourself!" barked Clara, wiping her cheek.

Nova belched in response.

"God, you two are disgusting," said Walter, carefully moving the bucket to a corner of the drawing room.

Clara had placed the pink hand back in her sweater sleeve and was using it to scoop up potato chips and ladle them into her mouth.

"Need a hand?" she asked Walter, waving the pink monstrosity in the air, sending chips flying.

And the afternoon passed. Three buddies getting plastered.

For dinner, Clara made a tuna casserole topped with Kellogg's Corn Flakes. The three of them ate it off the elk T.V. trays in the living room and watched *To Kill A Mockingbird* on television.

"Gregory Peck. Now there's a man," said Clara.

"I'm partial to Boo Radley, myself," said Nova.

"You would be," Clara said.

"Would you two shut up?" said Walter.

"Make us," said Nova.

"Don't say that," said Clara. "He *can* make us. He can make us into statues if he wants to."

Clara looked over at Walter who had moved his chair closer to the television.

"You'd need a helluva lot more of that plaster to capture these beauts," she said, hefting her bosom with both hands.

Nova cracked up. Walter hid a smile. Clara admired her boobs. And Gregory Peck looked extremely earnest.

By eleven o'clock, the evening had wound down to coffee and strawberry angelfood cake. Comfortable lethargy had set in and Clara retired to her bedroom to read her soap opera magazines, leaving Walter and Nova to clean up.

"I'll do it," said Walter. "You already helped me out by loaning me your foot."

"Okay," said Nova, who never was too interested in cleaning up anything. "I guess I'll see you at work tomorrow."

Walter hugged her, and closed the door behind his friend. He leaned against the door, feeling pretty good about everything. Tomorrow he would unveil Nova's foot mould. He was already running a list of available female acquaintances through his mind for other possible plaster feet. Then he heard a tapping at the door and Nova whispering his name.

"Walter," she hissed, her fingernails scratching at the door. "Walter. Open up."

He pushed himself off the door and opened it a crack, peering out into the darkened stairwell. Nova's face was pushed into the crack, her eyes wide.

"Open the door," she insisted, pushing at it.

Walter opened the door and Nova stepped into the hallway, her hands behind her back. She looked up and down the hall as if casing the joint for spies.

"Did you forget something?" Walter asked.

"No."

"Why are you whispering?"

"I don't know. It's...well. I nearly tripped over these. They were right outside your door on the landing," said Nova, bringing her hands out from behind her back.

The red ribbon shoes. Nova held them out to Walter like they were contaminated.

"Take them," she urged, pushing them on Walter.

He held his hands out and took the shoes as if he was afraid they might burst into flames.

"They're hers, aren't they?" Nova asked.

Without thinking about how odd it might look, Walter held one up to his face and breathed it in. He nodded, and brought it back down to his side.

"Yeah, they are," he confirmed, but it sounded more like a question.

"What the fuck are they doing outside your door?"

"I don't know."

"You don't *know*? Obviously, that chick knows where you live. And you told me you weren't with her last week."

Walter shook his head, his mind racing.

"I wasn't. I swear. I have no idea how these got here."

Nova stood there assessing Walter's tone of voice, her hands on her hips. He was telling the truth.

"Look, let's talk about this tomorrow," she said. "But all I've got to say is, that's one nutbar chick, y'know? Maybe she's stalking you or something."

For some reason, that hypothesis made Walter happy.

"I doubt it," he said, unconvinced.

"Well, how the *jesus* fuck does she know where you live then, huh? Christ, Spaz. This is weird, y'know? She could be a Mrs. Goodbar or something."

"Maybe someone at work told her my name and she looked me up in the phone book?"

"Well, why didn't she bring them back to the store? Why all this sneaking around bullshit, this clandestine drop-off?"

"I don't know. Maybe she was embarrassed to bring them back to the store."

Nova rolled her eyes. "Are you *defending* her? Some freak steals shoes and a week later, puts them outside your door. Why didn't she knock at the door and give them to you then?"

"Why are you asking me?" Walter said, his voice rising. "I don't know! I'm just guessing!"

Nova gave a dramatic shudder. "Well, I don't know about you, but this gives me the creeps. Look, I'll see you tomorrow okay?"

"Okay. Thanks for coming over."

"Okay. Be careful. She could be a psycho killer."

Walter grimaced and pushed her out the door. "I'll be sure to lock the door," he said.

He stood in the hallway, red ribbon shoes in hand, wondering what the hell to do. The shoes began to feel warm in his grip, like they were alive, blood pumping. One thing he knew for sure. These shoes were *not* going back to the store. They were staying right here, thank you very much. Besides, he rationalized, you can't sell shoes that have been worn.

After a few minutes, he pried himself off the spot he was rooted to and wobbled into the drawing room. He placed the red shoes on his drafting table, closed the door behind him, and went into the living room to clear up the dishes and turn the television off. When did Dixie drop them off? He wondered why nobody heard her coming up the creaky stairs, until he remembered how light on her feet she was. She could've pulled it off all right, while they were in the drawing room making moulds and drinking beer. Or later, while they were watching T.V. He was disappointed he hadn't sensed her presence. He felt like there should have been a moment when he had stopped whatever he was doing and froze. A moment when he would have felt a presentiment of some kind. But he couldn't recall any such instance, which pissed him off. He clumped past Clara's bedroom carrying the tray of dishes and noticed her light was off. The beers must have knocked her out. She usually didn't drink much, all her obnoxious behaviour pointing to the contrary. Walter washed the dishes as quietly as he could manage, still a bit unnerved from the discovery. A wind was rattling the screen door on the porch, sounding ominous, and his grandmother started up a series of loud, beery snores. He shivered, though his hands were deep in hot water. The red shoes were portentous, but Walter couldn't distinguish if their sudden presence made him feel good or bad. Good or *evil*. Nova's comments about Dixie had bothered him too, all that talk about his red shoe girl being a nutbar or a stalker. It didn't fit with his perceptions of her. It didn't fit with his longing.

He finished stacking the dishes in the cupboard and dried his hands on the dish towel, looping it over the handle on the oven door. Everything was rattling—Clara's snores, the porch door, and his nerves. It seemed like the entire hotel was vibrating. Walter poured a glass of water and turned off the kitchen light. The lights in the neighbouring buildings sprang into sharp focus like square yellow eyes. He stepped into the porch with the intention of stabilizing the door, but kept going straight ahead and onto the roof of the Fox. The movies were over and all was quiet except for the rattling. Walter walked to the southeast corner of the roof and perched on the low brick wall that ran around its perimeter, dangling his legs off the ledge. From here he faced Queen Street, looking towards the water. To his right, across the street, was the infamous Goof restaurant—a Chinese/Canadian diner-style eatery that had seemingly been in that location forever. Originally its lit-up L-shaped sign had read Good (vertical) and Food (horizontal), but the D in Good had been burnt out for years, leaving the vertical sign reading: GOO F. Despite its official name being Garden Gate, it had been known affectionately as the Goof ever since, and if the Beaches had any kind of funky landmark, the Goof was it. Apparently, the owners had replaced the missing D one year but the Beaches people raised such a stink that the owners removed it again. At least that's how the story went. Walter swung his legs and peered down at Queen Street. Not many people were out at this hour on a Sunday. Not much traffic. He craned his neck to the right, westward, but couldn't see GoLightly's from his position even though it was only a few blocks down Queen. He could see Nova's building, could see her window, but all was dark over there. Walter wondered if she would dream about the red shoes tonight. And there it was. That's what he was really doing up here. Trying not to think about them—impossible. They were kicking him with their pointy toes, they could boot him right off this ledge if he let them. Walter thought about falling off the roof, what it would feel like. It wasn't high enough that he would black out on the way down probably. That meant he would likely feel the splat. Until he felt his head split open like a melon, it would probably feel like a major episode of static. Spinning, tumbling out of control. All the king's horses couldn't put him back together again.

Walter looked over his shoulder to the buildings behind him. He wondered if Dixie lived in any of them. If she was watching him. He smiled and waved in case she was. So she would know he wasn't freaked out about the shoes. So she would know he could handle it. So she would know he knew.

He swung his legs over the ledge and walked under the clothesline back to the porch. A grease-stained rag served to tie the screen door shut and Walter eased his way through the darkened kitchen into the hall. It couldn't have been much past midnight, he guessed, far too early to go to bed. He stood at the end of the hall and stared at the door to his drawing room, took a deep breath, and marched towards it. He felt like the mother in *The Exorcist* must have felt, walking towards her daughter's bedroom door, bracing for what lay in wait on the other side. Maybe he would open the door and see the red shoes flying around the room, his sketches plastered to the walls and ceiling, and the desk lamp blinking off and on, off and on. An evil wind would slam him up against the wall and one of the red shoes would dive right at him, spearing him in the eye and grinding its heel into his brain. While he screamed in agony, the other red shoe would fly into his mouth, toe first, suffocating and choking him. And in the background he would hear Dixie snickering. Her disembodied face would hang in the center of the room, like the moon, or the wizard of Oz, brown hair dancing around her head, Medusa-like in the crazy fucked up wind. And she would say something to him. Her pale lips would form the words: I love you, Walter. And he would fall to his knees and pray for mercy.

He turned the doorknob and flung the door open wide, stepping back. But there was no evil wind. The red shoes stood right where he had left them on his drafting table. Walter took a step inside, holding his breath. But they didn't move. They didn't click their heels together. It was almost disappointing. The only cool thing was that he had placed them under his desk lamp and they were sitting in a circle of light, like they were on stage, poised to tap dance in the spotlight. He picked one up, turning it around in his hand, running the ribbon through his fingers. He brought it up to his face and stuck his nose inside, breathing deep. A musky bouquet, he thought to himself, savouring the olfactory taste. A precocious upstart, with a hint of tart fruit, maybe blackcurrant. He lay the flat of his tongue on the insole, the toe of the shoe pointing straight up between his eyes. And then he took the ribbons and tied them behind his head so the shoe stayed in place, sitting on his face like an oxygen mask. He sat on his stool, eyes closed, sucking in her scent. When he opened his eyes again, Walter noticed his reflection in the window. All he could see were his eyes blinking on either side of the shoe, and his hair standing up in tufts, caught up in the ribbons. I'm a freak, he thought to himself. I'm sitting in an old hotel room, a bucket of plaster foot beside me, and a shoe strapped to my face. And wait, there's more. I have a boner. Of course I do, why not?

He started laughing inside the shoe, but stopped himself because it caused warm moisture to build up and override her foot smell. Walter tilted his head at his reflection, thinking it looked like he had a beak. I look like a bird, he thought. A condor sprang to mind, although he wasn't exactly sure what a condor looked like. He stood up and began unbuttoning his shirt, because it felt like the right thing to do. Like being a condor felt right. He threw his shirt down on the floor with a matador's flourish and stretched his arms out to the side at shoulder level. Impressive, he thought to himself, admiring his wingspan in the window. Then he undid his belt buckle and unzipped his fly. *Zip-a-Dee-Doo-Dah*, he muttered, dropping his jeans and briefs and kicking them aside, one eye on the window at all times. His penis, although average size for a human male, seemed quite large for a condor. It was rigid, resembling a sturdy branch. He would have to disguise it, otherwise other birds might light upon it and peck it to pieces. *Peck*, he said aloud inside the shoe. *Peck my pecker. Peck a pickled pecker. Peckersnot. Gregory Pecker. Woody Woodpecker.* Now, there's a bird with a hard-on for sure. *Peckerwood.* Walter picked up the other red shoe and slipped it over his own wood pecker, his balls nestled partly into the heel of the shoe and partly flopping over the sides. He looped the ribbons underneath his scrotum and secured the shoe with a perky bow.

It felt—*fantastic.*

He took a step. His dick, heavy with shoe, dipped slightly.

Crap, this felt—*amazing.*

He took another step so he could feel the weight of his condor cock, the supreme heft of it. Soon he was striding around the room, his arms flapping up and down in time with every other step, his balls strapped up, excruciating sensation of his stomach dropping out. He tried a squawk, but the shoe muffled its legitimacy. However, it seemed perfectly reasonable that his walk wasn't as fucked up as usual. And every time he passed the window, he looked at himself. I'm a condor, he thought, then corrected himself. No, I'm a con*dork.*

It felt—liberating.

It looked—majestically insane.

But the fact that he understood this must mean he *is* sane. At least this is what Walter was thinking as he flapped his way around the room, his shod penis dipping and swaying and his tongue slurping the size seven-and-a-half right off the insole. He was pretty sure he read somewhere that if you think you're insane, you're not.

# 19 }

**The next day at GoLightly's was a blur.** Some talk from Nova about the red shoes, Walter ducking the entire issue. He didn't want to hear anything negative about Dixie. All day he looked for her. Thought maybe she might show up to explain the red shoes in the hall. He kept glancing out the front window, thinking she might be across the street watching him. Every time the store phone rang, he jumped. Thought maybe she would call him. It was stupid, but it wasn't. He vaguely remembered his antics of the night before and asked Nova on a break if she knew what a condor looked like.

"A condor? You mean like a giant bird?" she asked, when they were sitting outside behind the store.

"Yeah, I think it's a bird of prey or something. Do you know what it looks like?"

Nova shook her head.

"No. Am I supposed to?"

"No."

"Then why are you asking me that? Why do you want to know?"

"Because I turned into one last night."

"You're insane," Nova said.

"Actually, I'm pretty sure I'm not insane. I just wanted to know if I was a handsome bird or not."

Nova looked at him.

"You're a finch," she said. "Get over it."

And she walked back into the store like they had been discussing the weather.

Oh my god, she's right, thought Walter. I'm a finch. That never occurred to me last night. A condor? Who was I kidding?

He felt deflated. And embarrassed. Not about prancing around the room naked, flapping his arms, with shoes tied to his body. Not about that. He was embarrassed that he had had the gall to think he was a condor, when really, he was nothing but a tiny, insignificant finch. What a loser.

He scanned the backs of the other stores. Where *was* she? And what if he saw her again, anyway? What would he do about that? A condor could scoop up a little brown mouse with ease and carry her off to his nest in a towering tree. What the hell could a finch do? Nothing. That's what a finch could do. A finch was prey.

He pounded his fist once on his knee and got to his feet. No more lame fantasies for me, he thought. I'm done. And I'm going to stop thinking about Dixie and start concentrating on designing the perfect shoe. I'll line up some more foot models and buckle down. Buckle down and buckle up dem shoes, baby. Har-de-har-har.

And before going back inside, he took one more look around. Nope. Nothing. Just as he thought. Damn it.

The rest of the day took forever. Walter felt wrung out by the time he clumped up his apartment stairs. He looked up to the landing by his door, half expecting to see the red shoes sitting there again. He was sweating much more than the temperature would warrant. Thinking about not thinking about someone was hard work. He opened the door and almost smacked Clara in the head.

"Ow!"

"Did I hit you?"

"No, but you nearly."

"Are you going somewhere?"

"No, I always wear my coat and hat for sitting around."

"Well, sorry, I didn't mean to startle you," Walter said, stepping around his grandmother.

"I thought you were a rapist."

Walter hid a smile. "Where are you going?"

"Millie's, if that's all right with you. There's a lasagna in the fridge."

"Thanks...you're sure you're okay?"

"Don't wait up," she said over her shoulder as she stepped onto the landing.

Walter watched her descending the stairs, but her step seemed steady. He was beginning to realize the burden of having women you care about in your life.

First things first, Walter thought, heading for the drawing room. He was dying to see how Nova's foot turned out. Dinner could wait. Maybe he'd feel hungry after he saw the foot.

He hustled into the drawing room and pulled up the bucket, anticipating a good result. After worrying the bucket off, he gently peeled the alginate away, first chunks, then more finicky bits. He scraped with a fingernail at the last clinging bits of jelly, taking the utmost care, like an archaeologist brushing mud off a prehistoric fossil, or an art restorer dabbing at an ancient canvas. Respect was what was needed here. When finally he was done, Walter carried Nova's foot over to his drafting table and switched the halogen desk lamp on to examine it. It was a perfect replica. He tried to picture Nova's real foot, he had seen her barefooted often enough during the summers. But though he recognized this thing as her foot—there was her ultra long second toe, for instance—something had been lost in the translation. The plaster foot appeared more elegant. Like a sculpture, the foot of a Greek goddess. He set it on the floor, where a foot should be, and stepped back to admire his handiwork. If he squinted, it looked almost real, except for the stark whiteness of it. He pictured a long white robe, falling in luxurious folds, draping over the ankle. He visualized a sandal made of leaves and twine snaking between the toes and wrapping around the back of the heel. I should paint it flesh coloured, he thought. It will be more believable that way and easier to look at. I need more feet, though. I need feet in different positions, too. I need feet poised on their balls, standing on tippy-toe, arched, feet with toes spread apart so I can loop strips of leather through them, skinny feet, wide feet.

Walter put the foot on a wooden side table and opened his jar of flesh-coloured paint. His feeling of anxiety was lessening and he felt a little bit hungry. I'll paint the foot and have dinner while it's drying. Then maybe I'll take a walk to the beach. And he painted Nova's foot with loving care. His friend's foot. It felt a bit weird, if he had to admit it, verging on intimate. But it was fine until he got to the toenails. The foot was now a semi-believable flesh tone but the nails were still matte white. Nova usually wore black or dark blue nail polish and he considered painting them like that until he got blindsided by a blizzard of silver glitter, falling down like snowflakes in front of his eyes. Silver glitter that seemed to be hanging off his eyelashes, making everything sparkle and twinkle and dance. He blinked and sparkles fell onto the table, he looked up and sparkles rained down like a waterfall of diamonds. They were everywhere, winking and twinkling, and hypnotizing him. He held out his hands, palms up, to try and catch the glittering dust. And then it was gone. He blinked again and one last glittery snowflake fell off his eyelash and drifted in lazy circles down, down, settling on the big toenail of Nova's foot. It sat there, a speck of light, a twinkling point of reference. And Walter knew what he had to do. He had to go buy silver glitter nail polish. Lasagna could wait. But silver nail polish couldn't.

He turned off the desk lamp and looked at the window. There was no reflection at this time of day. He tried a big flap, his arms pumped once up and once down. Nothing. And then he remembered. I'm a finch. He stretched his fingers once up, once down. A little baby finch flap. It didn't have the same effect. There was no power behind it, nothing that caused his heart to swell. Nothing that could remove him, pick him up and set him down someplace else. Like in a nest in a towering pine. Nothing that could pluck the left side of his brain from his skull and set it aside for future use, allowing the right side free rein to hold a party unmonitored by the accusing presence of the restrictive left.

He padlocked the door behind him, grabbed his jacket, and left the hotel. On the hunt for silver glitter. Down the stairs, out the door onto Beech Avenue, west on Queen, striding purposefully, albeit wobbly, to the pharmacy. Head down, glitter everywhere. Bits of it in the sidewalk, traces of it glinting in the stucco on a storefront, sprinkles on the black asphalt of the street, and prisms reflected in the windows if you looked just so. Into the pharmacy now, flinging the door aside like a gunslinger, hello Mister Grant, I'm fine, how are you, clumping unerringly to the cosmetics aisle, hello Miss Clairol, past the eyelash curlers, the hair clips, the pinks and peaches of blush, the blues and greens of eye shadows, the reds of lipsticks, to the rows upon rows of nail polish with Eiffel Tower caps. He stopped. Nail polish had undergone a transformation since the old days. Sure, the pinkos and the reds still held the majority, the Commies of nail polish, but nowadays every other colour and stripe was represented too. Walter scanned the rows, his eyes sweeping over the matte finishes, the frosteds, and lighting upon the disco section. While reds and pinks may have ruled the regular polishes, the royalty of the glitter palace were silver and gold, and Walter's fingers found the princess and picked her up. Silver Stardust. He shook it and watched the sparkles shift like a fat river of glittering steel molasses. $1.99. Walter tossed it in the air and snatched it back. Mission accomplished.

Back down the aisle, hello again Mister Grant, yes I found what I was looking for, no sir, Clara wouldn't be caught dead in this colour, ha ha ha, well that's my secret, wink, wink, thank you, yes I'll say hello, goodbye now, and back out on the sidewalk, nail polish nestled in his jacket pocket, twinkling in musty darkness with old Kleenex and a sticky lemon cough drop.

Back to Queen and Beech, up the steep, creaky stairs and into the hallway. Into the drawing room, and without taking his jacket off, he unscrewed the cap of the nail polish and began painting Nova's plaster toenails. This he performed with great speed, aware that if he lingered over this particular exercise he could lose an hour or two to static. He could feel it picking at him as he swept the glitter on the plaster and smelled the fumes of the polish leaking into his head. He could see Nova's foot losing definition and softening up around the edges. And Walter knew what was going on. It was trying to turn into Dixie's foot for him. He hustled before the transformation could take place entirely. And as the last strokes were hurriedly flicked onto the last toenail, the baby toe, Walter sensed the static all around him, circling, hemming him in. The foot seemed to have the consistency of dough, and he felt like he could stick a finger right into it, like those faith healer guys who could reach right into your flesh and manipulate your organs. Freaky shit, but Walter didn't doubt it for a second. And the static hummed, low-like, in a regular rhythm as if it were a million boots marching in cadence. BUM-bum, BUM-bum, BUM-bum, BUM-bum. The foot was moving, shape-shifting, and Walter barely had the presence of mind to yank himself away from it. He didn't know if he had the energy to deal with what might come next, but he did know something would come if he didn't go. He screwed the cap back on the polish and shook his head, trying to dislodge the rhythm of the marching boots, just knock them off their stride long enough to march himself right out of the room. And with a supreme effort of will, he managed to do exactly that. A catch, a buzzing, something skipped. A BUH-BUM-bum slipped itself into the rhythm long enough to give Walter the opportunity to slip out. As he tottered down the hallway towards the kitchen, the image of the melting foot faded into something that couldn't harm him.

# 20 }

**After Walter's initial success** with Nova's plaster foot cast, he went on a mission for other models. Three weeks later, he had exhausted his list of female friends and acquaintances and now had a collection of twenty plaster feet in varying positions, shapes and sizes. Clara's foot had also made the cut, but only because she demanded inclusion. She had stood in the drawing room doorway one evening, watching Walter paint the toenails of his latest acquisition—a size five, AA-width foot. It was Mandy O'Toole's foot, a friend of Nova's, who had acquiesced after Walter promised to buy her a case of beer.

"So, when are you gonna do my foot?" Clara asked, leaning against the doorframe, watching.

Walter looked up, his eyes strained from the painting of Mandy's tiny toenails. "What?"

Clara cleared her throat and her necklace clattered. She nodded to his workbench.

"My feet. What are they—chopped liver?"

"What would you do with a foot?" he asked, screwing the nail polish cap back on.

She bristled. "Nuthin'. I wouldn't do nuthin' with a foot. I just thought you could use it. Y'know," she shrugged.

"But if my foot ain't good enough for your high and mighty designs, then never mind. I was trying to help, is all."

Walter spoke before she could storm off.

"Sure, I'd love to do your foot. Have you got time now?"

In reality, Walter had no practical use for his grandmother's warped foot. If he was to design orthopedic shoes, maybe, but his vision was of shoes fit for princesses and fairy queens, not ogres or ugly stepmothers, or big fat grandmothers with deviated metatarsals and fallen arches. But if she wanted to see her foot take its rightful place on display with the growing collection, Walter would oblige her. And even though he had painted all the toenails on all the feet with silver glitter, Clara insisted her own be painted red. She picked Red Rage. And when the process was completed and her swollen, cramped foot stood unevenly beside all the others, she was mighty pleased hers was the only one with red polish.

"Why don't you paint them all different colours?" she had asked. "Why are they all silver?"

"I got a deal on polish," Walter said.

Clara accepted his answer without question, but only because she was satisfied her foot stood out from the pack. And it did, like a sore thumb. Red Rage seemed an appropriate name for the polish. Walter wondered who came up with the names for polish. He thought about devising a line of macabre polishes. The reds would have names like Menstrual Cramp Red, or Blood Clot Red, or Gaping Wound Red. The pinks could be Dog Dick Pink, or Pussy Pink, or Dead Pig Pink. He couldn't think of any crude names for silver though. He refused.

And now, armed with twenty feet, Walter got down to business. Every night after work he would closet himself in the drawing room and immerse himself in designing. Sometimes he would go off on an automatic drawing spree with his sketch pad, and other times he would harness the energy and channel it into painting right on the feet. He had begun a collection of scrap materials gleaned from Remo and Reginald and he worked with the leather, the multi-coloured glass or wooden beads, strips of crushed velvet or brushed suede or strands of sequins, winding them through the toes of Nova or Mandy or Beatrice or Sue. These times, alone in his drawing room late at night, were the best times. These were the times he felt alive and energized and like he had a purpose. There was no question he would design a line of GoLightly shoes, all stamped on the sole with the GoLightly insignia—a sprig of holly. Walter wanted the first shoes off the line to be a statement, a signature. He wanted to design actual holly shoes. Dark green, dissolving to black, waxy, lustrous leather, with a cluster of small red glass berries somewhere on the shoe, and sharp points flaring out like leaves. They would be unveiled for the Christmas season. The berries could be detachable and come in different colours for different outfits. Black berries, gold berries, green or blue berries. Individual sprigs the women could snap off or on at their whim. And once the holly shoes hit the market, the rest would follow close on their stiletto heels.

Walter was doodling, thinking about fame. Drawing sprigs of holly on Sue Neidermeyer's foot, one by the ankle, one between her big toe and second toe, one at the back of her heel. Maybe GoLightly's could have a special shoe for every holiday, he thought. A pink and yellow Easter shoe, all frothy and springlike, custom made for the boardwalk or sitting at a sidewalk café. An earthy Thanksgiving shoe in shades of russet and pumpkin and autumn leaves. A rakish and cocky green shoe for St. Patrick's Day, and for Valentine's Day, a red shoe. A red shoe. He looked up from his sketch pad and saw them perched in their usual position. His guts twisted and his paintbrush stopped moving. He pictured Dixie's exquisite foot inside his own line of shoes. Her Easter foot, her Christmas foot. Sliding it in with a whisper of silk stocking, and Walter doing up a tiny rhinestone buckle at her ankle, just so. Dixie standing up and Walter watching her feet relax into the shoe he created. Hearing the new leather sigh as it welcomed the foot it was made to embrace. Walter lying on the floor on his back, his head turned sideways, the phantom shoes containing Dixie's feet standing beside his face. Looking up, the unbearable tension evident in her calves from the excruciating slope of the shoes, quivering of her inner thighs, from what? From lust for the designer. She lifts one foot and plants the spike-heeled holiday shoe on his chest. It is almost too much to bear. He can see right up her dress now. But he is pinned like an insect, unable to move. She begins lifting the hem of her dress up her thighs, and from his position he can't see her face, but knows she is watching him. He sees the white cotton now, he can't help it. Between her one lifted leg and her other straight leg, it emerges like a snow-covered landing strip. Walter gets an image of the Wright brothers and feels the heel of the holiday shoe sink deeper into his chest. She's relaxing, the pressure feels good. The pressure is everywhere. He thinks about going in for a landing, and how he would make his approach. It seems like he's been circling his entire life and now, finally, there it is. The clouds have parted and he sees it. And to make sure he sees it, she runs a finger down the length of the white cotton, silver glitter nail polish against the starkness of snow. When she takes the finger away and he starts to breathe again, he sees a trail of damp emerge from where her finger traced the cotton. It's so faint, no one else would see it. But to Walter's eye it is vivid. The heat from her finger has melted the snow to reveal a track, sluiced it open to show him something. He is riveted to the landing strip. The deceivingly insignificant line of melting snow is a hint. A promise. Walter senses what's beneath—a wet chasm, a wondrous magical cave, glowing and dripping. It's how his chest feels, like a hollow cave, her heel a stalactite spearing its cavity from above. Her shoes begin a rapid-fire series of changes, skipping from holiday to holiday, riffling through the colour spectrum, bows appearing and disappearing, straps snapping on and off, toes and heels there and not there, all the shoes he will ever design in his entire lifetime begin to flicker like a strobe light, a mad succession of styles interspersed with barely visible flashes of her naked foot. They are in his peripheral vision, a brilliant kaleidoscope. But he can't wrench his gaze from the strip of white cotton, he must keep his bearings if he's ever going to land. He wants to see his future, but he doesn't know where it is. He doesn't know if it's in the rainbow of shoes or the wet, white snow. The shoes or the snow.

He's torn.

Walter wants to look at the shoes, to see what he'll create, but he's afraid if he breaks his gaze, he'll never see the white cotton again. Shoes or snow. And then he thinks: Snowshoes. And the kaleidoscope screeches to a halt, stopped dead on white. The shoes are now white. They are winter shoes and white silk threads spin out of the shoes like a twister and snake up Dixie's legs, millions of fine threads, multiplying, overlapping, dancing up her legs, shimmering white threads, more and more flying out of the white shoes and swirling around her legs until they start to knit together, creeping white silk stockings up her legs, around and up. Walter is stunned. It's breathtaking. He watches the landing strip, he's circling, like the white silk, around and around. The wet track in the snow has widened slightly, an invitation. The white silk creeps up her legs and he is an insect. His mouth is dry. Cotton mouth, he thinks. He sticks his tongue out and wishes she would crouch lower or that his tongue could follow the silk threads. He thinks of the word "spelunking." The white chases up her legs, so many threads they look like one now, they're spinning faster, a gauzy blur, only an inch of skin left to be covered. He licks his parched lips, the white funnel circles upwards like the Tasmanian Devil, and the entire landing strip is dissolving. Ah, sweet relief, he thinks. It's melting, I can dive-bomb right in there. A kamikaze suicide mission. And he waits to see, waits for the white to completely melt away so he can see the mysterious dark beneath the light. Her skirt is up at her waist now, her legs are trembling. The threads of white silk lunge up in one ultimate effort, one final circumnavigation of her legs and then meet the landing strip in a connection that zaps into Walter's brain like sheet lightning. Everything goes white. There is no more colour, no distinction. He panics and begins to thrash about, but he is still pinned by her heel. It's nauseating. He's lost touch with everything. It's a white-out.

Walter floats in white limbo. Panic subsides, replaced with wonder. Nothing has ever gone totally blank before. He wonders when he will see colour, movement. He decides not to struggle. *Flow*, he thinks to himself. Flow. It is a good word. It is what he should do. Don't fight it. *Flow* with it. He closes his eyes and flows. With his eyes closed, he tries to recapture the images of the shoes so he can re-create them in his drawing room later. But it's like the dream you desperately want to retain on awakening, because it held the key to a question or a puzzle you had wrestled with. He cannot remember the shoes, only their essence. Maybe it's enough. The flow reassures him that it is. The flow tells him they are in his subconscious, they will emerge when he needs them. He is not to worry. He is a lucky man. This is what the flow promises him. He is special. He will prevail. Walter opens his eyes.

He is lying on the floor and doesn't remember how he got there. He is directly under the halogen spotlight pooling around the red shoes. It is bright, but not white. There is definition and the room comes back into focus. He knows the dream is over—a memory of it lingers. He is bathed in flow and he sits up, looking around as if with transplanted eyes. The red shoes are quiet. Walter sees the row of foot moulds lined up on his painting bench. He ticks off the names of their owners in order, left to right. It's an exercise. A *get a grip* exercise. Probably the type of recitation one does when coming out of a coma. Name, age, current prime minister. Or the type of thing a soldier recites when captured. Name, rank, regiment. He says the names out loud. When he comes to the end, Becky, he wants to say something else next. He wants to be able to say Dixie. Her foot should be there too. The collection is incomplete. He almost wishes he had never seen her, could take that moment back like a cruel joke. But that's not what you do when you're living in the flow. In the flow, there are no regrets.

Walter gets to his feet and brushes plaster dust off the seat of his pants. It wasn't surprising to observe that he had a semi-erection. He picked up a red shoe and fondled himself briefly, rubbing the shoe into his crotch— a surge of joy, but he had no energy or, for that matter, desire to indulge himself further. He felt spent, and put the shoe back down under the spotlight. And then he had a thought and it was this: *I need a woman.*

Naturally, Walter had entertained such a notion before, but this time there was an element of insistence to it. As he turned off the lights and packed away his brushes, he tossed the thought into the flow to see if it would stick or if it would get sucked into some vortex and vanish. Curiously, it stayed. It bounced around like it belonged there. He tried channelling his thoughts specifically to Dixie to see if she would obliterate the thought of another woman. She didn't. Apparently there was room for both in the flow. He considered this while he padlocked the drawing room door. He walked down the hall to the bathroom and surrendered himself to the flow. As he brushed his teeth, looking at himself in the mirror, he realized a couple of things. The saying "a watched pot never boils" came to mind. It seemed fitting. He spit. A string of clichés and axioms danced through his head.

*The grass is always greener.*
*When you're not looking for it, it will find you.*
*Be careful what you wish for.*
*You can't see the forest for the trees.*
*When you love someone, set them free.*

Walter rinsed and spit again. I need a woman, he affirmed. I need a woman to nudge Dixie out of my mind. It's only when I stop thinking about her, *obsessing* about her, that she will appear.

He flossed brutally.

*Tough times call for tough measures.*

Spit blood.

More women meant more feet.

*You can't have too much of a good thing.*

# 21 }

**And so begins the adult dating ritual** of the Lopsided Canadian Finch. Some have characterized this species as either lazy or indifferent, due to the length of time it spends in its nest without a mate. But once motivated, the Lopsided Canadian Finch gets down to business in what one could only describe as an orderly and decisive manner. There is no great display of emotion, ruffling of feathers, breast-beating or funky dancing, there is only clinical assessment of the task at hand. A mate is needed and so a mate is sought. Females don't naturally flock to the Lopsided Canadian Finch. Unlike other males, there is nothing dramatic about his plumage, nor does his singing voice cause any fluttering in the breast of the female. And there is the matter of his spastic hopping to consider. Perhaps the best thing to be said about the only card-carrying member of this species is that he is entirely nonthreatening. He wouldn't be likely to peck out his mate's eyes. He might be tempted to chew their feet off, but that's another thing altogether. There have been no documented cases of this, it should be noted.

Because the Lopsided Canadian Finch has never been one to go out on a limb, so to speak, in pursuit of mates, he initially places his trust in the taste of his friends. A flurry of hastily arranged dates ensues and before long, he is hopping from chick to chick. His friends agree that it's about time. They, however, don't hold out much hope, a sentiment shared by the finch himself.

These are three of the dates that last longer than an evening: Alice Kram, Faye Sinclair, Heidi Lemper. The Lopsided Canadian Finch gives it his best shot. Nobody knows why he has become keen on dating. Nobody knows about the *flow*.

Walter is sitting across from Alice Kram in a hipster bistro on Bloor Street. Of the three women he will date around the same time, she is what society would deem the most attractive. Alice Kram reminds Walter of the Mooney twins. She is very blond, very curvy, and very stupid. He discovers all these things on their first date. They are now on their third date. He has no idea why Alice has let things go on this far.

What he doesn't know is that Alice fancies herself a humanitarian. At least once a year she dates someone with an impediment of sorts. Last year it was Bruno, a guy in a wheelchair. The year before, Horace, a blind guy. Alice has entertained thoughts of writing a book about her exploits. A book about how guys who aren't whole, who are a bit *off*, are great fucks. The reason, she reasons, is because they're so grateful. She believes this study will not only be a boon to science and psychology, it will bring attention to the plight of the handicapped. It should also unearth a whole new dating ground for women who can't get the superior specimens. And because the book will have great sex in it, she figures it should be a bodice-ripping bestseller and will garner her the Nobel Prize for either literature or science or peace. Alice has thrown herself wholeheartedly into this cause. Also, she enjoys the looks she gets when she puts on her sexiest outfit and pushes around some guy in a wheelchair or leads a blind guy across the road. The only problem with her thesis thus far is that the handicapped guys haven't really been great fucks. Not *that* great. Of course, the blind guy couldn't see how *beautiful* she was. And the guy in the wheelchair couldn't get it up. Alice is rethinking her strategy. Maybe she's set her sights too high. Psychiatrists, for instance, probably begin by counselling disgruntled housewives before moving on to the serial killers and multiple personalities. Alice figures this may have been where she went wrong, so this year she is settling for someone whose deficiencies are less obvious. She will work her way up until she reaches her ultimate goal, the *coup de grace*, the day she can turn a gay man straight. But until that stunning moment, Walter has become her pet project. Walter doesn't know this, but if he did, he probably would have found Alice Kram way more interesting.

This evening, in the bistro on Bloor, they are getting around to discussing sex. It's a fairly safe third-date topic, particularly when the act has yet to be consummated. Alice is discovering, much to her satisfaction, that Walter has little experience in this area. She does not find this hard to believe and can't wait to share. For his part, Walter is trying to picture her feet that have been covered up in ankle boots on every date so far. She is a size eight. A decent size.

"So, you've never really had a long-term relationship then, have you?" asks Alice, hoping she is injecting compassion without pity into her voice.

"No, not really. I guess I haven't had a short-term relationship either," Walter says truthfully, wondering if she's painted her toenails.

"Are you looking for one?"

"I don't know. I guess so. Eventually," he replies, wondering if she has webbed toes.

"Have you had a lot of one night stands?"

"Not really. I don't date a lot," he says, adding, "But that's what I want to change. I'm settled in my career now."

Alice slides her hand across the table and scratches Walter's forearm with manicured peach-painted nails. This gesture reminds him of Daphne Fox and he gets a nostalgic image of her naked body, all glistening rolls and dimples, smelling of grease from the burger grill. He wishes it were Daphne sitting across from him. She may not have been his soulmate, but at least she was fun. He couldn't picture Alice sliding an onion ring over his cock and eating it off. And Alice's disquieting resemblance to the Mooney twins was more of a turnoff than anything.

"Do you think I'm attractive?" Alice asks, knowing the question is redundant or rhetorical, although if pressed, she would have no idea what those words mean.

Walter hesitates. He struggles to find a flattering answer that's truthful. Alice isn't offended by his hesitation. He's probably trying to find the words to describe my beauty, she thinks. It's not easy.

"Who wouldn't find you attractive?" Walter says.

"What do you like best about me?"

This is out of Walter's league. He hasn't seen her feet, so he can't comment on them. What do men usually say in a situation like this? He knows enough to not say breasts.

"Your eyes," he says. "They're an incredible shade of blue. Turquoise almost."

"Coloured contacts," states Alice. "What else?"

"Um. Your hair? It's very lush and very blond."

Alice is pleased. Lush is a good word unless you're using it to describe someone's drinking habits.

"Bleached. What about my boobs?" she asks, twining her fingers through his. "Do you want to touch them?"

Walter takes this in stride and squeezes her fingers.

"Who wouldn't?" he says again, making sure to stare at them with something resembling lust.

"Fake," she says.

"Oh. They look real."

"I know. You can't tell. But I'm not embarrassed about telling anyone that. Especially you. You don't seem judgmental."

What she means is, you have no right to be judgmental. You're no threat, so it doesn't matter what I say. They both know this.

Walter wonders if her feet are fake too. The possibility excites him and Alice picks up on it. They will have sex tonight. This is a forgone conclusion on both their parts. Once you mention breasts, it's a done deal.

Next up to bat is Faye Sinclair, a tall, nervous, skinny girl. She has no discernible breasts, which lets Walter off the hook on that score. But skinny hardly does justice to Faye's skeleton. After their first date, which was as simple a thing as a movie at the Fox and a hamburger at the Goof, Nova had called Walter to get the play-by-play. There wasn't much to tell except how skinny she was. He'd never seen anyone so skinny.

"She's *not* anorexic, if that's what you're thinking," Nova scoffed.

"But she's so *skinny*," he hissed into the phone. "It can't be healthy."

"She just looks skinny compared to Alice," replied Nova, unconcerned. Walter persisted.

"No, really," he insists. "She's *Auschwitz* skinny."

"Jesus, Spaz. What a thing to say," Nova said, then relented. "Auschwitz skinny. Christ, I never heard of such a thing. You're sick."

But Walter heard the trace of a smile in her voice and perhaps some amazement that he had said something bordering on rude. He knew Nova would use the line later and claim it as her own invention. He hadn't meant it as an insult, he was only trying to get his point across.

His third date with Faye "Auschwitz" Sinclair was at the Rivoli Tavern on Queen Street West. A credible jazz trio was playing, and the volume was such that the daters could converse without yelling. Auschwitz was drinking rye and water like it was plain water and she had to get her six-glass minimum in for Weight Watchers. Walter was nursing a few beers and marvelling at how sober she seemed. He was under the impression that skinny people got drunk quicker than fat people, a notion she was destroying with each round. He idly wondered if she threw up every time she went to the bathroom, which was often. Faye was a size ten. He had yet to see her bare feet but they were obviously as long and skinny as she was, and Walter was curious about them. He wondered if they would be as transparent as the tissue paper skin stretched over her bones everywhere else on her body. If she were naked, he believed he might be able to see her heart beating, or her lungs expanding in her chest. He hoped so.

As to their conversation, there was no worry that Faye would demand flattery. In fact, it was the opposite, but equally annoying. She constantly complimented him.

His hair: "The last two guys I went out with were balding. You've got a beautiful head of hair. You'll probably never go bald."

His clothes: "You look so *neat*. The last guy I went out with was a complete fashion disaster."

The gap between his teeth: "It's so cute. It makes you look younger, I think."

Walter wondered if the last guy she went out with had dentures, or maybe no teeth at all. He nodded and smiled and said thank you, and tried deflecting a few compliments along the way, a bad move that only served to increase Faye's insistence.

"No, *really*. Really. I mean it."

The entire fawning process was uncomfortable and made Walter feel pressured to return the flattery. It occurred to him then that maybe all women want to be complimented, but each has her own unique way of securing it. He scrutinized his date over the rim of his beer mug while she chattered away and threw drinks down her long skinny throat. Faye had mown her hair down to stubble, making it difficult to gauge its colour and further serving to enhance the concentration camp look. Her eyes looked large in her angular face, but any beauty they may have held was diminished by the dark circles floating under them. Her eyebrows were pencilled on. Walter struggled to find something to compliment.

"I like your ring," he said finally, swallowing with difficulty.

Faye stopped blathering and looked down at her bony fingers. The ring looked awkward and too big, but it was impressive nonetheless. A large, square, black stone, onyx, with a tiny emerald in the middle in what appeared to be a very old setting. It looked like an antique, an heirloom.

"Oh," said Faye, staring at the ring, seeming surprised to find it there.

"My ex-boyfriend gave it to me. I guess I really shouldn't be wearing it still, but Gord made me promise to never take it off. It was his grand-mother's ring."

Walter was unsettled by this. And it seemed to be making Faye Sinclair a bit wistful. Either that, or the multiple rye and waters were finally doing their job. There was an awkward silence.

"You're very thin," blurted Walter.

He braced himself, but Faye only looked at him with her large dark eyes and nodded.

"I know," she said simply. "Do you like thin women?"

And there it was. The asking. Walter was again at a loss.

"Not *too* thin," he said.

Faye relaxed back into her chair, and ran a hand over her stubble.

"Well that's a relief," she said.

What Walter didn't know about Faye Sinclair was that she went through boyfriends like rye and water. Newly dumped by Gord of the Ring, Faye was using Walter as her transition guy. She didn't see him as boyfriend material, but he would be useful to get her over the hump. And there was another thing about Faye. She was a failed ballerina. All those years of punishing cruelty to her body, of fasting and training and pushing herself to her limits, had literally come to a crashing halt when the no-talent asshole Rocco Gautier dropped her on her tailbone in the middle of a lift in *Swan Lake*. After months of tortuous physical therapy and rehabilitation, she was lucky to be walking, said the doctors. Dancing was out of the question. Faye had never quite gotten over it. She never went near a ballet again, and after years of addiction to painkillers and indiscriminate sex, she entered therapy. When she came out of therapy, she was a new woman. She shaved off all her hair, gave herself a therapeutic course of enemas, and picked up rye and water as her new prescription of choice. Walter appealed to her because of his walk. Beside Walter, she was once again graceful. She only hoped he wouldn't fall in love with her.

Faye ran the toe of her shoe up his pantleg and thought about having sex with him. Tonight. If it was good, she'd wear her tutu the next time.

Had Walter known about her dancing days, he would have fallen all over himself in his haste to pay the bill and get her naked. He'd heard about ballet dancers' gnarly feet.

Experimental date number three for the Lopsided Canadian Finch was Heidi Lemper. A Crown prosecutor, a feminist, and a real ball-buster. She had an opinion on everything and woe to anyone who dared question her motivations or ethics. She had an officious demeanour, a paralyzing stare and a clipped manner of speech. Even her physical stature was intimidating. Broad of shoulder, straight of back, and long of leg, Heidi could make the bravest of men tremble, both in and out of the courtroom. Her hair was silver and sliced in a severe bob. When Heidi had discovered she was going prematurely grey, she did the opposite of what most women would do. Rather than dying her hair back to its original colour, which in her case was dark brown, Heidi coloured the whole damn thing silvery grey. Although she was only thirty-seven years old, it suited her unforgiving personality. People complimented her on having the nerve. To her mind, it was efficient.

Heidi had decided to take her friend up on the blind date with Walter because she was sick of lawyers. Sick of professionals. Tired of their talk, bored with their egos, and disgusted with their constant one-upmanship and slickness. She hadn't dated all that much as a law student, intent on getting top marks and moving ahead like everyone else in the legal profession. And with her remarkable and quick rise up the legal ladder, she had to constantly battle perceptions she had screwed district attorneys or judges to get there. She hadn't. She wouldn't. And she despised anyone who thought she hadn't made it on her own merits. This put up an almost impenetrable shield between Heidi and potential suitors. The few men who dared ask her out were sized up by that glacial gaze, summarily cross-examined, and speedily sentenced. It would be a relief, thought Heidi, to date someone innocent.

Walter was not intimidated by Heidi at all. To Walter's eye, she was statuesque and classy and smart. This was a pleasant change and while they were out together, Heidi kept most of her ferocity in check. It was refreshing to be womanly for a change. On their third date, she wore a soft sweater and tights. Their outing was a simple stroll along the boardwalk. Heidi was comfortable and relaxed. She fantasized about bringing Walter to a law function and seeing the reaction of her buttoned-up, snide colleagues to her date. In Heidi's eyes, Walter was like a hapless puppy. He could thaw the coldest heart.

They sat on a bench to watch the lake roll in, Heidi enjoying a strawberry ice cream cone Walter had bought for her.

"Mmm. I can't remember the last time I had an ice cream cone," she said. "I forgot how good they are."

Walter was glad to hear it. He stretched his legs out and leaned back against the bench. Heidi was a size six—small feet for her impressive bearing. Walter couldn't wait to see them. Ludicrous little feet dangling off the ends of her long, muscular legs. He imagined she was militant about pedicures.

What he didn't know about Heidi was that her ongoing quest for perfection and success had left her wanting. She found Walter's imperfect gait endearing, his placid features reassuring, his job touchingly pedestrian. In her own way, Heidi was slumming. She was trying Walter on like a pair of cheap shoes. She wanted to feel the pinch, wanted to see what it would feel like to stumble. And for the moment, sitting on a boardwalk bench watching the water and enjoying the simple pleasure of strawberry ice cream, she felt insanely peaceful. She let her guard down and confessed a guilty pleasure, something her law buddies would never know.

"I play the harmonica," she said, burrowing her tongue deep into cold.

Walter sat up and looked at her. "You do?"

Heidi nodded, but couldn't look at him, kept staring at the lake, ice cream pressed hard against her lips.

"Mmhmm."

"Do you play in a band?"

A head shaking sideways, no.

Walter couldn't keep the grin off his face and continued.

"Well, what kind of music do you play?"

Heidi took a slurp and turned to face him.

"Blues," she said, ice cream smeared on her mouth.

Walter impulsively leaned over and licked it off her chin.

"Blues," he repeated, drawing back, savouring strawberry. "Like, what kind of blues?"

"You know, the blues. Little Walter, Muddy Waters, Sonny Boy Williamson. *The* blues."

Walter was delighted. What he knew about blues artists wouldn't fill a shot glass, but he believed he had felt the blues. Sometimes the static felt like the blues. The blues, as far as he knew, were all about loss. Losing someone or losing yourself. He was pleased Heidi was an expert. Maybe she could make some sense of things.

"I don't know much about the blues," admitted Walter. "But I'd love to learn."

"What kind of music do you listen to?" asked Heidi.

Walter shrugged.

"Nothing. Whatever. We play a lot of jazz at the store, but that's the owner's collection. I like all kinds of music."

Heidi sat up straight, crunching her cone.

"I guess I'll have to educate you then," she said. "I've got a huge collection of blues at my place. Why don't you come over and hear it sometime?"

"Will you play your harmonica?" Walter asked, picturing Heidi naked, lying on a bed blowing harmonica while he blows her feet.

He imagined he would feel the vibration right down into her toes. Blues should be able to do that.

"Sure, I'll play you a tune or two."

They would be having sex soon, thought Walter. Once you mention the blues, it's a done deal.

# 22 }

**All told, Walter dated the trio of women** about three months before things fell apart. Sexually, they couldn't have been more different and Walter learned the truth of the old credo: you can't judge a book by its cover.

Despite her frigid ice queen persona, Heidi Lemper consistently came like a bandit.

Alice Kram, all heat and flushed golden flesh, and curvy, womanly dampness, had multiple orgasms too. Sadly, they matched her tits.

Sex with Faye the stick ballerina was like fucking a mannequin. Walter had thought that with her dance background, Faye would be the most flexible of the three. She wasn't.

Then, there were the feet. Alice's size eights were close to perfect, but her ankles were a bit thick, which explained why she always wore multiple ankle bracelets under ankle boots.

Heidi's size sixes were, as guessed, immaculately cared for, but they didn't vibrate when she played harmonica. This was a let down for Walter.

Faye's size nines were broader than he had imagined, knobby and calloused. She never wore nail polish and cared nothing for her feet. In fact, she sometimes dreamed of cutting them off. She confided that thought once to Walter and he got such a raging, instant hard-on, he fucked her immediately and so viciously he thought she'd splinter into pieces and then crumble to dust. It scared him. Faye, as usual, laid there, her skull smashing against the headboard, her eyes rolled back in her head. Every now and then, she'd let out a squeak. After sex, she would get up and dance naked with scarves to Vivaldi. It was obscene.

Heidi, on the other hand, was a tigress. She'd buck and flail around and scream and dig her nails into Walter's back. This scared him too. He felt completely out of control of the situation. He was at the mercy of the Crown prosecutor and there was nothing he could do about it. Despite her desire to subjugate herself to the working class, Heidi couldn't quite bring herself to harness her controlling nature in the bedroom. Walter was becoming an expert at the blues though. Robert Johnson confirmed it. *You got them mean ole walkin' blues*, Robert would sing to him, while Heidi blew frantically on her harp and bounced up and down on Walter's lap like he had a pogo stick attached to his groin.

It was all an education. And what he learned was this. He wanted all of them to wear silver glitter nail polish on their toes and he wanted to make moulds of all their feet and he wanted to be with Dixie. The more he tried to replace her with other women, the more he craved her presence, her smell, her softness. He felt like throwing up sometimes thinking about her. And nothing, not Heidi's exuberance, or Alice's fakery, or Faye's brittleness, could obliterate his need. In fact, it seemed to intensify. After spending a night with one of the women, Walter would go home and rub Dixie's deck shoes on his dick. He'd come inside them now. And each time, he felt guilty for having been with someone else.

"It's you I really want," he would whisper, as he picked up her shoe.

He'd lock the door to his drawing room and turn up the music so Clara wouldn't hear him. Then he'd masturbate with the shoe, sometimes tying the laces tight around the base of his cock or under his balls like when he was a condor.

"I'm sorry," he'd say, panting and gripping the canvas tight around his length. "I'm sorry."

And he'd look at the row of plaster feet as he worked the shoe back and forth, the obvious incompleteness of the collection taunting him. These masturbation bouts were different than any others. They were not merely perfunctory. And they were not gleeful, crazy fun. They were urgent, poignant, desperate. They were voids. And he couldn't fill them, so he filled the shoes instead.

It was obvious to Walter that at one point during his mini-relationships, he would have to broach the subject of making foot moulds. When he got around to asking, Alice was all for it. Fake feet? Bring 'em on!

"Can you do it without including my ankles?" she had asked nervously, as she dipped her foot in the alginate, having refused to remove her bracelets.

"Sure," Walter lied.

Heidi was against it. Her lawyer instincts kicked in and she was suspicious. Maybe she was afraid she could be blackmailed later. Walter couldn't understand her reluctance. It's not like he was going to sell photos of them to a foot fetish magazine or display the moulds at a garage sale.

"Nobody else will see them," he promised.

"Forget it."

Heidi had visions of the feet sitting on a judge's bench. Exhibit A. Her undoing. She wanted nothing of herself left in his hands once they stopped seeing each other. Leave no evidence.

Faye was torn. On the one hand, these were her dancing feet. They should be immortalized. But on the other hand, she fantasized about cutting them off and tossing them over a bridge. Walter used her neurosis to his advantage.

"Just think," he said. "I'll make two sets and give one to you. They'll look like cut-off feet. Maybe it will stop your nightmares. You could throw the fake feet off a bridge if you want, or bury them. It might be good therapy. Like an exorcism or something."

Faye considered this, her large dark eyes blinking doubt. Walter knew she'd come around eventually. Vanity dies hard. For some women, it's the last thing to go.

Naturally, all sexual exploits were undertaken in the women's apartments. But they had all been to Walter's hotel on occasion and met Clara. Of the three, Clara's favourite was Alice. She couldn't believe Walter had snagged such a voluptuous beauty. Alice's hourglass figure reminded Clara of her own when she was younger. And also to be enjoyed was Alice's penchant for jingly jangly jewellery. Clara had never seen ankle bracelets before and was instantly smitten with the notion. She and Alice spent one evening choosing oversized wrist bracelets from Clara's jewellery box and trying them on their ankles.

"You're a girl after my own heart," Clara had said to Alice as they both shimmied up and down the hallway like belly dancers or shamans, rattling their feet and hands, shaking their boobs and hooting with laughter.

"Thank you, Clara," said Alice, who was having a grand old time.

Walter watched them with some sense of dread. He knew he'd never hear the end of Alice's virtues. Clara didn't disappoint.

"Now that Alice, *she's* a real woman," she said to Walter. "She looks like Marilyn Monroe, didja notice?"

"I guess."

"Don't let that one get away," advised Clara, already picturing the golden-haired great grandchildren.

After Alice, no one could measure up in Clara's opinion. Heidi, for instance, was too aloof for her liking.

"She's too tall," was her comment.

And Clara, of the Clairol number fifty hair, didn't trust anyone who would choose to dye their hair grey.

"It's silver," Walter said.

"Who would do that?" she said.

"She's a prosecutor."

"Mmph. Well, she walks like a man."

The thing Clara disliked more than anything about Heidi was her vocabulary, much of which Clara didn't understand.

"She talks like she's got a stick up her ass," Clara said.

"She's smart, that's all," said Walter.

"Too smart for her britches, is more like it."

As far as Faye was concerned, Clara thought she was a freak.

"There's something wrong with that one, mark my words," she confided.

"Like what?"

"Well for one thing, she needs some fattening up. There's no meat to her."

Walter sighed. "She used to be a ballerina. They're all skinny."

"Is she a ballerina now?"

"Well...no."

Clara sat back, satisfied.

"So, what's her problem then? She got something against beef? She's not one of them vegetarians, is she?"

"No. She eats meat."

Clara tried another tack.

"Well, what about her hair? She looks like she's got cancer."

It was a losing battle and Walter gave up trying to convince Clara of Faye's attributes. It was hard enough trying to convince himself.

Nova got in on the act too. Of the three, her favourite was Heidi.

"She's *great!*" Nova enthused. "She's smart, she's professional, she's got class...what's she like in bed?"

"God," Walter said.

"Well?"

The two were having breakfast at the Goof when the inevitable conversation came up. Nova was characteristically persistent. Walter wasn't used to divulging details of his sex life to anyone, mainly because he hadn't had one. He wondered how much to reveal.

"She plays the harmonica," he said.

That set Nova back in the booth.

"During sex?"

"Yup, sometimes. The blues."

"That's hilarious. But what's she like?"

"She's insatiable," said Walter, flinching with the memory of her take-charge attitude.

"Wow," breathed Nova. "Insatiable."

Walter leaned over his bacon and eggs.

"But, it's kind of scary," he confided. "It's like, I don't know. Like I'm not even present sometimes. Like she's off in a world of her own. I'm afraid to say or do anything to bring attention to the fact that I'm there."

Nova's eyes were wide. This was great stuff.

"So, she's like a dominatrix then."

"Yeah, kinda. But without the whips and leather."

"That's wild. God, she looks so together. But at least you're getting good sex. Right?"

Walter could only agree. There was no way in hell he would admit his longing for Dixie.

"What about Auschwitz and Alice? What are they like in the sack?" asked Nova.

Walter thought about them.

Faye's hairless, translucent twig body, rigid and unforgiving, her slightly medicinal smell, her sad dark eyes, and post-coital scarf dancing. How to explain the loopy feeling in his stomach when she raises herself up on her strong, hardened toes and twirls like the ballerina in his mother's old wind-up jewellery box. This, more than sex, is what captivates Walter. Her beautiful despair. It is this that always gives him an erection. Afterwards, he applauds enthusiastically and asks her to jerk him off with her hard, bare dancing feet to rid him of the nausea he feels. Faye is happy her feet are being put to use and appreciated again. She is thinking less about cutting them off.

"Faye dances," says Walter to Nova.

"What do you mean, she dances?"

"She used to be a ballerina. Sometimes she dances naked with scarves and she's really pretty good."

"God. One plays harmonica and one dances. What's next? One who recites Shakespeare? You sure know how to pick 'em, Spaz."

"You're the one who set them up, don't forget," said Walter.

"Well, whatever. Is Auschwitz as good at fucking as she is at dancing?"

"Not really," Walter said. "She's kinda awkward. But the dancing makes up for it."

Nova chewed on the information along with her breakfast.

"And Alice? What about her? She seems like a bit of a ditz, but she's pretty sexy in a gangster gun moll kind of way."

Alice Kram. Alice of the immovable breasts, the clanking ankle bracelets, and overly dramatic moans and sighs. Alice's golden skin and hair, both colours originating from a drugstore. Textbook orgasms, copied from a magazine. Walter plugging away in the missionary position, constantly having to respond to her breathy whispers. Her endless fishing.

*Do I feel good?* Yes, baby. Sure you do.

*Am I sexy?* The sexiest. Really.

*Am I the best you've ever had?* The best. Never had better.

*Tell me how beautiful I am.*

And Walter, eyes closed, going through the motions, thinks about Dixie. Like a ghost, her essence moves through him. He smells her spirit and transcends the fleshly body underneath him. He fucks by rote.

*Tell me.*

Dixie's feet twinkle out of reach. She smiles with her green eyes and parts her legs. He wants to breathe hot and damp against the white cotton, rip it away with his teeth. He will enter her with his tongue and glitter will flow out of her and into his mouth. It will taste like crystallized maple sugar. It will heal him. He will rise up and walk straight.

He fucks the body on the bed with an intense but otherworldly rhythm, probably the best he's ever been.

*Tell me how beautiful I am.* YOU MAKE ME WANT TO DIE.

"Alice? I think she fakes her orgasms."

"Figures."

# 23 }

**The experiment was a failure.** No amount of dating, toe-sucking, scarf-dancing or blues-blowing could purge Dixie from the thoughts of the Lopsided Canadian Finch. But it wasn't he who called an end to the relationships. It was Alice and Heidi and Faye. They all basically said the same thing—you're a nice guy, it's not you, it's been fun, see ya.

Walter didn't mind. He was grateful he didn't have to do it, because what would he say? You're too fake, you're too skinny, you're too scary?

The real reasons the girls had for dumping Walter would have been gratifying had he actually known them instead of the panaceas and platitudes offered in lieu of honesty. And although the women may not have fully recognized it at the time, Walter's influence had changed them all in a definitive way.

Take Alice Kram.

Walter was another chapter in the book she would never write. Once again, the misfit hadn't been a great fuck. She had hung in there for three months, taking meticulous notes and pulling out all the stops in bed in an effort to coax a great fuck out of him. God, she gave him multiple orgasms to work with, not to mention the privilege of ravishing her perfect body. Alice was beginning to seriously doubt her book idea, at least as it had been originally conceived. And she was, admittedly, pissed off. The whole point, the whole hypothesis, had been that the jerks would be grateful. Walter hadn't seemed grateful at all. Not as grateful as he should have been. He'd never get someone as sexy as her ever again. In fact, Walter's lack of unbridled enthusiasm for Alice's charms caused her to re-examine her research. When she did, she had a revelation and it was this: The great fucks weren't the gimps. No, on reflection, she realized the great fucks were the great looking guys. The guys that matched her. And the reason was that they *appreciated* her. Appreciation, not gratitude, must be the key. Alice readjusted her thesis. And because she still had that humanitarian streak, she decided to do the world a favour and write a book about how the handicapped should stick with the handicapped. Opposites *don't* attract, wrote Alice in her notebook. They don't *appreciate* each other. She could thank Walter for that epiphany. If she knew what epiphany meant.

In the end, Alice would eventually write a vanity book about how appreciation was the key to good sex. It would be financed by her new husband, a seventy-five-year-old millionaire who most certainly did appreciate her.

Take Faye Sinclair.

Thanks to Walter, she got her dancing feet back. They were, in fact, sitting on her mantel—the centrepiece in what had become a shrine. She tied her ivory toe shoes around the plaster feet, lit some candles, and placed a couple photographs beside them of her glory days of dance. Walter was right. She never again had dreams of cutting off her feet. She bought a ticket to a professional ballet to face down her demons through opera glasses from a seat in the balcony. Eventually, Faye would marry her A.A. sponsor and start teaching beginner ballet to kids. She grew her hair out, gained some weight, tracked Gord down and returned the ring. Every night she would pray and give thanks to the plaster feet.

Take Heidi Lemper.

Heidi discovered that life in the slow lane wasn't all it was cracked up to be. She was bored with the boardwalk. And she found herself missing the legal repartee she inevitably engaged in when she dated a colleague. She missed the challenge of arguing an ongoing case, defending a point of law, or speaking legalese as a matter of course. She couldn't be clever with Walter. Those reference points were missing from their relationship. He didn't *get* her. It got to the point where she began to resent his placid demeanour and she would try to stir things up. But he wouldn't rise to the bait. Heidi lived to argue. She was trained to argue, for godsake. Being with Walter had enlightened Heidi to the realization that she couldn't escape her true nature. She needed someone with an ego, with cutting wit, a sparring partner. She needed someone to do battle with. Heidi needed to win, always, but in order to crush someone with any degree of satisfaction, they had to be a worthy opponent. In the final analysis, her dalliance with Walter had reopened the possibilities within the legal dating pool, or scum pond, for Heidi. She dove in with a new appreciation for her slimy colleagues. She would never date an outsider again. And with that experiment out of the way, there was nothing stopping her from realizing her dream. Heidi Lemper would never become someone's wife, but she would become a respected judge. Everyone would know her name and marvel about some of her precedent-setting judgments. But no one would ever know about the nights she stood in front of her full-length mirror, naked under her judicial robes, blowing the blues until her lips were numb.

For his part, Walter got on with his life, which, after having been embroiled with the three women for months, seemed amazingly uncluttered. Clara and Nova were the only ones depressed about the break-ups. Nova, because she saw the demise of the gossip sessions. Clara, because she saw the abortion of the golden great-grandchildren.

Coincidentally, things were progressing rapidly with Remo now. The holly GoLightly shoes would be unveiled in time for the Christmas season. Reginald was thrilled with the concept and congratulated himself on recognizing and nurturing Walter's talent. He celebrated by purchasing a black wig and fishnet stockings and renting *Cabaret*.

With the loss of the dating obligations and the completion of the holly shoes, Walter found himself relieved of pressing responsibility. It took some time to adjust to having all his evenings free. Some nights he would immerse himself in designing and rejoicing with the shoe spirits, but other nights he would find himself aimlessly doodling and feeling restless. He was bored with his plaster feet and craved new material. It would appear that three months of dating was more trouble than it was worth with the end result only being two additional pairs of feet. And now, with the extra time on his hands and in his head, it was inevitable Dixie would flood his consciousness more than ever. This time, though, he welcomed her.

Dixie became his inner girlfriend and if that's all she would ever be, he resigned himself to that truth. Once he accepted her ethereal presence without remorse or self-recrimination, he found happy freedom. He could think about her objectively and allow himself to wonder about the connection he felt without getting tangled up in painful need. And if he ever felt a pang of longing, he would put on her knee socks and wear her shoes around his neck. He would talk to her late at night when he drew her feet as he remembered them. Sometimes he could fall dreamily into the static and find her there. There was no physical love in the static, only transcendence. If Walter had been a religious man, he might have thought he was undergoing a religious experience. But because he was not, he worshipped instead the *flow*. It's as if he had walked a few yards into Lake Ontario and stopped, letting the flow move around his legs, not going so deep as to drown.

Walter had taken to wearing desert boots for some reason. They were no longer in style, hadn't been since he was a teenager. Weird things like that were happening, little jagged occurrences that swirled around his ankles and tickle more than anything. His mother was marrying David Nussbaum in Vegas. Walter tried to picture Elvis in a yarmulke. Johnny had made a reappearance in his life lately, and Walter suspected the reason was because Johnny and Nova were getting involved. That didn't seem surprising, but if they were, they were keeping it a secret from him. Walter thought they looked good together, his two black-haired outspoken buddies. He wished them well. Walter saw Mr. Foster bend over in the backroom one day and caught a glimpse of lacy underwear. He wondered if his boss was either a cross-dresser or had a secret girlfriend and was wearing her underwear. Because Walter was often wearing Dixie's socks in his desert boots, he could understand the latter compulsion. This is what he chose to believe and was only mildly curious as to the woman's identity. Clara was taking a week's vacation with Millie beginning on Labour Day. They were going to a resort in Muskoka, owned by Millie's godson, where Clara was determined to try her hand at canoeing. Walter made her promise to take pictures and wear a life jacket. She agreed to the first request but believed her boobs would keep her afloat should she capsize.

All these events flowed around Walter as he stood firm. They didn't move him in any great way. If he took a step, they shifted with him. Nothing was difficult. Everything was adaptable. He felt at peace, unshakeable, content. His days had an easy rhythm. He sailed through them on quiet desert boots, selling shiny shoes to patent-leather women, eating greasy Goof lunches, and walking the boardwalk at night alone. Walter knew the pace of his life would pick up once the holly shoes went public and he was enjoying the respite. He felt as if he were in an air pocket, where time was suspended, and soon the tidal wave of publicity and demands for more shoes would thunder down on his head. He was simply treading water in the flow and was satisfied with that.

# 24 }

**Walter walked home from work along Queen,** looking forward to a night alone. Clara had gone canoeing and he was anticipating a quiet evening. Tonight he didn't want to go near his drawing room. He wanted to have a hot bath, order a pizza, crack open a beer and lie on the couch. He wanted to stare at the ceiling and maybe start a good book or do a crossword puzzle. He wanted to be alone with himself in the hotel. To own it. Maybe do some push-ups in the living room, or put on headphones and listen to old albums. Small stuff. The stuff he never got around to doing when Clara was home. He might smoke a couple of cigarettes. His grandmother would call it puttering. That's what he wanted to do tonight. He was more thrilled about this than he would be if he had tickets to the Stanley Cup playoffs. He was excited about fully inhabiting the hotel and listening to its voice. Saying howdy-do.

He turned the corner onto Beech and practically skipped up to the front stable doors. The stairwell was unusually dark and this pleased him. It meant he could screw a new lightbulb in—maybe he'd try a blue one for a change, or an orange one. Up he plodded in the dark, head down, mentally counting the stairs and trying to decide what kind of pizza to order. He didn't have to allow for Clara's tastes tonight, so he decided to get anchovies, though he wasn't sure he liked them. He would also get feta cheese, something Clara said tasted like puke. And maybe pineapple, a topping choice that sent Clara into an apoplectic fit about how fruit isn't meant to be hot and covered with cheese. Walter sensed the top of the stairs looming and fumbled in his pocket for his keys. As he pulled them out in the dark, he misjudged a step, and teetered to one side, waving his free hand around for the wall. He found it, cursed the fact that there were no railings, and steadied himself. As he refocused his gaze on the next step up, he froze. He was not alone. A shape materialized in front of him. He shivered as though a cold wind had sneaked inside his collar, and he shut his eyes and counted to five. But he could feel it. A presence. A life form, he thought to himself, as if this was a sci-fi movie. He opened his eyes, considered the logistics of bolting backwards down the stairs if he had to. And there, on the next step up, was a pair of bare feet. He looked up and saw the feet were attached to shadowy legs. Up further, and there, crouched on the landing, huddled into the corner, was a girl. She was silent but he could hear her breathing, because he had momentarily forgotten how. He knew she was a girl because she smelled sweet. She smelled familiar, and as his brain was clumsily collating the available information at a maddeningly slow rate, she spoke.

"Hello Walter."

He swallowed. Her legs retracted from the step, folded, and elongated, pushing her upright into a standing position. This movement stirred the close air in the hallway and allowed her scent to settle on him. He didn't know what to say. He could only stand like an idiot, looking up at her, his mouth open. It was, of course, Dixie. He had no words.

"Aren't you going to invite me in?" she asked in that voice he'd heard a million times in his head.

"I..."

Dixie reached a hand out, an impossibly fine hand, but he couldn't bring himself to take it, to touch her. Maybe he'd actually fallen down the stairs in the dark and cracked his head and was dreaming or dead. He was afraid to move.

Dixie said: "I'm real. You can touch me, I won't disappear. Come on."

Somehow Walter managed to step up to the landing. By sheer will, his fucked-up legs hoisted him up beside the vision. He couldn't look at her and instead busied himself with his keys, clattering and shaking as he tried to unlock the door. His main thought right now was only: thank god Clara went away. It was the best he could do. Other thoughts were fighting each other in the zoo that used to be his rational brain. There

were so many...howdoyouknowmynamewhatareyoudoingherewhoarey-
ouwhatisyournamewhatthehellisgoingonhereareyouforrealhelpmehelp-
mehelpme...help.

He unlocked the door and pushed it open. She walked by him like she
owned the place and turned around to face him, one hand on a hip, half-
smile. In HIS hallway. In his crooked, drafty, creaky hallway. Walter gave
his head a shake and stepped over the threshold to join her. He hip-
slammed the door shut and leaned his back against it, staring at her. He
still said nothing. He couldn't believe she was for real.

"Got anything to drink?" she asked.

Walter tried his mouth on for size.

"Uh."

He held onto her request as if he had been asked a skill testing question. Drink? Why, yesiree little lady. We got Scotch, we got beer, we got
wine. We got Kool-Aid, we got iced tea, we got coffee, we got water, soda,
tonic, pop, fruit juice, apple and orange, Red Rose, um, what else...maybe
some vodka.

"Uh. What would you like?"

*My name's Walter and I'll be your server tonight. But you already know my
name, which is weird because I'm not wearing a name tag. So—*

Dixie shrugged.

"Beer or wine would be nice. Do you have any?"

She was wearing a tight black jersey dress. Her hair was in a ponytail.
Walter couldn't bring himself to look at her feet. It would abso*lutely* send
him over the edge.

"Are you okay?" she asked.

"What?"

"Beer or wine. Got any?"

"Yes! Yes I do!" he practically shrieked.

"Great," said Dixie. "I'll be in the living room."

And with that, she did an about-face, bare feet squeaking on the hardwood as she strode towards the living room like she'd lived there for years.

Walter watched her back for a second or two and then ran in the opposite direction towards the kitchen, bouncing off the walls in his haste

and confusion. Once there, he stood in the middle of the room looking at the cupboards like a moron. He couldn't remember where the booze was kept. His hands were sweating and he wiped them on his pants, looking wildly around the unfamiliar kitchen. What did she say? Wine? Beer? He spied the fridge and threw himself at it, yanking open the door and sticking his face in, hoping the cold would stun him into some semblance of organized thought. He started grabbing beer.

The girl was strolling around the living room, swinging her arms back and forth, pausing now and then to look out the window or pick up a book and read the title. She could hear faint noises emanating from the kitchen and smiled to herself. She could picture his frenzy and she found it funny. After a few minutes, the girl settled herself on the couch, pulled up the new footstool Clara had demanded, and stretched out in comfort. She loved this place. Its oldness. Its smell. Its sparseness. She tried to see Walter in it. She knew his grandmother had gone away. Timing, she thought, as she laid her head back to stare at the ceiling, was everything.

Walter was clutching an armload of beer, at least ten bottles, when he remembered she also requested wine. He dropped the beers on the card table and lurched over to the booze cupboard. After pawing through various bottles, he pulled out two. One red and one white. He couldn't remember if she specified her preference and he stared dumbly at the bottles, one in each hand, as beer bottles rolled off the table behind him and hit the floor with a dull thud. The fridge, still wide open, was making a high-pitched whiny sound. He felt like he'd been in there for hours. He looked for a tray to carry the drinks and glasses, he needed wine glasses and beer mugs, a corkscrew. Fuck. Should he get snacks? It was all too much. He was sweating and trying not to think too much about the girl in the living room, but of course that's all he could think about. *Be careful what you wish for.*

He grabbed a bag of pretzels and ripped it open with his teeth like a crazed dingo. Pretzels went flying and he crunched them into the linoleum with his desert boots as he jerked himself around the kitchen, opening drawers and cupboards and banging into every available sharp corner. Now he needed a bowl for the pretzels. He was being a total klutz and it was probably the first time he felt that he deserved his nickname. He wondered what Dixie's real name was as he placed a couple beers and the wine on a serving tray. He couldn't imagine her being called anything else. Was it a plain name like Janet? An exotic name like Camille? An androgynous name like Lindsay? God, he thought, what if I slip and call her Dixie? Then I'd have to explain the whole land-o'-cotton thing. He rammed pretzels into a bowl and went on the hunt for the elusive Canadian corkscrew which could not be found in its usual habitat. He needed dress shields. He was hoping against hope that he didn't spring a boner when he went back out there.

The girl was thinking she would like to live here. She noticed three bedroom doors in the hallway. How convenient. She would paint the living room tangerine and buy a couple of Areca palms to sit by the bay windows. Maybe a nice tall wooden bookcase with glass doors. She had a lot of books, a lot of Agatha Christie, John Grisham, and nonfiction books about serial killers and true-life crime. Romance novels held no interest for her. She needed suspense, and had always thought she'd make a decent private eye. But other than a few additions, she liked this room the way it was. Spartan. Clean-looking and nothing fancy, like Walter.

She stretched her arms above her head and cracked her knuckles. She wondered where her brown deck shoes and knee socks were being kept. She knew they were here somewhere. The *suspense* was thrilling her.

The tray was loaded now and Walter wished he were. Two bottles of wine, two beers, two bowls of snacks, two slabs of cheese, two wine glasses, two beer mugs. He stared at the tray. Two of everything. Two. Like they were a couple already. Like it was the goddamn fucking *ark*. He pictured walking into the living room and setting down the tray like it was the most natural thing in the world to do.

Would you like to watch a movie, dear? Can I rub your feet? Did you have a hard day at the office? What do you think about going camping next weekend?

Walter arranged the tray, stalling, trying to compose himself into a humanoid. He couldn't think about all the questions he had.

Can I suck your feet tonight, dear? Would you mind putting on your red shoes and walking on my chest? How about I rip your white panties off with my teeth and taste your sweet glitter? How *about* that?

He took a deep breath and picked up the tray. Walked down the long hallway with care. He could see her legs stretched out, but the wall hid the rest of her. God, she was still here. He couldn't believe it. He was afraid that when he reached the living room, he would find out it was Alice-Faye-Heidi and it would be confirmed that he was delusional and paranoid. He was also fearful of the static creeping in. The shock of seeing Dixie was so great, he assumed it overwhelmed the static. But this could be a momentary respite. It could hit him at any time and the thought scared the shit out of him. He reached the living room and sidled in, balancing the tray on one hip. He walked sideways, crab-like, past her and laid it on the trunk. He avoided all eye and foot contact, slid the trunk over towards her. Pulled up a rocking chair and sat. He looked in her direction, but his gaze fell somewhere around her waist. If he looked up, he'd see the unbearable green of her eyes, down, and he'd see the feet. He was fucked and he knew it.

"I brought wine and beer. Please help yourself to whatever you like," he said to her hips.

"Thank you. I think I'll have a glass of wine."

He heard her pouring it and risked a look up. But she caught him. She was staring right at him as she poured. Green eyes. Yup. Green, greenie, green-green.

"Can I pour you a glass? I'm having red."

Walter nodded, and wiped his clammy hands on his pants.

"Sure, that'd be great. Thanks."

He wondered how the hell he'd be able to raise the glass to his lips without shaking and spilling wine all over his shirt. Was it too late to ask for white? The worst thing of all, he thought, was that this was so normal sounding. Just two friends having a drink. Very civilized and polite. Nobody seemed to be mentioning the fact that this entire situation was completely insane. He figured he'd play along until she enlightened him. After all, *she* started it. He leaned over and took the glass of wine. His trembling was hardly noticeable.

"What shall we drink to?" she asked, leaning over, wine glass out-stretched.

This forced him to look at her.

"Oh. Um. To surprises?"

She laughed and it thrilled the living shit out of him.

"To surprises," she said.

They clinked and he managed to not shatter their glasses somehow. So far so good. They drank—she a sip and he a gulp—and she settled back into the couch. He began a slow rock and tried looking her in the eyes to see if he could handle it. She was scanning the room.

"You've got a great place here," she said.

"Thank you. I like it."

She smiled at him and his heart exploded.

"Do you live around here?" he asked, wondering if it was too personal of a question.

"Not far."

They sipped their wine, he rocked faster.

"Don't you want to ask me anything else?" she said.

Walter thought about it. Part of him obviously had a billion questions. But another part of him wanted to answer no. No, I don't have any questions because that might spoil this. No, I don't have any questions because you're here and that's enough.

"Go ahead," she urged. "Ask me anything."

He took another gulp of wine and rocked faster.

"Well. What's your name?"

"That's a good start," she said. "It's Laura."

Laura. He said it in his head. Not Dixie, Laura. He liked it. It was a soft name.

"Laura," he said aloud. "Pleased to meet you, Laura."

"Likewise," she said. "Thanks for *not* inviting me over."

"You're welcome," said Walter, and actually managed a smile at the absurdity of the entire conversation.

She, Laura, smiled again too. It was a goddamn knockout of a smile. It was the best smile he'd ever seen in his life. But she beat him to the compliment.

"You've got a great smile," she said.

That flustered him and he could do nothing but take another drink of wine and try to think of another question. Why aren't you wearing any shoes, came to mind. But he decided to skip any mention of shoes or feet until he felt more sure of himself. Her damn feet were right in front of him though, and sooner or later he knew he'd relax and his gaze would slip.

"How did you know where I live?"

"You're not hard to find," she responded. "You're not sorry I'm here, are you?"

"No!" Walter spluttered. "God, no! I mean, no. No, I'm not. Sorry you're here. I'm glad you're here, actually. I mean, it's nice to see you again."

"Good. I'm glad I'm here too."

She leaned forward, her wine glass cupped in both hands.

"I've wanted to meet you for a long time, Walter. You interest me."

This threw him. He had no idea what she was talking about, but didn't care. He decided to risk a comment.

"I did feel a connection with you that day in the store," he admitted cautiously. "I've thought about you a lot since then."

"Me too," said Laura. "And now, here we are."

Here we are, indeed. Walter was soaring. This couldn't be happening, he thought. I can't be this lucky. There's got to be a catch.

"I really can't believe you're sitting here," he said.

"I can. I've pictured it."

She'd pictured it! What else had she pictured, he wondered. Probably nothing close to his own wild imaginings.

He started to relax and poured another glass of wine. This was going well, he thought. Who cared how bizarre it was? She was here, he was here, and they'd both been thinking about each other. If she walked out the door right now and never returned, these few moments were better than all his other dates combined. He decided to make the most of it, to be calm and enjoy the flow. In case this was it.

She spoke: "So, where are my shoes?"

Walter didn't understand the question at first. It was precisely what he was going to ask her: where are your shoes?

There was a lull while she stared at him with the same bemused smile she wore at the shoe store. Whereas only moments before he couldn't stand to look into her eyes, now he couldn't seem to stop. To stop would mean he would have to look at her feet and he couldn't go there yet. And then he got it. She meant her brown deck shoes. He thought of them sitting in his room, all crusty and rancid from his nocturnal activities. It horrified him. Is that why she was here? To get her shoes back? His hands started to sweat again and he slurped back more wine. His rocking picked up to a maniacal speed.

"You mean your deck shoes?" he asked, buying time.

She nodded, smiling.

"What else would I mean?"

A brainstorm.

"I thought you might mean the red ribbon shoes," he said, convincing himself that maybe she did mean them. They, at least, hadn't been flooded with his bodily fluids. The condor had, in fact, held back on that.

"You've still got those? I thought you might have taken them back to the store," she said.

Walter was not liking this conversation. Shoes were usually the safest topic in the world for him, but now he was faced with two shoe dilemmas. Well, I jerk off in the deck shoes and I kept the red shoes so I could tie them around my dick and my face one night when I was a condor. For a second, he thought about saying that to see her reaction.

"No, I didn't take them back to the store because they were worn," he said lamely.

She didn't buy it. He could see that.

"That'll fuck up your inventory," she stated, leaning over and topping up her glass of wine.

"Yeah, I guess it will."

"So, where are my deck shoes?"

"They're here somewhere. I just don't remember where I put them right now. You don't want them right away do you?"

Panic.

She wiggled her toes, an action he saw in his peripheral vision. That alone was enough to make him almost swoon.

"What am I going to wear home?"

God. What the hell was he supposed to do? He *couldn't* give her the shoes. He should have lied. He should have said they were lost. He was mugged in an alley and beat off his attackers with them. He threw them away. Gave them to a street person. Anything but the truth.

"You could wear the red shoes home," he suggested. "You can have them. I know exactly where they are."

And then he pictured her in them. Standing in his hallway in the screamingly high-heeled red shoes, her little black dress, ponytail. It caused him great pain. Hollow, achy pain. He fought it, knowing it was a precursor to a tumble into static.

"Okay," she said.

Relief so great, he felt like sobbing. He wouldn't be found out. Not yet. He was granted a reprieve and he was grateful to her. He would do anything for her at this moment, give her anything she wanted.

"There's cheese," he said, a pitiful offering.

"I see that."

The idiot poured himself another glass of wine. Might as well be a drunken idiot, he thought.

"Is that why you're here?" he asked, detecting a note of defensiveness in his voice. "Just to get your shoes?"

"No. Not just. Actually, the shoes were an excuse."

"An excuse?"

"Yes. An excuse to meet you."

Ah, this is way better conversation, thought the idiot at first. Then he actually *heard* what she'd said.

"Why would you want to meet *me*?" he squeaked pathetically.

She laughed. His throat swelled.

"Don't underestimate yourself," she said, leaning forward, her elbows resting on her knees.

"I wouldn't go to all this trouble if I didn't really want to know you. Don't you get that?"

*Flummoxed* was a word that came to Walter's mind. What a great word, he thought.

"I'm flummoxed," he said.

She didn't flinch. He thought she must be into words. She must be smart. He thinks anything at all to avoid thinking about why he would be worthy of her attentions. Maybe she was nuts. That would be okay. Everything's okay. She wanted to get to know him. He was flummoxed by that. And she was probably nuts. And it was all good.

"Look Walter," she said. "I want to get to know you. I hope that's okay with you. I thought maybe I could be assured of getting your attention by leaving the red shoes outside your door. I thought it might make you think about me."

She took a deep breath and he waited for her to continue. He was speechless anyway.

"I was hoping maybe we could see each other again sometime. Hang out together. Get to know each other. I know you probably think I'm nuts, but I'd like you to give me a chance. Do you think you could do that? Do you think we could see each other again sometime?"

Walter swallowed.

"I think that could be arranged," he said, fighting the urge to get up and dance.

Laura visibly relaxed and held her wineglass out again.

"Let's drink to it," she said. "Let's drink to new beginnings."

Walter held his glass out.

"To new beginnings," he agreed, picturing her naked for a second.

They clinked, sipped, and smiled at each other. Her smile felt like a mirror image of his. For a fleeting instant, she looked like him. The connection he felt in the shoe store was more insistent than ever, but this time it was comforting more than annihilating. It was fraught with possibilities rather than unrequited longings. He was ecstatic.

She put her drink down and smoothed her dress over her lap.

"I have to go now," she said. "But I'd like to see you again soon."

"Tomorrow?" he burbled too eagerly.

"I'd love that. If you're free."

Oh, I'm free, thought Walter. I'm a fucking bird.

"Would you like to see a movie?" he suggested. "Or go to dinner?"

She stood up and stretched, her dress inching up a bit too close for comfort.

"I'd like to actually take a walk on the boardwalk, if that's okay. We can talk."

It was more than okay and he told her so. She would meet him at seven at his hotel.

"Can I get those shoes now?"

"Yes, of course. Wait here, I'll get them."

He wobbled out of the living room and opened the padlock on the drawing room. Within a minute, he was back with the red shoes.

"What's in the locked room?" she asked.

"Oh. It's my studio. I design shoes for GoLightly's," he said, not without a trace of pride.

"I'd like to see it sometime."

"I'd like to show it to you," he said, holding out the shoes.

Laura sat back down and proffered a foot.

"Put them on me. Like you did before."

Walter's first instinct was one of immediate acquiescence and he got into his standard shoe salesman crouch. It was, after all, his job. But then he realized, too late, he'd have to see and touch her bewitching feet. He prayed he wouldn't lose it.

The next few minutes were a dream.

Her feet are more precious than he remembered. And now, he felt a possessiveness about them he didn't feel before. He felt he had to protect them. Her toenails were still glitter, but gold this time. Thank god. Silver might have conjured up images he couldn't afford to indulge himself in right now. The gold was warmer. Her feet were regal treasures, and he held them in his hands with the respect they were due.

He slipped a shoe on with tenderness. Wrapped an ankle with care. Took a moment to drink in the sight of her other naked white foot before regretfully slipping it into the other red shoe. He was fighting the static with everything he had. He would not, no way, look up. He tied the final ribbon with finesse and stroked her ankle. He remained kneeling at her feet, head bowed, hands in his lap. He felt like crying.

Laura's hand touched his head. She moved it through his hair, and he heard her breathing. No one spoke.

# 25 }

**Walter woke up at nine a.m.** It was Sunday, a day off. He stretched his body out and remembered Clara was away. He could sleep in if he wanted, she wouldn't be banging around the hotel. This was a relaxing thought and he turned his face into his pillow. It hit him then and he stiffened as if he'd heard a ghost, a trespasser. *She* was here last night. He frowned. Was it true? Had he dreamt it? Walter was afraid to move, as if that would crack the spell. He stopped breathing and thought back, sleepiness ripping away in sudden, quick jolts of memory. Snapshots of last night danced past him in a row, like they were pegged to a clothesline and someone was reeling them in. They started slow but picked up speed as each snapshot confirmed the next. Dixie—no, Laura—sitting on his stairs was the first image to flutter by, followed by his first glimpse of her in the hallway. He concentrated. Next, he was in the kitchen loading up a tray, and then the snapshots really started to move. They *snapped* like snapshots should. Laura on his couch, *snap*, two wineglasses clinking together, *snap*, *snap*, her voice saying she wanted to get to know him, BIG *snap* there, getting the red shoes, *snappety snap*, and putting them on her feet, *oh, snap!* Eyes closed, he recalled the sight of her feet. Gold glitter, he remembered. She *was* here. He opened his eyes. She *was* here. He sat up and breathed again. And then he remembered they had a date set for tonight at seven o'clock. Walter wouldn't believe it until he saw her. But all the same, the situation was good. He threw himself back down on the bed, on his back, and yelled something out to the world. A primal gut sound, no words. There was no one home, his dick was hard, and life was pretty fucking good. He felt as though his heart was beating outside of his chest.

Laura had been up since eight o'clock. While Walter was figuring out what had happened last night, she was sitting by her window having a cup of coffee. Laura had no such problem with her memory. It was all very clear. But it was always clear to the conductor of events. It had to be. You're leading the way, keeping people on track. They've got to fucking keep up. When you're in charge, you must have faith in your vision. And Laura was very clear on that. She thought about Walter. Initially, she had been worried that seeing him up close again wouldn't be the same as it had been in the shoe store. She wondered if she would still feel a tingle around him, or if she had only wished it. But she needn't have worried. Laura smiled into her coffee. He was better than she had imagined. He smelled good and had a calm aura, yet his hands on her feet were strong and sure. When he smiled, he looked boyish. Laura thought he looked like a Dickens character. A crippled shoe shop boy, she mused, with a gap-toothed smile and a shy awkwardness about him. The kind of boy you wanted to protect. But there was something else about Walter, something secretive. Like he was carrying around a quiet burden. Still waters run deep and all that. She believed he would fight for her, if he had to. And one day, he might have to, she thought, as she drained her coffee.

Walter didn't know what to do with himself all day. He felt rubbery and somewhat green, like Gumby, and wished somebody could bend his limbs for him, manipulate him into some kind of decisive action. He couldn't concentrate on designing, couldn't focus on reading, and barely tasted anything he forced himself to eat. The one thing he felt like doing was taking a long walk on the boardwalk to clear his head, but because that's what Laura wanted to do later, he would wait. He would give her that.

He had three baths throughout the day, for something to do.

*And thought about washing her feet.*

Did push-ups on and off for an hour.

*And thought about fucking her, sweaty, dreamy.*

He went to the corner store about ten different times.

*And bought her meaningless things each time, candy cigarettes, chocolates, a* National Enquirer *magazine, peanuts in the shell, a lottery ticket. Things he would never give her.*

He smoked cigarettes and paced.

He risked having a couple of beers to relax and immediately chased them with black coffee so he wouldn't be foggy.

He watched television but couldn't remember what shows he had seen five minutes after they were over.

He clipped his toenails.

*Pictured painting hers with precision and glitter.*

Laura had taken a shower. She walked around her one-bedroom apartment in a black Japanese kimono, wet hair piled on top of her head in a towel. Doing things. Tidying up. At four-thirty, she entered her darkroom and did some last minute dodging and burning on her latest prints. CBC radio played in the background. An oscillating fan scanned the room. When she was satisfied with the results, she hung the black and white photos by clothespins on a line. Turned the fan and the radio off and left the darkroom, flinging the towel off and ruffling a hand through her wet hair. The photos fluttered briefly with the closing of the door. They were good. She was getting better at capturing Walter's spirit.

At four thirty, Walter was standing in his drawing room looking at the plaster feet. He had bottles of nail polish in his hands. He had devised a project to keep him busy—repaint all the toenails in his collection. It had occurred to him that Laura might be a bit freaked if she saw all the moulds painted with silver glitter. And then he wondered if she would be upset by the moulds themselves. Naturally, he could explain. But he didn't want anything to fuck up her apparent, and still unbelievable, interest in him. He stared at the row of feet and tried to imagine hers in there. He hoped she would let him recreate her feet before she came to her senses and realized he wasn't worthy of her. Walter sighed as he opened Malibu Sunset and began repainting the toenails of Sue. He felt a twinge of regret as the silver disappeared under brush strokes of vibrant reddish orange. He hoped he wasn't making a mistake by assuming things.

Six thirty. Laura got ready. She spritzed herself with Paco Rabanne. Pulled on faded black jeans and a long-sleeved green T-shirt. She doesn't wear a bra. The weather was still mild and she slipped her feet into a pair of cheap plastic black flip-flops. The gold glitter was gone, replaced with pearly opal. At the last minute, she decided to braid her hair. Two braids, like a schoolgirl.

Walter started getting ready at five-thirty. Like a teenage girl preparing for a date, he tried on everything he owned, discarded it all as worthless, then tried it on again. His fingers reeked of nail polish and rubbing alcohol and he scrubbed them with Comet cleanser. He had at least an hour before showtime, but felt panicked that he'd waited too long already, that there were details he'd forget. He smelled everything to make sure it didn't stink because he'd forgotten which pile of clothes was freshly washed and which had been worn. His stomach was having an uninhibited party and at one point he felt so sick with anticipation and dread, he considered not answering the door at seven o'clock. But the thought of *not* seeing her made him feel sicker than the thought of seeing her, so he downed some Alka-Seltzer with a shot of vodka. In the end, he settled on blue jeans and a black shirt. He checked his socks a hundred times to make sure they were clean and they matched before finally sliding them into his desert boots which he brushed so vigorously, he nearly took the nap right off them. He brushed his teeth with the same viciousness. And shaved for the second time. By the time she arrived, he was raw.

Laura was punctual. At seven o'clock, Walter heard the bottom door bang shut. He heard this because he was standing at his apartment door, listening, quivering. As her steps drew nearer, he backed away from the door, tiptoeing, hoping she wouldn't hear the hall boards creak. By the time she knocked, he'd backed himself all the way into the living room and had picked up a magazine, pretending he was casually leafing through it and didn't realize the time. He heard the knock and glanced at his wrist, as if he was wearing a watch. He said, Is it seven o'clock already? And absently put the magazine down on an imaginary table. It slapped to the floor and he forced his legs to walk towards the door. She knocked again and Walter opened the door, a ridiculous part of him hoping it was a salesman.

"Hi again," she said.

Relief washed over him that it was not a salesman.

"Hi, come on in," he said, stepping back.

She stood in his hallway, a repeat of last night, and he absorbed the sight of her as if he were a sponge. She came back. She came *back*.

"Do you want to have a drink first, or do you want to leave right away?" he asked, still holding the door open.

"Let's go," she said. "It's beautiful outside right now."

Walter thought, yeah, but it's beautiful inside right now too.

"Let me grab a jacket in case it gets cool down by the water," he said, phrasing it like a question.

"Sure. Good idea."

"Should I bring something to drink?"

"If you like. Doesn't matter."

Walter smiled at her oddly and continued down the hall. Doesn't matter? Everything matters. Every fucking detail matters, because he'll replay them all later tonight when he's alone. He'll wear out the rewind button on his mental tape recorder.

He grabbed a blue nylon jacket off the pile of clothes on his bed and slipped a flask into his hip pocket. Already filled with Southern Comfort, a detail he'd worked out ahead of time. All this shit matters, he thought as he closed his bedroom door. It has to.

They didn't say much as they walked down Beech to the water. It was one of those companionable silences punctuated only by sporadic light commentary and the slapping of Laura's flip-flops on the sidewalk. It was like they were both waiting until they reached their destination to get real. As if the street were an escalator, a transition conveyance, on which you only engage in pleasantries because you're on the move to somewhere more profound. Walter allowed himself to feel joy in the stupendously normal things. The way her braids swung when she turned her head to look and point at something. How her green T-shirt accentuated her eyes. The fact he could see her bare feet and her toenails resembled smooth, shiny pearls.

Laura was content too. She was growing accustomed to the shuffling rhythm of Walter's walk and it made her want to hold his hand so she could feel it move through her. And she wanted people to look at them, to feel a bit unsettled by their presence. Laura sneaked a peek at Walter's face as he stopped and bent to pick a flower for her. She thought of camera angles, light and shadow, but mostly she thought how it was the best face she'd ever seen. She knew most people wouldn't be able to see it because nothing about him was obvious. It was what made him so challenging to shoot, and so hard to picture in her mind when she thought about him at night. But it was ultimately what made him so amazing and Laura thought he was the most handsome man she'd ever seen in her life. She could photograph a face like his forever and always find something new.

"It's beautiful," she said, accepting the flower.

"I think it's a weed," Walter said, hunching his shoulders.

Laura broke off the stem and tucked it in her braid.

"I love it."

She loves it. Walter felt as though his heart could split open and doves would fly out.

They continued walking, each of them picturing holding hands, but nobody suggested or attempted it. They both had completely different reasons for not making such a move. As they crossed the grassy park to the boardwalk, they noticed it was packed. It was the Sunday before Labour Day Monday and people were out in droves, cruising the boardwalk and having barbecues and picnics in the park.

"God, I thought everyone might go away for the long weekend," said Walter, eyeing the busy scene with dismay.

"No such luck," said Laura, as they both stopped in their tracks and surveyed the activity.

A Frisbee nearly clipped Walter's head as he looked down at Laura.

"Do you still want to do the boardwalk?" he asked.

"We don't have to fight the crowds on the boardwalk. We could walk further down and find a spot in the park that's more clear if you want."

"Good. Let's do that."

The thought of trying to navigate the hordes on the boardwalk left Walter cold, but curling up with Laura on a patch of grass passing the flask back and forth is an image he felt warm about. They tromped past families squatting on picnic tables, teenagers passing joints or making out under trees, solitary old men sleeping on the grass, young mothers rocking babies in carriages. The humanity didn't have an end in sight no matter how far west they walked.

"I've got an idea," said Laura, stopping. "Why don't we walk down there, and sit on some of those rocks. Nobody's out there."

She shaded her eyes and pointed to the water where a rock jetty jutted out from the beach, stretching into the lake. Walter was hesitant. The reason nobody's out there, he thought, is because you'd have to be insane to try and clamber out on those slippery, moss-covered rocks. It looked impossible to traverse and uncomfortable to sit on once you got to the end. *If* you got to the end. He looked down at Laura to voice his concerns, but she looked so excited about it, he didn't have the heart. Can't she tell he's no mountain goat?

"C'mon," she urged, grabbing his shirtsleeve. "I'll hold your hand. It's completely deserted out there. It'll be great!"

Walter allowed himself to be dragged down towards the beach and the rocks. All he could think about was, it's a helluva way to get to hold her hand. He wondered if she'd hold his head when he fell and broke his neck.

After much embarrassing slippage and near catastrophe, Walter made it to the end of the jetty, clamping onto Laura's hand with a death grip. And there they sat, barefooted, listening to the water slapping against the rocks and the distant sounds of people who didn't matter. Laura's flip-flops were stuffed inside Walter's desert boots along with his socks and he likes how this looks. Walter felt a calm sense of pride, and not for making it across the rocks. He felt proud to be sitting there with Laura. He felt like he had invented this day. He had created the lake, the air, the solitary drifting cloud. All this was his masterpiece. All this he designed for her pleasure and gratitude.

"See that sailboat?" he felt like saying. "I made that sailboat. I put it there for you to watch and enjoy."

He had no questions for her. He didn't care if she had a last name, a pet, or a criminal record. If a massive wave washed over them and dragged them under the lake's surface, it would be fine with Walter. They could drown together, locked in a final embrace. Years later, their skeletons would be found intertwined and people would wonder who they were—minstrels would write songs about the undersea mystery lovers and poets would glorify them.

"This is nice, isn't it?" Laura murmured.

Walter looked sideways at her. She had rolled her sleeves up and he looked at the fine hairs on her forearms. He wanted to lick them and watch his saliva dry.

"Yeah, I'm glad we came out here," he replied, feeling the beginnings of a stirring in his crotch.

"I wish we were naked," she said.

Instant huge boner. No transition. Walter felt hard and liquid all at the same time. He could only think in pictures, not words, and if he could stop being autistic, he was afraid of what he would say. Laura was chewing on the end of a braid. He felt like she was chewing the end of his dick.

"Do you ever go skinny dipping?" she asked, mouth full of braid.

Oh god. A question. This meant an answer was expected. Walter hoped he looked normal, aside from the monument that had sprung up in his pants.

"No," he managed, his voice like barnacles. "No, I've never gone skinny dipping. Have you?"

Fuck, why did I ask that, he thought. I don't want to know the answer. If the answer is yes, I'll picture her naked. If the answer is no, I'll picture her naked.

"Sure, lots of times. It's the best way to swim."

Naked. She's naked.

"You should try it sometime," she said, taking the braid out of her mouth and running it over her cheek. "It's liberating."

Still naked.

"You're not shy, are you?" she asked, leaning in, the tip of her wet braid poised close to his face.

His cock had burst through his jeans, split the seams, and was now the tallest freestanding structure in the world. How come she wasn't looking at it? It must be out. It must be splitting the heavens right now. Walter pictured her climbing his cock, her arms and legs wrapped around, inching her way up, her naked breasts pressing against it. On her way to heaven, astride his mighty beanstalk. He felt something on his face, realizes his eyes had been closed. It was the tip of her wet braid, tracing circles.

"Are you?" she asked again, her breath close and sweet.

"What?" he said, or someone said.

"Shy."

He opened his eyes and fell into green. It was a near-death experience. "I don't know."

The braid was on his lower lip now, running back and forth. He wished for a second that she had longer hair, more distance. And then he didn't wish that at all. As the braid explored his mouth, he stuck his tongue out to catch it. She played with him, winding it around his tongue, his chin, his mouth. She painted his teeth and he bit down. Their faces were inches apart, their breathing syncopated. She spoke.

"I don't think you are. Shy, I mean."

Walter didn't think so either, with her hair clenched between his teeth. He reached up and took the braid out of his mouth, but kept hold of it with one hand. With his free hand, he grasped her other braid. He moved his face closer until their noses touched.

"I don't feel shy around you," he said. "I feel safe."

Laura draped her arms over his shoulders and pressed her forehead to his.

"We belong together, I think," she said.

This made total sense to Walter. He knew someone was about to kiss someone soon and when it happened, it was Laura who took the initiative. It was Walter who splintered into pieces of glass.

Laura wasn't sure why she kissed Walter. She hadn't meant for it to happen. Things got out of control, something took over. Their connection was too insistent. The thing that did it for her, the one thing that sent her over the edge, was when she slid the tip of her braid through the gap in his front teeth. That killed her. It made her want to slide her tongue in the disarming gap between his teeth, and it made her want to straddle his lap and have him slide into her own gap. His erection was obvious and reassuring. It was solidity. Stability. The two things Laura craved, neither of which had anything to do with money or the things money could buy. Her need was more about belonging, not belongings. That's all she wanted from Walter. She had not planned anything physical. She had not intended to kiss him. And she had definitely not expected the teenage feelings she got when he kissed her back, holding tight to her braids. It took everything in her to resist laying her hand on his crotch, when all she could picture was lying back on the hot rocks and feeling him anchor her to this spot. To plant his flag and claim her. Laura knew she wanted too much from Walter. She was placing way too many expectations on him. But, what if?

The kiss was brief and startling and when it was done, they both drew back and lay against the rocks. Side by side, shoulders touching, they stared at the sky and passed the flask. Laura thought the cloud looked like a princess wearing a crown. Walter thought it looked like her. Nobody mentioned the kiss but it was out there, as big as the sky.

When they got up to leave the rocks, this time it was Walter who held his hand out. It was Walter who led the way back, having somehow gained sure footing. It was Laura who slipped once and Walter who steadied her. This simple act made Walter feel like a hero. He believed he could take her up in his arms and carry her over the damn rocks while dancing a jig if he wanted to. Nothing was impossible any more.

# 26 }

**When Walter wakes up the following morning,** he knows some things. Some things about her, about him, and some things about some things. It's all there inside his head. Clara would say it was percolating. Walter can picture his head as a clear glass bubble with rich aromatic thoughts bubbling and jumping around inside it. Thoughts brewing. He can smell them.

These are some of the things he now knows about Laura. She is a photographer. She lives a couple blocks off the Danforth in an apartment. She loves his plaster feet. Her last name is Booth. She has no brothers or sisters. Her parents are dead. She is twenty-seven years old. She likes cats better than dogs.

These are some of the things he knows about himself. He is attractive in her eyes. He has never felt this close to anyone in his life. Around her, he is a god. And these thoughts are more than enough. They splash up against his clear glass bubblehead in joyous abandon. They leap. They friggin' cavort.

Here's another thing he knows. She is sleeping in his grandmother's bedroom. Right now. They have an entire day to spend together, and this is how it will start. He will make French toast with icing sugar on it, and sausages. They will eat breakfast together in his kitchen while peeping Toms watch with envy from the neighbouring buildings. He will try not to sob with joy. And if she has a shower when she gets up, he will offer her one of his shirts to wear and hope to god that she will walk around his apartment in his shirt, her underwear, and bare legs and feet, with wet hair and shining green eyes that look at him with admiration as he moves sausages around the frying pan and pours her a cup of freshly brewed coffee. He wishes he had oranges to squeeze for her juice. And fresh strawberries to slice up and lay on her French toast. He wishes there were a cow out on the roof that he could milk, and chickens whose eggs he could gather in a basket. Walter wishes he could hear a rooster crow, and feels like he could do it himself if he put his beak into it. This is a fresh new day and he is a fresh new man and if he needed convincing, he had to look no further than the evidence pushing his sheet up into a teepee.

Walter smoothed the sheet down over the evidence and held it firm at its base with both hands. With his head propped up on two pillows, he looked down his chest with wonderment. Damn straight. It appeared bigger than usual to Walter's eye. Almost military in its rigidity and stature, official. He ran his hands down its length approvingly. A ghost cock waiting for its orders, at attention. A private, naturally. Walter considered putting it through its paces so it could be at ease. He didn't want the ghost cock haunting him through breakfast. But as he began the drill, he heard the hall floorboards creak and he froze. Pitter-pattering to his bedroom door and a tapping. He pried his hand off his dick: "Yes?"

"Are you awake?"

"Uh, yes."

Up goes the blanket over the evidence and Walter struggled into a sitting position, one hand still wrapped around the soldier as if to keep him from leaping out and bayonetting her.

"Can I come in?"

Oh shit. He put the extra pillow on his lap.

"Sure, come on in."

Laura pushed the door open and poked her head in. A sunny smile, green eyes still sleepy and sexy beyond belief. He could smell her sleep warmth. The pillow moved in response.

"Hi," she said. "Sorry to bother you, but is it okay if I have a shower?"

"Yeah, sure, go ahead. There's a clean towel in the wooden cabinet. Use whatever you want."

She flashed a glance at the lap pillow.

"Thanks. I didn't mean to wake you."

"You didn't. I was up," he said, mentally cursing the choice of words.

He wished she would crawl into bed with him. He wanted nothing more than to stick his tongue in her mouth before she brushed her teeth. Her hair was loose and wavy from the braids, and he was positive the pillow would shoot up off his lap and hit the ceiling any moment. He was glad he didn't have a ceiling fan because it would surely shred the pillow into millions of cloth ribbons and feathers would blanket the room. Laura looked at him with a half-smile as if considering whether or not to venture further inside. Yes, do it, he thought. Don't think about it, do it. Walter wanted to see her standing by his bed, disrobing in the dim light, a silent sepia movie. He pictured her removing the pillow from his lap and peeling back the sheet to reveal his soldier. She would be impressed, perhaps put a hand to her mouth for a second. Then she would lightly touch it with the tips of her fingers to make sure it was real. For his part, Walter would try not to think about that hot wet place, that sweet glitter place that she carried around within her. He would try not to think about her standing on the bed, feet planted on either side of his hips, lowering herself down into a shoe salesman crouch, balancing herself on the very tip of his impossible prick.

"Okay?" she spoke.

Walter shook his head and believed the pillow had risen off his lap a couple inches.

"What? I'm sorry, what?"

"Is it okay if I use your toothbrush?"

That does it. The pillow should be a foot in the air now, spinning madly around in circles, like one of those plate-spinning guys, thought Walter. *Can you use my toothbrush?* God, it's the next best thing to me brushing your teeth with my tongue.

"Yeah, no problem. Go ahead. Whatever you need."

"Thanks. I'll see you in a bit."

"Okay. Have a good shower."

Walter waited until he heard the water running and then whipped the pillow and the sheet off. He attacked his soldier with frightening speed and vigour. Manic, like he was on the clock. Oh my god, oh my god, he thought, his hand flying like he was beating egg whites into a meringue. Hearing the shower going didn't help. Now he pictured her naked and wet. It was worse in a way. Or better. He had to get his soldier in line, before the water stopped. No time for leisurely manoeuvres. Snap to it, bucko.

Laura hummed to herself as the water beat down on her head. Pretty good water pressure for such an old place, she was pleased to note. She soaped herself up with Ivory. If she decided to live here, she'd bring Pears soap. It's the only kind of soap she trusts to actually put inside her. She felt rested despite lying awake for hours in Clara's bed last night. Too much thinking is not a good thing, she thought, and adjusted the tap for more hot water. Yesterday and last night spent here with Walter was the best time she had had in years. The best. Aside from that hasty kiss out on the rocks, there was no more fooling around. Her choice. Fooling around was not part of the plan. She let her fingers wander south for a minute and closed her eyes to the hot water slamming into her face. Walter was getting to her. This morning, for instance. Who was he trying to fool with that pillow? Her fingers slid inside. Her fingers played. Every time she looked at Walter, he looked better to her, more vital, more intriguing. She slid her fingers out with regret and grabbed the shampoo to keep her hands busy. Head & Shoulders. Briefly thought about Walter joining her in the shower. Briefly wondered what he looked like naked. Dug her nails into her scalp to stop thinking about it. Her stomach growled and Ivory soap ran down her legs. She had wanted to take a picture of him lying in bed this morning. The lighting was warm, amber, and he had looked tousled and boyish and guilty. She could visualize the photograph as she raked her nails over her head. But there would be other opportunities now that he knew she took photos. He seemed as interested in her photography as she had been in his foot collection. Laura decided to get him some more feet, starting with her own. Pleasing him was important.

Walter dispatched his ghostly soldier in record time and scrambled out of bed and into his clothes. He grabbed one of his long-sleeved white shirts and hung it on the bathroom doorknob in case she wanted to wear it. By the time the water stopped running, he was making coffee and rattling pots and pans. Laura opened the bathroom door to let the steam out and saw the shirt.

"Is this for me?" she yelled from around the door.

"Yes, if you want to wear something clean," Walter yelled back.

The next time he turned around, Laura was standing at the kitchen door toweling her wet hair. She was wearing her black jeans and his shirt with the sleeves rolled up. Bare feet. He could smell his grandmother's moisturizing cream on her. The juxtaposition of Laura smelling like Clara made his stomach flip. It was like she belonged here, like she now carried something familiar and heartwarming along with her new strange mystery. An unbeatable combination, really.

"Can I help?" she asked, draping the towel over the back of a card chair.

"No. Sit down and relax. Let me wait on you."

Walter was beating eggs and milk for the French toast. Things were very under control.

"Coffee should be ready in a minute. You can go out on the roof if you feel like it. There's a good view."

Laura walked up behind him and peeked over his shoulder. Her nearness was unnerving and thrilling.

"Are you making French toast?" she asked, her breath all Pepsodent.

"Yeah. Do you like French toast?"

Laura resisted resting her head on his shoulder.

"I love it. But you don't have to go to this much trouble, y'know. Just coffee would be fine."

Walter turned around to face her and nearly bumped noses. She was glowy and dewy and damp and fresh. And she looked tiny in his crisp white shirt. He had an urge to open a couple buttons and slide his hands inside. To feel her bare skin, explore her shape.

"It's no trouble," he said. "I want to do it."

He smiled crookedly at her, feeling a bit unsteady. The smile slayed her. The gap did it every time.

"Well, thanks. I think the coffee's ready now."

And she moved away. Walter turned with relief back to the mixing bowl. He heard every sound she made. The coffee pouring into the cup. The milk, the spoon clinking. Her breathing, a tuneless humming which could have been her or him, he wasn't sure. Her bare feet walking over to the door, the creaking as it opened, her bare feet moving back into the kitchen, the scraping back of a chair, the rustling of a newspaper and the sipping of coffee. He busied himself at the counter, enjoying the background sounds of Laura waking up in his kitchen.

"Good coffee," she said.

It didn't require a response. Walter turned the stove on and got the bread and sausages out. He managed everything and by the time he sat down at the table, he felt good about his performance thus far. They ate breakfast together well. Enough conversation, a couple laughs, no awkward eating or food moments. It was as if they'd eaten breakfast together a million times before. It was fucking effortless, he marvelled. He would reach for the milk and pass it to her. She would reach for the syrup and pass it to him. He would talk when her mouth was full and vice versa. Everything was coordinated. It *flowed*. Walter tried to remember what it had been like eating breakfasts here alone or with Clara. He couldn't. This moment was every moment. He studied Laura sometimes as she was talking, her hands expressive or pushing wet hair off her face or holding a fork over her plate. Her eyes flashing green in the bars of sunlight coming through the drapes, one foot up on her chair, her knee brought up to her chest. His white shirt open at the neck, her collarbone. It was so fucking great, all of it, he couldn't believe it. And the best thing of all, the very best thing, wasn't how she looked to him. It was how she looked *at* him. Like he was important. Like she was enjoying this as much as he was. At this particular moment, Walter didn't give a shit about anything or anyone else. Not Nova or Johnny or his mother getting married or his grandmother coming back, not the shoe store or his new designs or Reginald. None of it mattered. He wished she had brought her camera so he could have a photograph of this moment to look at forever. For once, he wasn't thinking about dunking her feet in plaster. It was a miracle.

Laura was ravenous. She had watched Walter's back as he was cooking, sneaking glimpses every now and then. Her heart sang a song every time he had to move sideways in his jerky fashion. She loved the smells of cooking and coffee and she loved being in his shirt. It smelled clean and she felt cleansed. Walter's presence was like a pure river running through her. If he had told her about the flow, she would have had a name for this. And if she let go of her restraint, she knew the flow would likely turn into molten lava and if she let that happen, it would probably bury them.

She watched him eat, relieved he didn't chew with his mouth open or make smacking noises or speak with his mouth full. Once, he got a speck of icing sugar at the corner of his lips and she had to resist the urge to lick it off. There were a lot of urges she had to quell. But Walter was in the same boat. He realized too late that bacon would have been a preferable alternative to sausages. It was maddening watching her spear an entire sausage and then bring it to her mouth and wrap her lips around it. This simple act destroyed him with its implications and he would have to avert his eyes. He cursed the sausages while wishing he were the sausages. And he would stab his own sausages, hacking them into ragged pieces, as if this metaphorical act would kill his own impulses. It didn't work. He could only long for bacon.

But the small torturous moments were negligible when stacked beside the good stuff. The rhythm of two souls bouncing off each other across a breakfast table. The comforting clatter of silverware, murmurings, and the occasional bright flash of laughter. Mostly there was a subtle sense of ever-increasing recognition going on. Every new discovery took on an instant familiarity, almost the second it happened. There was a strong sense of déjà vu and no fear. When breakfast was done, Walter suggested leaving the dishes and sitting on the roof with their coffee. They grabbed two folding lawn chairs from the porch and carried them over to the far southeast corner where they sat, feet up on the ledge, talking about nothing and everything and growing into and around each other like creeping morning glory. Walter didn't ask the tough questions, the prying questions that Nova would have been all over. He didn't ask why he had been chosen, mostly because he didn't care and partly because he was afraid the answer could ruin everything. If Laura didn't see fit to tell him, then she probably had her reasons. Instead, they talked about things like growing up without siblings and how it felt. Walter got the sense Laura had been lonelier than he had. She told him she had made up an imaginary sister who she talked to late at night in bed. He told her about Johnny and Nina and Tina and Adelaide.

"Actually, I think I learned more from Adelaide than anyone," he said. "Y'know, she was the only person who really, truly didn't care or even notice my walking. That meant something to me, eventually. I still think about her."

"So, your friends were enough?" Laura asked, leaning back in her lawn chair. "You didn't feel something missing when you were alone in your room?"

"I guess I felt lonely sometimes."

"What would you do?"

He looked over at her and debated telling her about the static.

"I listened to the radio," he offered.

"So you liked to hear the voices I guess," she said.

"Yes. And the music. It was company."

Walter shifted in his chair and felt like he should elaborate.

"I didn't sleep much when I was a kid because I'd stay awake until the radio went off the air. I still can't get to sleep until really late, maybe because of that. I don't know."

Laura laid her head back, saying nothing. She was wondering if Walter would be able to sleep if they made love for hours and lay together afterwards. She could be his radio, his pacifier. Walter was wondering the exact same thing. Nobody spoke for five minutes, both of them sensing the imperceptible tightening of the morning glory vines as they envisioned an identical moment. When they spoke again, Laura stepped onto safer ground and asked about his shoe designs. She told Walter she would like to photograph the shoes and the plaster feet and he responded with such alacrity, she wanted to plant a big kiss on him right then and there. His enthusiasm was so infectious, Laura suggested they go inside and make a mould of her feet. The expression on his face was worth everything. He was like a big goofy puppy, drooling, eager, and grateful. She expected him to piss all over the floor. He fell all over himself in his haste to pack up the lawn chairs and waddle back inside as fast as his crooked walk would allow. Laura trailed behind, staring at her bare feet. It would be fun to dip her toes into Walter's passion.

In the drawing room, Laura snooped while Walter got out the alginate and bucket. She walked over to the row of feet and wanted to see her own among them.

"Whose foot is this?" she asked, running her hand over plaster.

Walter looked up.

"That's Faye Sinclair's foot," he said. "Why?"

Laura picked it up and turned it over in her hands.

"I don't know. It looks like a strong foot, that's all. Who is she?"

"She was a ballerina. I guess she used to twirl around on those toes. That's why it looks strong."

Laura put the foot back down. She studied Walter.

"Yeah, but who is she? To you."

"Nobody."

"Nobody? You walked up to some stranger on the street and asked if you could make a copy of her foot? And she let you?"

Walter wondered if Laura was jealous. That would be too good to be true.

"I dated her for a couple months. She's nobody to me now, is what I meant. I haven't seen her since. Why?"

Laura shrugged and ran her fingers over another foot.

"No reason. Who's this one?"

"That's Beatrice, a friend of Nova's. And no, I didn't date her."

"You think I'm jealous, don't you?"

"No."

She picked up Faye's foot and held it high over her head.

"What would you do if I dropped this on the floor and smashed it?"

Walter crossed his arms over his chest and smiled at her.

"Go ahead."

"You wouldn't care?"

"Nope."

Laura dropped the foot but caught it before it hit the ground. She began walking around him in circles, holding the foot above her head, teasing. Walter made a grab for it but Laura danced out of the way.

"Give me that," he said, hand outstretched.

"I thought you didn't care," said Laura, twirling like the foot's owner, out of reach.

Walter stood still and tried to maintain a solemn expression. He threw his hands up in the air in a gesture of surrender.

"You're right. Keep it," he said and turned his back.

But in a flash—in a move worthy of Nureyev—the spaz spun around and grabbed the foot from Laura. He held it above his own head and stepped back a pace, daring her. Laura took a step towards him, grinning. She was picturing the beginnings of a wrestling match, which was an exciting thought. And then she saw a look in Walter's eye that stopped her short. And like that, he heaved the foot against a wall where it smashed with an explosive sound in the high-ceilinged room. Laura stared wide-eyed at the wall. Walter laughed aloud and marched over to the foot collection. He picked up another foot. He kissed it.

"So long sweet Sue," he said, and slammed the foot into another wall.

Laura put her hand over her mouth and wasn't sure how to feel. Part of her was caught up in whatever adrenaline moment Walter was enjoying and part of her wanted to stop him from destroying his work.

"Walter," she said, walking towards him.

He had his hands on another foot. Mandy O'Toole's. He arced his arm back to pitch the foot but stopped in mid-throw. Instead, he marched over to the window and yanked it up and open. Stepping back, he hucked the foot out the window.

"Happy landing, Mandy," he yelled and snapped back around to face the dwindling collection of feet.

"Who's next?" he asked.

His eyes lit on one.

"Come to daddy, Alice," he said, striding over to the bench, rubbing his palms together.

Laura didn't know what to do. They were his feet, after all. She could only watch in awe. Walter picked up Alice's foot and turned to Laura.

"Alice," he stated. "I also dated her."

"Was she nice?" was all Laura could think to say.

"Nice? She didn't have a brain in her fucking head. She was narcissistic."

Laura walked over to inspect the foot.

"What's this?"

"Ankle bracelets. She always wore ankle bracelets because she thought her ankles were too thick," said Walter.

"Were they?"

"Yes, I suppose they were," said Walter, proffering Alice's foot.

"Here. Why don't you do the honours? Destroy Alice."

Laura took the foot, and looked around the room.

"Go on," urged Walter. "It feels good. Throw it out the window if you like."

"Are you sure you want to do this?" asked Laura. "Don't you need these?"

Walter seemed to think about it for a second.

"Are you still going to let me do your foot?"

Laura nodded.

"Well then. That's all I need."

Laura examined the foot in her hands. The foot with thick ankles and ankle bracelets. Alice's. That snotty bitch, thought Laura, and leaned into her pitch. The foot went sailing out the window and hit the neighbouring building with a satisfying thunk. Laura screeched with delight and clapped her hands.

"Take that!" she crowed, jumping up and down.

"Good one," said Walter, picking up the next foot in line.

"Who's that, who's that?" shrieked Laura, totally committed now.

"It's..." Walter began and stopped. "It's Nova's."

Laura sensed hesitation and calmed down a bit.

"Nova. That's your friend from GoLightly's, isn't it?"

"Yes."

He walked over to the drawing table and placed Nova's foot on it. Then he walked back to the collection and grabbed Clara's foot. He placed it with Nova's.

"Not those two," he said.

"Okay," agreed Laura. "Should we stop now?"

Walter seemed displaced, disconnected. And then he looked down at Laura's feet. The pearly opal polish had chipped and they looked like child's feet to Walter. They were the sweetest feet he had ever seen and the sight of them made his heart leap into his throat at the same time his stomach dropped out, leaving a big vacant torso in between. He pulled his gaze away and reassessed his collection. They were pathetic excuses for feet, he thought. Imperfect, odious feet that didn't deserve to be in the same room as Laura. Vile feet. They stunk.

"Let's trash them," he said. "I want these feet out of my fucking sight. They're grotesque."

Laura studied them. They looked okay to her.

"All right," she said. "What do you want to do with them?"

Walter thought about it.

"I want to put them all in a box right now and then later, I want to throw them in the lake. A sacrificial burial at sea. I want them gone. Right now."

"Why?"

He looked at her on his way out of the room to get a box.

"Because I've got your feet. I don't need anything else."

And he clumped down the hallway, leaving Laura alone with the feet. She walked over to the table and looked at Nova's feet.

"You're saved," she whispered. "For now."

And she looked down and wiggled her toes. Her feet were going to take the place of honour. This thrilled her in a strange and wonderful way. Walter's destructive act was her validation. Laura looked around the drawing room with its soon-to-be-empty foot bench and pieces of feet scattered about. A haze of plaster dust hung in the air, giving the room an industrial feeling. Like heavy work had been done here. Like it was a factory. She pictured her photographs tacked up on the bare walls, envisioned her tripod in the corner, spotlights and umbrellas and reflecting sheets of tin.

It looked like the only thing Walter would need in here would be his drafting table and space for his paints and pencils and scraps of material. With some rearranging, there was plenty of room for a photo studio too. Now that all those feet were about to be history, except hers. What had started as a glimmer of a thought in the shoe store that fateful red-shoe day now possessed her. She wanted to be part of all this, to belong to it. She wanted to be able to say: This is *my* place, step into *my* studio, can I fix you a drink in *my* kitchen? She wanted to paint the walls, arrange new plants, get down on her knees and varnish the wooden hall floor. This is *my* life, she wanted to say. She didn't know what she would call Walter:

This is my...something.

I'd like you to meet my...don't know.

This is Walter, my...my...what.

That part wasn't so easy. It hadn't come to her yet. Or it had, and she didn't want to acknowledge it. Walter was so much a part of this place, she didn't know if she could separate them. Didn't know if one had to come with the other. If they were a pair. If she could insert herself in between them or if she had to belong to both. And of course there was a wild card: Clara. Laura desperately wanted Clara to like her, almost as much as she wanted to like Clara. Maybe that would be the deciding factor. She picked up Clara's foot and closed her eyes, trying to get a vibe off it. *You will like me, you will love me.*

Walter watched her from the doorway. Laura's back was towards him, but he could see she was holding Clara's foot and appeared to be deep in thought. How did this happen, Walter wondered. It was surreal. A wind coming in through the open window was blowing particles of plaster dust around, swirling around Laura like a shroud. Why is she here, this girl with her head bent down, holding his grandmother's foot? Walter felt the beginnings of static scratching at him. A week ago, this room was orderly and contained. Now, it had taken on an entirely different character. Everything had been interrupted. The feet were in disarray, and a girl stood at his drafting table wearing one of his shirts. A girl who itched at him more than the static ever could. Walter looked at the box he was holding. The coffin for his feet. He felt no regret about their imminent demise. Now, they were but clutter in Walter's eyes. They were an insult to Laura's feet. He slid a glance around the room and spied the alginate and bucket. The static punched him in the eyes and he saw geometric patterns zigzagging across his vision. The box fell from his grasp and hit the floor. Laura spun around, still holding Clara's foot.

"Hey," she said.

Walter stared at her through black and red lines. She looked far away. He saw her put Clara's foot down and shove her hands in her pockets. He couldn't remember why she was here.

"Did you want to pack up the feet?" she asked.

Walter stepped into the room, kicking the box out of his way. No, that's not what he wanted to do. There was something else. He walked closer to her, feeling a static storm gathering in his forehead. She watched him approach. Something was off. It felt wide open in here, like anything could happen. It was that kind of electric energy that you typically try to cut off when you feel it creeping up on you because its immensity is too real. That kind of energy that once you've put the brakes to it, you always wonder later what would have happened if you had found the balls to let it happen, let it engulf you. This is how Laura felt as she watched Walter approach her, methodically, in his shuffling manner. He was staring straight at her, but through her. It was intimate and distant all at the same time, and Laura let him come. She knew this was a moment. His hazel eyes violated her and she let him come. She did not want to die wondering what might have happened if she hadn't.

Walter was on some sort of automatic pilot. He knew his feet were moving and his eyes were dry as plaster dust. He lost the room. It simply slanted away into nothingness. There was just him, or whatever he had become, and her. The crazy lines had shifted to the periphery of his tunnel vision, they circled Laura but she was clear and uncluttered. The white shirt was stark and impenetrable but Walter sensed the warmth beneath it, the blood pumping. The only other things he saw were her eyes, like cool green grapes. If he stomped on them, they would be wine. Perhaps enough to fill a thimble. He would drink it down and give the thimble to Clara for her needlepoint. Plaster dust tickled his nose as he shuffled closer. But he didn't feel awkward, he felt as if he was on roller skates and Laura was pulling him by an invisible thread. He was gliding, like a spirit, and once he reached her, their molecules would merge, their molecules would make a pact. They would share a heart, he believed. Like conjoined twins who are born knowing what it means to share from their very first breath. He wondered if conjoined twins were possessive of their toys. He felt possessive of the green-eyed creature before him and had only to recall the smashing of plaster feet to confirm this. But that seemed like another lifetime.

He was reeled in closer, and her green grape eyes were bigger now. Perhaps they would fill a demitasse. When there was only a foot between them he stopped gliding. He reached out his hands, one on each side of her head, and moved them close to her hair. The black and red lines danced, jabbing into his fingers. He couldn't ignore them, mostly. His hands touched her hair, dry now, and moved down to cup her face which felt tiny, like a doll's face. He tilted it up and absorbed it. Her eyes melted and her mouth opened, moist breath dampened his chin. Walter's fingers curled up in her hair and he knew he was in a position to do something now, but he couldn't seem to figure out what. He felt her shift closer and their hips touched. It sliced him in half.

Laura waited as Walter moved towards her, dazed looking but determined. Her toes clenched as if she were balancing on a branch, precarious, while his eyes pushed through her. It was impossible to read the intent behind them. Their colour kept changing, from grey to violet to blue-green, but it wasn't the colour that was disconcerting. It was the purity of his focus on her. She didn't know if she could bear his touch, if that is what he intended to do. And then he did and yes, she could bear it. His hands cupped her face and turned it up towards his own. She stared straight into the shifting hazel lights and thought she knew this moment. She parted her lips and moved in closer, because this is what she had always done. Her eyes closed. But it didn't happen. She felt his hands grip her shoulders and then move down her arms. There was an impression of empty space where his face had been and then she opened her eyes, seeing only the ceiling. He was halfway down her body, crouching lower as he ran his hands down her sides, over her hips and thighs, like he was peeling away a corn husk. There was purpose in his touch that travelled down her length until he was hunched over like a shoe salesman, hands around her ankles. Laura looked down at him. The moment had passed and she felt relief mixed with yearning. She felt stupid and stripped bare.

Something happened when Laura's hipbones hit Walter's upper thighs. The red and black lines went haywire, blasting off in all directions, then hanging for a split second in limbo, before rushing headlong into each other and colliding to form one straight black line, one straight black arrow that shot out of his head and dive-bombed into his groin. He buckled, but his vision was clear. He remembered what he was supposed to do. He was supposed to copy her feet because he had no more feet left. There was a bucket. There was alginate. He groped his way down her body, still unsteady from the static party, holding on like a child until he reached the floor, which is where he always felt safer.

"Walter?"

He needed a couple seconds to compose himself, get things back to normal. Get things right as rain, as Clara would say.

"What are you doing down there?"

He steadied himself before releasing her ankles. Cleared his throat.

"Looking at your feet," he replied truthfully. "Before I make the mould. We're still doing that, aren't we?"

"Yeah, sure. Do you want to do that now?"

Walter ran his hand down the front of her right foot and laced his fingers between her toes.

"No time like the present," he said.

"Any time you're ready," she said, flexing her toes around his fingers.

Finally Walter looked up and Laura was flattened by the vulnerability in his eyes. There was something pleading about the way he looked at her. She didn't know what to give him except her feet.

"They're all yours," she said.

He hung his head with gratitude or shame, she couldn't be sure.

# 27 }

**While Walter and Laura got busy** over a bucket of alginate and later trekked down to Lake Ontario to unload some feet, others were also finding this Labour Day to be significant.

After winning big at the slots, Joy Finch and David Nussbaum were going to the chapel. Robin Mooney and David's shrink friend Bernard had accompanied the pair as witnesses, and after the vows were vowed, the four would get pleasantly drunk watching the immortal Wayne Newton. Robin was planning an Agincourt after-party upon their return.

Clara was on her way back from Muskoka, sporting a sunburn and a girlish crush on one Clifford Klonsky, an eighty-year-old widower who was renting the cottage next to Millie's. This would also be the day she met Laura, although she did not know that yet.

Nova found herself in an unexpected position on Labour Day, that of having her knees up by her ears and Johnny Carmichael sweating it out between her legs. It's true she had found herself attracted to Johnny of late, and not just because he got contact lenses. They had been spending some time together in the last month or so, ever since he got a job in the Beaches as a short order cook and moved into the apartment below her. But she hadn't expected to spend a hazy Labour Day afternoon fucking him like a minx. Not that she was complaining. Johnny had been around.

This Labour Day would always be remembered by Reginald Foster as the day he brought home Sabrina, his new Jack Russell terrier. It was also the day he began planning a launch party to celebrate the new holly shoes. Sabrina watched attentively as Reginald wrote out lists and sipped a gimlet. Every now and then, he would pat Sabrina on the head and adjust her brand new rhinestone collar and Sabrina would lick his hand. Reginald added a crystal doggie dish to the list and showed it to Sabrina. She wagged enthusiastically.

All the people in Walter's immediate circle of acquaintances were experiencing some kind of love or a facsimile thereof on Labour Day. But at the time, nobody knew about any of the others. By the time secrets were divulged, the possible shock value of such information would be considerably lessened, as the recipients would be caught up in their own dramas and feeling quite benevolent. As long as Nova was getting plowed by Johnny, she wouldn't be as harshly dubious about Laura's presence in Walter's life. And as long as Walter was wrapped up in his exploration of all things Laura, he wouldn't feel awkward about his two best friends getting it on. Clara may have been way more critical of Laura, even suspicious, had she not felt a need to rush into her bedroom upon her return from Muskoka and pen a note on her lily of the valley stationery to Clifford Klonsky. Or write "Cliff and Clara" again and again, admiring how it looked and sounded. And both Nova and Walter may have been irritated by the new addition to GoLightly's that always seemed underfoot usurping most of Reginald's devotions, had they not been actually having a life outside the store. Once Clara and Walter found out about Joy's knot-tying spree in Vegas being official, they may have felt less charitable towards David Nussbaum, were they not mooning after Clifford and Laura in some dreamy fashion. As it would turn out, they could both afford to be pleased about Joy's happiness and managed to dredge up some kind words about David.

And Joy, who now had a new sparkling wedding ring to add to the collection of things she could twist around her finger, was so content she bore Clara no further ill will for leaving the nest. Once she heard about Laura, she was optimistic. Joy had secretly wondered for years if her son was gay, a notion David Nussbaum had not dismissed although not encouraged either. If Laura was more than a passing fancy for Walter, Joy was determined to love her like the daughter she never had. Flush with newlywed bliss, Joy wanted everyone to get married. When she was enlightened about all the dalliances, she wanted Clara to marry Clifford and Nova to marry Johnny. If Joy Nussbaum had her way, everyone would get married in one big honking group wedding. They would have the reception at the Tam O'Shanter golf course banquet room. Joy had attended several bonspiels at that facility and knew they did up a good prime rib buffet. And since Laura had no parents, Joy would pay for it all with help from her brand new husband's bank account. Her own wedding had been a hasty affair, and Joy decided Walter's wedding would be traditional and she could fill the role of both mother of the groom and mother of the bride. And it didn't escape her that she could wear the new peacock blue halter dress she bought in Vegas with her slot machine winnings. She might consider buying a matching hat, which she believed would be classy in an old-fashioned way. Clara would approve.

Joy would get her opportunity to examine all these potential marriage matches on Saturday at the party Robin was throwing for her and David. The new Mrs. Nussbaum was giddy about the impending festivities and busied herself all week baking squares and fudge for the grand event. The entire street was in on it. Robin had chosen to go with a barbecue, which seemed the easiest option and meant Allan would be doing all the cooking. Ivy was taking care of the salads and Evelyn Carmichael was bringing junk food and extra lawn chairs. All this help meant Robin didn't have much preparation to do, which left plenty of time for hair and nail visits to the beauty parlour. The days immediately following Labour Day were hectic for everyone and conversations were hurried and fragmented. Some of them went like this:

Clara met Laura and thought she was "pretty enough" but might have an agenda.

"An agenda?" Walter had asked. "What do you mean?"

"I don't know. She seems to be trying too hard, that one."

"Too hard at what?"

"At being liked."

"Liked by who?"

"By me, for starters."

"Don't you like her?"

"I didn't say that, did I? She's nice enough. If you were rich, I might be more suspicious. I'd get a food tester or something."

"But do you like her?"

"The important thing is, do you like her?"

"Yes I do."

"Then shut up."

And Clara would go into her bedroom and phone Clifford who had agreed to be her date for Joy's party on the weekend. He lived in Unionville, a small town outside of Toronto and not all that far from Agincourt.

When Nova found out about Laura's presence in Walter's life, she was only mildly annoying about it.

"Did she tell you why she left the red shoes?"

"So I would think about her."

"God. Did she tell you why she showed up unexpectedly? Why she's playing these games?"

"They're not games. It was her way of getting to meet me I guess."

"So, did she tell you why she wanted to meet you?"

"What are you saying? Nobody should want to meet me?"

"No, I'm not saying that. I'm saying it seems like a weird way to go about it."

"And having sex with Johnny isn't weird?"

"Fuck off."

Walter also had a conversation with Johnny, which Johnny initiated. If you're fucking your best friend's best friend, you should call.

"So I guess you heard."

"About you and Nova?"

"Yeah. It's kinda weird."

"That's what I told her."

"Yeah? What did she say?"

"She told me to fuck off."

"That's what I like about her."

"Me too."

"I hear you've been getting busy with someone too."

"Uh huh."

"Nova told me she's like a stalker or something. What's her name again?"

"Laura. And she's not a stalker. She's a photographer."

"Cool. So, you're not pissed about me and Nova?"

"No. I think it's great. Do you think it could be serious?"

"I dunno. Are you and the stalker serious?"

"I dunno. Yeah, I guess."

"Yeah, me too. Nova's amazing in the sack."

"Oh god. I don't want to hear about it."

"What about this Laura chick? Is she hot?"

"We haven't done it yet."

"Fuck OFF! You are SUCH a fucking SPAZ, I can't believe it."

And, naturally, Walter found out about Clifford Klonsky from Clara.

"So, tell me about him. What's he like?"

"He's retired."

"I figured that. I mean, what's he like?"

"He's tall. Taller than Nussbaum. But then again, who isn't?"

"Is he funny? Smart? Quiet? What?"

"He's a gentleman. He has manners and very nice nails."

"Does he have an agenda?"

"Hah! Touché, kid. I'm the one with an agenda."

"Really? What is it?"

"Promise you won't tell him when you meet him?"

"Cross my heart."

"My agenda is to live out the rest of my years on his hobby farm in Unionville. He has a goat."

"Really? You like him that much?"

"I don't know that yet. But I'd like to live on a hobby farm."

"Why?"

"Everyone needs a hobby."

"I guess you're right about that."

"I'm right about everything, kiddo."

David and Joy:

"I guess you're looking forward to seeing Walter on Saturday, aren't you?"

"God yes. I feel like we've really lost touch with each other."

"How does that make you feel?"

"How does what make me feel?"

"That you've lost touch."

"A bit sad. But I understand it. He's got his own life now. And I'm really excited about meeting the new girl in his life."

"Ah, Laura. Yes, me too."

"Are you happy, David?"

"Are you?"

"Completely. The only thing that would make me happier is grandchildren. What about you? What would make you happier?"

"If you would come over here and sit on my lap."

"That would make you happier?"

"Oh yes. No question."

"But I've got more squares to bake."

"Damn the squares, Mrs. Nussbaum. Doctor's orders."

"Whatever you say, Doctor Nussbaum. I'm not wearing any underwear."

"I'm counting on it, wife."

The days leading up to Saturday's party flew by for everyone. Joy was elbow deep in fudge, Clara was elbow deep in moisturizing cream, and Johnny was elbow deep in Nova. Reginald and Sabrina were busy getting groomed and scented, as was Robin Mooney. Clifford Klonsky was buffing his nails to a high gloss and trimming his nose hairs and David Nussbaum was licking chocolate icing off his new wife's fingers. Allan Mooney was greasing up the barbecue and stringing lights in the backyard. Ivy was peeling potatoes like she was a scullery maid and her husband was practising the accordion and selecting albums to play at the party. He had an enviable collection of 78s. Naturally, Tina and Nina Mooney would also be present for the gala occasion and both of them spent hours at

Scarborough Town Centre looking for the perfect outfit. Tina was also shopping for clothes for her now-fifteen-year-old "tumour" who she had named Tanya. Adelaide and her mother had been invited, but everyone doubted Lillian would show. Adelaide, who still lived at home, was now monstrous and giddy about seeing Walter again. Her pronunciation had improved over the years and she now called him Wadder Fint. It was something.

And Wadder Fint himself was nervous. He hardly saw Laura at all that week although they spoke on the phone every day. Laura told him she had a project she was working on and he had no reason not to believe her. But not seeing her made him nervous. His drawing room, empty of feet except for the three preferred guests, made him nervous. Adjusting to having Clara back made him nervous. At work, Nova made him nervous whenever he thought about her and Johnny and especially whenever she broached the subject of Laura. Sabrina running between his legs made him nervous. But what made him the most nervous of all was bringing Laura to Agincourt to meet the street. What if they didn't like her? What if she didn't like them? What if she took one look at where Walter came from and hightailed it out of there? He still didn't know anything about her past, about where she came from. What if people started pestering her with questions she didn't want to answer? What if everyone made *her* nervous? And the static made him nervous. What if he had a major attack of it? He began biting his nails which Clara noticed, slapping his hands away from his mouth.

He forgot about the positive things. He forgot that he had designed some fabulous shoes and could go back to Agincourt a proud man with a beautiful young woman on his arm. He forgot that most of the attention would be focused on his mother and his new stepfather, not him.

He longed for Laura and felt sick without her around. This too made him nervous. He waited every night until he heard Clara snoring and then locked himself in his drawing room with Laura's plaster feet. He would put his dick between her soles and masturbate with them. He would kiss them and wonder what it would feel like to kiss the real things. And wonder why he hadn't yet. Nervousness turned into anguish.

Laura was edgy too. She had a pretty fair idea what she was in for at the party. A lot of questions from people Walter had described in detail. The person she was most afraid of meeting was his mother. She wanted Joy to like her and although she had pestered Walter for information about her, he wasn't very good at explaining his mother. All Laura really knew about her was that she was tall. She was afraid of meeting David Nussbaum too. Laura didn't trust shrinks. But despite her misgivings, she was looking forward to meeting Walter's past. It had to be done. She would make them love her.

On the day of the party, Robin Mooney shot one more blast of Final Net hairspray on her platinum coif. She was now wearing it in a perky pageboy, and thought the new style made her look younger. She had chosen a filmy white pantsuit to wear for the festivities and you could see her legs right through the sheer material. The top was sleeveless, long and flowy, and her husband told her she looked like a pixie. Joy and David were already here, outside talking to Allan at the barbecue. Tina and Nina were in the kitchen finishing up forming all the hamburger patties. Tanya was somewhere, being bored and fifteen. Robin was feeling positive. She was born to be a hostess and relished her role. She looked out the bathroom window at the backyard. The new above-ground pool twinkled blue and sunny, and the patio lanterns swung in the breeze. Allan was tinkering with the barbecue and talking to David and Joy. Everyone had taken a beer from the cooler and the sounds of Nina and Tina laughing in the kitchen floated down the hall. Family. It was a solid thing, thought Robin, as she lit a cigarette. Allan looked good today. She had forced him onto a diet the past month and he looked trim and handsome in his white slacks and navy blue golf shirt. In Robin's judgment, David looked a bit nerdy. He was wearing khaki shorts and a short-sleeved tan shirt. He looked like an archeologist. His legs were white and skinny and Joy towered over him in her blue wedgie sandals. Robin never did understand what Joy saw in David, but knew her friend well enough to realize it wasn't his money. Joy didn't buy into things like that. She had alluded to his voracious sexual appetite though. And Joy looked stunning today, Robin graciously noted.

She was wearing her new halter dress that flared out at her knees. A pretty shade of blue, Robin couldn't pinpoint what shade exactly, and she was wearing a darling pillbox hat that she must have pinned to her curls because it sat on such a jaunty angle. Robin was feeling very loving of her friends today and was mighty pleased she had thought of throwing this bash. She leaned her head against the window frame and took another drag of her cigarette.

"Robin?"

Robin turned and saw Tanya slouching at the door. Sometime during the past year, Tanya had dropped the grandmother label.

"Yes honey?" she said, tossing her cigarette in the toilet and flushing it.

"Can I go for a swim?"

"Sure you can. Anything you want, sweetie."

"Thanks."

And Tanya loped down the hall to change into her bathing suit. She was a real stunner, like her mother and her twin auntie. Long blond hair, long skinny legs and boobies that would have felt at home on a twenty-year-old's chest. Robin watched her go and then looked in the mirror. Tina had never told anyone who the father was. She had been totally unbending on that score. Robin had always suspected one of the older Carmichael boys and every time she saw Tanya she would squint real hard, searching for a resemblance. But the Mooney genes were all over her. There was nothing of her daddy, whoever that might be, unless he was a truly blond Scandinavian. And there was no one like that in Agincourt. It must have been some boy at Stephen Leacock, Tina's high school. Maybe some Nordic basketball player. Robin wondered if it would always be a secret, and although she and Allan had hammered at Tina for the boy's name at the time, she now grudgingly credited Tina with her obstinance. The last thing any of them needed was some goofy guy hanging around trying to horn in on the family. Robin patted her hair and reapplied lip gloss. *Her* family. *Her* beautiful blond family. The doorbell rang and Robin heard Tina yell out:

"Mom! Can you get that? Our hands are all covered in hamburger!"

Robin straightened her back and flowed silkily out of the bathroom.

"Coming!" she trilled.

Walter and Laura were standing with Nova and Johnny on the front steps of the Mooneys' home. They had carpooled in Johnny's beat-up 1972 green Gran Torino, and spent the better part of the drive up the Don Valley Parkway telling Laura what to expect. She had been fairly quiet and sat in the back holding Walter's hand and smiling her mouse smile. He couldn't help her out at all because the closer they got to Agincourt, the more dislocated he felt. And now standing here, looking at his old house across the street, it all came blasting back to him. He remembered playing with Nina and Tina on this very same front lawn, the Cinderella game and Ali Baba and painting their toenails. He saw Adelaide's house, still deserted looking. Naturally, there had been some changes—the trees were taller, some houses were different colours, there were newer cars parked in driveways, but aside from those predictable advances, everything was as it had been. Walter could swear everything smelled like it used to. He didn't know how much use he was going to be for Laura and could only hope she would fit herself in somehow. It was all a bit much. She had only met Nova and Johnny for the first time on the way up and Walter was relieved Nova seemed to be behaving herself. But then again, she hadn't started drinking yet. Johnny had only managed a wink and a whispered *not bad* in his ear on their way to the car. And on the drive up, Walter had to keep shaking his head at the sight of Nova and Johnny in the front seat, talking and laughing like they had been intimate, which they had, and Nova sliding across the bench seat to lean her head on Johnny's shoulder.

"Kids!" sang Robin as she opened the door and clapped her hands together.

"Come on in!"

And so it began.

"Walter! My god, it's been a while. Where have you been hiding? You look wonderful!"

"You too, Mrs. Mooney."

"Johnny! Gracious, we haven't seen you around for a while either. Aren't you looking handsome. Where are your glasses?"

"I got contacts."

"And Nova, hello dear. I think we've met a couple of times before, haven't we? Of course, you're right. You look lovely."

"Thanks for inviting me."

"And who's this? Laura? Welcome to my home. I'm Robin. Please make yourself comfortable and help yourself to anything you like. My girls are in the kitchen and everyone else is outside."

Walter had to admit that Robin Mooney still looked really good and possibly tinier, if that were possible. They moved as one unit up the couple stairs and into the kitchen where Nina and Tina were throwing raw hamburger at each other.

"Spaz! Johnny!" they squealed in unison and ran to the sink to wash their hands.

They were still identically gorgeous. Walter couldn't tell them apart at first. For a joke, they had dressed in the same outfit for the party. Snug green jumpers with zippers down the front and matching green barrettes in their blond locks. Walter noticed their fingernails and toenails were painted the same shade of green. They were dazzling and bubbly and Walter hoped Laura wouldn't be intimidated by the dual assault. Nova could hold her own.

"Walter, you look totally the same!" said Nina, throwing her arms around him, while Tina ruffled Johnny's hair and grinned wickedly.

"You guys," Tina said. "You guys. This is just like old times."

But it wasn't like old times, thought Walter. Johnny had never been a big fan of the twins and Walter couldn't recall them ever socializing or playing together. And Tina had a teenage daughter who must be around here somewhere. Nova and Laura were new additions to this scene, this picture, and of course there was David Nussbaum and Clara's date, Clifford. If this were just like the old times, the Finch clan would be solo. While Tina and Nina were jabbering away to him and Johnny, Walter noticed that Nova was taking Laura out the door to the backyard.

"We'll go amuse ourselves while you guys catch up," Nova said.

People started filing into the party shortly after Walter's arrival. Clifford Klonsky had insisted on driving all the way from Unionville down to the Beaches to pick up Clara and then all the way back up to Agincourt. The trip would take him hours, but Clifford not only loved driving, he was a gentleman and old-school manners dictated he pick up his date in person. Everyone was concerned about him driving on the insane Don Valley, but as all would discover when they met him, nothing rattled Clifford Klonsky. He loved new experiences, he said. You take things one minute at a time, he said. You only live once.

After Cliff and Clara showed up unscathed, it didn't take long for everyone to fall in love with the sprightly silver-haired gent whose smooth face and bright blue eyes belied his eighty years. He had crazy white hair and a neatly trimmed moustache and reminded Walter of pictures he had seen of Albert Einstein. Everyone was as smitten with Clifford Klonsky as Clara was. He was dapper, there was no other word for it. A smart black blazer, pressed grey slacks, and a polished walking stick only added to his courtly charm. He appeared both serene and mischievous and Walter knew that if anyone could handle his grandmother, Clifford Klonsky would be up to the task. Clara had gone all out on her ensemble for the occasion and clanked and clinked every time she moved. Today she had squeezed herself into a dress that showed off her considerable crepey cleavage, something she seldom revealed to such a brazen extent. The low-cut emerald green dress was at least a couple of inches above her knees and her legs were displayed to good advantage. She had gone a bit overboard on the makeup and jewellery for a backyard barbecue and was choking in Chanel No. 5 perfume, but she beamed. The sight of Clara and Clifford Klonsky together made Walter feel optimistic. He still hadn't completely reconciled his feelings about David Nussbaum, and shuddered when he saw his stepfather cop a quick feel of Joy's ass when he thought no one was looking. Once the neighbourhood started swarming in, armed with food and two-fours of beer, it got easier to dissolve into the background and observe. While Nova was walking Laura around the yard, Walter found an unlikely ally in Tanya Mooney. He met her for the first time when he walked over to the pool to feel the water. She was suitably cynical and looked exactly like how he remembered Tina and Nina as teenagers.

"So, you must be Tanya," Walter had said to her when she lifted herself out of the water to lie on the pool deck.

"Who are you?" the nymph said, staring at him with haughtiness and boredom.

"Walter Finch," he said. "I used to play with your mom and your aunt."

"Oh, you're Spaz," said Tanya in a matter-of-fact voice. "I heard about you."

"Yeah? What did you hear?"

Tanya assessed him. He looked gormless.

"Not much," she said. "Nothing bad."

Walter felt let down. He had told Laura vivid stories of Tina and Nina. Had the twins remembered nothing of their childhood together? Had he been that inconsequential?

"So, your mom didn't tell you much about her childhood, about her friends?" he asked.

Tanya combed her wet hair and gazed around the backyard.

"She told me Johnny was a pig. And his brothers were convicts."

Walter stifled a smile. He was dying to ask Tanya if she knew who her father was, but resisted.

"Is she your girlfriend?" Tanya asked, pointing at Laura who was still talking to Nova.

"Yeah, I guess so," said Walter.

"You guess so?"

"Well, we haven't known each other that long, but I guess I'd like to think so," Walter admitted.

"She's pretty. I like her," Tanya pronounced. "What's her name? She suits you."

"Laura."

Tanya hugged her knees to her chest and looked at Walter.

"So how do you feel about your mom getting married? Do you like your new stepdad?"

"I don't really know him. If my mom's happy, then I guess I am. Does your mom have a boyfriend?"

"Not today," she said.

"Do you have a boyfriend?"

"Sort of."

Walter wondered if Tanya was still a virgin and realized Tina hadn't been much older than her daughter when she conceived her.

"How come your boyfriend isn't here?" asked Walter.

"My mom doesn't like him," said Tanya. "She thinks he's too old for me."

"How old is he?"

"Twenty-one. My mom doesn't get that I'm really mature for my age."

"I'm sure she's only trying to protect you," said Walter, believing the virgin question had now been answered.

"I don't need protecting. I'm way older than she thinks I am. Inside, I mean. I know stuff that she has no idea I know. Did you ever feel like that when you were a teenager?"

Walter looked at Tanya and realized that though she had inherited her mom's looks, she must have got her brains from her father. He wondered again who that would be.

"Yeah I did," Walter said. "I felt like that since I was a kid."

"You did?" Tanya asked. "Did you feel like you could protect yourself? You didn't need anybody else to do it for you, because nobody else could *get* you?"

Walter nodded in agreement.

"Totally. It was all up to me."

"Thank God," breathed Tanya. "Now I know why my mom didn't tell me much about you."

"Why?"

"Because she didn't get you."

Walter considered this. Tanya was probably right about that. Then Tanya grabbed his arm.

"Look," she whispered. "It's Adelaide. Mom told me all about her."

Walter looked up and saw a monster crashing into the yard. Adelaide was enormous. She looked like she should be wearing a collar and a leash. Like a circus animal.

"Have you met Adelaide before?" he asked Tanya, watching as people cleared a path for Adelaide.

"Not really. She's never around when we come over to visit," she said, still whispering. "But I feel sorry for her. My mom said everyone was mean to her except you."

"Really? Your mom said that?"

"Yeah, that's when I decided I'd like you."

"Thanks," said Walter, watching Adelaide with narrowed eyes, remembering.

Somebody dragged a huge wooden lawn chair over to Adelaide and seemed to be urging her to sit. But she was looking for Wadder. She had dressed up, and was the only one wearing more makeup than Clara. Walter thought: Now we know what happened to Baby Jane. Her hair had remained bright yellow, not dulling with age, but it was cut short and uneven. Then Walter noticed she was pulling an oxygen cylinder and had thin plastic tubes running into her nose. He felt a jolt, not static, but a punch of memory or sympathy. He said to Tanya: "There's someone who couldn't protect herself. It was her I wanted to protect."

"I totally see why my mom didn't like her," Tanya muttered.

Walter couldn't argue with that. And then Adelaide spotted him, flushing red underneath all the beige spackle liberally trowelled on her face. Ignoring all the neighbours trying to corral her into the deep chair, she heaved her way over to Walter, oxygen cylinder bumping along behind her on the grass. Walter and Tanya watched her approach.

"God, she's huge," breathed Tanya. "Poor woman."

And that's when Walter realized Adelaide was a woman. It hadn't occurred to him. After getting over the initial shock of seeing her, Walter had slotted her back into being a tubby girl. But she wasn't merely chubby or a girl anymore. She was a gargantuan woman who was moving towards him, blue eyes alight with recognition, dark sweat stains under her fat arms. Walter was mesmerized and couldn't move. Some people were standing stock still, watching. Others were ignoring her progress, trying to pretend she was a regular party guest, thinking it a kinder approach.

Adelaide was about two yards away from him and Walter fully expected her to throw herself at him in a suffocating hug. He braced himself.

But she didn't. She stopped short, at a respectable distance, and gave him a smile of such force it could have split an atom. Her breasts were somewhere down around her waist, unencumbered by a brassiere, hanging loose and large, and they heaved with the effort exerted from her walk. For what seemed like an entire minute, she simply stood there staring at him, her mouth hanging open in what looked like a silent laugh. Walter wondered if she had lost the ability to speak. Maybe she forgot how because nobody ever talked to her.

"Hi Adelaide," he said, taking a step towards her, hand outstretched.

She ignored his hand and stared, her pale gaze more focused than he remembered. She seemed to be trying to collect herself, or catch a breath, and for an instant Walter felt like crying.

"Wadder," she said finally. "Hi Wadder."

Her voice was deeper, more mature. It surprised him with its resonance.

"How have you been Adelaide?" he asked, smiling at her.

"I mitt you," she said.

"I missed you too," said Walter.

"Look," said Adelaide, bending her head to the ground and planting her feet further apart.

Walter looked. She was wearing low-heeled white leather pumps, the tops of her fat white feet bulging out like water balloons.

Adelaide moved her right foot forward.

"Wed," she said, looking up at Walter and grinning like a lunatic. "BAHA! Member?"

Walter kneeled down at her feet. It was an involuntary reaction. He put his hands around her huge ankles that were overflowing the shoes and he squeezed them.

"I remember," he said, looking up at her.

She wheezed with delight.

"I smart now," she said, nodding her head up and down.

Walter got to his feet.

"You certainly are," he agreed, and his hand made its way through the air to settle on her shoulder.

From there, it went to her face where he brushed her hair back. He had no idea why he was touching her, but felt he should. He wondered when the last time was that Adelaide had ever been touched.

"Wadder?"

"Yes, Adelaide," he replied, smoothing her hair back and wanting to hug her but afraid he'd pull the lines out of her nose or be crushed to death.

"I lub you," she said, pronouncing each word distinctly.

"Oh my god," whispered Tanya behind him.

But it didn't bother Walter in the slightest. He leaned forward and kissed Adelaide on her powdered damp forehead.

"I love you too," he said. "You're my special friend."

Adelaide's pale eyes filled with tears, but her smile remained fixed.

"I hab a job," she said. "I hab a good job."

"You do?" asked Walter, pleased. "Where do you work?"

"I hab a job at the senner. I fode close and put them in boxes for Mitt Back."

Adelaide stopped to catch her breath and Tanya leaned towards Walter.

"What did she say?"

"She said she works at some centre for a Mrs. Black. She folds clothes and puts them in boxes. She has a good job, she said."

"I know who that is," said Tanya. "It's the homeless shelter she's talking about. Mrs. Black runs it. It's on the other side of Birchmount. Mrs. Black is like, some kind of saint. Everyone knows her."

Adelaide had harnessed her breath and continued, obviously thrilled to be imparting something of her new life to her best friend. She spoke with deliberation.

"I go to the senner on a bus. I hab lunch at the senner and Mitt Back says I am best worker."

"Mrs. Black sounds really nice," said Walter.

"Mitt Black is my fend doo," said Adelaide. "Mitt Black and you."

"God," said Tanya.

"I'm so happy for you Adelaide," said Walter. "It sounds like a great job."

She laughed loudly, a brash donkey sound reminiscent of her earlier years. Adelaide probably would have said more, but Robin Mooney showed up looking like a speck of lint next to Adelaide.

"Adelaide honey," she said. "Wouldn't you like to sit down? Have a drink of lemonade?"

Adelaide looked down at Robin's tiny frame. It was Mitt Moo. Adelaide was very thirsty, now that she thought about it.

"Kay," she said agreeably, allowing herself to be directed back to the only chair that could withstand her weight.

"Bye Wadder," she said. "I hab lemonade."

"See you later Adelaide," said Walter, waving.

When life hands you a lemon...

"God," said Tanya. "That was amazing."

"What was?" asked Walter, watching Adelaide lurch her way to the wooden chair.

"I dunno. She loves you. You were great with her."

"I'm glad she has Mrs. Black in her corner," said Walter.

"Yeah, Mrs. Black," said Tanya. "I wish more people were like you and her. I wish more people would care about people like Adelaide."

Walter looked at Tanya and could see her fifteen-year-old mind working on it. He sensed true compassion. It didn't surprise him when he found out years later that Tanya had marched herself right into the homeless shelter and gotten herself a volunteer job there too. It didn't surprise him that she became social worker later. And although nobody knew it at the time of the party, Adelaide had made herself another special friend, one who would be there for her until the day she died at age sixty, far outliving what the doctors had predicted.

The next interruption came from Joy who magically materialized beside Walter.

"You haven't introduced me to Laura," was her pointed comment.

"Hi mom," he said, hugging her. "Congratulations."

"Thanks honey, but that's old news now. I want to meet Laura."

"Did you meet Cliff yet?"

"Yes I did. He's fantastic, isn't he? You'd never guess he's eighty."

"I know. Clara seems happy."

"I've never seen her like this," agreed Joy. "Maybe there will be another wedding."

She looked at Walter.

"If you don't introduce me to Laura, I'll start planning your own wedding."

"Mom."

"Laura Finch. Has a nice ring to it, doesn't it?"

"Christ mom," he said. "Okay, okay. I'll introduce you."

Joy smiled down at her son and patted him on his head.

"Good boy. Now where is she?"

"Over there, talking to Nova and Johnny."

"Great. How about those two anyway?"

Walter started walking towards them, towed by his mother.

"Yeah, why don't you start bugging them about getting married?"

"You know, I used to think you and Nova would get together. I never imagined her and Johnny."

"Me neither," said Walter, catching Laura's eye with a warning look. *Here we come. Get ready.*

Laura was more than ready. She'd been prepping for this moment for a long time and actually relished its imminent arrival. She'd been watching Joy Finch since she arrived. Walter was right. She was tall.

Nova spotted them and tugged Johnny's arm.

"Let's vanish," she said. "It's meet the mother time."

Johnny grimaced.

"You know, my mother is supposed to be here soon. You're gonna have to meet her too."

"I don't have to do anything," Nova said, but was curious about meeting Evelyn Carmichael. "Are any of your brothers showing up?"

"I have no idea. I doubt it."

"Are they as sexy as you?"

Johnny blushed.

"Shut up," he said, pleased.

Walter couldn't have predicted the instant camaraderie between Laura and Joy, but it could have been guessed by anyone who was intimately acquainted with the souls of the two women, like God. Or the devil would have known. Here was Joy Finch who had always wanted a daughter. Joy Finch who had always wanted to see her son married. Joy Finch who had once speculated about the sexual orientation of her uncoordinated son. It should come as no surprise to anyone with that knowledge of Joy Finch that she would be predisposed to fall in love with any girl who captured her son's attentions.

And Laura. Anyone who knew Laura's history could have guessed. Laura, whose mother died when Laura was way too young to have a dead mother. Laura, who craved a family. Laura, who had reasons for wanting Joy's acceptance at the very least, her love at best. Ordinary people, had they taken the time, may have been able to speculate about Joy's desires. But nobody could have guessed Laura's true motivation. God or the devil would know, but only the latter entity would have been happy about it.

Later, after a few drinks, Joy would tell Robin that she felt she had known Laura for years.

"I don't know, she has a way about her," Joy said. "It's like she fits right in."

Robin rolled her eyes and sucked back a gin and tonic.

"Please don't say she's like the daughter you never had," said Robin.

"Why not? Why can't I say that?"

"Because that's too weird, for one thing. That would mean your daughter is fucking your son, wouldn't it? And besides, daughters aren't all they're cracked up to be."

"You're just saying that because you have them," said Joy.

"Well, duh. Listen sweetie, they could break up tomorrow. Don't get all attached. That's all I'm saying."

Joy nodded and disregarded everything Robin had said. She looked at Laura who was talking to Johnny, shading her eyes with one hand. At first glance, she almost appeared plain until you got close enough to catch her unbelievably green eyes. And her hair had subtle pale streaks that showed up if she tossed her head. Joy noticed these things that brought her to life, that made her pretty. She had a slim, almost boyish figure and Joy guessed she had been athletic in school. Track and field probably. Or swimming. But mostly it was her eyes and the way her eyes looked at Joy that cinched the deal. It was a daughterly look, mixed with polite respect. Joy was drawn to this green-eyed girl in ways she couldn't articulate.

"You'd like anyone who liked Walter," Robin had stated, dragging on her long cigarette and blowing a smoke ring.

"I wouldn't like it if he dated a speed freak," said Joy, dragging her finger through the smoke ring.

"Well sure, a speed freak. That's extreme, isn't it?"

"I wouldn't like it if he dated someone as old as us or as young as Tanya, either," said Joy.

"Well, Tanya's jailbait. But what's wrong with an older woman? Someone like Anne Bancroft in *The Graduate*? Or, what if she was really old and rich and eccentric and died after a couple years and left Walter all her money? What about then?"

"Well okay, maybe if she was rich and had a terminal disease, that would be okay," she said.

"So, barring juveniles and delinquents, I'm right. You'd like anyone who liked Walter," said Robin smugly.

"I guess...but I really like Laura. That's all I'm saying. She seems real." Robin crunched a gin-flavoured ice cube.

"Real is good. At least she's not a blow-up doll."

David Nussbaum took this moment to show up at the ladies' sides.

"Talking about me?" he asked.

"You wish," they both said at once.

Joy slung her arm around her new husband's waist but her thoughts were still on Walter and Laura. She was planning what she'd make for dinner when she invited them over. Maybe have Cliff and Clara too, she thought. Nova and Johnny. A nice pork roast would be good, she decided. With mashed potatoes and some of her homemade applesauce on the side. Something light for dessert, like trifle. While the new Mrs. Nussbaum pondered her menu, David's hand crept up her left side, swooningly close to her breast. He was a sex maniac.

Other partygoers trickled in, bringing plates of food, bottles of booze and extra lawn chairs. Joy was pleased and surprised to see wedding presents piling up. Reginald and Sabrina waltzed in, Reginald lugging a cooler filled with multi-coloured sorbet balls and gourmet doggie treats. He deposited a neatly wrapped gift alongside the others, two sterling silver wine goblets engraved with naked Cupids. Reginald was wearing casual yet stylish summer clothes, the only obvious affectation being a silk powder blue ascot that matched the one Sabrina was sporting around her neck. Sabrina was a hit, the perfect icebreaker. Evelyn Carmichael and her red-faced salesman husband Clay made a rowdy entrance, giving everyone else permission to loosen up. Ivy was laying salads out in the shade while Mr. Q and Allan Mooney began rigging up a record player to accommodate the 78s of swing music. The pace was picking up, in direct proportion to the amount of booze being consumed. This was the moment Walter had waited for. He felt blended in enough to hang with Laura and not feel they were on display.

"I really like your mom," she said, popping the cap off a beer and passing it to him. "She has a kind of dignity about her."

Walter gulped down some beer and looked sideways at Laura, who was too perfect to be true.

"Dignity? Are we looking at the same people?" he asked, waving one arm at the colourful suburban backyard display.

There they were: Adelaide the monster, huffing oxygen and spilling lemonade down her top, Reginald looking like he'd be more at home at Wimbledon, Tina and Nina, the identical Stoner Barbies, David Nussbaum the sickly white archeologist trying unsuccessfully to hide his lust for his bride, Robin who was beginning to resemble a tipsy Tinkerbell, the loud Carmichaels, Cliff and Clara, the hyper Sabrina, and the list went on.

"I see a certain dignity to all of this," Laura said. "But I was talking about your mom. She must have had it rough, raising a kid alone and living with her mother. But she looks really serene. She's very beautiful, you know."

Walter looked at his mother, all dolled up in her new dress and hat, laughing. The woman of the hour.

"She doesn't think so," he said. "She's always hated being so tall."

"None of us think so," said Laura. "None of us women."

Walter looked at his date and something slipped out of his mouth. Something he didn't plan on saying.

"Did your mother think she was beautiful?"

But Laura seemed to take this first mention of her mother in stride.

"No, but everyone else thought so. I thought so."

"She must have been," was all Walter could think to say.

"She was dignified," said Laura, sipping her beer. "She was a singer and I always remember her wearing long dresses. Gowns and gloves. I remember her getting all dressed up at night to go to work and tucking me in before she left."

Walter stared at her. He didn't know whether to press the point or not. A singer?

"What did she sing?" he ventured.

"She was a lounge singer. Classical, jazz, standards. She usually worked with a piano player. And she'd stand by the piano, like you see in the movies, singing to guys in suits with their wives or their mistresses, usually in hotels. She made a few albums. I've got them still."

"Wow," breathed Walter. "That's great. I'd like to hear them sometime."

Laura appeared not to hear him.

"I was brought up with dignity. I know it when I see it, and your mom has it too. She has a different kind of dignity though, not the showy, glamorous kind like my mom had. But a quieter, gentler kind. I recognize it. That's probably why I like your mom."

Walter swallowed. He had never thought of his mother as dignified before, but looking at her now, surrounded by the eclectic characters of Agincourt, he thought he might be able to see it. He still didn't see what she was doing with Nussbaum. She was far too dignified.

"He's probably good in bed," said Laura, reading Walter's thoughts by following his gaze.

"What?"

"The shrink. My bet is that he's good in bed."

Walter's gut contracted. On the one hand, the thought of his mother having sex with the shrink disguised as an archeologist was frightening and disgusting. But on the other hand, Laura had mentioned sex, which gave him instant stomach flips. She had used the words "good in bed." Which means, Walter thought uneasily, she must have some kind of sliding scale on which she rates a sexual performance. She must know what "good in bed" means. God, he had no idea if he was. He wished she had never said that.

"Does the thought of your mom having sex bother you?" she asked, peering at his face which was probably as green as the jellied salad Ivy was uncovering.

"No, I guess not. The thought of her having sex with *him* does though," said Walter.

"Yeah, shrinks. Do you think he psychoanalyzes their sex life?"

"God, I don't know. Let's stop talking about it," said Walter, feeling uncomfortable about anyone's sex life being analyzed.

"Okay. Do you want to go say hi to your boss?"

Walter looked at Reginald who was surrounded by the Agincourt regulars exclaiming over Sabrina. He looked well taken care of and pleased to be the centre of attention, even if these weren't exactly his people, whatever his people were.

"Not really," said Walter. "I'd rather talk to you, as long as we stop talking about my mother and David."

"Okay," said Laura, leaning against him and casually slipping her hand in Walter's back pocket like it was the most natural thing in the world to do.

Her hand is on my ass, thought Walter. My ass is in her hand. His knees dissolved and he didn't know what to do with his own hands. They felt large and jerky, like he had no control over them. Like his fingers could snap open at any moment and clamp onto her breast without his permission. His ass was on fire. His dick was surging, like a dolphin breaching the waves. And for some insane reason, all he could think about was: How would David Nussbaum psychoanalyze this?

But David Nussbaum was off the clock and didn't give a shit. He was too busy psychoanalyzing his own stiffening dick and wondering if there was any way he could get Joy alone for a minute. He pictured her sitting at the picnic table, and himself underneath it on all fours like Sabrina. He imagined prying Joy's knees apart and nosing his way up between her thighs. He licked his lips and swore he could taste her on them. David Nussbaum thought he was the luckiest man in the world and if he allowed himself one thought to his psychiatrist's couch today, it would be to picture his brand new bride lying naked on it, long limbs draped loosely over the sides. And he, the esteemed Dr. Nussbaum, getting inside more than her head—pushing his professional prick inside his patient, tape recorder rolling, picking up his best doctor voice: "How do you feel today Mrs. Nussbaum, how do you FEEL, how do you *FEEEEEL?*"

He may have looked nerdy, but there was a reason David Nussbaum was wearing baggy shorts today. And despite Joy's belief that he was a sexaholic, the good doctor knew he wasn't. The luscious Mooney twins, for instance, didn't create so much as a stir down below. Nor did the fresh teenage charms of Tanya, or the see-through petiteness of Robin. Dr. Nussbaum only had eyes and ardour for one woman: the statuesque Mrs. Nussbaum née Finch. There was only one dress he wanted to rip off with his teeth, and it was a peacock blue halter dress. This was his one and only Joy.

Joy wasn't so single-minded in her focus today. David's presence was always encircling her, his desires apparent every time he stood close behind her. She was grateful she aroused such passion and devotion. But she gave no thought whatsoever to indulging in any sort of quickie during the party. If she thought about sex at all with her new husband, she would visualize it happening later, in their new bed when they got home. If they made it that far. Knowing David, she'd be half naked before they got the key in the lock. She smiled, thinking about it. He was the devil.

But she had other things on her mind. Her son and Laura, mostly. After observing them the entire afternoon she guessed correctly they hadn't had sex yet. She wondered why. Walter was obviously head over heels and Laura seemed natural and open. She didn't seem like an uptight princess, or a frigid virgin. She seemed organic and artistic. Joy sensed a great passion beating in Laura's breast. A great sadness maybe, with the loss of her parents. Whatever it was, it was an empty space that needed filling. Joy believed her son could do that. Unlike Walter, who would rather die than picture any intimacy between his mother and his new stepdad, Joy visualized her son and Laura together. She wished it for both of them, maybe because she was getting so much. Walter needed something to devote himself to, besides shoes. He had his creative outlet, now he needed an emotional one. This is what Joy believed. She couldn't have been more right.

And right when she was thinking about wandering over and talking to them, David sneaked up behind her and whispered: "I want to taste your Joy juice."

Aside from Joy's random speculations and motherly curiosity, there wasn't nearly as much critical attention being directed at Laura as Walter had feared, and for this, he was thankful. The two women he had been most worried about as potential interrogators were Nova and Clara. Thank christ for the presence of Johnny and Clifford at this backyard shindig. He could have kissed Clifford Klonsky. Walter entertained an image of Clara moving to the hobby farm and Laura moving into the hotel. And then he caught his mother's eye and he knew she had been thinking the same thing. He smiled bashfully at her and she lit up. Then David whispered something in her ear and she turned a thousand shades of red. Walter looked away, embarrassed.

Laura was feeling as snug in this setting as her hand was in Walter's pocket. It surprised her, this feeling of belonging, because her mother's friends had been nothing like this. They had been all show biz. Glitzy, but good-hearted, looking after her backstage while her mother performed. And although her father also worked a lot of late nights, he definitely wasn't show biz.

"I could never marry a musician," her mother had confided to her once. "One big ego is enough around here."

So she married a carpenter, which seemed safe and normal enough, until he began refurbishing and renovating yachts. That's when the late nights started up. The long hours, the meetings with rich men, and the beginnings of an elite boat refinishing business. Laura's father had a knack for shmoozing and an eye for design, and together those qualities soon made his talents indispensable in a certain naughty nautical crowd. But while his business picked up speed, his marriage began sinking. And as far as Laura's place was concerned, her nights were often spent alone while her parents pursued their different paths. They loved her, of course. Her mother showed it with extravagant gestures, public displays of affection, and expensive gifts. Her father was more low-key. His gifts were things he made with his hands, wooden dolls when she was a child, and later, handmade jewellery. He didn't kiss her much, except when she went to bed at night, whereas her mother was forever leaving bright red lipstick marks on her cheeks and forehead and hugging her until she felt she would break in two. From her father, Laura would get a quiet smile when he was proud of her. Like the first time he took her out on a boat and let her have the wheel. He stood beside her, tall and silent, one hand resting on her shoulder, both of them facing into the wind and feeling the salty spray from the Pacific Ocean. Laura had glanced up at her father once and he had been looking down at her with a mixture of pride and love and something else that looked like regret. At the time, Laura figured he was sad that her mother wasn't there. She was wrong about that.

"You've got a knack for this, Lolo," he had said.

And her heart sang a song of sixpence and it was the best day ever. From that day on, most of her time spent with her father was on a boat. Her mother would get seasick in a Jacuzzi.

Laura observed the Agincourt creatures with keen interest. It didn't escape her attention that of everyone here, Walter came closest to what she had grown up with. He had her mother's creativity and her father's work ethic. And as far as she knew, Walter was the only one here with a nickname. Nicknames were big in the Booth household. Laura's mother, known in entertainment circles as Delilah Booth, was called Lila around the house.

"Lolo and Lila, my two best girls," her father would say, and always in that order.

He had been saddled with Boo, a pet name bestowed upon him by

Lila and eventually picked up by everyone who knew them. It was an un-shakeable moniker and made for fun games when Laura was a child.

"Knock knock."

"Who's there?"

"Boo."

"Boo who?"

"Why are you crying?"

Or when her father would jump out and yell "BOO!" and then sweep her up in his arms if she looked too startled. Laura missed them both dreadfully.

It's natural to compare, thought Laura. And here was Walter who could draw as well as her mother could sing, and who could design shoes as well as her father could design boats. And he had a nickname and it was Spaz. It all made sense to her.

"My dad used to call me Lolo," she said, slipping her hand out of Walter's pocket.

Walter looked down at her, feeling like his ass had caved in. This was really something, he thought. First her mother, now her father. Maybe this party was a good idea after all. It seemed to be drawing her out.

"Lolo," he said, trying it out. "I like it. What was your dad's name?"

Laura smiled at him, picturing her dad's face superimposed on Walter's.

"Boo. We called him Boo. And my mother was Lila, but her singing name was Delilah. We all had pet names for each other."

Walter didn't want to ask any more questions. Instead he reached out his hand and looped Laura's hair behind her ear.

"Lolo and Lila," he said. "That's nice."

"And Boo."

He thought about his own nickname and it didn't seem like such a bad thing anymore. Laura may have lost Lila and Boo, but she still had Spaz. And he wasn't going anywhere.

The party raged on, with the usual mishaps and comedies. Adelaide sat on a woven lawn chair and fell right through it, causing Tina and Nina to shriek with laughter, like the old days. Tanya was the first one at

Adelaide's side, shooting looks of disgust over her shoulder at her mother and her auntie. Sabrina was the second one at the scene, jumping and licking and yelping. Clay Carmichael mooned everyone from the pool deck and then fell over face first into the water, still clutching his beer. Mr. Q tap danced on the picnic table to an old song called "Paddlin' Madeline Home," and put his foot right into the potato salad his wife had spent an hour making. Ray, Johnny's brother, actually put in an appearance and Tina and Nina greeted him by unzipping their green jumpers and simultaneously flashing their identical boobs at him. Robin eyed Ray critically, wondering if he was Tanya's dad. Nova and Johnny ducked into the house and had what they thought was surreptitious sex in the bathroom, but everyone could hear them and began hooting and throwing food at the open window. Jaunty old Cliff got into the action, stripping off his shirt at one point to show off a huge ship tattoo on his chest and flex his pecs like Jack LaLanne. Clara beamed as if she had stuck the needles into his skin herself.

Walter swam in the flow of the party. He mingled, asked and answered questions, did what he always did at a party. He was the perfect cheese platter. But after a few hours, he realized he had moved on. At first he had tried to get it up for the past. When Mr. Q mentioned the old wing shoes, Walter had a fleeting moment of nostalgia. But when he tried talking about his new holly shoes, Mr. Q's eyes glazed over.

"But how about those wing shoes?" he repeated. "Those were sure something. I thought by now you'd have made real flying shoes."

Walter could only smile and say things like: "Yeah, I'm working on it."

After talking to Nina and Tina, Walter soon realized that any common ground they had once played on together was now nothing more than artificial turf. As far as the twins were concerned, the Beaches seemed like another country. They seldom got out of Scarborough, unless it was to make a trip to downtown Toronto and shop at the Eaton Centre. And they were not impressed by Walter's job. In their eyes, he had always been a shoe salesman, and still was. Big whoop. From the twins' perspective, Walter hadn't done anything remarkable. From his perspective, the only remarkable thing about the twins was Tanya.

He did get a glow seeing Adelaide again. Walter believed she had made more strides than anyone else in Agincourt. She had a job that made her feel good, for one thing. She had pride. And she had a loving spirit. Maybe her mental handicap didn't allow for cynicism. Maybe it was impossible for her to feel jaded. Walter wondered. Every time he glanced at her during the party, she had a big stupid smile on her face. She was morbidly obese, had tubes running out of her nose, and food all over her blouse, but she was smiling to beat the fucking band. Any time she caught Walter looking at her, her smile grew. He felt happy and re-assured. The girl least likely to succeed had fooled everyone.

It was around seven o'clock when Laura said to Walter: "Why don't you come back to my place tonight?"

Eight billion thoughts rushed through his head. He would get to see her place. He would have to tell his mother they wouldn't be staying over. They would have to call a cab. Laura was inviting him into her private domain. And overriding all these thoughts was the big one. *What does that mean? Does that mean sex? Does that mean he would have to be "good in bed"? Oh god.*

He said: "I'd love to."

"Good," said Laura, putting her hand on his leg. "I'd like some time alone with you. So we can talk."

Walter covered her hand with his own.

"I'd like that," he said. "I'd like to see where you live."

He was thinking about her last four words: So we can talk. Maybe that's all she wanted to do. Maybe now that she had started opening up about her parents, she wanted to talk more about her past, her family. Maybe she was drunk. Maybe he was a fucking moron.

"Will your mom be disappointed we're not staying?" asked Laura.

"Probably, but I'm sure she'll understand if we want to go," said Walter, feeling more ready to leave with each passing second, now that the idea had been planted.

Joy was totally okay with it. The more time her son spent alone with Laura, she mused, the more chances of potential grandchildren. David

Nussbaum was thrilled. Two less people in the house to hear his love-making. Nova and Johnny were getting pretty gunned with Ray, and Walter's defection didn't seem to register. Clara and Reginald said they would see him soon. And everyone else simply said goodbye and went back to their conversations. The only two people who seemed genuinely sorry to see Walter go were Adelaide and Tanya. He kissed and hugged them both with great affection, and when he left to call a cab, Tanya grabbed Adelaide's hand and held onto it.

Walter gave them all one last look, walked back through the house with Laura, and closed the door.

# 28 }

**Laura's apartment was much smaller** and more compact than the hotel. Walter walked around it, running his hands over books and plants and wooden carvings like a cat leaving his scent, while she opened a bottle of wine at the kitchen counter. She could have lived in a cave with bats for all he cared. He heard the cork pop out of the wine bottle, a gunshot to his crotch. The wine gurgled and splashed into glasses, and he felt like he was wetting his pants.

"Do you want to put something on the stereo?" asked Laura.

She was standing behind the counter, looking into the living room at him.

"Maybe you should do that," he said. "My taste in music isn't that great. But is there anything else I can do to help?"

Laura tossed him a lighter.

"Sure. Any candle you see, light it. I'll take care of the tunes."

Walter missed the lighter like a true spaz and was on his hands and knees looking for it when Laura breezed into the living room. She set the wine down on a low coffee table and looked at him with amusement. He found the lighter under a chair and snatched it up.

"I know," he said, getting to his feet. "Can't walk, can't catch. I guess you've figured out I wasn't a jock in school."

She began flipping through CDs. "That's okay. I wasn't a cheerleader."

"Great," said Walter, beginning to light candles. "It's a match made in heaven."

Laura selected a Miles Davis CD. "Or hell," she said, pressing play.

He looked at her, but she only smiled at him and shrugged.

"If it's a good match, who cares where it's made," she said. "I think heaven might be highly overrated."

"Hell, yeah," said Walter, who would agree with anything that came out of her mouth.

"Do you mind if I change?" Laura asked.

"Into something more comfortable?" asked Walter, daring to dream.

"Something without barbecue sauce on it," she said, moving behind a bamboo room divider. "Relax. Have some wine."

Walter sat on a futon couch and stretched his legs out. God, he was here. The Agincourt party was a distant memory. He was here, listening to Miles Davis by candlelight while Laura slipped into something more comfortable. What could be better? Nothing. If someone offered him a million dollars to get up and leave this cloud he was sitting on, he would laugh at the very idea. If this was heaven, it wasn't overrated. If this was heaven, Miles Davis was Gabriel, Laura Booth was an angel, and he, Walter Finch, was most definitely God. If this was heaven, everyone else could go straight to hell.

Laura had planned on changing into her kimono, but thought it might look too suggestive as it had a habit of coming untied. She settled on the next most comfortable thing and slipped a baggy cotton sundress over her head that buttoned all the way down the front to her ankles. Humming along to the CD, she twisted her hair up into a loose knot on top of her head and secured it with a couple of bobby pins. She felt a bit nervous. There were things she wanted to talk about with Walter tonight. Serious things. But she also wanted to simply enjoy the evening in his company. Shadows from her rubber tree snaked across the bamboo divider, flickering from the candlelight in the other room, and Miles' trumpet underscored her mood that also flickered. The beers she had drunk at the party made her feel mellow but not out of it. She was craving a glass of red wine and a cigarette. But more, she was craving a good outcome, whatever that might be.

God was sitting on the couch feeling pretty good about himself when she appeared like a vision from behind the screen. He actually stood up for her entrance, as if she were royalty.

"Sit, silly," she said, and floated down onto a cushion on the floor.

Gabriel's trumpet wept and God crumbled into dust in her presence.

The angel picked up her wine and tilted her head at Walter who had plunged from holy grace and was now struggling with an entirely mortal erection. In the shadowy room, her eyes looked darker than usual, with points of light floating in them. He couldn't see the green—everything had turned to shades of dark and light. Her dress white, her tanned skin dark against it. Her feet, bare for the first time today, sparkled with toenail polish. It did not escape Walter's attention that she was wearing silver glitter again. It seemed like a good omen. Laura was holding her wineglass out for a toast and he remembered the first day she had been at his apartment. They had toasted to surprises, he recalled. He believed they had moved beyond surprises into something else now. Discovery, maybe. Surprises are unexpected, but discovery can be a process. Walter liked to think they were now in a process, on a path. And maybe there would be surprises along the way, but the important thing was, they were moving. He held his glass out.

"To discovery," he said, pleased with his choice.

Laura hesitated and then clinked his glass.

"To discovery," she affirmed.

Walter drank and watched her over the rim of his glass. Her eyes were closed as she drank her wine and he wondered what she was thinking about. He wished she would get up off the floor and sit beside him on the couch. Of course he could join her on the floor, but that would look awkward. She was so much more fluid than he was. And he wanted this entire night to be fluid. He stretched his legs out again and Laura, sitting cross-legged, pulled his feet into her lap. She began undoing the laces on his desert boots as if she had done this before.

"Do you mind?" she asked, before pulling them off.

"God, no," said Walter.

And off they came. Grasping the tops of his socks, she looked at him questioningly.

"Go ahead," he said, hoping his feet weren't rank.

And she unrolled the socks, tucking them neatly in his boots. She laid her hands on his bare feet and he shivered.

"Do you dance?" she asked.

"Yes."

"Do you want to?"

"What, dance?"

"Yes."

"Now?"

"Yes, right now. I feel like dancing."

"Okay, sure."

Walter didn't really feel like dancing but he did feel like touching her. And if dancing was the way to go about it, then count him in. Besides, he was good at it. She released his dancing feet and stood, holding out her hand. He leapt up like a cat and assumed the traditional waltz position. She curtsied and stepped into it, keeping the respectable and formal distance between their torsos. They stood poised, Laura on tippytoes.

"Madam," said Walter solemnly.

"Sir."

And he took the first step forward and she followed. He guided her effortlessly around the cramped space without mishap and she marvelled at his grace and rhythm.

"You're a really good dancer," she murmured, relaxing into it.

"Only as good as my partner."

"Did you take lessons?"

"I grew up with two women, remember?"

And for the next couple of minutes there was no more talking, only the sound of Miles Davis and the swishing of Laura's dress. She let herself go with it, dropped her guard. Eyes closed, she imagined herself at a grand ball as Walter guided her with finesse. She felt guilty for thinking he would be clumsy, for thinking she would be the one in control. *To discovery.*

Walter was riding the flow, his lady love in his arms. He was masterful, a barefoot prince. He alternated between losing himself in the moment and wondering if he should be planning the next one. Should he dip her at the end of the song, lean over and kiss her? Should he sweep her up in his arms and carry her to the bed, wherever the hell that might be? Or should he simply bow and kiss her hand like a gallant gentleman? His personal favourite was the bed idea. But if she didn't go for it, he would feel like a loser and the night could be ruined. He spun her expertly and tried to concentrate on the moment, on her. In the candlelight she was ethereal, an elfin princess, a beam of light. She was radiance in his hands and this should be enough. If it weren't for the erratic surging in his crotch every time her dress brushed his bare foot, it would be enough.

All these thoughts collided and cancelled each other out when the song ended. Without any premeditation, he dipped her because it was a natural move, an automatic *denouement*. They hung there, bent over, and her hair spilled out of its hastily pinned knot as her head fell back. She was weightless. He could have held her forever like this, staring at her outstretched neck. This is what he kissed, her white neck. And then swooped her back upright to face him, one arm still around her waist, steadying her. She was out of breath from the rapid ascent, her hair dishevelled, eyes glowing. She reached out a hand and touched his face, like he was a wax museum replica. Like she didn't believe he was real. Whereas his clunky walking had become endearing, his dancing shattered her. In her mind, he had transformed from shy, crippled shoeshine boy to suave and classy gentleman. How had this happened? She could deal with the former, but the latter was disconcerting at best. He removed her hand from his face and pressed the inside of her wrist to his lips. He didn't know what else to do. He was a man without a plan.

And Miles Davis started up again. A cue. He took a step back, executed a bow and held out his arms, an invitation to dance another. Laura obliged and he swept her up and away, his feet steady on course, his thoughts all over the map. The longer they danced, the more Laura was enthralled. She remembered wanting to talk to Walter tonight about important things. She wanted to enlighten him, lay her cards on the table so to speak. It would have been so much easier discussing these things with the average boy who had drank beer with her earlier at a suburban backyard barbecue. But to tell this man who danced her like a fantasy, whose face looked so stunning in candlelight? She didn't want to break the spell, and against her better judgment, she surrendered to the dance.

Walter felt it rip through him. Whatever she had been holding back, she had given it up. He didn't know this in so many words. He sensed it, the same way you know your heart is beating without actually hearing it. He acted on it spontaneously and pulled her in, twirling in intricate circles, her body now pressed up against his, following, around and around, their faces inches apart, spinning into what would surely have to end in a major kiss. The power balance had shifted and for once Walter not only had it, he knew he did. This time when the song ended, he wove his fingers through her hair, lowered his face and kissed her deeply before he could change his mind. When he felt her acquiescence, Walter grew. There was no other word for it. His chest opened up and warmth poured out. Walter had the sense that he was finally being fitted into his own skin. He felt solid, complete, and if someone cut his flesh, it wouldn't be blood that would escape. It would be lava. Self-confidence was coursing through him, an entirely unnatural feeling for the Spaz-man, unless it came to shoes. He relished it. His cock felt superhuman at the moment, a cross between godlike and satanic. And all this time, his dance partner's mouth was wet and receptive and following *his* lead, and why? Because he was the man, goddammit. He *is* the man.

Midnight. A cliché. A naked man and a naked woman sitting up in bed, sharing a cigarette after sex. To anyone else's view, the scene would hardly be worth commenting on. It's a scene played out countless times in bedrooms in countless countries, cities, towns, villages, hamlets, castles, shacks, wigwams and igloos. But in Walter's view, it's as bright and shiny and new as the original sin. He is the first man to walk the earth, Laura is the first woman, and nobody can take this moment away from him. He would kill anyone who tried. He took a drag and passed the cigarette to Laura. Their fingers touched. She took the cigarette and draped her leg over his, sighed. He was hard again. Already. It's unfuckingbelievable, this. He was filled up. All the empty corners and spaces that he wasn't aware he possessed were flooded. But Walter sensed within himself an infinite capacity to keep receiving. Bring it on, he thought. More, I can take more of this. And the reason, he believed, is because whatever this goodness is—this golden light, this warmth—it was pouring out of him as quickly as it was coming in. He was giving up buckets of himself. She passed the cigarette back and he took a drag, blowing the smoke out luxuriously. What's more, he thinks with great satisfaction, I was good in bed. In fact, I was *more* than good in bed. I killed it.

Laura wasn't thinking as figuratively as Walter was. She was far more literal, ticking off details. His mouth, his hands, his cock, his smell, his skin. And she was thinking about how she literally got swept away by his dancing. And how he fucks like he dances. Otherworldly, she thinks. There was no obvious transition that she could pinpoint. One minute they were dancing in the living room and the next, waltzing under the sheets. But it was no Minute Waltz. She snuggled closer and slipped her hand under the sheet. This time, she wanted to lead. He turned his body and pulled her close. Laura felt like she belonged to this moment. Walter felt like he owned it. And talking was out of the question.

# 29 }

**Walter woke up to find** a girl's arm lying across his chest, a girl's head on his shoulder, a girl's thigh resting on his groin. *His* girl. Had he ever not had a boner in the last fifteen hours? Whose life was this? She moved, a sleepy sigh escaped. He wanted to welcome her to this day, pin her to it. He trailed his fingers up her thigh and rested his palm on her ass. He couldn't believe she was naked beside him and moving into his touch. This is permission, he thinks with relief, this is proof that last night happened. He found her mouth first, said hello like a lover would, and continued the conversation down her body. If she answered, he would taste it. If the answer was yes, he would drink until he was blind.

Two hours later the new lovers had pulled themselves off each other. Laura had made a breakfast fit for truckers, enjoying the kitchen ritual, the wifely role. Pancakes, scrambled eggs, fried potatoes, ham and toast and blueberries. A post-fuck feast. Walter was sitting on her couch, thumbing through one of her detective novels, hair still wet from a shower. They ate at the coffee table, sitting on the floor side by side, their backs against the couch. Walter was wearing Laura's kimono and she wore a plain white slip. They fed each other, kissed, tumbled onto the floor, took a cigarette and coffee break, ate more, touched each other, gulped juice, laughed and wondered. They wanted to say things like *you move me*. But they didn't. They said things like *pass the syrup, please*. They wanted to make love again, but they didn't. They licked butter off each other's fingers. They wanted to ask *what are you doing later today?* But instead they asked *do you want another coffee?*

Finally, they were full.

**282**

Walter looked at Laura who had lain down on the floor, fingers interlaced over her tummy. His erection had parted the black kimono and he glanced down at himself with disbelief. The curtains were still drawn and the room was dark enough to light a candle, which he did, and heard Laura murmur *that's nice*. He surveyed the scene. Leftover food on plates, empty wine glasses from last night, the smell of stale cigarette smoke, and he remembered the dancing. He could almost see it, two ghost dancers waltzing around the room, his big break. The Spaz-man had seized the moment and effortlessly, flawlessly, steered them both into bed where the rhythm continued. He sipped some lukewarm coffee and replayed whatever he could remember. There was nothing specific. They fit, that's all he could think. One day it was just him, and then it wasn't. And now, sitting in this afternoon room, all hazy and messy, he was super horny. Everything before breakfast had been dream-like, surreal. But right now he was feeling very real. Right now he was of this blood and bone world, hyper aware of every nerve ending twitching under his skin. If she touched him right now, he was positive his skin would crackle. Walter had to do something with this energy, this pent-up whatever the fuck it was. He looked at her lying on her back, eyes closed, in her short white slip. She looked too peaceful to ram with his heat-seeking missile, which is what he felt like doing. Annihilation wasn't called for now, something subtler was needed. Walter's eyes travelled down her boyish body, rested on the preferred target, and moved further down to the inevitable. Of course, what else? Her perfect size seven-and-a-half feet, her silver glitter toes. His stomach dipped and he crawled over on his hands and knees like a jungle cat.

"You have the most perfect feet I've ever seen," he said, taking them in his hands.

"Mmm. Thank you."

"You do," he insisted. "I've seen a lot of feet."

"I'll bet you have."

Walter examined each toe with awe. Had he not spent hours ravishing the rest of her, this close proximity to her feet would surely have struck him down in some fashion. But luckily their power was diffused, absorbed into everything else he was experiencing. As it was, he could handle them without fainting or freezing. He pressed his thumbs into the balls of her feet, knowing which parts of a woman's foot took the most pressure. He knew where to rub, how to make them breathe.

"That feels good," Laura said.

It doesn't get much better than this, Walter thought for maybe the twentieth time. In the last twenty-four hours he had consistently proven himself. Dancing, sex, foot massage. Important things that pleased a woman. And he was good at them all, surprised at his own gifts. Her feet were dry and smooth and he ran his thumb down her arch, admiring its curve, its balance and form. He brought both feet up to his face and inhaled them, his nose touching her toes, the tip of his tongue on her skin. She breathed something quiet, approval. Walter laid her feet back on the floor and picked up the maple syrup bottle, unscrewing the cap. Not that her toes could be any sweeter than they already were, but he drizzled the syrup over them and lay on his belly, propped up on his elbows. One by one, he savoured her toes, sliding his tongue around and in between, taking each in his mouth and sucking like they were candy, scraping the glitter with his teeth and not caring if it was poison. He took as much of her foot into his mouth as possible, wished he could swallow them whole. In response, Laura moved her feet further apart and while he was blissfully inhaling her feet, Walter was not unaware of the view he had been afforded. What a decision. Feet, or *that*. He kept an eye on her movements for clues. Some form of writhing is what he was waiting for. He watched and kneaded and sucked and then it happened, like he imagined it would. Regretfully leaving the feet behind *for now*, he crept up her body, almost being waylaid by her toes again as they made a grab for his penis. His mouth bore traces of glitter that he transferred to her mouth. He felt tears on his face and was awash in amazement and pathetic gratitude.

Sharing another après lovemaking cigarette, Walter was thinking about addiction and thinking it wasn't such a bad thing.

"I've never smoked this much before," he said, passing the smoke to Laura.

"It's a filthy habit."

"Maybe we're a filthy habit," said Walter, reaching for her.

Laura sat up abruptly. "Why would you say that?"

"What? I don't know, I was kidding."

"Well, don't say that about us."

She rubbed her arms and stood up. "I'm getting chilly. Let's get dressed."

"Are you okay?"

Laura looked at him and relented. "I'm totally okay. Sorry, I was thinking about something else."

"Are you sure?"

Laura sat back down and hugged him. "I'm more sure of this than anything. I mean it."

Walter held her and looked around the room, as if it could offer a change of topic. And his eyes lit upon a familiar sight, a padlocked door.

"What's in the locked room?"

"Oh, it's my darkroom," said Laura. "It used to be my bedroom."

"Can I see it?"

"Sure."

"Can I see some of your photos?"

"I'd like you to see my work. I'd like to know what you think."

Walter sat up and pulled the kimono over his shoulders.

"What are you doing?" asked Laura, running a bare foot down his chest to his groin.

"Can I see it now?" he asked, putting his hand over her treacherous foot and holding it.

"Okay. But let's get dressed first. I really am getting chilly."

In five minutes, Walter was rejuvenated and ready for anything. Bathed and dressed and fed and sexually satiated. He was standing at the door while Laura opened the padlock. He liked the fact that she had a padlocked room, like his grandmother's old room and his drawing room. He liked hearing the snap of the key turning, the scrape of metal as it slid out of the hasp, the pop of the door as she turned the handle. These sounds were usually precursors to an interesting room. A room that reflected its owner better than any other. And in his experience, something momentous always happened inside a locked room. Walter felt a thrill of anticipation as he followed her inside, into another dimension of black and white.

Laura looked different in this room and not because her face took on a sexy glow when she flipped a red light on. She moved with assurance in here, this was her domain. Walter saw her passion reflected in her body language, her respectful touch as she handled her cameras. She spoke with feeling, but authority. It turned him on. Right now, she was digging around in a drawer.

"I hope this doesn't scare you off," she said, pulling a photograph out and handing it to Walter.

He took it and turned it over. It was him. An eight by ten, black and white glossy of his face.

"When did you take this?" he asked, not sure what to think yet.

"The day after I met you in GoLightly's," said Laura. "I snapped it from across the street when you were leaving work. Are you mad?"

"No," said Walter, realizing he wasn't.

As a matter of fact, he was flattered. And the photo was good. He looked almost handsome, like a younger Harrison Ford maybe.

"I honestly didn't plan it," said Laura. "I was sitting at the restaurant patio having a drink. And I saw you. I always have my camera with me, so I...I don't know...I couldn't help it. Please don't be angry with me."

She looked fragile, worried. He shook his head.

"I'm not angry. I'm not. I love it," he said, meaning it.

"So, you don't think I'm a freak? You don't feel violated or anything?"

Walter put the photo down on a table and his hands on Laura's hips.

"You can violate me any time you feel like it," he said, staring straight into her red-orange face. "I'm here to be exploited."

Laura dropped her gaze.

"Exploited," she repeated, staring at her feet. "I'm sorry."

"Relax," Walter urged, tilting her face back up. "There's nothing to be sorry about. It's a beautiful picture. I love it."

"You do?"

"Yes, yes I do. God, don't worry about it."

Laura seemed to relax a bit.

"Do you feel like a beer?" she asked.

"If you're having one, sure."

Laura seemed anxious to get out of the darkroom and moved towards the door.

"I'll be in the living room," she said. "Come on out when you're ready."

"Okay. I'll be out in a minute. Can I look at more photos?"

"Yeah, help yourself. My portfolio is over there on the table."

And she left. Walter waited until she was gone and started flipping through the prints that were scattered about. He liked it in here. It reminded him of his boyhood bedroom late at night, all black and white with a red tinge. He hoped to find a photo of Laura somewhere, a photo he would ask to keep for himself. Laura had turned a radio on and the low murmur of a phone-in talk show rippled through the room, a comfortable backdrop. Today's topic was flirting, favourite pick-up lines. Walter smiled as he rifled through some fantastic images of Lake Ontario being whipped up by a lightning storm. Thankfully he wouldn't need pick-up lines anymore, not that he ever had any.

He opened a drawer. Inside he discovered a spectacular hardcover book of nudes taken by a photographer whose name he didn't recognize. God, nude photography. Walter's mind filled with possibilities and his gaze skittered over to a tripod leaning in one corner of the room. In his mind, he saw photographs of Laura entwined in silk sheets on the bed, lathered up with bubble bath in the tub, slick with baby oil stretched out on a beach or on a sun-bleached wooden dock. He lifted the book out of the drawer with care. The photo on the front cover was of a woman sitting on a high stool wearing nothing but a black leather beret and high heels. She was smoking a cigarette in a long black holder, and the smoke swirled starkly white against a flat black background. Walter opened the book. The next photograph was of a black woman grooming a white horse. She and the horse were muscular, their haunches taut. Walter felt the unmistakable beginnings of yet another erection, as he turned the page. He wondered if Laura had ever taken any nude photographs, if she would. He pictured a series of photos of Laura naked, wearing nothing but different types of shoes. GoLightly shoes, his designs. She could wear the holly shoes and a Santa cap, standing by the fireplace at the hotel. They could send them out as Christmas cards, hah. He turned the page.

"What are you doing in there?" Laura called.

Walter swallowed.

"Uh nothing," he yelled back. "Looking at your prints. They're amazing."

"I've got a beer here for you when you're ready," Laura said.

"Be right out."

Walter stood up with the book and fanned quickly through the pages, catching glimpses of breasts and legs and buttocks. As he was about to close the cover, something fluttered out of the book and fell to the floor. He looked down and saw the back of a small square photograph. He squatted and turned it over. It too was black and white, but old. Taken back in the days when there was only black and white. Walter stood up again and moved it under the light, examining it. It was a photograph of a man wearing big rubber boots and a plaid shirt, his face partly shaded by a hat. He was holding dead birds upside down by their feet. Walter squeezed his eyes shut, then dared to open them again. His world tilted and screeched to a halt, dumping him off the edge. What the...?

Laura had taken this time to change again. She felt guilty about the surreptitious photos she had taken of Walter and wanted to do something nice for him. When he came out of the darkroom she would be waiting for him, dressed in a sheer red teddy that barely cleared her ass and on her feet, the red shoes. Laura arranged herself into a provocative pose on the couch, and waited for Walter to emerge from the darkness. She took a sip of beer, leaving bright red lipstick on the rim of the glass. She licked her lips and smiled, anticipating his reaction.

Walter was paralyzed. He felt like he was on the verge of a stroke and couldn't take his eyes off the photo. It was identical to the one in his mom's underwear drawer. Exactly. How the *fuck* did Laura get her hands on it? What the *fuck* was it doing here? He felt like his brain was going to vomit. He was shaking so badly, he didn't know if he could walk. Worse, he didn't know why he was reacting so violently to the photo. Was it because it brought up unresolved feelings about the man in the photo, or because he couldn't wrap his brain around why it was here? There were certainly enough reasons to pin it on, all of them wrapped up in that queasy feeling you get when you suspect you have heard the very first lie from your lover's lips.

Laura glanced over at the darkroom. She was getting antsy. She missed him already, wanted him here beside her. Wanted to see his unbearable smile. She stretched one leg out on the coffee table and admired the red shoe, moving her foot from side to side. He would love this. And then she heard the creak of the darkroom door and propped herself up to see his expression. It wasn't exactly what she had hoped for, but it was good. He looked completely stunned. She smiled coyly at him and put one hand between her legs, rubbing herself. God, he looked white, slack. He must be in shock, she thought, pleased her outfit was eliciting such a strong reaction.

Shock was the right word for it. Laura's sexy attire registered, but the photo obliterated any pleasure Walter would normally have experienced. His overriding feeling was one of confusion, but a strong and unnatural anger was boiling up underneath. He stepped towards her, jerky. Laura sat up straighter and frowned. Something was off.

"Walter?"

He walked over to the couch and stood in front of it, his eyes locked onto hers with a death grip. He held his hand out and a photo wafted down onto the coffee table. Laura looked up at him, puzzled, and then down at the photo. She caught her breath and saw the life punched out of any happiness she might have envisioned with Walter. How could she have been so stupid, how could she have, even for a fucking minute, thought she could make this work? She stared at the photo as if it were a blackmail shot. Which, in a sense, it could be. She couldn't bring herself to look at Walter.

For his part, he was swinging in the fucking wind. He needed answers and hoped there was a rational explanation but feared there wasn't. What the *fuck* was she doing with a picture of his dad? What possible explanation could she have? Just please, please have one. Make this make sense. Please. He willed her to look at him.

"Where did you get that?" he managed to croak out.

Laura felt ridiculous in her transparent slut outfit and put a big cushion on her lap, sitting up straight. Seven hundred lies zoomed through her head, but she didn't have the energy or the time to create an intricate maze of deceit. She settled on the truth, knowing it would probably set her free. Free and alone.

"From my mom," she said in a whisper.

Walter shook his head. What? He managed another question.

"That's my dad," he said flatly, trying to keep his voice controlled. "How did your mom get a picture of my dad?"

Laura bit her lip.

"Because she married him. He gave it to her," said Laura, flinching.

Walter tried to filter this information but it had become far too complicated.

"What?" was all he could manage. "What?"

Laura took a deep breath and committed herself.

"That's my dad too," she said.

"What? No it's not."

"Yes it is. We have the same dad, you and me."

Walter shook his head again.

"No we don't. That's impossible."

Laura willed her tears back. She couldn't fall apart yet.

"No, it's not impossible," she said, enunciating every word. "That's Bradley Finch. He's my father. And your father."

"I thought..." said Walter, flailing. "I thought your last name was Booth."

"That's my mom's maiden name," said Laura.

Walter still didn't get it. And until he did, he thought there still might be some hope.

"I thought your dad's name was Boo. Short for Booth. Was that a lie?"

"No, not really. We did call him Boo, but it wasn't short for Booth. Did you ever see *To Kill a Mockingbird*? It was our favourite movie."

Walter stared at her. She wanted to talk about movies now? Well, good. Maybe this is all one big movie. One big horror movie.

"As a matter of fact, I watched it the other night," he said, trying to contain his own growing horror.

"Gregory Peck was great," he continued. "But what the hell does that have to do with any of this?"

"The character Boo Radley. Do you remember him?"

"Yes, yes of course I fucking remember him. What about it?" Walter said, beginning to pace.

"Well, we called my dad Boo Radley, you know, like Bradley, if you say it fast. So, I don't know, it got shortened to Boo eventually. It had nothing to do with the name Booth. You just assumed that."

Walter stopped pacing.

"Apparently I assumed a lot."

Laura shrank into the couch. She had never seen Walter upset before and it didn't suit him. Not that she blamed him. And she watched as the implication hit home. His pleasant shoeshine boy face transformed into something twisted. A darkness overcame his features, as he grappled with one undeniable fact that had occurred to him.

"So, you're my sister?" he wheezed. "You're my fucking *SISTER*?"

Laura gulped her beer.

"Half-sister, actually," she said in a small voice.

Walter threw his hands up in the air and shouted.

"GREAT! GREAT! I always wanted a sister, did I ever mention that? And now I find out I've got one and I've *slept* with her?"

"I know," said Laura. "I didn't know how to tell you. I never should have let this happen. I'm so sorry."

Walter leaned in close to her face. He was dangerously close to losing it. Gone was any control he thought he had gained the night before.

"You didn't know how to tell me?" he practically shrieked. "You didn't know how to fucking *tell* me? How about: Hey Walter, I'm Laura. I'm your sister. Your dad's dead. Thought you might want to know. How about that?"

Laura could feel tears coming on.

"I'm sorry," she whispered. "I was going to but I waited too long. I started to have feelings for you."

Walter was back to pacing.

"Feelings. You got feelings? What about my fucking feelings? What about those, anyway? I was falling in love with you, or is that too weird to say? Meanwhile, you were playing me like a violin. No, strike that. More like a banjo, when you think about it, huh? Christ! Christ, I can't believe this!"

Walter stopped pacing, crossed his arms over his chest and stood still, studying the ceiling. It was a white ceiling with swirls of stucco. He stared hard at it, trying to make sense of the shapes in the stucco patterns. But they all looked like spinning funnels to Walter, like vortexes he was being sucked into. Like he was circling a white toilet bowl and being flushed down like a piece of shit. To join all the other pieces of shit, all the other men who had been betrayed, lied to, shattered. Walter wondered what happens to shit once it's been flushed. You can see what happens to it in outhouses. Flies eat it.

He wrenched his gaze from the ceiling and looked at the girl huddled on the couch, wearing a sexy red teddy and clutching a big cushion. He barely recognized her. He could hardly remember anything he had said. Walter opened his mouth and asked a question, perhaps the most important question.

"Now what?"

Laura didn't look at him. Head down, she said only three words.

"I don't know."

It wasn't good enough. Walter needed more than that. He *deserved* more than that, goddammit. He couldn't look at her anymore. Sister-lover, sister-lover, sister-lover—liar. He was very tired.

"I have to go," he said.

Laura put her hands over her face and nodded. Walter turned and headed towards the door. He felt a sense of desperation about getting back to the hotel where he could get some space. If you could gulp space, that's what he wanted to do.

"Walter?"

He stopped, hand on the doorknob.

"Will you call me?" asked the tiny person on the couch wearing the red shoes.

He said nothing. Shut up, he thought. I can't talk to you right now. I have to get home. I have to go to MY home where there is no mother or father or brother-fucker sister.

"I'd like to explain some things," her voice continued. "I'm sure you have a lot of questions and I'd like to help."

It's difficult to talk when your brain is exploding, Walter realized.

"Maybe," he managed, and walked out the door leaving it open.

# 30 }

**Midnight. Walter sat on his couch** in his living room with no lights on. So much can change in twenty-four hours—too much. He had been sitting here for hours, the only interruptions being trips to the bathroom. There was a bottle of Scotch on the trunk in front of his knees. But he was not drunk. He was, like the bottle of Scotch, half empty. It would take something stronger than booze to hack through the dense wall of information that has sprung up between what used to be and what will be. Walter felt like he was bricked up inside this wall, like something out of the Edgar Allan Poe stories he used to read. This is all very Poe-esque, he thought as he lit another cigarette in the dark. *Filthy habit.* The new information is the pendulum, swinging ever lower in long lazy arcs, a glinting blade intent on slicing his guts into ribbons when it finally and inexorably sinks in. And he is helpless to stop it, because he is either strapped to a table or bricked up inside a wall or his heart has been ripped from his fucking chest and is beating under the floorboards in another room. Yes, he mused, Poe knew what he was talking about. Poe had obviously been shit on. Walter poured another shot and made a mental note to re-read Poe. Anything to keep the information outside the wall for as long as possible, because it's too much to absorb. One brick at a time, he thought, dismantle the information one brick at a time. But which brick to start with, there are so many. Does he start at the top, dealing with his feelings about Laura, or does he go all the way to the bottom and dredge up his feelings about his father? Or does he say *fuck it*, and stay sealed up inside the wall in the dark forever, or until someone eventually finds him and pulls him out, half crazed and blind or something? It's the only kind of scene Walter could bear to imagine at this point. He couldn't think happy thoughts right now. He couldn't imagine Laura moving into the hotel anymore and hosting nicey-nice dinner parties while wearing her simple black dress and a single strand of pearls and bare glitter toes. No, not now. That particular scene brought sharp pain. It was, instead, pictures of pendulums and suffocating that bring some measure of relief to him. They are where he belongs, where he lives at the moment.

He took a drink of Scotch, swung his legs around and stretched out on the couch. Not surprisingly, the static was humming along like a soundtrack. He wasn't having a full-blown attack or anything, it was there like white noise. It was comforting. It was an enabler.

"Laura Booth," he said aloud, then corrected himself.

"Laura *Finch*."

Funny how he had dared to dream that she might one day bear that name. It *is* funny, he thought. Nova will bust a gut when I tell her. Nova will say something like: Well at least she won't have to change her driver's licence if you ever get married.

Yeah, funny. Har de har. What did Johnny used to say when we were kids? It's so funny I forgot to laugh? Yeah, like that. It's that kind of funny.

There was a message on his answering machine, the red blinking was the only light in the room except for an indirect glow from the street lamp outside his window. He has not played the message because he was afraid it would be Laura, his sister. Okay, *half*-sister. Walter wondered which half is related. If it was the top half, then maybe he could have incest-free intercourse with the bottom half. And with that one small thought, his own lower body instantly betrayed him. This was not the brick he would have chosen to start with. Walter tried to shut it down, but all he could picture was Laura's lower torso. In his mind, she has been hacked in two at the waist, maybe by the same pendulum, and he is madly fucking the half that isn't his sister. He couldn't stop the image any more than he could stem his arousal. He put his drink down on the trunk and fumbled his pants undone. Then he kicked his pants right off. His dick felt engorged with rage, not love. And he couldn't stop the mental image that glowed in the darkness. He is standing, doing her from behind. He has to keep a firm grip on her hips and move them back and forth to his desired rhythm because she obviously can't balance herself without any upper body. He begins slowly, so he can watch. But his horror and excitement get the better of him and soon he is thrusting with frenzy, rocking her hips faster and faster, and he feels sick and dizzy and mean and he can't stop. He felt bile coagulating in his throat and thought: That is what I will ejaculate. Bile.

He closed his eyes because he was afraid her other half would show up to taunt him, or cry. She would judge him, probably tell him he's been a bad boy. Or worse, she'd be a supportive sister and forgive him. He couldn't bear that. And still he continued to fuck her like a maniac, the bile continued to rise, his fingers dug into her hips, and his breathing was erratic and harsh.

In the real world, he was a half-naked guy lying on his couch beating off. In the static world, he had become a creature with two torsos and it wasn't clear to Walter which one he was actually abusing. What was clear was that he had to get this over with before he could begin to think about anything else. He sensed flies encircling him.

Laura sat huddled in a blanket on the couch, staring at the photo and biting her nails. *You went too far, Lolo.*

She kept hearing Walter's last question: Now what? Now what? Now what?

An image of David Nussbaum appeared. He was sitting in a chair, legs crossed, staring at her. He tapped a pencil against his notepad and leaned forward. *I think we need to work on your abandonment issues, Laura. Don't you?*

I didn't mean it.

*He's not coming back, you know.*

Who's not coming back?

*You tell me, Lolo.*

Joy Nussbaum slid a fingernail under the flap of an envelope. Party photos. David was mixing martinis in the kitchen.

"How do they look?" he called into the living room, over the shaking of the ice.

"Come see for yourself," Joy invited, flipping through the pictures, a half-smile on her face.

She stopped at a photograph of Laura and Walter, a candid shot taken without their knowledge. Walter is standing behind Laura, his hands gripping her shoulders, his chin resting on the top of her head. It looks like they are listening to someone who isn't in the picture, their heads tilted at the same angle. Joy hasn't had a picture taken of her son in years and is grateful someone, maybe David, snapped this photo. Walter is quite handsome, she thought, looking at him as if for the first time. Laura must bring it out in him. And she looked at Laura's face, immediately below Walter's. Her smile grew. David sat beside his new wife, poured a couple of martinis and glanced at the photo.

"They make a good couple, don't they?" Joy asked.

"Yes they do," David affirmed. "They look like they belong together. Like a matched set."

And then Joy saw it. For the first time since her son was two years old, she saw Walter's resemblance to his father. It caught her off guard and she peered more intently at the photo. Yes, there's Bradley's squint, and those shallow dimples noticeable only to a wife or mother. David was still babbling away, oblivious to the fact that Joy had stopped breathing. He wouldn't shut up about what a likely couple Walter and Laura make. But Joy was only listening to her memories. The photo blurred and she saw Bradley's hands gripping *her* shoulders, Bradley's chin resting on *her* head.

"They almost look alike, don't they?" David was saying now.

"Yes they do," murmured Joy.

David continued his analysis, enjoying the sound of his voice.

"People are often attracted to people who look like them. It's some kind of subconscious thing, strengthening the gene pool, purifying it."

"Mmmhmm," she replied, having no idea what he was talking about.

"Except us, of course," David said, meditatively rolling an olive around on his tongue.

Joy remained riveted to the photo. Walter has turned into Bradley and Laura has become the reason he left.

"I guess in our case, opposites attract," stated David. "I wonder what that says about our commitment to the gene pool."

"Jean Poole?" Joy asked, wondering if that was the other woman's name.

"Yes, but maybe that gene pool attraction isn't such an imperative when you're not having kids," David said, sipping his martini, fascinated by his own logic.

Joy was confused. Does that mean Bradley and Jean Poole didn't have any kids? All these years she had been convinced he had knocked someone up. This was worse. This meant he left because he didn't love her anymore. He left because he loved someone else. What had David called it? The Jean Poole attraction.

"No kids," Joy repeated dully and licked the rim of her martini glass.

David reached up and moved her hair behind her ear.

"I'm okay with that, you know," he said. "You're all I want. But if we were young enough to have children, I would pray they looked like you. Especially if we had a daughter."

"A daughter?" asked Joy, taking another look at Laura.

David finally realized his wife was still absorbed in the photo and not really listening to him. He pointed to the picture.

"Maybe you'll have a daughter soon anyway," he said, tapping Laura's face. "She could be Laura Finch someday."

Joy downed her martini and held her glass out for another. What is David saying? Who is Laura Finch?

She looked at her second husband, bewildered. He took the photo from her hands and moved in to claim her mouth before she could speak. The photographs fell to the floor as David Nussbaum's full weight pressed his wife along the length of the couch. His right hand grappled with her underwear, pulling it down past her knees in one urgent motion while his left hand unzipped his fly and pulled out his ever-ready prick.

"You are so incredibly hot," he said hoarsely against her lips, inserting a knee between her long legs and parting them. "I can't wait. I want to fuck you right now. Can I do that? Tell me I can fuck you now. Tell me."

Joy looked into the eyes of her husband. But it wasn't Bradley. It was David.

"Fuck *me*," she said, closing her eyes.

Walter sat in his drawing room in total darkness but for the light from a single candle. He was looking through his sketch pad, thinking about shoes. Every time he flipped a page over, the candle flame wavered and the drawings appeared to move, the shoes to dance. In here, he is safe. Shoes have never let him down. Right from the beginning, shoes have supported him. Walter picked up a pen and began to draw. He had a need to design a new shoe. A shoe that fit his mood. His first strokes were harsh, thickly black and jagged, evil stepmother shoes, witch shoes. His pen tore a hole in the paper and he stopped, shaking. The few brutal strokes had captured something. Walter peered at the drawing, moved it closer to the candle. The flame flickered, the black shoe rippled, and Walter shuddered. It was a raven. He picked up the pen with a trembling hand and wrote at the top of the page: *Nevermore.*

Laura had changed into a bulky sweater and sweatpants and moved from the couch to her bed. She sat cross-legged, a pad of yellow legal paper on her lap. A bedside lamp shines on the page that has only two words written on it: *Dear Walter*

On the floor beside the bed were crumpled up balls of yellow paper that all start with the same two words. It was the rest of the words that Laura was having trouble with. She didn't know how to construct an apology within an explanation, describe an emotion within a history. There was too much stuff to say, too much he didn't know. There were facts and there were feelings. Where do you start with that? She chewed on the end of her pen, tasted ink. The yellow pages gave up nothing, no information.

"Dear Walter," she read aloud, and placed her pen beneath the formidable salutation.

"There's so much I have to tell you," she said, scratching her pen along. "I'm so sorry about everything...except how I've come to feel about you..."

Laura stopped writing, re-read the page and sighed. Another ball of yellow hit the floor. She began again.

"Dear Walter. I didn't plan any of this. I only wanted to find you, find my brother. But I ended up finding so much more..."

Gag. Crumple.

"Dear Walter. Please forgive me. Please don't hate me. I don't want to lose you now that I've finally found you..."

Blech. Toss.

"Dear Walter. I'm a fucking idiot."

"Dear Walter. It's not really incest, is it?"

"Dear Walter. Get over it."

"Dear Walter. Can we start over?"

"Dear Walter. I want to ~~fuck you~~ make love with you again. I don't care."

The pile of yellow balls was mounting in direct proportion to Laura's frustration and anxiety. She pushed the pad of paper off the bed and stepped into the wads of yellow on the floor. In a few moments she returned, clutching one of her photos of Walter. The paper balls crackled as she stepped through them again and hopped back into bed. She laid the photo on the pillow and kissed it.

"Goodnight, dear Walter," she said and turned out the light.

# 31 }

**It was the drawing room floor** that first came into focus when Walter woke up. He was lying on his side, his right cheekbone numb from pressing into the hardwood. Blinking, he rolled over onto his back, turned his head and saw daylight streaming through the window. This is not a good day, he thought. Everything ached, his legs, his eyes. Some inner monitor reminded him he didn't have to work today, a relief because he didn't know if his cramped body could straighten up, let alone crouch and balance, crouch and balance. He had a vague unsettling feeling of loss. It swirled around the perimeter of his waking thoughts, elusive and sickening. Walter decided it was a hangover because he remembered drinking Scotch on the couch last night and because his mouth tasted foul, like blood or shit or rot. He swallowed with effort and closed his eyes to the sunlight, frowning with the awareness that he had to take a severe piss. This knowledge obliterated everything else. Aching limbs, swollen tongue, a sense of foreboding—all are crushed under the weight of a bloated bladder. Walter groaned and, with tremendous effort, grabbed the leg of his drafting table and pulled his way up off the floor, hand over hand, until his head reached the tabletop. One last heave and he was standing and swaying. He turned to mince his way into the bathroom with legs crossed, but was stopped short when he caught a glimpse of his sketch pad. The fierce black drawing from the night before took him by surprise and immobilized him. Walter stared at the black raven, the torn paper, and was pummelled with hard hits of memory. Line drives to the brain, fastballs coming at him with no time to swing. Hard, mean curveballs. And as they smacked into him—BANG, BANG, BANG!—he did the only thing he could do. He pissed his pants.

Dear Walter:

*I am not a strong person. I am a photographer. I can tell stories with pictures but I have a hard time putting my feelings into words. So I will just give you the facts. I was born in Toronto but raised in Vancouver. My father taught me how to sail. My mother taught me how to love. They died in a boating accident when I was sixteen. From a very young age, I knew I had a half-brother. As a young girl, I didn't care. Boys didn't matter much to me. I had my father and he was enough and I guess, if I were honest, I didn't want you to be found. I wanted to be enough for my dad. I thought a son might take him away from me. When they died, I was a mess. I was sent to live with my godmother, who was a friend of my mom's, and she was super nice but always on the road. She was a singer too. Sometimes I went with her and she let me take photos of her singing to keep me entertained. That's how the photography thing started.*

Now bathed and clad in a flannel bathrobe, Walter began to wipe up the growing lake of piss. What began under his drafting table had flowed across the entire room and into a corner. His knees were sore and red from crawling around and, despite the warm bath, he was not relaxed. He didn't know what he was. There was a huge pressure inside his chest and head that he was afraid would erupt if he didn't vent it. And Walter knew what would help. Drawing would help. Face the fear. Face the raven. But first, he had to mop up piss. You have to crawl before you can fly.

*I lived with my godmother, Felicia, until I finished high school. I didn't go to college or university. I went to work for a wedding photographer. Then I started taking pictures on my own time of local bands and concerts and I began to start selling a few of them to the local newspapers. To make a long story short, I ended up employed at a local entertainment magazine as their staff photographer. I was living on my own, making enough to eat and pay rent, and thought I was happy. I didn't know it, but my parents had left me a trust fund for when I turned twenty-one. Felicia didn't tell me until my twenty-first birthday. I hated her for not telling me sooner and I've never talked to her again. But I had enough money to do whatever I wanted then. I went a bit crazy with my new freedom. But who wouldn't?*

Walter wrung out the piss-soaked rag and threw it in the garbage. He washed his hands until they felt raw and then made a pot of Red Rose tea, probably because he hated tea. These are details. They must all be tended to before he sits down to draw. While the tea was steeping, he walked into the living room to retrieve the bottle of Scotch and noticed the answering machine light blinking. Another detail. He pressed Play and his grandmother's voice soared into the room, giving him a feeling of relief so powerful it nearly levelled him. He had forgotten all about her. And there she was, chattering away, saying she wouldn't be home for a few days. She's going to be staying at Cliff's farm, indulging in her new hobby for a while. Walter erased the message and took the Scotch back to the kitchen. He fixed himself a mug of tea with honey and lemon and strode into the drawing room, his crooked step intent with purpose.

*I started going out a lot. I was meeting a lot of people through my work and staying out late because most of the crowd I was hanging out with were musicians. Anyway, that's not important. What I'm saying is that I began a lifestyle of drinking and partying and thinking I was having a good time. I left the magazine in what was a "mutual decision" and began to freelance in music photography. By this time I had a name and I got quite a bit of work even though I didn't need the money. I might as well tell you I slept with a lot of guys and pretty soon I stopped freelancing and just lived off my trust fund and took pictures for fun. I was having a blast and soon I didn't give a shit about anything, not even taking pictures. I went from relationship to relationship, all of them short-lived. It's hard to explain and it sounds really corny to say I was obviously looking for something, but I guess I was. I know what your stepdad would say about it. Basically I was in a haze for years. And then something happened and I woke up.*

Walter cracked his knuckles, shook his hands out, and flipped his sketch pad to a clean new page. He picked up a pen and closed his eyes, trying to summon the shoe spirits or the ghost of Edgar Allan Poe. There was a big danger zone in his head that he was trying to ignore. A bad place in which a sister lived, joined at the hip with his girlfriend. *Ex-girlfriend.* It was not a place he wanted to dwell right then, but its essence would surely move him to draw the raven shoe. He began with a single black line, curved and aerodynamic. It was a beautiful stroke. Clean and powerful. Walter was pleased and relieved. He thought of tiny hollow bones, so easy to crush but strong enough to elevate a bird into the heavens. His pen moved with precision. The thing about a raven, Walter thought, is all in the perception. It can be both sinister and magical at the same time. He could think of no other bird that embodied both those qualities. This is what he would strive for. These shoes would either intimidate or enchant, depending on the woman who wore them. A bleak shadow of a smile drifted across his face as his pen moved with grace and surety. He could do this.

*It doesn't matter what happened. What's important is that I suddenly realized part of me had died with my parents. Even though I was surrounded with people now, I had nobody. I stopped drinking, stopped seeing the guy I was with at the time, and stopped going out. I started taking pictures again. Tons of pictures, but not pictures of bands and musicians. Pictures of flowers and trees and people on the street, pictures of buildings and rocks and even pictures of me. And then I started looking at pictures. I pulled out my parents' old photo albums for the first time since they died. I finally wanted to see them again and I ransacked boxes and boxes of their stuff. And I found home movies that made me cry. And guess what, Walter? There was a home movie of you, when you were just a little kid. I guess my dad must've taken it with him when he left. You were so cute with your funny little walk, I think I fell in love with you then. Nobody could love the way you walk more than me, because it helped me find you.*

Tiny baby bird bones. Walter was sweating, but didn't notice. He was meticulous with his pen strokes, his face mere inches from the paper. He drew individual feathers, each one overlapping just so. The whole was lost at this close scrutiny. The whole was swooping and circling somewhere else while Walter concentrated on each perfect slick feather. He could feel them building up, smooth and glossy, layers upon layers, and it thrilled his soul. Such fragile lines, barely whispers on the page, but they were strength when connected. Walter sensed a faint pulsing arising from underneath the feathers. Maybe he was gripping his pen too tightly and his fingers were throbbing or maybe it was his own tell-tale heart. He took extra care now—the feathers could not be only flat adornment. There was warmth underneath them. There was life. He must protect it at all costs.

*After seeing the movie, I became obsessed with connecting with you. It was like you were a missing link or something. But I was also afraid. I didn't know what I would say to you and I didn't know if you would even want to know me. I didn't know if you hated your dad for leaving you. I didn't know anything, Walter. And I especially didn't know that I would fall for you. I can't explain it in a letter. I feel deeply connected to you in ways I can't articulate. I don't know if it's because we share blood or if it's something else more powerful. Whatever it is, I don't want to lose it but I also don't want to upset you anymore. You are the only man I have ever felt this close to. You are my knight, my prince. Please don't push me away. Please try to understand why I didn't tell you these things before. Please see me again. I don't care that we're related. It doesn't matter to me. We don't have to tell anyone.*

It was night and the sketch was done. Walter sat back in his chair and stretched his arms to the ceiling. His stomach was growling and his fingers were cramped. The raven shoe was a masterpiece. Sleek and elegant, but ominous. Not just any woman could carry it off. There were details he would have to work out with Remo, like how to protect the feathers, how to keep the sheen alive. But it was indeed a sinister, magical shoe. It was his best work ever and Walter knew it. He entertained the notion of a supermodel wearing the shoes, strutting down a catwalk, all high-stepping attitude and haughtiness, turning on a dime, the feathers catching the lights in dazzling blue-black rainbows.

He was exhausted and turned off the desk lamp. He headed for the kitchen where he was going to make a cheese and lettuce sandwich and eat it while sitting on the roof. He needed cold air and darkness. He needed biting oblivion.

*That's all I have to say for now. I'm sure you have other questions and I am willing to answer anything you want. I am here for you, Walter. I will always be here for you. You know what they say...you can't pick your family. We didn't choose this. We are innocent. I know we can work something out, if you give us a chance.*

*Call me. I'm here for you. I don't want to lose you now that I've found you. Love, Laura*

*PS: I know my dad (our dad) loved you, if that makes any difference. He wouldn't have kept the movie if he didn't.*

The peeping Toms weren't getting much of a show that night. Walter sat alone, balanced on the northern ledge of the roof, chewing his sandwich that felt like putty in his mouth. From there, he could see right into the apartments in the next building. There were no curtains on the bedroom window of one of the second floor suites, one right below him and to his right. They probably don't know about the roof, he thought. They probably don't know it's my backyard. He swallowed a cold lump of bread and cheese and stared into the room, hoping something would happen. Usually he would not sit on this side of the roof for the precise reason he would sit here tonight. Tonight, he was all about invading privacy when his own has been attacked. Boundaries don't seem to matter much any more. And then, as if he had scripted a movie, someone did enter the room. He stopped chewing and held his breath. It was a woman, probably in her forties. She looked familiar and Walter realized it was Judith, his shoe store customer who runs the boardwalk. He scanned the bedroom, automatically looking for the GoLightly sneakers, and while he was doing this, Judith took off her blouse. He was stunned when he realized what she was doing. He started chewing at hyperspeed and swallowed another bite with an audible gulp. Judith was wearing, what else, a sports bra. She is in really good shape, he thought to himself, and mentally urged her to take off her bra. He wanted to see her breasts that were mashed beyond recognition within the confines of the tight black Lycra. She slipped off her skirt and tossed it on the bed. She was wearing snug black bicycle shorts, all shiny and clingy, wet looking. Walter bit into his sandwich, eyes glued. Her legs were strong, her bare midriff flat and taut. Judith had a tan, probably fake. She turned her back to Walter and pinned her hair up, muscles moving around underneath the skin of her strong back. He chewed frantically and swallowed again. This can't be happening. And then Judith lay on the floor and closed her eyes. She began to move, and at first Walter didn't know what she was doing. Then he realized it was yoga. He was mesmerized. She was fluid and strong, like the raven, and when she got up on all fours, balancing on her fingers and toes, her ass facing him, he got an erection so fast it nearly toppled him off the roof. He took a sharp breath in as he steadied himself, and nearly choked on the wad of congealed bread and cheese lodged at the back of his throat. He started to gag and splutter, trying to muffle the choking sounds. He has one hand over his mouth, eyes bulging out, and one on his dick trying to beat it down. A good gust of wind and he'd be a goner. He hacked up the bread and spit it out over the rooftop, nearly keeling over with the effort. By the time he righted himself and began to breathe normally, Judith had changed position. She was now facing the window, balancing on one leg, holding the other bent and up to her chest. Walter admired her coordination, knowing he could never in a million years stand steady on one leg. He wished he had a drink but couldn't risk making any noise by leaving and crunching back across the gravelly roof. He began to shiver, whether from the cold air, the stress of holding himself steady and quiet, or from the sexual arousal he was experiencing with this unexpected show. He had never found Judith attractive before, but now she was about the best damn thing he'd ever seen. Take off your clothes, he urged. Take off your clothes for me. I'm a disgusting, hideous pervert.

And she was looking right at him.

He froze.

She grasped the bottom edge of her sports bra with both hands and pulled it up and over her breasts but she didn't take it right off. She pulled it up until it covered her face and left it sitting there, like a black mask. Walter didn't know what to think about this, but he was glad her face was covered and she was not looking at him anymore. Her breasts were larger and fuller than he imagined, with enormous dark nipples. Judith left the black top on her face like an executioner's mask and began to pull her shorts down. Walter believed he was dreaming this. No way this would happen in real life, he thought. It's too perfect. And there are no witnesses. But down went the shorts and Judith was standing in her bedroom, naked but for the mask, her hair sticking straight up in tufts. She had shaved, or more likely waxed, her pubic hair right off. His jaw dropped at the sight and he pulled his dick out into the cold night air.

Judith stepped up to the window—she must be able to see something through the black Lycra—and opened it wide. Her nipples hardened instantly and she touched them with her fingertips. Walter couldn't decide if she could see him or not—if she was putting on a show for him or if this was some crazy-ass thing she does every night. He wrapped his hand around his peeping Tom perv dick. Now Judith stepped back from the window a few paces, turned her back to Walter again, and bent over at the waist, legs spread wide. She began to play with herself and he watched her finger slide in and out of her bald pussy which, even from this distance, he could see beginning to glisten. This nearly sent him over the edge. After a few minutes of this contorted masturbation, Judith stood back up and walked over to a dresser. She picked up a tube of lipstick and returned to the window. Pulling it back down a few inches, she wrote on it backwards. She wrote a big number 6. Then she lay on the bed and continued to masturbate, undulating like a snake. Walter got it. She was in apartment number 6. This is good information.

# 32 }

**Nova watched Walter move** around the shoe store in his usual efficient and non-invasive manner.

*Can I help you? Would you like some waterproofer with that? Have a nice day.*

There was nothing she could put her finger on, but she sensed a detachment about him. He hadn't really looked her in the eyes all day long and had definitely been avoiding the topic of the Mooneys' party. What cinched it for Nova was when she tried to say something nice about Laura and got only a blank stare in return. She didn't know whether to be concerned or pissed off, but was leaning towards the latter. Nova didn't like being left out of the loop and she couldn't imagine what could have happened between the party and now. Laura and Walter were sickening at the party. They might as well have been the newlyweds, the way they hung onto each other, mooning into each other's eyes all afternoon. So what was his fucking problem today? She was also pissed off because she wanted to hang with Walter and tell him all about meeting Johnny's parents and staying over at their place. She wanted to talk about his new stepdad and Adelaide and, well, rehash the party and the people. Have a good old-fashioned gossip session. It was a *party*, for Christ's sake. You're *supposed* to deconstruct it. But he was acting like an android.

She looked down at her customer who had sneakily grabbed a size eight shoe off the display shelf and was trying valiantly to ram her Clydesdale hoof into it.

"It's too small for you," Nova snapped. "You're a size ten. Get over it."

The woman flushed and looked up at Nova, the open-toed pump hanging off the end of her foot.

"Give me that," Nova said, holding her hand out. "There's no way."

The woman leaned forward and slipped the shoe off, guiltily handing it over.

"It looked like it would fit," she said.

"Yeah, and I look like Michael Jackson," said Nova, taking the shoe and tossing it over her shoulder, nearly beaning another customer. "Stay put. I'll be right back with your size. I think we have one pair left. It's your lucky day."

"Thank you."

"It's my job."

"Thank you."

And Nova flashed a dazzling smile at the woman before she turned towards the backroom.

While she was sliding the size ten shoebox from its stack, Nova noticed the back door open and went to investigate. Walter was outside having a smoke.

"Hey," she said, poking her nose out. "Gimme a drag."

He wordlessly handed the cigarette over.

"What's your problem, Spaz?" Nova asked, inhaling then handing the smoke back.

"Nothing," he said.

"You're full of shit. Something's going on. What is it?"

And then Nova got hit with a look of such naked confusion, she forgot all about being pissed off.

"Oh my god," she breathed, holding her fingers out for the cigarette. "Something's really wrong, isn't it?"

Walter passed it over, not looking. He could only shake his head and stare at the ground. Nova took a drag and nudged him, passing the smoke back.

"No thanks," he said in a small voice.

She dropped the cigarette and poked him.

"Hey. Talk to me. I'm not going to freak out, whatever it is."

Walter said nothing. Nova frowned.

"I'm also not going to give up on this. You're gonna tell me and we can do it the easy way or the hard way."

Walter smiled a bit at that.

"Well, maybe..." he began.

"Maybe nuthin'," Nova stated. "I'm coming over to your place after work and we're gonna talk. Okay? Maybe we could have dinner or something."

Walter shrugged.

"I'll take that as a yes," said Nova. "Now, I've gotta go. I've got a stupid customer."

Walter looked at Nova's retreating back with a mixture of trepidation and relief. By eight o'clock that evening, the verdict would be in.

Judge Nancy Nova didn't show up alone. She brought Johnny the juror with her, an addition that initially made Walter uneasy but one whose presence he ultimately was grateful for. He supplied his team with egg rolls and chow mein from the Goof and Johnny brought a twelve-pack of Molson Export and a couple joints. Although the three of them seldom smoked pot, Johnny had suggested it to Nova as a way of loosening Walter up and making him talk freely.

"Yeah, or make him completely paranoid," she said.

Truth of the matter was that Johnny didn't much relish the idea of having a sit-down with his buddy and prying into his affairs. That was Nova's territory. The pot was really for Johnny so he could loosen up, in case something was really going down. He thought Nova was way overreacting though. Walter was probably in a bad mood. It happens.

Chow mein, six beers and one joint later, Walter testified. As the story unfolded, Nova's jaw dropped lower and lower in disbelief and Johnny actually started to grin. Nobody interrupted. Walter recounted the sequence of events, from finding the photograph of his father to storming out of Laura's apartment. When he was done, he cracked open another beer and waited. It was out in the open now, and he was glad.

Uncharacteristically, Johnny was the first to speak.

"Man," he breathed. "You did your sister."

Nova punched his arm.

"*Half*-sister, you jerk."

Johnny rubbed his arm and glared at her.

"Hey, fuck. It's still weird."

"Only half as weird," Nova stated, taking a slug of beer and process-ing the information.

Walter watched them, not caring what they thought. The pot had taken care of that. He closed his eyes and saw Judith lying naked on her bed, face covered. He saw himself approaching the bed and slipping her Go-Lightly sneakers on her feet.

"Would they have deformed kids?" Johnny asked Nova, as if Walter wasn't in the room.

"God, what a thing to say. I doubt it," replied Nova without much conviction. "Besides, he's not going to see her again. She lied to him, for fucksake. A BIG lie."

*Walter did the laces up. They were green laces.*

"Well, I'd lie about something like that too," Johnny said, bracing for another punch in the arm.

"If you lied about something like that, I'd be gone so fast your head would spin," said Nova, sparking up the last joint.

*Walter walked around to the side of the bed. He could see the black mate-rial moving in and out where Judith's mouth would be. It was getting damp.*

"Oh come *on*," Johnny protested. "I thought you said I could tell you anything."

"Yeah, but I meant right away. You don't wait until someone falls in love with you before you lay something like that on them. It's feeble."

*Walter's eyes travelled down her athletic body. He was particularly fasci-nated with her hairless pussy. It looked so vulnerable. It made her powerful body look powerless and Walter felt himself grow harder and hardened.*

"So, if I told you I was your brother, you'd leave me? Is that what you're saying?"

Nova looked at Johnny before she spoke. His black hair was falling into his eyes in the way she loved and she reached up and pushed it aside. She saw the jagged white scar on his left temple that sliced his eyebrow in two and her stomach flipped. And for maybe the first time, she saw that Johnny was hers.

"We do kind of look alike," Nova said, entranced by Johnny's hot black eyes and maybe the pot. "Have you ever noticed that?"

"Not until now," he said, leaning in close.

"I bet some people would think I'm your sister if they saw us together," whispered Nova, touching her nose to Johnny's.

"Does that turn you on?" he asked, lips touching hers.

"Sort of," she breathed, her head swimming.

*Walter sits on the edge of the bed wondering what to do next. Judith decides for him and begins to pull his T-shirt up. He stops her when it gets to his shoulders and he pulls it over his face and leaves it there. Walter stands up and takes his pants off. They are both naked and faceless. His dick is like petrified rock and his head is spinning. Judith has not said a word and this is a fine thing. She lies back down.*

"Hey Nancy Nova," whispered Johnny.

"Yeah?"

"Shouldn't we be talking to Spaz?"

"Who?"

*Walter doesn't want to ally himself with Judith, he wants to invade her. Her body language suggests this is what she wants too. It's a movie, he thinks. I'm in a David Lynch movie and it's called Stockinghead or Black Lycra. Judith tilts her pelvis and Walter climbs aboard. He pictures himself sitting on his rooftop watching himself. He decides to give himself a helluva show and for an instant thinks about how Laura would photograph this. It's enough to push him into Judith. He is unforgiving.*

"Walter? Hey, Spaz."

He opened his eyes reluctantly and saw Nova and Johnny on the couch. They looked odd.

"I guess the main question is this," Nova began. "Are you actually in love with Laura?"

Walter swallowed and tried to think.

"Does it matter?"

"Yes, I think it does," Nova said, reaching for Johnny's hand.

Walter shifted in his chair and tried to think past the pot.

"I don't know if I can think about that right now," he said.

"Because you're too fucked up about the sister thing, right?" said Johnny.

"Right."

Johnny leaned forward, eyes like slits. He reached out a hand and crooked a finger.

"Hey man. Blood brothers."

"Yeah, so?" Walter asked, but grasped Johnny's finger with his own, remembering.

"There's nothing stronger than blood," Johnny said, as if it was the most profound thing in the world.

"Yeah, so?"

"So, you asshole. If you got blood, you're already halfway there. You can conquer anything when you got your blood looking out for you. You don't mess with blood."

"You can't stand Ray," Walter stated.

"Yeah I know. But I also know he'll be there for me if I need him. I can't get rid of him even if I wanted to."

"So what are you saying?" Walter asked, his finger beginning to hurt.

"I'm saying, make peace with it. Make peace with Laura. Personally, I wouldn't give a shit about going out with my sister. I mean, if I found her later, not if I had grown up with her or anything."

"But you don't have any sisters."

"That's not the point. Think about it. If you find the love of your life, then she's probably the most important thing in the world. The next important thing is your family, right? Fuck man, you've got both those things all wrapped up in one chick. It's kinda awesome. It's like Romeo and Juliet. Weren't they related?"

"No."

"Well, whatever. It would be like that."

"Cleopatra married her brother," Nova interjected.

Both guys looked at her.

"Really?" they said together.

"Yeah. It was standard practice back then. At least in Egypt. I've read a lot about Cleopatra because people have told me I look like her."

"You do," said Johnny.

"You mean Antony was Cleopatra's brother?" asked Walter.

"No, it was some other dude, I forget his name. But they all inter-married in those days."

"So," Walter said. "Are you telling me I shouldn't have a problem with this? Is that what you're saying?"

Nova leaned against Johnny's shoulder.

"Hey, Spaz. I don't think it's the worst thing in the world. I think you should be more worried about why she lied to you about it. And you've gotta deal with all that shit about your dad too. I think you've got more important things to worry about than fucking your sister."

"*Half*-sister," said Johnny. "That's only half as bad as Cleopatra, right?"

"I guess so," said Walter. "But we're not in Egypt, man. We're in Toronto."

# 33 }

**Walter didn't get a lot of phone calls.** There was Nova and Johnny of course, and sometimes his mother or Reginald. But when Walter was on the phone he was efficient, not chatty, not prone to aimless meandering discussions. People who used to phone him, acquaintances he met in the Beaches or from the store, soon stopped calling unless they had something specific to ask Walter. And because he never called anyone unless he had a reason, some people got their noses bent out of joint and would stop calling him altogether. Walter hardly noticed. Except for the entire week following Nova and Johnny's visit. He would find himself staring at the phone, hoping it would ring as much as he was afraid it would. And if it did ring, he would break out into a sweat and pace back and forth before snatching the receiver up in a panic, sometimes just in time to hear a dial tone. Occasionally he would pick the phone up when it wasn't ringing, when it hadn't rung all day, to check and make sure it was working. Some days it didn't ring at all and those days he felt sick. The first time he noticed his new obsession with the phone was the day after Nova and Johnny had been there. He had been sitting in his drawing room sketching pictures of shoes with heels suspiciously shaped like pyramids, when the phone rang and caused his heart to slam up against his ribcage. He just sat there, mouth-breathing, listening to the screaming ring of the phone in the living room. Had it always been that fucking loud? He felt every nerve ending recoiling as if each ring of the telephone was stabbing at him. But there was another feeling too, one of grim hope or anticipation. It was all wrapped up in sick anxiety and he felt like he was going to puke as he put down his pencil and wobbled his way into the living room. By the time he reached the phone, it had rung four times and he stood staring at it. If it rings one more time, I'll pick it up before the machine kicks in, he said to himself. And it did.

"Hello?"

"I'm living in sin," the voice said.

"What?"

"Are ya deaf? I'm living in SIN, I said."

Walter's heart slowed.

"Clara?"

"Who'd you think it was? Mother Teresa?"

"I don't know. What do you mean, you're living in sin?"

"Jesus. You kids invented it. You should know."

And a loud cackle assaulted Walter's ear, reassuring him that it was indeed his grandmother and all was good.

"So, can you make out all right without me?"

"What?"

"Christ, what's the matter with you? I'm trying to tell you that I'm moving in with Cliff. Whaddya call it...living together...shacking up... getting a hobby. That okay with you mister?"

Walter said yes, that's okay with me.

"So, I'm coming into town tomorrow to pick up my stuff."

"Okay."

"You don't sound surprised."

"I guess I'm not."

"Well, we're not spring chickens y'know. We don't have a lot of time for courtin'."

"I know."

"Aren't you gonna miss having your old granny around?"

"Of course I am, but I'm happy for you."

"Well you could say so."

"Didn't I? Okay, I'm really happy for you Clara. I am. I like Cliff a lot."

"Not that. You could say you're gonna miss me."

"I will miss you."

Walter hung up the phone and thought about it. He didn't know how much he would miss Clara. Having the hotel all to himself was appealing. Already, with Clara's brief absence, it had started to take on a bachelor's look. Towels were lumped on the bathroom floor, a few dishes were still in the sink, some half-empty cups and glasses in the living room. Walter wasn't a slob by nature, but he had a lot on his mind. This is what he was thinking as he lurched down the hallway and kicked a stray sock to one side. When he got halfway down the hall, he saw it. A white envelope poking out from under the apartment door. He stooped to pick it up, not thinking, and opened it.

*Dear Walter*

Leaning against the wall of his crooked hallway, Walter sunk to the ground, reading. Speed reading as if his life depended on it. And then re-reading as if it were someone else's life. And it was someone else's life, but it was also his, and he struggled to understand where he fit in. The words were flat, but the feelings they conjured were multi-dimensional and huge. Too huge. Too many words. He read it a third time and felt like he was choking. Like all the words had become a big ball of shit. It was all too hard to swallow. He crawled into the bathroom and dry heaved.

The next day, Walter did something he had never done in his life. He called in sick to work. He said he didn't feel quite right and that he also had to be around to help Clara get her things together. Reginald was fine with it and so impressed with the raven shoe he would have given Walter a week off if he had asked. Nova was suspicious and called Johnny.

"Why don't you go over there later today," she suggested. "Check up on him."

Walter dragged his ass around the hotel half-heartedly picking up his clothes, doing the dishes, and tidying things before Clara's arrival. He had folded the letter up the night before and stuck it inside his Edgar Allan Poe book. He couldn't bring himself to look at it again. He needed to ignore it for a while so he could have a clear head when he decided to think about it. This of course was impossible, and he couldn't shake random images that would pop unbidden into his head. Laura on a sailboat, her hair flying the breeze, standing beside his dad. Looking at the words on the page, he would picture her writing it. Was she in bed when she wrote it? On the couch? The floor? Some images made him smile despite himself. Other images made him feel like he was rotting inside. Like Laura as a little girl, her hair in braids, playing hide and seek with their dad, and their dad throwing her up in the air and catching her. Things like that. Things Walter never got to do. Resentment would intervene, slicing angrily into a careless moment of fond fantasy, shredding it. And Laura's happy face would melt and transform into something ugly. Walter would feel feverish. He would bite his nails. This is why he had to banish all thoughts of the letter, at least for now. Things were too vivid, too close. He needed some distance, some perspective. He needed a drink.

Walter was having a rum and Coke and eating a grilled cheese sandwich in the kitchen when Clara knocked on the door and simultaneously fit her key into the lock.

"Anybody home?" she yelled. "Walter? Walter?"

"In here Clara," he called out. "The kitchen."

She made her usual racket coming down the hallway, Clifford Klonsky in tow. Walter had never heard anyone make their presence known as boldly and officially as Clara did. He could almost hear her raspy breathing, feel the floorboards vibrate with her heavy tread. And he could hear a girlish tittering whisper underneath the clattering of her bracelets and the deep rolling tones of Cliff's voice. She was like a big fat travelling carnival, thought Walter. A glittery, loud midway ride that thrills, excites and scares the shit out of you. He swiped a corner of his sandwich in some ketchup and took a bite, waiting for Clara's appearance. They seemed to have stopped in the hallway for a second, talking in low voices. He wondered if they were making out, if Clifford was playing grab-ass with Clara—a preposterous notion and highly unlikely considering the industrial strength girdle she perennially wears which makes her ass look like a big flat square, impossible to get a grip on. He swallowed his sandwich and took a gulp of rum and Coke, allowing a small belch to escape.

"Hey," said Clara loudly, stepping into the kitchen. "Got anything to drink? I'm parched."

Walter looked up and smiled.

"You're a sight for sore eyes," he said, meaning it. "Hello Cliff. Good to see you again."

Mr. Clifford Klonsky stepped forward, hand extended. He looked unruffled, well pressed, and clean. He looked solid and Walter leaned into it as he clasped the older gentleman's hand.

"Walter my boy, you're looking well," said Cliff.

"You too," said Walter. "Any problems on the drive down?"

"None at all. Crazy drivers in Toronto, but I take my time. Precious cargo, y'know?"

Walter got up to mix some drinks and couldn't help but notice the fond look exchanged by Clara and Cliff. It made him feel lightheaded.

"What are you drinking?" he asked.

"Nothing alcoholic for me," said Cliff. "But maybe Clara might like a snort, would you sweetheart?"

"Well, it's kind of early," Clara said.

"I'm drinking rum and Coke," said Walter.

"Already? Well, can't have you drinking alone. That's not seemly. Have you got any of my sherry left?"

"Sure do," said Walter. "Cliff? Tea or coffee? Juice? Pop?"

"I'd love a cup of tea if you're offering," said Cliff.

"Why don't you two go into the living room and make yourselves comfortable while I fix some drinks," said Walter.

"Fine with me," said Clara. "I guess I'm a guest now, ain't I?"

Walter gave one of Clara's crystal sherry glasses a quick wipe with a dishtowel and waved her off.

"You can move back in any time you want," he said.

Clifford steered his precious cargo out the door and gave a parting comment.

"She won't be moving back here anytime soon if I can help it," he said to Walter with a boyish wink.

Walter watched them leave and plugged the kettle in. He poured a sherry and took some cheese out of the fridge. All this took a few minutes, time that he was grateful for. Time he was not thinking about the letter. He found some chocolate wafers and arranged them on a plate with the orange cheese and some green grapes. Old people like food, he thought to himself as he took his time overlapping the different colours. You could never serve an old person a cup of tea or a glass of sherry without some kind of snack or dessert on the side. They need crumbs. Walter imagines that this is how he will know when he's old. It would be the first time he asks for a cookie when he's over at someone's house for coffee. He hoped he would remember this bit of wisdom when the time came. He would like to know the moment he is officially old. He would ask for a cookie, and say:

"I am now officially old, did you know that?"

And his host will say: "What are you talking about?"

"I asked for a cookie. That's what it means."

And his host will say: "I have cookies. What does that mean?"

And Walter will say: "That doesn't mean anything. Have you ever asked for a cookie when you're at someone else's house?"

"I don't know."

"Well then. You might be old and you might not. Most people don't know the moment it happens. Don't worry. It's just something I know."

And his host will probably look at Walter like he's weird and go get him the cookies. But when they take the cookies down from the shelf, they will look closely at the bag and they will wonder. They probably will not eat one.

But Walter will. He wonders what it will taste like, if he'll notice a difference. If it will taste as good as the first cookie he ever ate as a child. He picks up a chocolate wafer and takes a bite off the end, chewing with his eyes closed. It tastes like sweet sawdust and he is relieved he is not yet old. There are too many things he needs to do.

Walter and Cliff were sitting alone in the living room while Clara was packing up her old room. Cliff was smoking a pipe and Walter lit a cigarette to join in the manly smoking ritual. Clara would smack him if she saw him smoking, but Walter risked it. He wondered if she ever gave

Cliff any grief about pipe smoking and guessed not. Cliff allowed Walter
to doctor his tea with an ounce of brandy and they both sat back in their
seats, puffing. Walter couldn't remember the last time he relaxed like this
with an older man. He felt good about it.

"She's some woman, your grandma," said Cliff now, sucking on his
pipe.

"I know," said Walter, exhaling a thin ribbon of smoke. "She's one of
a kind."

"Yup. I'm gonna take good care of her, y'know. You don't have to worry
none."

"I know. I've never seen her this happy."

Cliff chuckled to himself but didn't elaborate.

"You looked pretty happy at your mom's wedding party with Laura,"
Cliff said. "She's a right lovely girl. Almost as lovely as Clara."

Smoke catches in Walter's throat and he coughs, grabs his drink and
takes a big hit.

"Y'all right there?" Cliff asked, leaning forward.

"Yes sir, I'm fine. Swallowed wrong, that's all."

"Uh huh. If that's what you think, then that's what it is."

Walter cleared his throat and gave Cliff the thumbs-up.

"So, is Clara going to be milking goats or anything like that?" asked
Walter.

"Not unless she wants to," said Cliff.

"Hey sonny," he said now. "Your mom and your grandma, they want
you to be happy. You know that don't you?"

Walter looked at Cliff with surprise. Where did that come from?

"I guess so," he said.

"Well," said the old man. "I may be speaking out of turn here, or
maybe I'm an old fool who's giddy in love, but I don't want you to make
a mistake."

"I don't want to either," said Walter, not entirely sure where Cliff was
going with this.

"Don't let it pass you by," said Cliff. "You'll always regret it."

"Don't let what pass me by?"

"Anything. Anything that you really, really want."

"What if I don't know what I want?"

Cliff re-lit his pipe and studied Walter.

"I think you do," he said, puffing. "I think you do. Maybe you don't want to admit it."

Walter stared at him, not knowing what to say. He nodded, unsure. Cliff continued.

"Don't let nobody else keep you from what you want. Nobody, y'understand? Not your mom or her new husband or Clara or your friends. We're all alone in this life until we find someone to share it with. And then sometimes they die and you're alone again until you find someone else. And sometimes you don't ever find anyone. All's I'm saying is don't let nobody tell you what to do."

"Even you?" asked Walter.

Cliff grinned at him, dentures gleaming around the stem of his pipe.

"Except me," he said. "'Cause I don't have a stake."

Walter didn't know what to say except: "Want another cookie?"

By six o'clock, they were gone. The hotel seemed empty without their presence and Walter stood at Clara's bedroom door looking in. He could still smell her perfume. He stepped inside the room and ran his fingers over the top of the dresser. There wasn't a speck of dust. The pink hand was gone. He pictured Clara running after goats and chickens, waving the pink hand in the air, scaring the crap out of them. He wished he had made a blue hand for Cliff. Walter sat on the bed. He wondered what to do with the room now that Clara was gone. He'd wait until her smell disappeared and then come up with a plan. Maybe a den or a study. Sitting with Cliff earlier had made him think of gentlemen's clubs with leather wingback chairs, old books lining the walls, brandy snifters, cigars, and bowls full of walnuts. It occurred to him that he didn't have a lot of male friends and not nearly enough books to pull it off. Maybe he could make it into a formal dining room. Every hotel should have one.

He looked up at the ceiling, envisioning an old-fashioned chandelier. He would buy some floor-length velvet or brocade drapes for the window, a long wooden table lined with high-backed chairs, and he would need silverware and pewter wine goblets and big heavy candlestick holders running down the length of the table. The ceiling works its usual magic, sucks him in. His eyelids begin to droop as visions of scantily clad serving wenches dance through his head. They look suspiciously like Nina and Tina dressed in their Swiss Chalet uniforms. He is sitting at the head of the table gnawing on a bone and gulping ale from a tankard, spilling it down his ruffled shirt front, wiping it with greasy fingers. He sees Nova to his right barking orders at the wenches, dressed like Cleopatra, a live snake wound around her upper arm flicking its pointy tongue at her neck. And Johnny to his left, dressed like an Indian with a full headdress and a quiver of arrows strapped to his back. His face is painted and smeared with blood. Walter smiles to himself. There are other dinner guests, but they are hazy. His mother, David Nussbaum, Clara and Cliff, Reginald, and Adelaide and Tanya are there. Sabrina scoots about underfoot, foraging for scraps and yipping incessantly. Walter boots her in the ribs and pounds his fist on the table, causing the silverware to jump and clatter. Adelaide starts laughing, her big mouth hanging open, revealing half-chewed lumps of brown mush sitting at the back of her throat and green spinach clinging to her teeth like moss. Her breath smells like carrion. David Nussbaum keels over and hits the floor with a thud where Sabrina sets into licking food off his face and fingers. Joy is dressed like the Bride of Frankenstein and she flutters a fan, looking down with dismay at David's motionless body. "Oh dear," she says.

Walter is enjoying the display. It has gusto, he thinks. Why did he ever think he had boring friends and acquaintances? Look at them all. They're mad.

He continues his surveillance. Tanya is wearing a pointed cap with stars painted on it and Walter can see that she is naked underneath her dark blue cloak. Her eyes are like jewels and when she laughs, diamonds spill out of her mouth. She is magical and sinister, like the raven. She is maybe the most powerful one at the table and that is the way it should be. Reginald is Audrey Hepburn with a pencil moustache and he is eating his food with white gloves on, eschewing the use of a utensil altogether. Sabrina is nudging Walter's leg and he looks down. She has one of David's fingers in her mouth, and her stub of a tail is wagging so fast it unscrews itself and pops right off her ass. He reaches down and takes the finger, then glares at Sabrina who slinks off in search of her tail. Walter holds the finger up in front of his face and examines it, turning it around and around, wiggling it. He points it at the guests one by one and as he does, they disappear in a poof and a cloud of sparkles. Soon he is sitting alone at the head of the table, his heavy crown slipping down over one eye. He surveys the mess. Glasses are turned on their sides, burgundy wine pooling onto the table like coagulating blood, chunks of meat ripped from haunches of mystery beasts sit rotting on plates. All is silent except for the faint buzzing of flies. Walter looks around the table, still hearing echoes of the laughter and the belching and the talking and the screeching. He listens as it recedes into nothingness and the flies get louder. He can't help but laugh. And he does, loudly. It feels good, therapeutic. This is his kingdom and it's funny. There are crazy people in his kingdom. It's fucking hilarious.

With tears streaming from his eyes now, Walter sweeps the table one more time, picturing his departed guests. Each empty chair he spies, he laughs louder. Until he gets to the chair at the foot of the table. His laughter slows. He shakes his head. He can't remember who sat at the other end of the table. Who was there? He wipes his eyes and takes a deep breath, trying to remember. Counts all the guests in his head and still can't think of who was sitting directly in his line of sight.

But he knows. He knows nobody was, because that particular guest sitting in that particular seat of honour wasn't invited. Pain claws at his heart. Walter stares at the empty chair, conflicted. He decides to invite her and see what happens. Silver glitter begins to swirl around the chair and Walter sits back, entranced. She appears first like an illusion, shimmering and translucent, rising up from inside the glittery cascade. And the sparkles slow down, attaching themselves to her form. It is astonishing and Walter has no will to stop it. In seconds she is sitting there, fully realized, and glowing with a radiant inner light. He savours the sight of her as if she is an elixir. She is dressed like a princess, and he has never before beheld such beauty. She smiles at him. It is a shy smile and its sweet simplicity breaks his heart. He rises from his chair, adjusts his crown, and steps towards her, his hand out. There is only one thing to do. They must dance.

# 34 }

**Walter wasn't sure how he got from his new dining room** to his old kitchen. But here he was, and there was no mistaking who was sitting across from him this time. It was Johnny Carmichael and he was wearing his usual black T-shirt and jeans. Walter had a dim recollection of seeing blood on Johnny's face. And instead of a tankard of ale, there was a six-pack of Carlsberg beer on the kitchen table with two bottles missing. Johnny was sucking one back and Walter realized he had one in his own hand. He took a tentative sip to make sure it was real. It was warm but it was real all right.

"Smoke?" said Johnny, holding out a pack of Player's.

Walter took one and put it in his mouth, biting into the spongy filter. It was real too. Johnny snapped his Zippo open and Walter leaned into the flame, drawing on the cigarette. He settled back into his card chair and inhaled harshly, holding the smoke in longer than normal. When he exhaled, hardly any smoke escaped. This was the second time Walter had sat with another man and smoked in company. At least he thought it was the second time. He thought maybe it was the same day. Johnny wasn't saying much and Walter wondered what he was doing here.

"Clara moved out," said Walter, taking another slug of warm beer.

"Everything go okay?"

"Yeah," said Walter. "I've been thinking about what to do with the room now that she's gone."

Johnny said nothing.

"I was thinking about turning it into a dining room. What do you think?"

Johnny raised his broken eyebrow.

"A dining room? What for? You planning on throwing a bunch of dinner parties or something?"

Walter thought about saying: I already did. You were there. But instead he said: "Well, what would you do with it?"

"God, I'd make it into a poker room, unless it's big enough for a pool table."

"I never thought of that," said Walter. "A poker room would be good."

"Yeah, you could start a weekly poker night or something."

Walter now saw himself wearing a visor and smoking a cigar, dealing cards. He pictured Johnny as a gunslinger.

"Would it be a boys' night?" asks Walter.

"Wouldn't have to be. Nova's a killer poker player."

Walter nodded, knowing he would have to brush up on poker hands. He had no idea if a full house beat a royal flush.

"So, have you decided what you're going to do yet?" asked Johnny.

"Yeah, I think I'll make a poker room."

"Not that. Have you decided what you're gonna do about Laura?"

Walter recognized what Johnny was saying but hearing the word Laura come out of Johnny's mouth sounded all wrong. It didn't sound like English. It sounded like an album played at half speed, all guttural and drawn out and indistinguishable. *Lllorrrahhhhhgghhgh.*

Walter stared at his friend, mouth half open. He didn't know how to respond. He wasn't prepared for this question.

"Hey man, you don't have to know," said Johnny. "I was just wondering if you were okay. I mean, you took the day off work. Forget it."

"No," said Walter, figuring out how to talk. "No, it's okay. I'm not sure. What would you do?"

Johnny cracked his knuckles and tilted his chair back on two legs.

"Fuck, Spaz, I don't know. There are plenty of other chicks in the sea."

"Fish," Walter said, correcting him.

"Fish?"

"Yeah, fish. There are plenty of other *fish* in the sea."

"Yeah, well there are plenty of whales in the sea too. And sharks and barracudas, don't forget."

"So, are you saying I should go fishing but stick to the lakes?" asked Walter.

Johnny laughed. "Well I dunno," he said. "What are you using? Live bait or a lure?"

Fishing was safe territory for Johnny who had spent countless summer days with his brothers fishing the lakes of Northern Ontario. Things like metaphors and analogies weren't so easy. What Johnny was really thinking was that Walter didn't have a great track record with the chicks, or the fish for that matter. He couldn't afford to be too picky if he wanted to get laid on any kind of regular basis. If you snag a beaut, you reel 'em in and show 'em off. Johnny was never big on catch and release. Not anymore, anyway.

Walter, who had only fished a couple times, was thinking about Johnny's last question. He guessed he was probably live bait. He never considered himself as having allure.

"Live bait," he announced. "I'm a worm."

The more he thought about it, the more Walter was sure. He did feel like he was wriggling on the end of a hook.

"Okay," said Johnny. "That's good. So, you could troll for chicks."

Walter didn't correct his friend again.

"I'm not very good at fishing," he said.

"Maybe not. But don't forget, you've already landed one. I guess the question is, do you toss her back or smack her in the head with a hammer and keep her."

Walter looked at Johnny, startled. But Johnny looked placid as he took a drag of his cigarette.

"Hey man, it's a metaphor," he said proudly.

Walter groaned.

"This isn't getting us anywhere," he said. "I appreciate your concern, but this is something I'm gonna have to work out on my own."

"Do you have any tequila?" asked Johnny.

"Uh, yeah. I think so."

"Let's do a shot."

"Okay, sure."

Walter found a bottle of tequila with enough left for two shots. He poured them and they held their glasses up.

"What are we drinking to?" asked Walter, licking salt off his hand.

"To blood, brother," said Johnny.

Walter hesitated, then clinked Johnny's glass.

"To blood," he said.

They downed the tequila simultaneously and Johnny smacked his shot glass down hard on the table. He leaned forward and pinned Walter with his intent black gaze.

"Okay, fuck the fishing. Here's the thing, Spaz. If I found out now that Nova was my half-sister, or even my fucking whole sister, I wouldn't give a rat's ass. And as far as your old man goes, fuck it. He left you high and dry years ago. Fuck *him*. And if you still give a shit about the prick, then why the hell would you want to give up the only person who can tell you about him?"

Johnny belched and sat back, chasing the tequila with a gulp of beer.

"Let's face it," he continued. "The babes aren't exactly beating down your door. You spend half your life drawing *shoes*, for chrissakes. You don't go out to the clubs, you don't do sports. What do you think? Another one is gonna walk into the shoe store and stick her foot in your face?"

Walter's face felt warm.

"You're right," he said. "You're right about everything. It's just..."

"Just nuthin'," said Johnny. "What the fuck are you afraid of? It's not like you have to marry her, if that's even legal."

Walter's face felt hot now.

"In fact," Johnny continued, "who gets married now anyway?"

"My mom," said Walter, something new occurring to him.

"My mom," he repeated, looking at Johnny. "How would I tell my mom? What would she think?"

"Oh god," moaned Johnny. "Your mom is happy again. Don't blow it."

Walter felt cold now. He pictured his mom looking at the old photograph of his dad in her underwear drawer. The same photograph Laura has. Walter again felt like he was one of the birds being held upside down by his feet, his fucked up feet, and his shadow of a father was the one holding him there. He was dangling and the only way to land on the ground was if his father let go.

"Hey man, I've gotta go," Johnny was saying. "Are you all right?"

"Yeah, sure. I'm fine. Thanks for coming over. And say hi to Nova for me."

Johnny got up and shrugged his black leather jacket on.

"I will, but you should call her. She worries y'know."

Walter got up to walk his friend to the door.

"She told you to come here today, didn't she?"

They walked down the creaky hall.

"Yeah she did, but I would have called anyway if I knew you had taken the day off."

Walter held the door open and gripped Johnny's shoulder.

"I know you would. And thanks, man."

"For what?"

Walter punched Johnny on the shoulder.

"For the beer, what else?"

Johnny grinned at him and headed down the stairs, his boots loud. Halfway down, he turned around and looked up at Walter who was watching him descend. Johnny gave a wave.

"Hey, anytime you want to go fishing, you let me know," he said, and turned back, thudding to the bottom of the stairs.

Walter waited until he heard the front door close before he moved back into his hallway and closed his own door. My father *did* let me go, he thought. I must have landed on my head.

Walter walked back down the hall, stopped at Clara's old room and leaned against the door frame, studying the room's dimensions. A pool table would be a tight fit, he thought. But a poker room might do nicely. He would buy one of those lamps you can pull down from the ceiling to light the table. Maybe set up a wet bar in one corner, get a small icebox. Instead of the floor-length drapes he would have chosen for a dining room, he'll get venetian blinds. Walter could visualize hazy slats of light scoring the intent faces of the poker players. He will get a ceiling fan to dissipate the inevitable cigar smoke and a trolley cart for snacks. Walter marvelled at how easy it was to imagine any number of purposes and decors for this one room. How easily it could accommodate any purpose he chose. Clara's personality had been stripped and relocated to some other room in a farmhouse in Unionville, and Cliff would be the one listening to her snore now. Why, this room could be anything, thought Walter. It could be a grim torture chamber with a rack and meat hooks hanging from the ceiling. It could be a colourful arcade with pinball machines and a jukebox. It could be a meditation room with nothing but a mat, some candles and incense. It could be a...

*It could be a darkroom.*

*Just like that.*

*It could be a darkroom, dear Walter.*

*No. Walter curses the thought. No. It will be a poker room. But as he stares into the room, it begins to darken. He can't stop it. It starts around the edges and creeps into the centre. But it isn't entirely dark. There is a red glow moving into the middle of the room. He can hear soft voices now, speaking in the muted tones peculiar only to CBC radio hosts, unmistakably Canadian talk radio. The red glow pulses and bathes the room with an eerie light—everything appears to be in negative. Walter doesn't want to see this. He tries to will back the poker room, the gunslingers sitting around the table, the saloon girls, the smoke. But it is impossible. The darkroom has turned him inside out, like he is a negative. The soft siren babble of the CBC radio people beckons. The red light is consoling and the darkness on the edges is safe. Walter licks his upper lip and tasted salt. He feels a tear drying on his cheek but doesn't feel sad. He feels nostalgic. He doesn't want the voices to go away, he doesn't want to have to turn the dial, keep frantically spinning the dial as the stations go off the air. Then all that will be left will be static and the one lone red light to keep him company. Everyone on earth is not dead, he thinks. Not as long as the radio keeps going and I can see the light. He takes a step inside the room, half expecting the darkroom to vanish, to poof into nothingness like his dinner guests did. But it doesn't. He realizes whose darkroom this was, of course. And still he steps into it. If he is indeed a negative, then he must bathe himself in the light and see what develops. That much he knows about photography. The* red light is steps away from him, it is the heartbeat of the room—the tell-tale heart, the heart that has been pierced by a hook, it is his heart and he must own it. He takes another step closer to the centre of the universe, tears now running freely down his cheeks, his hands outstretched like he is a blind man. The CBC voices murmur a soundtrack that rises and falls in cadence, in time with the beating of the red light. And then he is in it. It surrounds him, and he is standing in a shadow of blood. The rest of the room is dark, but he can make out the odd thing, the bed and the dresser stand black and skeletal, like they have been charred. They are one-dimensional, but he isn't. He is developing here in the red light. He can feel it happening. He is coming to life, he is number one with a bullet on the Hit Parade, and the hits keep on coming. He looks down at himself as his hazy body takes on a more substantial form. Soon he is no longer a negative. Of this, he is positive. He takes a deep breath so the blood-light can enter his body and mix with his own. It does not make him sick as he feared it might. It is a match.

# 35 }

**"Does this come in any other colours?"**

Walter nodded at his well-dressed customer and took the white display shoe from her hands.

"Yes, it comes in plain black, and black and white," he said. "What colour are you looking for?"

"Could I see the black and white?"

Walter glanced at her feet, shod in expensive black Italian-made pumps.

"Sure," he said. "Size six and a half?"

Her eyes widened: "Yes, exactly! Thank you. I'll sit over here."

Walter wobbled off to the backroom, humming. He was floating through this day. He was in the flow. All his customers had been dreams today. This one will be no exception, he could sense it. She'll have a nice compact foot that will slide into the black and white shoe and she'll be pleased. He pulled the shoebox out from its stack and didn't bother with alternative choices. Within a minute, he was at her feet, slipping off her pumps. Her stockings were silky and expensive and her toes boasted an immaculate pedicure, as he expected. Her toenails were painted with clear gloss, but he imagines she paints them red when she goes out dancing. She can probably tango.

She liked the shoes.

Walter watched her walk up and down the store, twirling on the balls of her feet, pausing to examine the shoes in a mirror, turning her ankle this way and that. He sat on his haunches, rocking and waiting. He knows she will buy these shoes. They are made for each other.

"These are perfect," she said, sliding back into her seat.

"They look good on you," he said honestly, sliding them off and tucking them back into their box.

She leaned over to slip her Italian pumps back on and Walter caught a glimpse of cleavage and a whiff of perfume, something that smelled like lavender. It did not turn him on, but it did make him smile. The woman reminded him of a movie star, a Sophia Loren or Ann-Margret. The kind of woman who is completely unattainable and out of your league, but who makes you feel happy to do nothing but gaze upon her. This customer is such a woman. She knows what she wants and she always gets it. And men, like Walter, are here to serve.

"Can I ask you a weird question?" Walter said, completely confident.

"Sure."

"Do you know how to tango?"

"Yes I do. Why do you ask?"

Walter got to his feet, shoebox in hand.

"I don't know. I pictured you dancing when I watched you walk around the store. You look like you would be a great dancer, that's all. You're very graceful."

She stood and put her hand on Walter's arm.

"Thank you. That's about the nicest thing anyone has said to me all day."

As Walter rung in her shoes, he began to hum again. He was ready for the next customer to enter his flow. One in. One out. The woman watched him bag her shoes and toss in some free polish without mentioning it. She felt sorry for him, for the way he walks. He probably had polio as a kid, she thought. He will probably never be able to dance, let alone something as intricate as the tango. He handed over her purchase with a smile big enough to show the gap between his front teeth.

"Thanks," he said. "Hope to see you again."

"My pleasure," she said, returning the smile. "I'll be back."

She *will* be back, Walter thought as he watched her exit the store. He knew this as sure as he knew her foot size. What he didn't know, but would be thrilled if he did, was that she would be the first customer to buy his raven shoes. And she would tango the living shit out of them.

"You're in a good mood," said Nova, as they both took a quick break out back.

"Yeah, I am."

"Any particular reason?"

"Nope."

"Did Johnny visit you yesterday?"

"Yup, but I'm sure you already know that."

"And Clara is gone?"

"Yup, and I'm sure you know that too."

"Anything else happen that I should know?"

"Nope. Business as usual."

"What about Laura?"

"What about her?"

"Are you going to talk to her again?"

"I already have."

"You have? When? Where?"

Walter gave Nova an inscrutable look, and turned to head back into the store.

"In my dreams," he said and laughed.

Nova watched him go, dumbfounded.

"In your fucking dreams if you think I'm settling for that answer," she muttered to his back and followed him in.

Walter's customer flow was steady, easy, like waves rolling in and out. He helped a young girl buy her first pair of high heels without so much as a whimper from her mother. Everyone was under his spell today. He could do no wrong. He brought a flush to the lined cheek of an old woman as he complimented her and sold her some smart suede-trimmed ankle boots. She left the store knowing her calves were being enhanced by the slight heel and fashionable cut of the boot. She pranced down Queen Street, forgetting for a moment the throbbing of her varicose veins and the creaking of her replacement hip. The only blip in his day was when Judith sprinted and cartwheeled into the store. Whereas Walter's initial reaction might have been to hide in the backroom, he decided against it. He believed the flow would keep his head above water, no matter what. As it turned out, Judith was only there to buy insoles and laces, all of which she could purchase at the front counter where Nova happened to be at the time. Walter stopped straightening the chairs and looked over. Judith spied him and gave him a wave which Walter returned. Not so bad, he thought. Nothing speared his brain, no black-hooded images. It's all very civilized. Another test passed. Another wave breaks the shoreline and recedes.

At the end of the day, Walter had sold more shoes than Nova. He volunteered to vacuum the store and lock up. Nova watched him plugging in the vacuum and shook her head.

"Hey, Spaz," she called out from the counter. "What are you doing after work?"

Walter stopped humming and looked over.

"Going home, why?" he said.

"I thought maybe we could go for a drink."

Walter pushed his hair back off his forehead and appeared to think about it.

"Thanks, but I think I want to go home and hang out. Maybe another time?"

Nova tried again.

"Well, won't it seem really empty at home with Clara gone? Do you want some company? I could bring a bottle of wine over or something."

"No thanks," said Walter. "I think I'll enjoy the space for a change. You know how it is."

Nova didn't know how it is, but before she could say anything else, the vacuum roared to life. She watched Walter run the machine around the carpet. His lips were moving and she believed he was singing. After a few minutes of observing him, Nova walked over to the wall and pulled the plug on the vacuum. As the sound died away, Walter looked around to see Nova with her hands on her hips.

"What?" he asked.

"You're too happy," she said. "If I didn't know better, I'd think you got laid last night. You didn't, did you?"

"God, can't I be in a good mood for no reason?"

"No."

"You're nuts," said Walter. "Plug in the vacuum, will you?"

Nova stood firm.

"You didn't answer my question," she said.

"Okay. No, I didn't get laid. No, there's nothing wrong with me. I'm fine. Really, I am. Now, could you plug in the vacuum? I'd like to get out of here before midnight. Why don't you go home and I'll lock up."

"Are you sure?" Nova asked.

"Yes, I'm sure. Now get the hell out of here."

Nova gave him one last searching look before plugging the vacuum back in.

"THANKS," Walter yelled.

Nova mouthed goodbye to him and walked out the door. *Johnny has some splainin' to do. What did those two talk about, anyway?*

It was six-thirty when Walter finished tidying up the store. A half-baked idea had been swirling around his head ever since he woke up on the floor of Clara's old room. He woke up feeling more rested than he had in a long time. But more than rested, he felt purposeful again. And he felt strangely romantic. Gone was the pulsing blood-red darkroom light of the night before, but its effects were still with him. He was filled with it, he was warm and loving and had no static cling. And he was horny, but not in the usual way. This was deeper. It wasn't localized in his dick. His entire being was horny. His entire self needed to plunge into someone. He felt raw and brand new and ready to take and be taken. And he was the man who would be king. Which, when he thought about it, would make him a prince.

He lay in the pool of dawn for at least half an hour feeling quite princely and charming and able to think about his beloved princess. His first thought was to call her, but that didn't seem a very regal thing to do. Only peasants would call. He considered sending a letter, but knew words would fail him. What he needed was action. Decisive, manly action, befitting that of his princely station. What he needed to do was sweep her off those perfect size seven-and-a-half feet. Claim his princess with a flourish and an act of chivalry.

It is this notion that has put a smile on Walter's face all day and a tune on his tongue. There can be nothing finer than running romantic scenarios through your head in which you are the leading man who gets the girl. They come and go within the flow, considered and then discarded as unworthy. The standard ideas are briefly entertaining—flowers, chocolates, serenading under a window—but all are found wanting. Prince Walter of Spazdom needs a more unique form of declaration, one that tests his creativity and seals his commitment. He kept coming back to the phrase "sweeping her off her feet." It's the most appropriate thing to do, considering. But you need a grand gesture. A *sweeping* gesture. Something worthy and noble and irresistible. These were the things Walter was thinking about as he vacuumed GoLightly's. Plenty of grand gestures involve feet. Galloping by on a white charger and sweeping a maiden off her feet. Laying a cloak over a puddle to save her feet from getting muddy. Feet are the key.

He unplugged the vacuum and put it away in the backroom, enjoying the head movies that he hoped would lead him to the perfect act of nobility. As he prepared to leave, he spied a stray shoe underneath one of the chairs and tottered over to scoop it up and put it away for the night. He knelt down, grunting a bit as he reached for the shoe, curling his fingers around the heel and pulling it out. It was a silver evening pump, one of Nova's customers he recalled, who was looking for something to wear to a wedding. For the first time since hearing about his mother's Vegas vows, the thought of a wedding did not completely disgust him. He clasped the shoe to his chest like a bouquet and did the wedding walk towards the backroom—step, stop, step, stop. The store was dimly lit now, with only a few spotlights shining on selected displays and it gave the room a surreal glow. When he was almost at the backroom, he caught his reflection in a full-length mirror and it stopped him cold. A spotlight caught him, lighting up his hair as if it were a crown. The light also hit the silver shoe and it sparkled in his hands like a fiery crystal. A sound escaped him, *ahhh*, and he could not move, could only stare. The head movies spooled out like crazy, overlapping with visions past and present—Laura rising from the dining room table resplendent in her princess dress, gloved hand taking his as they danced in delirious abandon, skirt flying, while he, the charming Prince Walter, guided her with a steady step and expert hand. Walter blinked at his shining visage and saw his answer. It was right there in his hands. With this realization, the visions collapsed around him in a pretty heap. He now knew what had to be done, and his step was sure as he marched into the backroom. It's so obvious, he thought. I don't know why I didn't think of this before. Duh.

# 36 }

**Walter stood in his drawing room,** excited, almost feverish. An album was playing *The Sound of Music* soundtrack in the background. Right now it was on "My Favorite Things" and he sang along while unpacking his new purchases. He'd been busy, as evidenced by the shopping bags on the floor and the growing pile of items he was heaping on his table. It was beginning to look like Santa's workshop, with glue bottles and strings and glass cutters and mirrors and pieces of coloured glass and beads and tinfoil and sequins and paint and brushes and cookie cutters and stencils and metallic stars.

*Brown paper packages tied up with strings*
*These are a few of my favourite things*

Walter sung and unpacked, his eyes glowing. It's so *perfect*, he thought. I'm a genius.

The sky darkened as he hunched over his drawing table, laboriously cutting pieces of mirror and glass, tongue lodged in the gap between his teeth. He only paused to sketch something on his pad of paper or get up and play the album again. He was warm and had thrown off his bathrobe, wearing only underwear and socks, his forehead glinting with sweat as he ran X-Acto knives and cutters along the slick glass surfaces, and broke them up into piles of multicoloured shimmering pieces.

*Follow every rainbow, 'til you find your dream.*

The mound of irregularly cut pieces of mirror and glass grew and Walter fiddled with them occasionally, trying to fit them together like pieces of a jigsaw puzzle. There were still many decisions to be made, but getting there was half the fun. He will not rest until the end result is exactly what he has envisioned and he doesn't care how many prototypes he will have to fashion in order to achieve perfection. It will be worth it.

*Better beware, be canny and careful*
*Baby, you're on the brink.*

He felt like a child, sitting on his high stool, elbow deep in craft supplies. His stockinged feet were curled around the legs of the stool, and he knows the words to every *Sound of Music* song. He played this album constantly when he was young, and was not aware that while he leaped and danced to it, his mother was having her first misgivings about his impending sexuality. That was when she took him in hand and taught him how to dance properly, how to lead like a man because that's what you are becoming Walter, a MAN. You are not going to become a ballerina.

And in his head he danced on, while Maria sung of her favourite things and glinting glass was shuffled and matched and his pen skittered across the paper. Tonight he was not summoning the shoe spirits—he didn't need them. His focus was more corporeal than spiritual. It was exquisitely female.

At four a.m., he accidentally cut his finger on a bit of glass. It was a minor slice, and he squeezed the tip of his finger, letting the blood drip onto the sketch paper in a random pattern. He stared at the droplets of blood, fearing they would magically form a damning word, but they didn't. They were only drops of blood, nothing more. Walter sucked his finger and decided it was time to stop for the night. He had done a lot of the preparation work already and was pleased.

*I flit, I float, I fleetly flee, I fly*
*The sun has gone to bed and so must I.*

He turned off the record player and walked to the doorway where he stood for a moment with his hand on the light switch, surveying his supplies, wondering if he'd forgotten anything. But everything seemed to be there, including a lot of things he may not need. He turned the dimmer switch down, and the light gradually faded on the pile of glinting glass and baubles and the four identical pairs of silver evening pumps lined up in a row across the top of the table.

*So long, farewell*, sang Walter in a quiet voice as the dimmer clicked off.

And he wobbled into his bedroom, tired and satisfied, anticipating royal dreams.

Every evening for the next week found Walter in his drawing room, cutting and gluing and listening to the *Sound of Music* for inspiration. All else had slid far back in his mind while he concentrated on his project. He flitted, he floated, he flew through his days at GoLightly's, rising above Nova's insistent pestering questions and consistently selling more shoes per day than he'd ever managed to sell before. Thoughts of Laura had been pushed back, despite the fact that she was the driving force behind his nocturnal creations. So obsessed was he with sweeping her off her feet, he gave no regard to the time that was elapsing while he devoted himself to the making of his grand gesture. If he thought of Laura at all, it was to picture her face at the glorious moment of his offering at her feet. It was to picture them waltzing into the sunset while the hills were alive.

On this particular night, there was but one pair of silver evening pumps left untouched. The other three had been used for practice, and Walter was now confident about his direction. At first, he wasn't sure about colours. The glass slippers in Cinderella books always looked like clear unbreakable glass, a manufacturing feat beyond even Remo's capabilities. Walter was doing the next best thing—creating the illusion of glass by gluing pieces of it onto a ready-made shoe. This was his grand gesture. This is what he will offer up to his princess as he kneels at her feet, head bowed, and slips the size seven-and-a-half glass slipper on. It will prove beyond a doubt his belief in their own perfect fit. It will be a truly magical moment and this is all he could envision as he prepared his final pair of shoes. After experimenting with different colours of glass, he had settled on using only mirrors and clear glass. The shoes will take her breath away. He will fill in the gaps between the pieces with tiny silver sequins and metallic threads and glitter and cover it all with several coats of clear acrylic into which he will sprinkle silver sparkles. They will indeed be shoes fit for a fairytale, his most precious achievement. Other women can wear his holly shoes, his raven shoes, and all the other shoes of his design, but only one woman will wear the glass slippers. If there were a mould to break, these shoes would stomp it to smithereens.

And so Walter cut and filed rough edges and glues, eyes on the craftsmanship, brain elsewhere. Brain indulging itself, roaming from the moment of the offering to the acceptance and further. To a wedding, yes, even that. She could wear the shoes, be a princess bride. To their first dance, their wedding night, and on. To nights curled up on the couch, with Laura telling him stories of his father, showing him photographs of their life. Slaying the secrets. As the glass slippers took shape, Walter couldn't remember why he had doubts. He could only remember the green of her eyes and that first day in GoLightly's when he saw her feet and knew something. He holds onto that and releases everything else, and so consumed was he with his self-indulgence, he neglected to think she might be waiting to hear from him.

He decided not to call her first. The grand gesture should be done in person, he thought, as he got dressed for the occasion. He took great care with his wardrobe, found a cloak in a second-hand store that he fastened about his neck. Going for the princely look, he was wearing his tightest black jeans tucked into knee-high black boots. He had tied a white sash through the belt loops and was wearing a white tuxedo shirt and a deep purple tailored velvet jacket, all found at thrift shops. Having studied Reginald's wardrobe for years, he had added an ascot, pale yellow. As he examined himself in a full-length mirror, Walter wished he had a sword strapped to his hip, or at the very least a silver cane to flash about. He couldn't decide if he looked like a prince or like Mr. Hyde. But no matter, the effect was outstanding and definitely not average. He put one of the sparkling glass slippers in the palm of his hand and went down on one knee, watching himself in the mirror. He offered it to his reflection and was smitten with the image. She will be overcome with emotion, perhaps cry. There could not possibly be a better way to declare his intentions, not in a million years, and he couldn't wait to slide her foot into this shoe. The thought had given him an erection that strained uncomfortably against his tight black pants. All the years of bending and crouching at women's feet had come to this. He was the master.

But in his single-minded focus, he had either underestimated or completely disregarded Laura's pride and her regret. Unbeknownst to Walter, she had given him a week—one long torturous week of waiting for the phone to ring, or a letter to be slipped under her door, or to hear a knock. She could not bear the silence any longer. Worse, she could not bear running into him by accident, seeing his face, hearing him fumble for words. She had misjudged him. It was too risky to stay.

Walter ignored the stares as he plodded unevenly down her street, the glass slippers in his knapsack with a bottle of champagne. His cloak flapped in the breeze and he strode as manfully as he was able, swinging the knapsack and whistling. He had chosen dinnertime to lay his surprise on her, hoping he would catch her alone at home with no company. It was only while thinking this that he got a minor brain skip. A skip that made him wonder how long it's been since the letter, what she's been doing all this time. For an instant he wondered if she would have guests, if she'd been going out a lot. But that didn't feel right, not when he considered all the trouble she went through to meet him. He was a bit unsettled and picked up his pace, willing her to be home and alone. Willing her to be waiting for him. She had to.

He was sweating under the collar of his cloak as he knocked repeatedly on her apartment door, finally pounding with his fist, yelling her name. It is madness, she might only be at the corner store after all, but something sunk within him when she didn't answer. A dread certainty that she had left kicked in. She had tired of waiting for him, and worst of all, probably believed he was sickened by her. Not true, he moaned, as he lay his face against the door. Please.

"Mister?"

He looked to see a young girl standing in the hallway.

"Are you looking for Laura?"

Ah, sweet child. You are truly a delightful girl, he thought, dropping to his knee. He felt like grabbing her shoulders and shaking the information from her, but resisted the impulse and tried to look kindly.

"Yes, do you know where she is?" he asked. "Has she gone to the store? Away for the weekend? Is she babysitting you?"

What, what? Speak, he thought impatiently. Speak, you demon girl.

"She left," said the girl, twirling her hair. "What's in the bag?"

"She left? Well, when? Where?"

"What's in the bag?"

Walter clutched his knapsack to his chest and tried not to glare at the girl.

"Nothing. A bottle of wine. Nothing fit for you. Now where did Laura go?"

The girl studied Walter and folded her arms across her chest.

"She moved out."

"What? When?"

"Um. I dunno. A week ago."

Damn petulant girl. Impudent brat. She should be shot.

"Do you know where she moved to?"

The girl shrugged her shoulders, bored now. There was nothing in the bag for her and she took a step backwards. Walter got up off his knee and waved his hand at her.

"Go on then," he said.

Off with you, tormentor. Out of my sight. There is only one girl I want to see.

The girl walked backwards down the hall, staring at Walter.

"You could ask Mrs. Cobb," she said.

He turned, heart picking up speed.

"Who?"

"Mrs. Cobb, the landlady. She's in apartment one, downstairs," said the beautiful wondrous creature. "She might know."

Oh, where would we all be without the goodness of children, thought Walter.

"Thank you, sweetheart," he said. "Thank you. I'll try that."

And he bolted down the stairs, leaving the girl walking backwards and thinking adults are stupid.

Mrs. Cobb had a Woody Woodpecker knocker on her door, which Walter took as a good sign. He tapped its beak in a tentative knock, though he felt like slamming it right through the thin door. He expected to see a grey-haired old lady with curlers in her hair, but instead the door opened to a woman not much older than he. A reasonably attractive woman with dark red hair who was wearing a dressing gown that clung to her slight body. She was smoking a cigarette and peered at Walter with the safety chain still attached to the doorframe. She unhooked it when he stated his business and because she recognized seeing him with Laura once. She wondered if he was going to a masquerade party, but didn't ask. Instead, she offered him a drink, which he refused at first, so anxious was he to leave and track Laura down. She insisted he sit on the couch with her, which he did.

Mrs. Cobb didn't have good news. To her recollection, she said, crossing her thin legs and allowing the dressing gown to fall open, Laura might have gone out West.

"Yes, I think she's from there," said Mrs. Cobb, pulling her dressing gown back over her bony knees only to have it immediately fall open again.

Walter was hot. This was a bigger apartment than Laura's, probably a two-bedroom, but it felt close and stuffy. He undid the top couple of buttons on his shirt and pulled the ascot free. Mrs. Cobb scrutinized him through slitty eyes.

"Hey, you sure you don't want a drink? You look hot. I just made a pitcher of mint juleps," she said.

Walter had sunk into Mrs. Cobb's couch and didn't know how he would get out of it. His pants seemed to be getting tighter by the second.

"Mint juleps?" he asked, wondering who the hell makes mint juleps.

Mrs. Cobb rose easily from her side of the couch and sashayed into the kitchen. She came back with a pitcher of booze and ice and set it on the coffee table with two tumblers.

"Yeah, mint juleps," she said, speaking around her cigarette and pouring the drinks, ice cubes clinking into each glass.

Walter strained to reach his glass and took a big sip, coughing as he swallowed.

"This is a mint julep?" he croaked, wiping his mouth.

Mrs. Cobb laughed.

"Yeah, without the mint...or the sugar...or the water, for that matter."

"So, it's...?"

"Straight bourbon."

Walter took another drink and squirmed within the depths of the couch.

"So, Laura said she was going out West? Where out West?"

"Hmm. Vancouver I think. I'm not sure though. I remember her sayin' something about it. She paid me for an extra month's rent, so I ain't complaining. I don't like to ask a lot of questions, y'know, as long as I got my money."

Walter didn't believe her for a minute, about not asking questions.

"Well, when did she leave? Did she say how she was getting there?"

Mrs. Cobb butted her cigarette into a pink ashtray shaped like a fish. She smoothed her hair, and took another drink.

"What's the matter? She dump you or something? Maybe she don't want to be found. Maybe I should keep my trap shut."

Walter felt a bit dizzy, but wasn't sure if it was the bourbon or the airless room or his circulation-destroying pants or Mrs. Cobb's hairspray that smelled like kerosene.

"No, she didn't dump me. I have to get in touch with her about a family matter," he said.

"Oh. *Family* matter," said Mrs. Cobb, lighting another cigarette.

"Yeah, family matter," repeated Walter, wondering where Mr. Cobb is.

"You her brother?"

Walter was startled.

"Yes I am. Why? Do you think we look alike?"

"A little. It was just a guess. So all I can tell you is that I believe Laura said she was going out West, maybe Vancouver. Well hell, she said she's from there. You must be from there too then. Maybe she went to visit your relatives or some old school friends or something."

"Yeah, maybe," said Walter, taking another big hit of bourbon. "If she calls back here for any reason, could you tell her that her brother is looking for her? My name's Walter."

Mrs. Cobb held out a skinny hand with super long manicured fingernails painted hot pink.

"Cecile," she said. "I'm Cecile. Nice to meet you."

Walter shook her hand.

"Will you give her the message?" he asked.

"Of course I'll give her the message, but I don't see any reason she'd call me. Want a cigarette?"

Walter shrugged and said okay and disappeared further into the couch while Cecile Cobb topped up his drink and lit him a smoke, leaving hot pink lipstick on the filter. He was beginning to get used to the stuffy atmosphere in the room and needed time to digest the fact that Laura was gone—something that hadn't really sunk in yet, at least not as far as he had sunk into the sofa. He was stunned and helpless and a bit stupid in his prince get-up. And despite everything, he didn't feel like leaving yet. A tiny part of him thought Laura would return at any minute, maybe for something she forgot. Like him, for instance. And this news, this news has sucked the energy out of him for the moment. Cecile Cobb has bourbon and cigarettes and seems in no hurry to kick him out, not that he could dig himself out of this couch anyway, so maybe he'll numb out here for awhile. He has nowhere else to go, except maybe Vancouver.

By eight o'clock, Cecile and Walter were getting drunk. He was so committed to the couch, it seemed unlikely he would ever surface. Cecile had made devilled ham and relish sandwiches which Walter ate only out of politeness. He was glad to be getting drunk and glad to be in the same building that Laura once inhabited. Cecile had become somewhat amusing and apparently had no inclination to end his impromptu visit.

She was trotting out her life. Walter had now seen her collection of swizzle sticks from Reno, her Siamese fighting fish, and her wedding album. Mr. Cobb, Arthur, looked to be at least twenty years older than Cecile and she told Walter with pride that she is what is known as a trophy wife. Mr. Cobb, she said, is a salesman of unspecified items and out of town on business a lot, which is where he is now. She said he was supposed to be in Winnipeg and it was her job to stay home and look after the building. She said she was very handy with power tools, a statement that unnerved Walter. At some point, perhaps after the sandwiches, Cecile seemed to think she wasn't dressed appropriately for company and left the room to change into something "less comfortable." When she returned, she was wearing a blue halter top and orange toreador pants and he could see her ribs. It didn't look less comfortable but it did make him more comfortable to know her dressing gown wouldn't keep gaping open. He sunk further, along with the level of faux mint julep in the pitcher. Cecile kept a steady stream of chatter going, in between tiny bites of the sandwiches and huge belts of booze. Walter wondered if she was planning on making an advance. He entertained the notion of having sex with Mrs. Cobb but was afraid he'd get hurt by any number of sharp protruding bones and couldn't help but visualize Arthur Cobb coming home early from his travels and strangling him with a vacuum cleaner hose. Yet, it was safer to imagine anything other than what he was going to do about Laura.

Soon enough, the inevitable happened. The liquor ran out and Mrs. Cobb looked dismayed.

"Now what?" she asked, looking at Walter. "You don't have any booze in that bag, do you?"

Walter had all but disappeared into the couch, but managed a nod.

"Actually, I do. I've got a bottle of champagne in there but it's probably warm."

"Champagne?" Cecile squeaked. "Why didn't you say so? I've got ice."

And she lept off the couch again, toreador pants billowing as she strode into the kitchen, singing "I Get No Kick From Champagne." Walter watched her return with two champagne flutes and a bucket of ice. He wondered if people ever called her C.C. It would suit her.

"I can't get up," he said.

"Can I go in your knapsack and get it?" she asked.

"Sure," said Walter, but then remembered what else was in there.

He struggled to heave himself upright, arms flailing.

"No wait," he said, but it was too late.

Cecile had unzipped the knapsack and hauled out the bottle, but she was transfixed with what else she saw.

"What's this?" she asked, pulling out a glass slipper and holding it up to the light.

Walter gave up and sunk back.

"A shoe."

"I can see that," said Cecile, digging the other one out and holding both aloft.

"These are beautiful," she sighed, turning them this way and that. "I've never seen anything like them. Where'd you get these?"

Despite himself, Walter felt a flush of pride.

"I made them," he said. "I made them for...my sister."

"Wow," breathed Cecile, the champagne forgotten. "They almost look like..."

Walter waited.

"Like...Cinderella's glass slippers," she finished.

He was relieved.

"Yes, they're supposed to," he said. "I'm glad you like them."

"They look like my size," said Cecile, kicking off her own, less spectacular, slippers. "They're not," said Walter. "They're seven and a half."

Cecile looked at him, indignant.

"I'm a seven and a half," she retorted.

"No you're not. You're at least an eight and a half."

"I am NOT," she huffed. "I'll prove it."

And before Walter could protest, she was trying to force her feet into the glass shoes. He felt horrible about this, but couldn't get out of the couch fast enough to stop her. By the time he struggled to the edge of the couch, Cecile Cobb was standing in the shoes, holding her toreador pants up to her knees, admiring them.

"See?" she said. "I told you I'm a size seven and a half."

And she began to mince back and forth, her toes probably fracturing. Walter freaked out. He could almost feel the straining of the shoes, and was worried about the pieces of glass shifting out of place or the acrylic cracking. But more than that, he was horrified that he had let someone else wear them.

"Those aren't YOURS!" he bellowed now, giving one final mighty push off the couch. "Take them OFF!"

Cecile stopped, teetering. She looked at him like he was an idiot.

"What's your problem?" she said, doing can-can kicks with them. "They look good on me."

Walter stood, swaying from the effort, the lack of fresh air, and the bourbon. She laughed at him and continued her high kicks.

"It ain't midnight yet," she said. "I get to keep these on till midnight."

It was too much. Everything closed in and Walter lunged, tackling her. They both went down onto the floor, Cecile screaming and Walter grabbing for her feet.

"You're insane!" she screeched, punching and kicking at him.

But he managed to wrench the glass slippers off and crawl over to his knapsack while Cecile hurled epithets at him. He had to get the fuck out of here. What was he thinking? How could he have defiled Laura's shoes with that woman's feet? How could he have let this happen? He felt like bawling as he zipped up his knapsack and got awkwardly to his feet. He turned to face Cecile, sheepish.

"I'm sorry," he mumbled. "Are you okay?"

"You're sick," she spat out, brushing herself off.

"Thanks for the drinks," Walter said. "I've gotta go. I'm really sorry."

"Yeah, you're sorry all right," snapped Cecile to his back as he neared the door. "Those shoes were for your *sister*, were they?"

Walter opened the door and stepped into the hall, but Cecile was right behind him.

"I know something about your so-called sister," she sneered, which stopped him in his tracks.

He stood still, his back to her, waiting.

"I heard you up there in her apartment, you two," said Cecile. "Either Laura isn't your sister, or you had SEX with your sister, you sicko freak."

Walter hunched his shoulders and fled the building, hoping nobody could hear Cecile screaming after him.

"You're a fucking PERVERT! Don't EVER come back here again!"

And Prince Walter, who had never been good at running, began to do a very good imitation of it. His ascot flew off and fluttered to the ground behind him. He didn't stop, he kept running and gulping the air in ragged snatches of breath. Everything felt tight—his brain, his heart, his chest, and especially his fucking pants. The glass slippers clunked together in his knapsack as he ran, but he didn't care if they got chipped. He didn't care about anything. He only knew he had to get home before he turned into a rotting, festering piece of pumpkin pulp.

# 37 }

LOCAL SHOE DESIGNER A HIT WITH THE LADIES
GOLIGHTLY SHOES GOLOVELY
FINCH DOESN'T PINCH

"Did you see these reviews?" shrilled Reginald, waving a batch of newspapers in Walter's face.

"Yeah, they're good, huh?"

"They're fabulous, my boy! You're a wonder!"

"Thanks, Reginald. Remo deserves most of the credit."

"You're right. I should thank him. Where is he?"

"Uh, I think he's scarfing down the prawns."

"I'll go show him. He'll be thrilled!"

Walter watched Reginald glide across GoLightly's, easily moving in and out of the well-dressed people attending the gala showing and launch of the first shoes off the GoLightly line. Walter watched it all with a sense of detachment. Reginald was right—the shoes *are* a wonder. He didn't know how Remo managed to get them done in a year. And they were everything Walter imagined on paper and more. The raven shoes sleekly sinister, the holly shoes waxy and festive. In the last year, Walter hadn't done much else except designs. He had not only been summoning the shoe spirits nightly, he'd been living with them. They had been drifting in and out of his body like smoke, helping obscure a great loss. Some nights he sat at his drawing table, his head lying on one arm stretched across the paper, his other hand doodling. Other nights he got manic, going through sheet after sheet of paper, ideas pouring out of him for lines of theme shoes or boots. For one month, he only concentrated on colours. A line of inexpensive candy-coated shoes, all the same style—striped humbug shoes, pink bubblegum shoes, green spearmint shoes, butterscotch shoes, and licorice shoes. Or fruit shoes—candy apple red, lemon lime, pink grapefruit. He went mental, thinking of themes and colours and passes everything by Reginald who clapped his hands like a schoolgirl with every idea that Walter proposed. These happy colours were coming at Walter straight from his childhood, zooming at him from the depths of Clara's shoe closet so many years ago. He was dimly aware of this, but didn't dwell on it, didn't try to force a meaning or a connection. He let it flow, a river of colours that wound from candy and fruit and tumbled into frothy streams of ice cream and frosting. These were the nights he played. But other nights were darker, and on those nights he usually ended up in an ornithological orgy. Much like how the raven shoe came about, his hand swooped and dove and birds flew out of his brain. Winged shoes. From pearl grey pigeons to stark white seagulls and shimmering peacocks, they clawed their way onto the paper through Walter's pen.

And when he was not drawing, he was walking with his head down. He's worn out two pairs of desert boots in a year. Everywhere he went, he looked at women's feet, searching for size seven and a half. When he spotted them, he looked up with anticipation only to have his hopes flattened. He carries a knapsack constantly now, the glass slippers always in it, in case. Once he tried slipping the glass slipper on Laura's plaster foot but of course, the foot wasn't pliable enough and he almost threw the foot and the shoe against the wall in frustration and pain.

And now, GoLightly's was teeming with press and potential shoe buyers and he should be happy. Not only were some of his shoes realized and on display, Reginald had cleared a wall for Walter's sketches and designs that were in the making. He had become a mini-celebrity and had been asked for interviews at least three times today. Nova was beaming as if she designed the shoes herself and had been chatting up the writers, telling stories about Walter. Everyone was there. Joy and David and Clara and Cliff. The two women were being grilled about Walter's childhood, and the original wing shoe invention had made it into several reporters' notebooks. They were naturally eyeing the raven shoe and the bird designs and drawing their own conclusions. Walter would have to find an answer at some point to their inquisitions. For his part, he's avoiding everyone as much as possible. He felt oddly deflated, sapped of energy. He had asked Reginald for a month off, which his boss had granted grudgingly upon Walter's promise to do some interviews during his time off. Reginald didn't know that Walter wouldn't be around to do that.

As Walter leaned against a back counter, ducking eye contact and listening to people's comments about his shoes, he had one hand in his pocket clutching his plane ticket to Vancouver. He leaves tomorrow. No one knew, not even Nova or Johnny. But after the birds all flew out of his head, after a year of staring at the empty glass slippers, Walter was clear on one thing. He had to go. There were a few places to try. Sailboat charters, bars where Lila may have sung, places that might eventually lead to some people who may know where to look next. He was looking forward to the trip, to the plane ride. And as he gripped his ticket and watched the milling crowd, his eyes scanned his bird designs. Funny that he's never actually flown before, he thought. Now, finally.

**Walter was staring out** the murky scratched window of a 737, gazing in wonderment as they breached the clouds, his tongue resting in between his front teeth like a fat slug, causing a barely audible whistle as he breathed open-mouthed. While he was climbing into the heavens, a woman was on earth looking at his photograph. She had finished packing up a parcel addressed to Walter, and hoped he was still at the same address in the Beaches. She had to pack it very carefully, and made sure to plaster the box with Fragile stickers. When the courier showed up, she handed it over anxiously. She hoped it didn't freak Walter out.

"Be careful with that," she said to the delivery guy.

He dipped his head and stuck the package under his arm. The woman watched him walk to his van and toss it in the back with disregard. She closed her drapes and turned to the other person in the room.

"That's that," she said.

And within a few hours, the package is in another plane winging its way to Walter. For all anyone knows, the planes could have passed each other in the air. He won't be home to receive the parcel, but Nova will. He left a note in her mailbox telling her he was leaving for a while and asking her to check his mail. She didn't get around to it for a week after his departure. When she finally decided to tackle the job, she was sitting out on his roof having a beer. The bills she tossed into a GoLightly's shoebox sitting to the right of her lawnchair, the junkmail into a green garbage bag at her feet. And she was left with a small box wrapped in brown packing paper. The return address was from Vancouver and she tried to recall if she knew anyone who lived there. She didn't recognize the writing and held the package up to her ear, shaking it. Nova bit her lip and stood up holding the package, debating. She walked over to the southern ledge of the roof and sat on it, looking across the street to her old apartment, the box in her lap. Johnny would be home from work in an hour. It was his night to cook dinner and she knew it would be something barbecued. They would eat it out on the deck of their new place, a few blocks east of GoLightly's. He would probably make steaks.

She looked down at the package on her lap and realized she had opened the paper and one flap of the box. Guiltily, she pried open the other flap and saw tissue paper and bubble wrap. She would have to really dig in if she wanted to see what was inside.

"Damn," she muttered, poking at the bubblewrap with one finger and reaching for her beer with the other hand.

Her fingers grazed the neck of the beer bottle sitting on the ledge beside her, but her gaze was square on the package. The bottle tilted as her fingers fumbled for a grip, but she didn't look over right away because she was beginning to see a glimpse of the parcel's contents. Then, too late, she felt the bottle start to go.

"Shit!" she shrieked, grabbing for the bottle before it could smash onto the sidewalk below.

She saved it, but her sudden twisting motion caused the package to slide off her lap. She could only watch as it plummeted to the ground.

"FUCK!" she swore, hoping it wouldn't hit someone on the head.

It landed right in front of an elderly couple and even from her height, Nova could see that the box had split open and whatever had been inside was in pieces on the sidewalk. The elderly woman knelt down while her husband looked up to see Nova perched on the ledge, waving her arms around and yelling something at them.

The man waved at her, we're okay, and knelt beside his wife who was picking up the pieces and putting them back in what was left of the box.

"What do you think it was?" she asked.

He stroked a piece and rubbed his fingers together, smelled them.

"Whatever it was, it was plaster," he stated.

"Oh dear," clucked his wife. "I hope it wasn't too precious. Do you think it belonged to that girl on the ledge?"

"I suppose so," said her husband, looking up to see the ledge empty. "She must be on her way down."

"Why, look at this piece," said his wife, handing him one of the bigger chunks.

He turned it over in his palm and grunted.

"Well, I'll be darned. Looks like a little toe, don't it?"

"Yes, yes, and here's another one I think," said his wife, cradling another piece of plaster.

"They're so tiny," she breathed. "So perfectly formed."

"What a shame they're broken," said her husband.

"Do you think they could be glued back together?" asked his wife.

"Not a chance in hell," said her husband, shaking his head. "Whatever these were, they ain't never gonna be whole again."

"Are you sure, honey?" asked the wife, tapping her toe-like piece along the sidewalk.

"I'm afraid so," her husband replied, watching her. "There's too many pieces. I don't think nobody could put this back together again."

His wife looked over at him and smiled.

"Not even all the king's horses?" she asked, trotting the toe up his pantleg.

"Nope. Not even all the king's men," he said.

## Acknowledgements:

There are a few specific people to thank for their support, and a few who are nameless but no less appreciated. Specifically, I'd like to thank my publisher, Brian Kaufman, editor Aimee Ouellette and any and all Anvilites who put finger to keyboard in the making of Spaz. Big nod to The Canada Council for the Arts for much-appreciated funding that allowed me some free months to write, unfettered by the demands of a job-job. And speaking of job-jobs, a tip of the hat to the good folks at Mount Sinai Hospital in Toronto who gave me unlimited time off from a contract job during the deadline crunch times. Kudos to the talented Malcolm Jamison for having the balls to draw a caricature of me, and to Lisan Jutras for enduring a grueling photo session with an ornery subject. A gracious bow to Barbara Zatyko, esteemed patron of the arts and all-round swell gal. To the instructors at Emily Carr, especially Camrose Ducote: Thanks for introducing me to the powers of alginate and for immortalizing my middle finger in plaster. Finally, I'd like to acknowledge all the people who work in shoe stores, especially during the winter months when the clammy boot feet come out.

## About the Author

**Bonnie Bowman** grew up in Agincourt, Ontario, like Spaz did. When she was in Grade 5, she got a gold star for a story she wrote called: "If I Were A Scrub Brush." When she was ten years old, she was writing novels about horses with "taut, sweaty flanks" and reading them to her parents at the dinner table. Decades later, in journalism school, she got a "metaphor" assignment handed back to her in magazine class with the words "I refuse to mark this" scrawled across the paper. The story she wrote was called: "Oral Sex in the Barnyard of Life, or, I Bet You Didn't Eat Broccoli as a Kid Either." (You can see the progression.) Her biggest fear is being pronounced dead when she's not really dead, so she wants to be propped up in someone's apartment until she starts to smell. She actually has people who have agreed to do this for her. She wears black a lot and not because it's slimming. She despises the colour pink. When she was a restaurant critic in Vancouver, she developed an adult allergy to shellfish, which didn't stop her from being a restaurant critic. What did stop her was when they implemented a smoking ban in restaurants. She has perfect feet.